Simon Scarrow's passion for writing began at an early age. After a childhood spent travelling the world he pursued his great love of history as a teacher, before becoming a full-time writer in 2005. His Roman soldier heroes Cato and Macro first stormed the book shops in 2000 in UNDER THE EAGLE, and have subsequently appeared in a number of other bestsellers including CENTURION and THE GLADIATOR.

Simon Scarrow is also the author of a quartet of novels about the lives of the Duke of Wellington and Napoleon Bonaparte. YOUNG BLOODS, THE GENERALS, FIRE AND SWORD and THE FIELDS OF DEATH have been published to great acclaim. In addition, he writes a young adult Roman series and develops projects for television and film with his brother Alex.

To find out more about Simon Scarrow and his novels, visit www.scarrow.co.uk and www.catoandmacro.com.

By Simon Scarrow

The *Roman* Series

Under the Eagle
The Eagle's Conquest
When the Eagle Hunts
The Eagle and the Wolves
The Eagle's Prey
The Eagle's Prophecy
The Eagle in the Sand
Centurion
The Gladiator
The Legion
Praetorian

The *Wellington and Napoleon* Quartet

Young Bloods
The Generals
Fire and Sword
The Fields of Death

Sword and Scimitar

SIMON SCARROW

Sword & Scimitar

headline

First published in 2012 by
HEADLINE PUBLISHING GROUP

First published in paperback in 2013 by
HEADLINE PUBLISHING GROUP

4

Cataloguing in Publication Data is available from the British Library

ISBN 978 0 7553 5838 0 (B format)
ISBN 978 1 4722 0190 4 (A format)

Typeset in Bembo by Avon DataSet Ltd,
Bidford-on-Avon, Warwickshire

Printed and bound in Great Britain by Clays Ltd, St Ives plc

Headline's policy is to use papers that are natural, renewable and recyclable products and made from wood grown in sustainable forests. The logging and manufacturing processes are expected to conform to the environmental regulations of the country of origin.

HEADLINE PUBLISHING GROUP
An Hachette UK Company
338 Euston Road
London NW1 3BH

www.headline.co.uk
www.hachette.co.uk

ACKNOWLEDGEMENTS

My main thanks, as ever, go to Carolyn for supporting me through the writing process and then carefully reading through and commenting on the final product. I would also like to thank Chris Impiglia for letting me read his dissertation on the defences of Malta at the time of the siege. And Isabel Picornell provided some very useful background detail on the historical setting and together with Robin Carter checked through the final draft for me. Thanks to all.

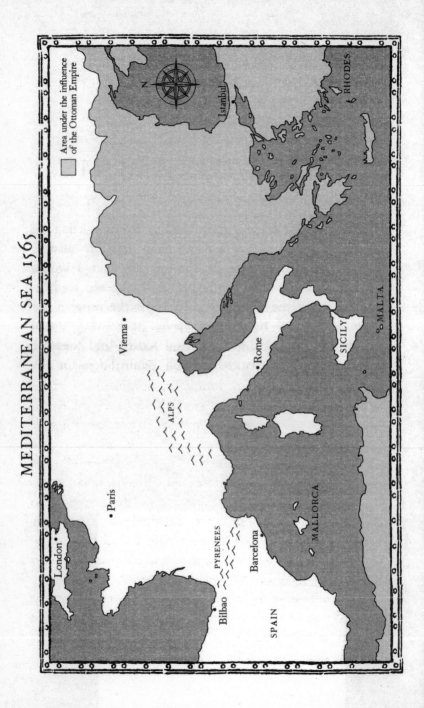

MEDITERRANEAN SEA 1565

Area under the influence of the Ottoman Empire

London
Paris
Vienna
Bilbao
PYRENEES
Barcelona
SPAIN
MALLORCA
ALPS
Rome
SICILY
MALTA
Istanbul
RHODES

CHAPTER ONE

The Mediterranean, July 1545

The sea was pitch-black in the night and the galley rose and fell gently on the slight swell outside the bay. The *Swift Hind* was hove to half a league from the shore, just beyond the dark mass of the headland. A young knight stood alone on the foredeck, one hand clasped tightly around the shroud that arced down from the top of the foremast. The air was uncomfortably humid and he raised a hand to wipe the beads of sweat from his brow. At his back were two long brass cannon, their muzzles plugged up to keep out the spray. He was long used to the motion of the galley and had no need of a handhold on the calm sea, yet he held the rough tarry cord in a clenched fist as he stared intently across the dark swell. His ears strained to pick up the least sound above the rhythmic slap of the wavelets against the hull beneath him. It had been more than three hours since the captain and four of the sailors had taken a small boat ashore. Jean Parisot de La Valette had patted Thomas lightly on the shoulder and there was a dull gleam of teeth as he smiled reassuringly and told Thomas to take command of the galley in his absence.

'How long will you be, sir?'

'A few hours, Thomas. Just long enough to make sure that our friends have settled down for the night.'

Both men had instinctively glanced in the direction of the bay the other side of the headland. No more than three miles away the Turk merchant ship would be lying at anchor not far from the beach, just where the fisherman they had encountered the day before had told them it was. Most of the crew would be ashore, sitting around campfires while a handful of men remained aboard the galleon, watching for any sign of danger from the sea. The waters along the African coast were plagued by corsairs but it was not the fierce pirates that the Turks would be looking out for. The writ of Sultan Suleiman in Istanbul protected their vessel from the depredations of the corsairs. There was a far greater danger to Muslim vessels journeying across the White Sea, as the Turks called the Mediterranean. That danger came from the Order of Saint John, a small band of Christian knights who waged ceaseless war against those who followed the teachings of Mohammed. The knights were all that remained of the great religious orders that had once held sway over the Holy Land, before Saladin had driven them out. Now their home was the barren rock of Malta, gifted to the Order by the King of Spain. From that island the knights and their galleys ventured on to the sea to prey on the Muslims wherever they might be found. On this moonless night one of the galleys of the Order was poised to attack the large merchant ship lying at anchor no more than three miles' distance.

'There will be rich pickings . . .' Thomas had mused.

'Truly, but we are here to do God's work,' the captain reminded him in a stern tone. 'Whatever spoils we take will be put to good use in fighting those who follow the false faith.'

'Yes, sir. I know,' Thomas replied softly, shamed by the thought that the older knight might think he was after plunder.

La Valette chuckled. 'Easy, Thomas. I have come to know your heart. You are as devout a member of the Holy Religion as I am, and as fine a warrior. In time you will have your own galley to command. When that day comes you must never forget that your vessel is a sword in the right hand of God. To him the spoils.'

Thomas nodded and La Valette turned to ease himself through the gap in the ship's rail and down to join the four men in the small craft bobbing beside the bow of the galley. The captain had growled an order and the other men had set to the oars, stroking the small craft across the sea. They had been swiftly swallowed up by the darkness as Thomas stared after them.

Now, hours later – too many hours, it seemed – Thomas's mind was filled with fear for his captain. La Valette had been gone for too long. Dawn was not far off and unless the captain returned soon, it would be impossible to take advantage of the cover of night to spring their attack upon the Turks. What if La Valette and his men had been captured? The unbidden thought caused a deep chill in Thomas's heart. The Turks often delighted in the torture and protracted death of any knights of the Order who fell into their hands. Then another alarming thought occurred to him. If La Valette was lost then the burden of command would fall on his shoulders and he knew with a sickening certainty that he was not ready to captain the galley.

He sensed movement close behind him and quickly looked over his shoulder as a tall figure ascended the short flight of steps to the small foredeck. The man was bareheaded and his body was bulked out by a padded gambison beneath a dark surcoat whose white cross was faintly discernible in the light from the stars. Oliver Stokely was a year older than Thomas but had joined the Order more recently and was therefore his junior. Despite that, the two had become friends.

'Any sign of the captain?'

Thomas could not help a faint smile at the needless question. He was not the only one whose nerves were being exercised by the long wait.

'Not yet, Oliver,' he said, affecting an untroubled air.

'If he leaves it much longer then we'll have to call it off.'

'I doubt he will do that.'

'Really?' Stokely sniffed. 'Without the element of surprise we risk losing more men than we can afford.'

It was a fair point, Thomas mused. There were fewer than five hundred knights still with the Order on Malta. The unending war against the Turk had its price in blood and it was proving increasingly difficult to replenish the ranks. With the kingdoms of Europe at war amongst themselves, and the strict entry requirements for those joining the Order, the number of young nobles presenting themselves for selection was dwindling. In the past, a veteran like La Valette could have gone to sea with a dozen younger knights on his galley, eager to prove themselves. Now he had to make do with five, of whom only Thomas had faced the Turks in battle.

Despite that, Thomas knew his captain well enough to know that he would not refuse a fight unless the odds were overwhelming. La Valette's heart burned with religious zeal, enflamed still more by the thirst for vengeance for the suffering he had endured as a slave chained to a slim wooden bench in a Turkish galley many years ago. La Valette was fortunate to have been ransomed. Most of those condemned to the galleys were worked to death, tormented by thirst, starvation and the agony of the sores caused by the heavy iron used to shackle them in place. For that reason, Thomas reflected, La Valette would fight, whether he succeeded in surprising the enemy or not.

'What if something has happened to him?' Stokely glanced round to make sure that they were not overheard by the men on the main deck. 'If the captain is lost, then someone will have to take command.'

Here it comes, Thomas thought. Stokely was about to stake his claim. He must assert himself before his friend did so.

'I will take his place, as his appointed lieutenant, in the event of his death or capture. You know that.'

'But I have been a knight somewhat longer than you,' Stokely replied in a restrained whisper. 'It would be best if I was captain. The men would prefer to be led by someone with more experience. Come, my friend, surely you can see that?'

Whatever Stokely might think, the truth was that Thomas's fighting prowess had been noticed from the outset by his superiors. In his first action he had commanded a raid on a small port on the coast near Algiers and captured a galleon laden with spices. After that he had been posted to serve La Valette, the most daring and successful of the Order's captains, to wage war on the Turks. This was his third campaign at sea and he had forged a close bond with the crew and soldiers of La Valette's galley. He had no doubt that they would prefer him to take command rather than a knight who had only joined the galley a month earlier, fresh from the offices of the Order's quartermaster.

'Be that as it may,' Thomas replied, sensitive to his friend's feelings, 'the matter need not concern us. The captain will return, soon, I have no doubt.'

'And if he doesn't?'

'He will,' Thomas said firmly. 'We must be ready for battle the moment the captain rejoins the galley. Give the order for the rowers to be muffled. Then have the men prepare their weapons.'

Stokely hesitated briefly before he gave a curt nod and returned down the steps on to the broad deck that ran along the centre of the slender galley for almost fifty paces before it reached the covered stern where the knights and senior officers shared their quarters. Above the deck the two broad yardarms crossed the twin masts of the galley, bowing slightly under the weight of the furled sails. Thomas heard his orders being relayed and a small party of men went below to fetch the cork plugs and leather straps from one of the chests in the small hold. A moment later a ripple of bitter murmurs rose from the men chained to their benches. Their protest was silenced by a harsh snarl from the officer in charge of the rowing deck, and the sharp crack of dried leather on bare flesh.

Thomas could well understand the feelings of the

hapless creatures who manned the galley's long sweeping oars. In order to ensure that none of them could shout a warning to the enemy as the galley glided towards its prey, the captains of the galleys on both sides had adopted the expedient of fitting a cork plug in the mouth of each man, held in place by leather thongs fastened by an iron shackle. It was horribly uncomfortable and suffocating once the men began to exert themselves at the oars. Thomas had seen men choke to death after some of the battles he had taken part in. Still, he reasoned, it was a necessary evil in this crusade against those who held to the false religion. For every man who choked on his muffle, lives of Christians were saved for want of a warning given to the unsuspecting enemy. The only other telltale sign of the presence of a galley would be the stench of excrement and urine that lay beneath the rowing benches, where it was left until the vessels were hauled out of the water at the end of the campaigning season. If it was not for the steady offshore breeze, the foul odour might carry far enough to alert the enemy.

Above the rowing deck the soldiers of the Order – Spaniards, Greeks, Portuguese, Venetians and some French, mercenaries all – rose to their feet. They struggled into their padded jackets and buckled on the small guards that protected their exposed joints. Their equipment was cumbersome and would be stifling when the sun was fully risen. Normally the order to prepare would not have been given until the galley began to close on its prey, but Thomas had sensed the tense mood of anxious expectation amongst the men and judged that it would be better to offer their minds some diversion while they awaited the return of the captain. Besides, it provided an opportunity to exercise his authority over Stokely and remind him of his place in the chain of command.

Thomas's ears pricked up at the sound of a splash away towards the dark mass of the headland. At once all other thoughts vanished from his mind as he strained his eyes and ears, searching the shifting black shadows of the sea for any sign of movement. Then he saw it, the almost invisible shape of a small boat, the men working hard at the oars. A thrill of relief surged through his heart as the craft edged closer to the galley, accompanied by the faint splash and swirl of the oar blades.

'Rest . . .' La Valette ordered in a low voice and a moment later there was a gentle bump against the solid timbers of the galley's side. A rope snaked through the air and was grasped by one of the sailors. La Valette climbed over the side as Thomas descended from the foredeck to join his captain. The other knights and officers gathered round.

'Is the galleon still there, sir?' asked Stokely.

'She is. The Turks are sleeping like babes,' La Valette announced. 'The men of the galleon will give us no trouble.'

Stokely clasped his hands together. 'Praise be.'

'Indeed.' The captain nodded. 'Our Lord has blessed us with good fortune, which is the reason for my delay in returning . . .' La Valette paused to make sure that he had the full attention of his followers before he continued. 'That galleon won't be the only prize we shall seize tonight. She's been joined by a pair of corsair galleys. They're at anchor, close by. A rich haul, gentlemen.'

There was a moment's silence as the other men took in the news. Thomas glanced round at the faces of his companions and could just discern that some were exchanging nervous looks. The galley's sailing master cleared his throat anxiously. 'That's odds of three to one, sir.'

'No. Two to one. The galleon is of little account. Once we have dealt with the galleys, she'll fall into our hands easily enough.'

'Even so, it would be reckless to attempt it,' the sailing master protested. 'Especially with dawn fast approaching. We shall have to withdraw.'

'Withdraw?' La Valette growled. 'Never. Any man who serves the Order is worth any five Turks. Besides, we have God on our side. It is the Turks who are outnumbered. But let us not test providence too severely, eh? As you say, the morn will soon be upon us. Therefore, gentlemen, there's no time to be lost. Is the galley ready?'

'Aye, sir.' The sailing master nodded.

'And the men?'

'Yes, sir,' Thomas replied. 'I have already called them to arms.'

'Good.' La Valette looked round at his officers and raised his fist. 'Then let us do the Lord's work and visit his wrath upon the Turk!'

There was already the faintest hue of lighter sky on the eastern horizon as the *Swift Hind* began to round the headland. Beyond, the bay opened out into a broad crescent some three miles across. The outlines of the galleon and the two galleys were clearly discernible against the pale loom of the sandy beach and a tiny faint orange glow showed where the embers of a campfire still warmed those huddled about it.

'We're too late,' Stokely said softly as he stood beside Thomas on the deck. 'The dawn will be upon us long before we reach them. The Turks are sure to see us.'

'No. We're approaching from the west – the darkness will shroud us for a while yet.' Thomas had seen La Valette use the tactic before in his raids on the enemy and it was a proven way of concealing their approach until the last moment.

'Only if the Turks are completely blind.'

Thomas bit back on his irritation. This was Stokely's first 'caravan', as the Order called their sea campaigns. The young knight would learn to trust the experience of the captains who had spent many years at war with the Turks – provided he lived long enough, Thomas reflected. There were many ways in which a knight might meet his maker while in the service of the Holy Religion. Combat, disease and drowning all took their toll, with no regard to whether a man was from one of Europe's most noble families or raised in the sewer. Drowning was a particular danger. The plate armour that protected a knight in battle, and the rest of his equipment, was heavy enough to send him straight to the bottom of the sea should he tumble into the water.

Thomas glanced down the length of the galley, taking in the clusters of soldiers, some armed with crossbows, and saw La Valette on the stern deck, standing tall and erect, with the stout shape of the sailing master at his side. No man spoke above a whisper and the only sound was the dull crash of the ocean swell against the rocks of the headland, and the rhythmic creak of the oars and the splash as the blades bit into the sea. Once the galley had cleared the headland, the steersman turned the *Swift Hind* in towards the shore, in line with the nearest of the galleys. Thomas had become accustomed to the captain's habit of keeping his plans to himself but could nonetheless guess at his intentions. La Valette intended to attack the nearest galley first. Even if the galleon managed to weigh anchor and clear the bay before the galleys were dealt with, she would be easy enough for the Order's sleek warship to run down and capture.

To the east the light was now distinctly stronger and the outline of the opposite headland was stark against the sky. A stinking waft of the enemy's galleys carried across the deck of the *Swift Hind*, adding to the foul smell of the Christian vessel.

The galley had closed to within half a mile of the enemy before the shrill blast of a horn carried across the water, sounding the alarm. Thomas felt an icy twinge of anxiety snatch at the back of his neck and he grasped his pike more tightly in his hands. From the rear of the galley La Valette's voice carried clearly to his men.

'Paceman, battle speed! Gunners, prepare your port fires!'

As the drum began to beat out a steady, insistent rhythm below the deck, a dull glow appeared at the bows as the first length of the port fires emerged from its small tub. For an instant it flared brightly as a gunner blew on it and then the other gun captain took his turn and both men stood poised by the breaches of their cannon waiting for the order to fire.

Thomas's heart quickened with the increased pace of the time-keeping drum and the deck lurched slightly beneath his boots with each sweep of the oars. Off the port beam he could see tiny figures scrambling to their feet around the glow of the fire on the beach. Some simply stared at the galley cutting across the surface of the bay towards them. Others began to run to the water's edge and wade out towards the galleon, then splash forwards as they swam towards their vessel. Those who could not swim began to heave the ship's tenders into the gentle surf and scramble aboard. Over on the nearest of the corsair galleys dark figures began to line the sides of the vessel. Many wore turbans and gesticulated wildly towards the oncoming danger as they snatched up their weapons. Their shouts carried clearly across the intervening sea.

Meanwhile not a man on the Christian galley spoke a word and the only sounds were the beating of the drum, the rush of the water along the sleek lines of the hull and the muffled grunts of the men straining at the oars. Thomas looked back along the deck to the stern and could just make out his captain's expression in the thin pre-dawn loom. La Valette was standing quite still, his left hand resting on his sword hilt, his features, framed by a closely clipped beard, fixed and unyielding. It was his custom to lead his men into battle in silence, knowing that it would unsettle the enemy. Only at the last moment would they let out a deafening roar as they fell upon their foe.

A sharp crack sounded close by and Thomas flinched as several splinters exploded from the side rail. A puff of smoke from the nearest corsair galley showed where an arquebusier had fired at them a moment earlier. He had already lowered the butt of his long-barrelled weapon to the deck and was reloading. Thomas glanced to each side to see if anyone had noticed his flinching but the men around him were staring ahead and Stokely's lips moved as he prayed under his breath. His gaze flickered towards Thomas and he stilled his tongue and averted his eyes when he saw Thomas looking at him.

There were more puffs of smoke and the lead balls zipped overhead before another shot struck the galley on the bow. Thomas forced himself to stand still as he watched several more shots fired from the nearest enemy vessel, each one a lurid red bloom in a swirl of smoke that died away in a moment.

'Crossbows!' La Valette called out. 'Make ready!'

The soldiers of the Order still used the outdated weapon. It lacked the range and power of the Turks' firearm but it was less cumbersome and could cause terrible injuries when it was aimed true. A small party of men moved forward and took up position along each bow rail. Using the small windlass on the butt they wound back the bowstring and carefully placed a bolt in the channel running along the top of the weapon.

'Shoot at will!' The order carried clearly from the stern of the galley. The loud cracks of the enemy's arquebuses were answered by the dull whack of the released bowstrings and the bolts leaped across the water in a shallow arc before disappearing amid the men crowding the deck of the corsair vessel.

There were now no more than a hundred paces between the two galleys, Thomas estimated. Scores of turbaned men lined the side rail, shouting their challenges at the Christians as they brandished their scimitars and pikes. Below the side rail the first oars were being run out as the crew frantically struggled to get their vessel under way. Thomas braced himself for the imminent order to fire the galley's cannon, and he saw one of the gun captains glance over his shoulder. 'Come on, come on,' the man growled.

La Valette waited a moment longer then cupped his hands to his mouth and bellowed, 'Open fire!'

CHAPTER TWO

At once the gun captains touched the glowing ends of their slow matches to the paper cones filled with gunpowder that protruded from the vents. There was a crackling hiss as the powder flared and then an ear-splitting roar and thump as a jet of fire and flame leaped from the muzzle of each cannon. The violent recoil caused the deck to lurch beneath Thomas's feet and he staggered forward a step before he recovered his balance. Each weapon had been carefully loaded with a mixture of large iron nails, linked chains and cast lead shot, captured from an enemy ship months earlier. There was a savage satisfaction in seeing the enemy's ammunition used against them, Thomas mused. The deadly cone of metal fragments blasted into the side of the corsair vessel. Splinters spat in all directions as the side rail was chewed up in two places. Behind, the turbaned warriors were swept away like children's dolls and left in tangled heaps on the deck.

'For God and St John!' La Valette bellowed and his men echoed his cry with a great roar that tore at their throats, their mouths agape and their eyes wide with crazed excitement. 'For God and St John!' they shouted again and again as the galley surged forward, directly towards the side of the enemy vessel.

'Brace yourselves!' La Valette shouted, his booming voice just audible above the cheering of his men. Thomas stilled his tongue and gritted his teeth as he lowered himself into a crouch, grabbed the side rail with one hand and spread his feet wide. The others around him, those with the wit to understand what was to come, followed his example and waited for the impact. The deck seemed to leap beneath him and the soldier standing behind Thomas slammed into his shoulder before pitching on to the deck, along with several others. The foremast groaned in protest and there was a loud crack as one of the shrouds parted. Below deck there was a muffled chorus of cries as the terrified rowers were hurled from their benches and brought up painfully by their chains. The bow of the *Swift Hind* had been heavily reinforced to withstand the impact of a ramming attack and now rode up with a terrible grinding and splintering as the corsair galley tilted under the impact. There were cries of terror as scores of the enemy tumbled down the sloping deck and fell against the side. Several continued over the rail and splashed into the sea.

'Jesu!' Stokely muttered as he clambered back on to his feet close by Thomas.

The *Swift Hind* had stopped dead in the water and there was a brief moment of stillness as the stunned crews on both vessels recovered their wits. Then La Valette's voice cut through the chill dawn air.

'Grappling hooks! Aim for the far side and cleat home!'

'Come on.' Thomas lowered his pike to the deck and beckoned to Stokely to follow him as he raced forward and snatched up one of the heavy iron hooks lying on a coil of rope. Letting out a short length he swung the hook up and then swirled it overhead before releasing his grip. The hook arced across the enemy deck and disappeared over the far side. At once Thomas snatched up the rope and pulled in the slack. As he bent down to fasten the rope round a cleat, more hooks flew across the enemy vessel and lodged in the woodwork.

'Back oars!' ordered La Valette. 'Quickly now. Pace master, use your whip!'

The rowers struggled back on to their narrow benches and grasped the shafts of their oars, worn smooth over the years by those who had gone before them. The order for the first stroke was given before every rower was ready and the blades splashed down clumsily on either side. Having fastened their ropes, Thomas and Oliver returned to their position at the head of the band of armed men on the main deck. For a moment the *Swift Hind* did not move and her bows continued to press down on the side of the enemy vessel. Then with a gentle lurch she began to ease back, and the ropes attached to the grappling hooks snapped taut across the enemy deck. There was a cry of alarm from the stern as the corsair captain realised the danger. Some of his men began to slash at the ropes stretching overhead, but because of the canted deck only the handful who struggled up to the far side could hack into the ropes.

But it was already too late. The *Swift Hind* began to draw clear, dragging the far beam of the corsair vessel after them. The near side dipped beneath the water and then, with a graceful flow of movement, the galley capsized, pitching the crew and unsecured equipment across the deck and into the sea. Thomas caught a quick glance of the terrified expressions of the rowers through the deck gratings, still chained to their benches. Then they were gone, rolled under the surface of the sea, and the barnacled hull of the galley glistened on the disturbed waters of the bay. The grappling hooks were cut loose and the ropes slapped into the sea. Around the hulk, dozens of men thrashed as they tried to stay afloat. Those who could swim were making for the safety of the beach, a short distance away. Others clung to whatever floating debris they could find, or tried to find purchase on the hull.

A cheer rose up from the men on the Christian galley but Thomas could not find the heart to join in. He could not free himself of the spectacle of the faces of the rowers as the enemy ship had turned over. Most of those men were Christians like himself, taken prisoner and condemned to the galleys, only to die, dreadfully, at the hands of men of their own faith. Even now, Thomas could imagine them trapped under the water, thrashing about in the cold and darkness, held down by their chains until they drowned. He felt sick at the thought.

A hand slapped him on the shoulder. He glanced round to see Stokely beaming at him, until he caught sight of Thomas's stricken features, and frowned.

'Thomas, what is it?'

He tried to answer but there were no words to describe the horror that chilled his heart. He tried to thrust the feeling aside and shook his head. 'Nothing.'

'Then join in.' Stokely gestured at the other men on the deck as they cheered wildly.

Thomas looked over at them briefly and then turned

towards the remaining enemy galley, less than a quarter of a mile away. The corsairs had cut their anchor cable and turned the vessel so that it was now pointing directly at the *Swift Hind*. Thomas nodded his head towards the enemy. 'There'll be no chance of surprising them in the same way.'

Movement caught Thomas's eye and he turned to see the crew of the galleon swiftly climbing the ratlines and spreading out along the spars as they prepared to unfurl the sails. They would be under way shortly but there was no more than the lightest of breezes and they would be lucky to clear the bay before the duel between the two galleys was decided. Time enough to deal with them later, Thomas decided as he returned his attention to the corsair galley.

Once the *Swift Hind* was clear of its first victim, La Valette gave the order to move ahead and the rowers strained at the oars to get the galley moving. Slowly, then with increasing speed, the slender vessel swept forward. There was a brief cry of terror as one of the corsairs in the water saw that he was in line with the oars but then a great blade smashed down on his skull and drove him under the water and abruptly cut off his scream.

On the foredeck the gun crews hurriedly sponged out the barrels of the two cannon and began to load the next charge, ramming down the stitched bag that carried the powder charge, and then packing in the second bag carrying the assorted pieces of iron shot that were so deadly at close range. On either side of the main deck the crossbowmen were working their winding mechanisms and preparing their next bolts. Thomas could see the turbans of men above the bows of the approaching corsair galley as they readied their arquebuses. Below them, protruding from gun ports either side of the prow, were the barrels of two cannon, the dark spots at the end of the muzzles looking like two black eyes, staring remorselessly at their prey.

'This is going to be a bloody business,' one of the men behind Thomas muttered.

'Aye,' one of his comrades answered. 'The Lord have mercy on us.'

Stokely turned on them angrily. 'Quiet there! The Lord is on our side. Our cause is just. It is the faithless heathen who should be begging for mercy.'

The men fell silent under the knight's fierce gaze and he turned away and raised himself to his full height as he stared towards the enemy. Thomas edged closer to him and spoke under his breath. 'I've not yet discovered a prayer that is proof against the bullet of an enemy or the shot from his cannon. I'd bear that in mind when they open fire.'

'That is profanity.'

'No, it is bitter experience. Save your prayers and set your mind to the matter of killing, or being killed.'

Stokely made to reply; then he clamped his jaw shut and pressed his lips together as he looked towards the corsair galley, surging across the calm water towards them. The eastern horizon was ablaze with the liquid glare of the sun just beyond the black mass of the far headland. A moment later the details of the corsairs were thrown into sharp outline as the first rays of sunlight lanced across the sea, causing Thomas and the others to narrow their eyes. The enemy were close enough for the sound of their cheers and the clatter of their blades against the sides of their round shields to carry clearly across the sea. The gap between the two galleys closed swiftly and now Thomas heard the first crackle of shots as the more excitable of the arquebusiers shot at the Christian vessel. Even though the range was long, still over two hundred paces, one of the gunners was struck in the head and his skull exploded as he tumbled back, showering his companions in droplets of blood, brains and bone splinters.

'Why doesn't La Valette give the order to shoot back?' asked Stokely.

'The captain knows what he's doing.'

Another shot struck home, striking one of the soldiers in the stomach with a high-pitched clang as it pierced his breastplate and burst through the padding of his gambison. He dropped his pike as he collapsed on the deck and rolled on to his side, groaning in agony.

'Get him below!' Thomas ordered and one of the soldiers set down his weapon and dragged the man over to the hatch just behind the foredeck and down the steps into the small hold where the galley's food and water was stored. There he would lie until his wound could be seen to after the fight. If the corsairs won the day then that was where he would drown or be killed as the ship was looted.

By the time the soldier returned to his post, the distance between the ships had halved and still the cannon had not fired, even as musket balls whirred overhead or cracked into the timbers of the *Swift Hind*. Thomas saw the nearest gun captain raise his slow match towards the powder quoin and he shouted to the man.

'Wait for the order!'

21

The gun captain looked round with a fearful expression, just as a brilliant flash came from the bows of the other galley. An instant later another. Then the air around Thomas was filled with a cacophony of cracking, clattering and the sharp ring of metal striking metal. Several of the crossbowmen at the bows were swept away, together with most of the crew of the larboard gun. Thomas was jerked round as something glanced off his breastplate and he staggered to the side to regain his balance. There was a brief hush across the deck before the cries and screams of the wounded broke out. Thomas glanced over his body but there was no sign of any wound. He looked up and saw Stokely clutching a hand to his cheek. Blood welled up beneath his gauntlet and dripped on to the polished steel of his gorget.

'I'm wounded . . .' he said in a shocked tone. 'Wounded.'

Thomas pulled his hand away and saw that a chunk of his cheek had been torn away. 'It's a flesh wound. You'll live.'

He turned to look over the deck and saw that perhaps a dozen men had been downed. Just then the surviving gun captain touched his slow match to the quoin of his weapon and there was a savage flash, a billowing cloud of smoke and a concussive thud that passed through the timbers of the galley and the bodies of those aboard her. Thomas saw the match in the lifeless hand of the dead gun captain and ran on to the foredeck to snatch it up. Crouching down beside the barrel he waited a moment until the smoke had cleared enough for him to see the corsair vessel looming directly ahead. There was just time to spring back and touch the glowing slow match to the powder, and the gun bucked violently as it discharged its weight of iron into the faces of the enemy.

'Ship oars! Helm hard to port!' La Valette's voice cried from the stern.

The rowers instantly pressed down on their handles to raise the blades clear of the water and then began to haul them in as the rudder bit into the water and forced the bows round to pass down the side of the corsair vessel. A moment later there was a jarring collision and a long rumbling groan as the two hulls ground along each other. Some of the oars from each vessel had still not been withdrawn through the sides and there was a series of sharp splintering reports as the long lengths of wood shattered.

Before the *Swift Hind* had stopped moving La Valette had rushed down from the quarterdeck, sword in hand, and raced to join the party of armed men led by Thomas and the other knights. The captain glanced round to check that his men were ready and then pointed his sword over the bulwark towards the enemy. 'For God and St John!'

CHAPTER THREE

La Valette clambered up on to the side rail and leaped over the narrow gap between the hulls and on to the enemy deck. Some of the crew had already begun to lob grappling hooks over the small gap and draw the two galleys together.

Thomas sucked in a deep breath, grasped his pike tightly in one hand and echoed his captain's cry. 'For God and St John!'

Then he, too, climbed on to the rail and jumped after La Valette. The veteran knight had already made his way into the middle of the corsair's deck, swinging the long blade of his sword before him in a vicious arc to drive the enemy back and clear a space for the men following him. A handful of shots sounded from either side as the arquebusiers discharged their weapons and then cast them aside before drawing their scimitars and charging into the fight. Thomas thudded down on to the deck and looked quickly from side to side, then turned towards the nearest threat, a large turbaned man with skin as dark as coal. His eyes glittered above a thick beard. He carried a heavy scimitar in one hand and a brass buckler in the other. He charged across the deck towards Thomas, swinging his blade to knock aside the steel point of Thomas's pike. Thomas let the point drop and cut under the corsair's blade before he thrust at the robes covering his opponent's chest.

Instinctively the corsair smashed his buckler against the shaft of the pike, knocking it aside so that it missed its target and ripped through the folds of his robe instead. Thomas snatched the pike back and presented it to his enemy again, feinting to keep the man at bay. On the periphery of his vision he was aware of La Valette's sword cutting down into a skull in a welter of blood. On the other side, Stokely was leading a small party of men in a charge along the bulwark. A small gap had opened up between Thomas and the black corsair, as if to provide a stage for their duel.

The corsair suddenly screamed something at him and lunged forward, hacking at the pike and knocking the tip down. He charged on and punched his buckler into Thomas's breastplate. The impact was absorbed by the padding beneath the armour and Thomas released his right hand, balled it into a fist and slammed it into his opponent's face. The small plates of the mantlet tore at the corsair's flesh and there was a dull crunch as the bones of his nose gave way. He let out an animal roar of pain and rage and thrust his buckler out again, knocking Thomas back, as he swung his scimitar in a high arc towards the knight's head.

Thomas saw it coming, a curve of steel, glinting in the light of the rising sun, and leaped to one side. The scimitar hissed close by and then struck the deck with a splintering thud. Before the corsair could straighten his body, Thomas viciously thrust his pike. The point caught the man squarely on the shoulder and knocked him off his feet. He fell heavily on his back and Thomas thrust the pike again, into his chest, high up just below the collarbone. The point tore through the white robe, pierced the flesh beneath and shattered bones as it plunged on, deep into the corsair's body. His face contorted, eyes and mouth tightly shut so that his features looked like charred wood. Then he sank back on to the deck, his hands clasped over the wound as blood welled up and spread through the stained folds of his robe.

Thomas placed his boot on the corsair's chest and ripped the point of his pike free. He glanced round, ready to strike again. La Valette and a party of men were fighting their way towards the stern where the corsair captain and his officers stood, determined to defend their station. In the other direction Stokely and some men had gained the foredeck and were cutting down the gun crews. Elsewhere the deck was a chaotic battlefield. The superior armour of the knights and the mercenaries they led gave them the advantage. The enemy's fanatical faith in their prophet's teachings gave them fierce courage but it was of little avail. Their scimitars glanced off the plate armour and only a fortunate blow at the joints or a thrust towards the face caused injury to the Christians. A handful of Thomas's comrades had fallen but the rest were steadily cutting their way through the corsairs.

Some of the enemy still presented a formidable challenge. Thomas picked out a tall, thin, well-armoured fighter with a large shield and a finely decorated scimitar who appeared to be standing guard over a hatch leading down into the galley's hold. A body lay sprawled at his feet, the white cross on a red surcoat revealing that it was one of the knights. The corsair grinned and held up his sword so that Thomas might see the bloodied edge. He ignored the taunt. The corsair was light-skinned, perhaps one of those taken as a child from the Balkans and raised as a Muslim, like the infamous Janissaries who formed the elite corps of the Sultan's army. A plume of black horsehair shimmered from the point of his helmet, which was covered in a gleaming black lacquer, as were the small plates of armour that had been stitched on to his quilted jacket. A livid scar on his cheek told of his experience, and also that once a foe had got the better of him, Thomas realised.

He presented the point of his pike as he approached the man and feinted towards the corsair's face. His opponent did not even blink, just shook his head mockingly.

'Very well,' Thomas growled through clenched teeth. 'Then try this!'

He threw his weight behind his pike and leaped forward. The corsair nimbly stepped aside and then slashed his fine blade towards the side of Thomas's head. Thomas ducked and the honed edge glanced off the curved steel of his helmet with a sharp ringing impact that stunned him for an instant. He stepped back and shook his head, weaving his pike from side to side to keep the corsair back. The other man grinned briefly, then the lips closed into a tight grimace and he stepped forward, the blade whirling, almost too fast for human eyes to follow. Thomas ignored the scimitar and abruptly changed his grip to hold the pike out like the cross staff he had used as a boy back in England. He was strong and well-built as all men who had been raised to become knights must be and now he charged forward.

The bold, and crude, tactic caught the corsair by surprise and he could not move fast enough to get out of the way of the length of the pike. Thomas crashed into him, driving the corsair back and causing him to stumble as he struggled to remain on his feet. Then he slammed against the bulwark, the impact driving the breath from his lungs so forcefully that Thomas blinked as the odour of the man's morning meal washed over his face. The corsair released his grip on his sword and shield and let them slip to each side as he grasped the shaft of the pike and pushed back. Thomas met his thrust and with every muscle and sinew in his arms he pressed down on him, steadily forcing the corsair on to the deck. The shaft touched the top of the man's chest and then Thomas pushed it up, under his chin and against his throat. The corsair's jaw opened and he squirmed as he desperately tried to stop his opponent choking him.

'Curse . . . you . . . Christian,' he uttered in accented French. 'Damn you . . . to hell!'

Thomas's face was now scant inches from that of the corsair and he could see every detail of the man's features and the sweat pricking out from his brow as he fought for his life. His breaths were now laboured and harsh and his eyes rolled up and then something gave in his throat with a soft crunch. The corsair spasmed, his eyes snapped open, wide and fierce, as his mouth worked in a series of dry clicks and gasps. Thomas felt the other man's strength fading but he kept pressing down on the pike, until at length the corsair's head slumped back on to the deck, his hands slid from the shaft and he stared blankly at the pink sky, the tip of his tongue protruding from between his teeth.

Thomas rolled to one side, his pike held ready in case there was another enemy about to attack him, but he had only the dead and wounded for immediate company. The fight for the ship was almost over. Stokely and the men with him had cleared the foredeck, while La Valette and the other soldiers were pressing across the stern of the galley. The corsair captain and a handful of his men were up against the stern, savagely hacking at the armoured men in front of them. As Thomas watched, La Valette raised his sword above his head and slashed it violently down at an angle. The veteran knight was a powerfully built man and the enemy captain's attempt to parry the blow did nothing to alter the course of the sword. An instant later the sharp steel cut through his turban and deep into his skull, right down to the jaw.

When the corsairs on the stern saw that their captain was mortally wounded they threw down their weapons and fell on their knees to beg for mercy. Swords and pikes hacked and stabbed at the men on the deck for a few more moments and then the fight was over. La Valette wrenched his blade free, wiped it on the robe of the corsair and sheathed the weapon then turned to survey the carnage on the deck of the galley. He caught sight of Thomas.

'Sir Thomas! Over here.'

Thomas quickly picked his way over the deck towards the stern, stepping over the bodies sprawled and heaped across the bloodstained deck. He stopped at the foot of the short flight of stairs leading up to the stern and looked up at his captain. La Valette had taken a blow to the head and his morion helmet had a deep dent in the wide brim, but there was no sign that he was wounded or even dazed as he calmly regarded his subordinate.

'Take command here.'

'Take command? Yes, sir.'

'I'm taking the *Swift Hind* and going after the galleon.' He gestured with his hand and Thomas looked round to see that the sails of the big cargo ship had filled with the light dawn breeze and she was about to clear the bay. If she got far enough out to sea then she would be more weatherly than the galley and might yet escape if a heavy swell picked up along with the increasing breeze.

'I'll leave Sir Oliver and twenty men with you,' La Valette continued. 'Free any Christians you find amongst the rowers. Take care, mind you. I don't want any of the Muslims claiming that they are of the faith.'

'Yes, sir.'

'Chain the prisoners to the rowing benches. Then make the necessary repairs, clear the bodies away and set course for Malta.'

'Malta?' Thomas frowned. There was still plenty of time before the end of the campaign season. It was too early to return to the home of the Order. But the captain had made a decision and Thomas had no right to question him. He stiffened his back and bowed his head curtly. 'As you command, sir.'

'That's right.' La Valette regarded him with a stern expression for a moment before he relented and continued in a lower voice that was meant for the young knight alone to hear. 'Thomas, we have sunk one galley and taken this one. I hope to take the galleon in due course. We must take our prizes to Malta where they will be safe and revictual the *Swift Hind* before we continue. By noon we shall have three vessels and barely enough men to crew them. We cannot take the risk of any further clashes until we have returned our prizes to Malta. Do you understand?'

'Yes, sir,' Thomas replied flatly.

'There are few enough of us left now. Some in Europe think that the Order is the vanguard of the Church's struggle against the Turk. The truth is we are the rearguard. Never forget that. Every man we lose brings the enemy one step closer to victory.' His eyes bored into Thomas's. 'In time, if you live long enough, you will command your own galley and be responsible for the lives of the men who serve under you. It is not a duty to be taken lightly.'

Thomas nodded. 'I understand, sir.'

'See that you do.' La Valette backed off a pace and looked over the men standing along the deck. 'Sergeant Mendoza!' he called.

A portly figure trotted up to him and saluted. 'Sir?'

'You and your men are staying aboard, under the command of Sir Thomas. The rest of you, back to the *Swift Hind* at once.'

The party following the captain made their way along the deck until they reached the place where the bows of their ship were bound to the corsair galley by the grappling hooks. They climbed up on to the bulwark and crossed back over to the other vessel. As soon as the last man had left the corsair, Thomas gave the order for the grappling-hook lines to be slackened off so that the iron points could be worked free and carefully tossed back to the deck of the *Swift Hind*. A gap opened between the two galleys as La Valette gave the order to unship the oars and back the vessel off far enough to allow them to turn the bow in the direction of the fleeing galleon. Then the oars, working in a steady rhythm, powered the sleek galley after their prey. Thomas watched for a moment and then turned his attention to his temporary command.

CHAPTER FOUR

T he first priority was to deal with the men imprisoned below deck. He turned to the sergeant. 'You and two others come with me. The rest are to dispose of the bodies. Make sure our men are set aside for a proper burial.'

He and Mendoza made their way over to the grating above the entrance to the main hold. As Thomas approached he could hear muttering from below and a terrified keening that was hurriedly silenced. A bolt fastened the grating in place and Thomas knelt down to draw it back, noting the thoroughness of the corsairs, who chained their rowers to their benches and then locked them into the hold for good measure.

'Help me with the grating.'

With the sergeant's help they lifted the grating and slid it on to the deck beside the entrance to the hold. Thomas peered over the edge and winced at the warm blast of the foulest stench he had ever encountered. There was movement below and the clink of chains as limbs stirred. Then he saw faces turning towards the pallid light entering through the hatch. Wild locks of filthy hair and straggly beards hung over their emaciated features. Most were white, but there were darker hues of skin there as well, though it was hard to tell for the filth that covered them.

A ladder descended on to the narrow walkway that stretched between the lines of benches running along each side of the galley. He climbed down and saw a figure holding a small whip standing towards the stern, beside the pace keeper still chained next to his drum. Thomas and his men had to bend their heads as they strode aft, under the gaze of glittering eyes on either side.

'Praise the Lord . . .' a voice croaked. 'They're Christians . . . Christians! Come to set us free!'

His words set off many of his comrades who raised their hands imploringly towards their rescuers. Some simply hunched over the oars and wept, their shoulders wracked by sobs.

The overseer dropped his whip as Thomas approached and clasped his hands together, begging in French, 'Please, sir . . . Please.'

'Where is the locking pin?' Thomas demanded.

The overseer jabbed a finger towards a ring bolt on the deck just beyond the reach of the pace setter. 'Th-there.'

Thomas brushed him aside. He fought back his nausea at the overpowering stink rising from the bilges. How could any man endure this? he wondered. He reached the ring bolt and saw that the locking pin was just beside it. He took out his dagger and began to work it free. A moment later it fell out of its sheath and then Thomas fed the chain back through the ring bolt and laid it at the foot of the nearest rowing bench. He stared at the faces of the men sitting there.

'Who amongst you is Christian, if any?'

'Me!' The nearest man nodded emphatically. 'Me, master. I'm from Toulon.'

'Set him free,' Thomas ordered.

'And me!' said the rower's neighbour.

'Liar!' the first man snapped. 'You are a Morisco. The corsairs took you from Valencia.'

'Sergeant, free this Frenchman. The other man stays in chains.'

The Morisco, descended from the Arabs who had once ruled Spain, opened his mouth to protest but then, seeing the implacable expression on Thomas's face, he closed it and bowed his head over his oar in resignation. Thomas looked round as more voices called out, proclaiming their faith. If all were telling the truth, only a third would be left at the oars, too few to work the passage to Malta. As the tumult of desperate cries rose, he drew a deep breath and bellowed down the length of the galley, 'SILENCE!'

The rowers, long since cowed by the whip of the overseer, obediently stilled their tongues. Thomas turned to his sergeant. 'Set the Christians free, and only the Christians. Any man who claims the faith and is found to be a liar will be put to death.'

'Yes, sir,' the soldier replied tonelessly.

'Carry on.' Thomas could not bear the smell of these creatures and their surroundings any longer. 'I'll be on deck.'

'What about him?' Mendoza gestured at the overseer who was standing towards the stern, not daring to meet anyone's gaze as he awaited his fate. Thomas stared at him briefly and noted the short length of whip still in his hand. 'Him? Let the men you set free deal with him.'

Thomas turned away and strode quickly back down the

narrow walkway towards the ladder, fighting the urge to run and escape from this hellish hole as quickly as possible. He climbed on to the deck and hurried across to the upwind bulwark and breathed as deeply as he could to expel every last tendril of the foul air in the hold. Although he had known what went on below the deck of a galley, he had only been below on a handful of occasions. What he had seen had disgusted him, but the men who crewed the Order's galleys were criminals, pirates and followers of false faiths. As foul as the circumstances were on the Christian galleys, he had never before seen men as pitifully treated as here on the corsairs' galley. He felt a deep rage as he thought of the enemy, a burning desire to wipe Islam from the face of God's earth.

A splash close at hand made Thomas look round; some of his men were heaving the bodies of the dead over the side. The corpses had been stripped of their weapons and items of clothing that might fetch a decent price in the markets of Malta. Two more men guarded a handful of wounded prisoners sitting on the deck around the base of the aft mast. As he gazed at them, Thomas felt his heart harden like a cold stone in his breast. He turned away from the bulwark and strode towards them, gesturing to a handful of the other soldiers to follow him. As he reached the prisoners he stopped and stared at them with hatred. There were over twenty of them, most still wearing some armour, empty scabbards hanging from their belts and baldrics. Most had wounds which had hastily been dressed with torn strips of cloth. The wounds were superficial and they would recover, well enough at least to take their places on the galley's rowing benches.

'Leave the officers here. Take the rest down to the oars,' he ordered in a flat tone. His men separated the prisoners, herding most towards the hatch while a handful remained sitting on the deck. Thomas stared at them for a moment before he spoke again. 'Kill them. The bodies go over the side.'

One of the men who had been guarding the prisoners glanced at his companion before he cleared his throat and responded. 'Sir? The officers are worth good money.'

Thomas felt a tremor in his hand and clenched it tightly. 'I gave you an order. Kill them! Do it!'

Footsteps sounded behind him and then Stokely stepped between Thomas and the prisoners. 'You can't kill the officers. They are prisoners.'

Thomas swallowed and answered bitterly, 'They are the enemy. They are Turks, infidels.'

'They are still God's creatures,' Stokely answered, 'even if they have not yet embraced the true faith. We accepted their surrender. We cannot slaughter them. It would offend any notion of chivalry.'

'Chivalry?' Thomas frowned and then smiled. 'There is no place for it in the war against the Turk. Death is what they deserve.'

'You can't—'

Thomas raised a hand to silence him. 'We're wasting time. I want the galley under way as soon as possible. First, we get rid of these . . . vermin.'

He drew his sword and before anyone could intervene he ran the blade through the nearest of the corsairs, a youth in a finely embroidered jerkin, too young to grow a beard. The corsair gasped and slumped back on to the deck as a crimson stain quickly spread over the white cotton of his jerkin. He feebly clawed at the rent in the cloth and tried to press at the wound as if to staunch the flow of blood. Thomas stood over him, blinded by all but the desire to kill. He struck again, this time at the youth's neck, cutting deep into the spine and almost severing the head. Thomas looked round at his men. 'Now, carry out your orders! Kill them all. You first.' He pointed at one of the men who had been guarding the prisoners. 'Do it.'

The soldier lowered his pike and thrust it into the chest of the nearest corsair. The others began to cry out, begging for mercy in French and Spanish as well as their native tongues. Once the first two were dead, the rest of the soldiers standing around them joined in with the slaughter. Thomas stood apart, and Stokely looked on, his lips curled with disgust and horror.

'This is . . . wrong.' He shook his head. 'Wrong.'

'Then perhaps you had better reconsider your membership of the Order.' Thomas shrugged and turned away as the last of the prisoners was killed. 'See to it that the bodies are removed.'

As he walked towards the bows, Thomas felt nothing for a moment. He had expected to feel a sense of release, the draining of the tension that had built up during the battle, and then in the hold. But there was just a chilling numbness. The blood on the deck around him and on discarded weapons was just a detail, and his recollections of the battle were fleeting images unfreighted by emotion, remorse or even the smallest ray of triumph. All he knew was that he still lived and his comrades had won a small victory. No more than a pinprick to the vast Leviathan of Turkish might that was steadily making this sea, and the lands that bounded it, the domain of Islam. Blood would continue to flow, men would continue to die by the sword or from starvation and exhaustion chained to the oars of the galleys that swept this troubled sea. Women and children would continue to be taken as slaves to become whores or be raised as Muslims to wage war on those they had once called family. In turn the knights of St John and those who shared their cause would fight for survival. And so it would go on. Sword and scimitar locked in an endless, bloody duel whose only prize was the misery upon misery heaped upon man.

Thomas went over to the small hatch over the forward hold where he had killed the man dressed in black. He sat down heavily and unbuckled his mantlets and pulled off his gloves before fumbling with the buckles of the chinstrap of his helmet. It took a few attempts before he pulled the helmet off and placed it beside him on the deck. Sweat plastered his hair to his scalp and the morning breeze felt cool on his exposed skin. He leaned back for a moment, resting against the bulwark, until a shadow fell across his face. He blinked his eyes open and saw Stokely standing before him.

'I've carried out your orders. And the Christians have been freed.' He gestured towards the rear of the deck where forty or so skeletal figures in rags were gathered around some baskets of bread, frantically scrabbling for a loaf, and ripping chunks off and chewing vigorously. Stokely watched them a moment. 'They weren't so hungry that they didn't tear the overseer to pieces first. Still, *he* deserved his fate.'

'If you say so.'

Stokely glanced at the hatch. 'Have you searched down there yet?'

Thomas shook his head.

'Might be some more food we could give that lot.'

Thomas waved a hand towards the narrow coaming. 'Do as you wish.'

Stokely lowered himself down the ladder into the small storage hold. A moment later Thomas heard him swear in a surprised tone, before he called up.

'Thomas!'

'What is it?'

'Come down here!'

The urgency in his tone caused Thomas to quickly shift himself over the edge of the hatch and drop down into the confined space. 'What is it?'

He turned and looked forward to where Stokely was crouching down, not far from a bundle of rags. There was not enough room to stand and Thomas shuffled over to his side. The bundle stirred and in the shafts of light that penetrated the hold through a small grille Thomas saw that it was a woman. A thin strip of cloth covered her and as she began to turn towards them, it slipped and exposed the raw welts across her shoulders and back. Her hair was long and dark and one hand was chained to a bolt in the side of the hold. She looked at the two men, eyes narrow with suspicion. Her skin was pale and there was a bruise on her cheek. Her lips parted and her tongue briefly moistened the chapped skin before she whispered, 'Who are you?'

'Christians,' Sir Oliver replied. 'We've taken this galley.'

'Christians,' she repeated, looking them over searchingly.

There was a brief silence as the woman and the two knights stared at each other. As he looked at her, Thomas realised that she was beautiful, even here, beaten, bruised and chained in her own filth. Something stirred in the coldness of his hardened heart. He shuffled round so that he could reach the ring bolt and then pulled out his dagger. The woman flinched slightly at the sight of the blade and he motioned towards the pin fastening the chains to the bolt. 'I'll get you out of here.'

She nodded and Thomas inserted the point of the blade and began to work the pin free. He paused briefly and looked at her.

'What is your name?'

She licked her lips again and replied hoarsely, 'Maria de Venici.'

Thomas nodded and again he felt something stir in his heart as he regarded her.

'Maria,' he repeated slowly, savouring each syllable of the name. 'Maria.'

CHAPTER FIVE

Malta, two months later

Thin streaks of silvery cloud ringed the bright gleam of a crescent moon over Malta. A glittering finger of reflected light stretched across the waters of the harbour towards the mass of the Sciberras ridge, and the air was still and hot. Thomas paid little attention to his surroundings. On another night he would have been sensitive to the sensual aesthetics of a summer night in the Mediterranean and paused to drink in the sights and sounds and surrender to the moment.

But not now.

His heart was beating with impatience and anxiety as he stood in the shadow of the walls of Fort St Angelo, the home of the Order, built on the rocky tip of the Birgu peninsula. The fort guarded the entrance to the harbour and loomed over the small town whose red roof tiles appeared dull and grey in the moonlight. A small path ran along the base of the wall, leading down to the landing stage at the edge of the water, where Thomas stood waiting. He started nervously as the cathedral bell tolled the half-hour after midnight. Maria should have been here long ago. Edging away from the rocks beneath the wall,

Thomas strained his eyes as he stared along the path, but nothing moved there. He felt a stab of fear at the thought that she might have changed her mind and decided not to take the risk of meeting him alone again.

They had already been warned not to pursue their relationship. La Valette had approached Thomas at the morning weapons drill and taken him aside for a quiet exchange. Maria de Venici, he reminded the young knight, was waiting for her brother to retrieve her from the island and pay over the reward to the Order for her rescue.

Thomas's lips twitched with amusement. Ransom was a more accurate word for it. Not that such an infelicitous term played any part in the exchange of messages between the Order and the Venici family.

'Your mutual affection has not gone unnoticed,' said La Valette. 'And I must warn you that it is inadvisable, Thomas. Maria is betrothed to another and there is no future for this . . . friendship that has grown between you.'

'Who told you, sir?' Thomas asked.

Before he could stop himself, La Valette's gaze instinctively flickered towards the other young knights practising their attacks against wooden dummies set up in the courtyard of Fort St Angelo. Thomas looked beyond him and saw Oliver Stokely watching them. As their eyes met, Stokely turned his attention back to the dummy he had been attacking, which was painted to resemble a Turk, complete with a crudely depicted face with dark features and black eyes.

So, Thomas thought, it was the man he had considered a friend. It came as little surprise. Their friendship had cooled in the weeks since the galley had returned to Malta as it quickly became evident that the woman they had set free preferred the company of Thomas. She had been grateful and friendly towards Stokely, but her expression became far more lively in the presence of Thomas and it was him she asked to accompany her in her walks about Birgu, and then in the surrounding countryside.

That was where it had happened, Thomas recalled, with a quickening of his pulse. In the shadow of one of the island's rare trees on the heights of St Margaret, which overlooked Birgu and the harbour. She had stumbled against him, her brow brushing his cheek as he caught her by the arm to prevent her falling. Maria had looked up, and smiled, and then they had kissed. It had been an instinctive act, and Thomas had been shocked by his impulsiveness, until she reached her hand behind his neck and pulled him closer to her and they kissed again. They found a hidden corner in one of the stone walls and Thomas had laid his cape on the ground and they had remained there for the rest of the afternoon, before returning to Birgu, flushed with passion, and trepidation. It was a dangerous liaison and both knew it. Yet they could not, and would not, constrain the heat that coursed through their veins.

That had been several days before La Valette had issued his warning. Days in which Thomas had endured his daily duty as if it had been an eternity in purgatory. Afterwards he ran to meet her at the place they had agreed upon, a small garden close to the town gate. It had belonged to a Venetian merchant who had bequeathed it to the islanders. The garden offered shade and the sweet scent of flowers and herbs to visitors. A more fertile ground for the meeting of lovers was not to be found anywhere else on the island. That was where they had been, in a shady bower, when Stokely had appeared, standing foursquare upon the path, in the direct glare of the sun. He stared at them in silence as they self-consciously leaned away from each other. The scar on his cheek was still livid and had stretched the skin at the corner of his mouth into a faint sneer.

'Oliver,' Maria smiled. 'You surprised us.'

'I can see that,' he replied coldly. 'So, this is where you have been running off to, Thomas.'

Thomas rose from the bench he had been sharing with Maria. 'Listen, this is our secret. I would ask you not to tell anyone of this.'

'Ask and be damned,' Stokely said angrily. 'This is wrong. You swore an oath of chastity, Thomas. As has every knight.'

Thomas snorted. 'The oath is meaningless. Honoured more in the breach than the obligation, and you know it. Grand Master d'Omedes is content to turn a blind eye when it suits him.'

'Nevertheless, it is an oath. It is my duty to report this.'

The two glared at each other and Thomas was surprised to see the anger, and even hate, that blazed in the eyes of his friend.

'You must not speak a word of this, Oliver. If not for the sake of our friendship, then out of chivalry to Maria.'

'I will take no lessons in chivalry from you!' Stokely spat.

Thomas gritted his teeth and pressed his lips together as his hands balled into fists. But before the confrontation could go any further he felt Maria gently stay his arm. She stepped between them and smiled nervously at Stokely. 'There is no need for this. Not amongst friends.'

'I see no friends here,' Stokely responded in a strained voice.

Maria frowned. 'I consider you a friend, Oliver, and you have my heartfelt gratitude for saving me from the Turks, as does Thomas.'

'Is this how a friend shows gratitude?'

'Do not be angry with me.' She reached out for his hand but Stokely took a step back. Maria let out a small gasp. 'Oliver . . . I speak direct from my heart when I call you my friend. My dear friend.'

'Then why do you betray my friendship like this? Both of you.'

'In what way have I betrayed you? Have I lied to you?' she reproved him.

When he did not reply she lowered her head sadly. 'I had thought you my benefactor and friend, just as I regard Thomas. And now, even though he is more than my friend, that does not make you less of one. Dear Oliver, please understand.'

'Do not call me that! Not unless you mean it as I wish it to be meant.'

'You have my affection. Please do not abuse it.'

Stokely growled something under his breath and with a last bitter glance at Thomas he turned on his heel and strode off through the garden. Thomas watched his retreating back and let out a sigh. 'There will be trouble for us. Mark my words.'

Maria shook her head. 'Oliver is a good man, and a good friend. He will come to his senses.'

Thomas thought for a moment and shrugged. 'I hope you are right, my love.'

As soon as he had uttered the words he felt his heart jump anxiously and he quickly glanced at Maria. She was smiling at him in delight as she whispered, 'And now I know . . .'

'Thomas, did you hear me?' La Valette snapped.

Thomas's mind raced to recall what his superior had just said to him, but to no avail. His mouth opened, but no reply came. La Valette let out a hiss of exasperation and ran his hand through his thick dark hair. He leaned forward.

'Stay away from the woman. If you do not, there can only be misfortune for you both. Great misfortune. Do you understand?'

'Yes, sir.'

'I could ask you for your word that you will not see her but I would not wish to place you in a position where your soul was put at risk for the sake of your more animal instincts.' Thomas felt a moment's anger at this characterisation of his feelings. 'I am therefore ordering you to remain away from Maria de Venici until her brother removes her from the island,' La Valette continued. 'Is that understood? Keep away from the house where she is staying.'

'I understand.'

'Good.' La Valette stretched up to his full height with a smile. 'I shall let her know what has been agreed. Let that be an end to it.'

Why has she not come? Thomas fumed. She had got his note and replied that she would meet him, despite the warning from La Valette. So what could have delayed her? A change of heart, or some other cause? Dear Lord, let it be another cause, Thomas prayed silently, then felt ashamed that he had called on divine favour in pursuit of an end he knew that others would see as ignoble.

He decided to wait until the bell tolled the first hour of the morning. If Maria had not come by then he would take it that she would never come and that this first love of his life was doomed.

The night edged on and as the deep note of the bell sounded, he drew a sorrowful breath and slowly paced back along the path. Then she emerged from the gloom and hurried towards him and without a word they embraced and kissed and all his fears vanished.

'What kept you from me?' Thomas asked at length.

'I'm so sorry, my love. The wife of the merchant tasked with accommodating me is a suspicious old shrew and watches me like a hawk.'

'With good cause.' Thomas chuckled.

Maria pushed at his chest. 'Do not mock. I had to wait until I was sure there was no movement in the house before I dared creep out. I came as soon as I could. We haven't much time. I have to be back in my room before the servants stir at dawn.'

She kissed him again and Thomas sensed her tension and drew back.

'What is the matter?' he asked.

Her skin looked pale in the moon's glow as she stared at him, and he felt her tremble. 'Thomas, what is to become of us? We are sinning, there is no other word for it. I am to be married to another man, and yet I give you my heart and body. What good is that? My brother will arrive any day. After that we shall never see each other again.'

'So we should make the most of the time we have.'

'We have already made more of it than is prudent,' she replied nervously.

'Damn prudence. We should follow our natures and our hearts.'

She shook her head and spoke softly. 'You fool. You dear fool. We are as the smallest cogs in an intricate mechanism. We must turn on the whim of larger forces. We have no say in it.'

'But we do,' Thomas responded earnestly. 'We could leave Malta. Come home with me to England.'

'Leave Malta? How? Do you think to steal yourself a ship as easily as you have stolen my heart?'

'It was not stolen, as I recall, but freely given.' Thomas rubbed his jaw as he considered their plight. 'We could stow away aboard a merchant ship. Make for France and travel on from there.' He was speaking without much thought and his words sounded foolish and hopeless even to him. Maria would be missed at once, and when it was discovered that he was also gone, it was not hard to imagine the consequences. Maria was in the safekeeping of the Order. They could not be seen to have failed in their duty. A fast galley would be sent in pursuit of any ship that had left the island. They would be overtaken before the first day was out and brought back to face the wrath of the Grand Master. He knew this but still his heart argued for fleeing with Maria.

'What can we do?' he asked angrily. 'I will not give you up!'

'Yes, you will.' A voice spoke from the shadows further along the track. 'Sooner than you think.'

They turned towards the sound and Thomas saw a figure emerge into the wan moonlight. A man, his hand resting on the hilt of his sword. Several more men appeared behind him.

'Oliver . . .' Maria whispered.

Thomas swallowed and tried to sound calm as he addressed his former friend. 'What are you doing here?'

'Don't be an even bigger fool than you already are, Thomas,' Stokely responded. 'You know precisely why I am here.' He turned and gestured to the men behind him. 'Arrest them both. Take the lady back to her quarters.'

Two men approached and Thomas stepped in front of Maria and raised his fists.

'No, Thomas!' she said urgently. 'It's too late for that. Far too late.'

'Maria is right,' Stokely intervened. 'It is too late. It is over between you. Now let the lady be escorted to her keepers . . .'

Thomas stood his ground and Maria edged round him, taking his hand and giving it a quick squeeze before they were parted. Thomas watched in anger and despair as the three figures padded back along the path towards Birgu. Then Stokely gave a curt command and two men grasped his arms and pinned them behind his back. Stokely stepped forward and shook his head mockingly. 'Dear Thomas, what is to become of you now?'

CHAPTER SIX

The expression on the face of Grand Master Jean d'Omedes darkened as he listened to Stokely. The Grand Master had been roused from his slumber shortly after the second hour and had berated his servant angrily until the cause of his disturbance eventually penetrated his sleep-encumbered mind. Then he had dressed hurriedly and summoned Romegas, his senior galley captain, and Jean de La Valette to the council chamber of the Order in the heart of Fort St Angelo.

Flickering candles illuminated the hurriedly assembled hearing. Thomas stood between two armed guards in front of the three men sitting behind a long table. To one side Stokely stood and gave his account. When he had finished there was a tense silence before the Grand Master cleared his throat and glared at Thomas.

'Do you have any idea how much damage you have done to the Order? The Venici family will never forgive us when they hear what has happened. Nor will the Duke in Sardinia to whose son Maria was betrothed. Our position is precarious enough without making new enemies.'

Romegas growled, 'If we are denied permission to replenish our galleys from the ports of Naples and Sardinia then our ability to strike at the corsairs and the Turks will be hit hard, sir.'

The Grand Master sucked in a breath. 'What are we to do?'

'I don't think there's any choice, sir,' Romegas replied. 'We must punish Sir Thomas, in an exemplary fashion. The Venici family will expect nothing less.'

'Wait.' La Valette half turned to address the other men seated at the table. 'There is no need to act rashly. It is not too late to hide this affair from outside eyes.'

'I wonder,' the Grand Master mused and then looked at Thomas shrewdly. 'Is it too late? Sir Thomas, is the lady's honour still intact?'

Thomas flushed and his defiant gaze dropped and he stared at the stone floor in front of the table.

'I see,' d'Omedes said flatly. 'Then we must do as Romegas says. Punishment must be swift and severe. The Order must be seen to have acted against this miscreant.'

'He has broken a sacred oath,' said Romegas, 'and betrayed the honour of the Holy Religion. The Venicis will want his head. I suspect nothing short of that will assuage their anger.'

La Valette snorted with derision. 'You are not seriously suggesting that we execute Sir Thomas?'

Romegas nodded. 'That is precisely what I am suggesting.'

'For what? For succumbing to the weakness of the flesh? That is no reason to hang a man. By God, if it were then half the knights of the Order should be strung up alongside him for having mistresses or ravaging the women of our enemies.'

The Grand Master raised a hand. 'Pray, be quiet. We are not here to judge other knights. Just Sir Thomas.'

'Unless there is a common standard then I suggest that we have no code of honour worth preserving, sir.'

The Grand Master's brow furrowed angrily. 'You go too far, La Valette.'

'No, sir. It is you who are stepping beyond the bounds.' La Valette gestured towards Thomas. 'I know this knight well. He has fought at my side for these last two years. I have not seen his equal for courage and devotion to the Order. Sir Thomas is one of the most promising knights of his generation. It would be foolhardy to eradicate such talent when we are in sore need of fighting men. Punish him, yes. A public flogging perhaps. That should do to remind our men of the need to act with honour and chivalry. That is all that is necessary.'

'It is not enough,' Romegas replied. 'If we did that and permitted Sir Thomas to stay in the Order, he would be a constant reminder of our shame and, worse, our leniency and indulgence of ill discipline and lax morality. Our younger knights need to be taught a lesson. They need a reminder of the depth and solemnity of the oaths that bind the Order together. Let Sir Thomas's death reaffirm the bonds that tie us. I urge you to have him executed, sir.'

La Valette shook his head. 'Kill him, and you risk discouraging other good young men from joining the Order. Sir Thomas's crime is that he is a young man, and we all know full well the powerful desires and needs that we once shared with Sir Thomas. If he is executed for a temporary lapse of judgement then men like him, men whom we need, will refuse to join us. There is a better way,' La Valette continued. 'A way that shows we will not tolerate such indiscretions. I say that we expel Sir Thomas from the Order.'

'Expel him?' The Grand Master frowned. 'What kind of punishment is that?'

'There is nothing more shameful.' La Valette turned towards Thomas. 'I believe I have the measure of this man. He counts his membership of the Order the highest honour a man can attain in this life. It is the Order that gives shape and value to his existence. Withdraw that and he lives on in shame, and knows the full weight of his loss every day. That is the punishment that should be imposed. Besides, while he lives, he can still put his talent for war to use in the service of Christendom somewhere, if not here.'

Thomas was grateful for La Valette's intervention. It might save his life. But the words of his mentor were true enough. There was no dishonour greater in his mind than being cast out of the Order. What would he do then? His honour would be held cheap in the eyes of all those who came to know his fate.

The Grand Master was silent as he pondered the young knight's fate. At length he drew a deep breath and spoke. 'I have reached a decision. Sir Thomas Barrett will be stripped of his rank and all privileges pertaining to his membership of the Order. His coat of arms is to be removed from the quarters of the English knights and he will be taken from the island as soon as passage on a ship can be arranged for him. He is never to return here upon pain of death, save by express permission of the Order. He is an exile, and shall remain so until death claim him or it is the will of the incumbent Grand Master to remit his exile, on terms set out in such an eventuality.' He rapped his knuckles on the table. 'Take the prisoner away.'

'No!' Thomas cried out. 'Let me see Maria first.'

'How dare you?' Romegas said furiously. 'Take the insolent swine away! At once.'

Thomas felt his arms grasped by the soldiers on either side once again. He struggled as they dragged him towards the door. 'Let me see her! One more time. I must see her. For pity's sake!'

'Get him out of here!' d'Omedes shouted.

Thomas writhed but the men held him tightly and thrust him towards the door. 'What is to become of her? What are you going to do with Maria?'

'Her turn will come,' the Grand Master told him. 'She, too, will be judged and punished accordingly. You can be sure of that.'

Thomas felt as if his heart was being torn asunder and he looked pleadingly towards Stokely as he was led away. 'For the sake of our former friendship, Oliver, swear that you will take care of her. It is I who deserve your wrath, not Maria. She is innocent. Swear that you will protect her!'

Stokely stood still and silent, and only a faint smile of satisfaction betrayed his feelings as Thomas was dragged outside and the door closed behind him.

CHAPTER SEVEN

Barrett Hall, Hertfordshire
13 December, St Lucia's Day, 1564

The first message arrived at dusk, on a cold, bleak evening.

Thomas was sitting on an old carved chair in his study, gazing out through leaded windows. A blanket of snow covered the meadow that stretched down from the hall. Distorted glimmers of red and gold shimmered on the panes of glass as they reflected the glow of a dying fire in the hearth. Outside, the light was cool and blue and comfortless and he stared into its depths without moving or, indeed, showing any sign of life. It was as if his heart was as cold and still as the world outside, wrapped in a shroud, waiting for a rekindling of warmth and growth when the season changed. Though spring would return, just as sure as the rising and the setting of the sun, the prospect was of little cheer to Thomas. The years had unravelled around him like old worn cloth and he cared little for their passing. His spirit had long since turned to stone – hard, unyielding and unfeeling. But even if his heart had shrivelled, he still cared for his physical well-being and ate sparingly and exercised every day whatever the weather or his state of health. He was a creature of habit.

In all the years since he had been banished from the Order of St John, Thomas had kept himself lean and fit and put his considerable fighting skills to use. He had spent much of the time as a mercenary fighting in the interminable wars that raged across Europe. Death, from disease, hunger and battle, had been at his side throughout and yet had spared him, a few wounds notwithstanding. In addition, continual reading and studying kept his mind agile. He would not succumb to the self-indulgent foolishness that seemed to consume the English nobility who lounged indolently in their ornamental gardens and great houses. They called themselves lords and knights yet not one in ten was capable of taking his place in the battle line.

At forty-five Thomas still moved with an easy grace. Even though there were streaks of grey at his temples and in his beard, and his face was weathered and starting to wrinkle, most people instinctively knew he was not to be trifled with. There were times, though fewer and fewer these days, when he attended a court event and attracted the unwanted attention of a drunken fop, who had heard some story about Sir Thomas and determined to put the quiet knight to the test. But Thomas had long since mastered the art of deflecting fools in a polite and self-effacing manner. Sooner a display of mature tolerance than any confrontation that could only result in a very public humiliation of a younger man. Thomas had tasted the bitter shame of humiliation himself in his youth and had learned the value of self-restraint. It was a lesson paid for alone in the darkness when he had buried his face in a coarse bolster to hide his misery from others. He had no wish to win new enemies so he let the oafishness amongst these soft English aristocrats ride over him and did his best to ignore it.

Only once had he been forced to harm another in order to defend himself. It was over ten years before, at a feast for the Lord Mayor in London. Thomas had been confronted by a loudspoken youth, tall and broad and far too full of some misguided sense of his martial prowess. Yet even he had been nervous when he confronted Thomas. His young eyes were wide and alert, his hand trembling ever so faintly as it slid from the pommel of his rapier and grasped the handle. Before his blade had rasped more than a few inches from its finely decorated scabbard, Thomas's hand had clamped round the boy's wrist like an iron manacle, and he shook his head with a gentle, warning smile, before turning away. But the fool had shouted with affronted rage and continued to draw his sword. Thomas spun back and pinned the youth's arm to his thigh with a slender dirk that had seemed to come from nowhere, so quickly had it materialised. The boy had collapsed to the floor. Thomas had calmly retrieved his blade and dressed the wound, before making his apologies to the host and quitting the feast.

He shook his head at the memory, still angry with himself for not reading the lad's expression in time to prevent the incident. There was enough blood on his hands already and he had no desire to add to the suffering he had already caused so many others, heathen and Christian alike. The memory of it had tormented him in the years after his return to England. Now it had become just another scar fading with age and familiarity.

Thomas drew his coat closer about his shoulders and rose from the window seat, crossed to the hearth and carefully placed two more split logs on the fire. He watched them for a moment in idle fascination as steam hissed from cracks in the wood, and then there was a sharp pop and flurry of sparks before a bright yellow flame flickered up from the glowing embers below the logs. He returned to the window seat and sat down again, staring into the gathering shadows outside.

Above the crackling of the firewood he heard sounds of a commotion in the hall and his curiosity was piqued. Only a handful of servants still lived in the hall. He had no need for more. Certainly no need for the dozens that had waited on his parents and brothers long years ago, in childhood, before his father had secured him a place in the Order. Both parents had died shortly after Thomas had left England, and he had received only a terse letter from his older brother, Edward, informing him of the illness that had killed them within days of each other. Then Edward had been killed in a hunting accident and, a year later, young Robert had died at sea, serving on a privateer whose only booty had been the dysentery that had swept through the crew and left in its wake a handful of skeletal figures who finally reached Dartmouth several months later. On his return to the hall Thomas had been told the story by the maid who had served as Robert's nurse. Robert had always been the family favourite, fair-haired and fair-humoured with a wild adventurous streak, quite unlike the dour, quiet Thomas. Thomas had never resented him, nor wished to emulate his popularity. He had simply loved his brother.

Now he was the last of them. He lived alone, apart

from his manservant, John, the elderly maid, Hannah, and a young stable lad who managed the remaining six horses and riding tackle in the yard behind the hall. Stephen rarely spoke to the others, and was more horse than man, according to Hannah. Beyond that, the only other family retainer was the steward of the estate who now lived in Bishops Stortford and oversaw the tenants on Thomas's land, collected their rents and banked the income for his master, sending him a statement of the accounts twice a year.

The hall in Hertfordshire had been in the family for eight generations. Thomas was the last in the line of the Barrett family. He had not married and had no heirs. On his death, the estate would pass to a distant cousin, a man Thomas had never met, and cared nothing about.

From time to time attempts had been made by friends of his father to arrange a union for Thomas. He had politely but insistently declined the opportunities that were steered his way. Some of the women had been well connected, attractive enough, and even intelligent. But not one had borne a moment's comparison to Maria and they only served to remind Thomas of what he had lost and could never regain in this life. And such was the nature of their parting that there was little prospect of any divine power permitting their reunion in the afterlife. It was in this spirit of perpetual loss that Thomas lived out his life. After Maria there was nothing, only the gnawing ache of recollection of touch, gesture, smile, expression and fragments of moments shared in each other's arms.

For an instant the memories were overwhelming and Thomas shook his head angrily, clenching his fists and glaring sightlessly through the window at the quiet serenity beyond. Then the moment passed and he sighed, the tight exhalation of one who has just come out from under the surgeon's knife.

There was a quiet knock at the door of the study and Thomas turned away from the window.

'Yes?'

The latch lifted and the dark oak door gently swung into the room as John entered. He nodded to his master and gestured back towards the darkened corridor outside the study.

'A messenger has arrived, sir.'

'Messenger?' Thomas frowned. 'Who is he?'

'A foreigner, sir,' John said, narrowing his eyes suspiciously. 'He called himself Philippe de Nanterre.'

Thomas was silent for a moment. 'I do not know the name. Did he say who sent him, or what the message concerns?'

'He said the message was for your ears alone, sir.'

Thomas felt a faint pang of anxiety. What was a Frenchman doing here in England, in his house, if not to stir up some aspect of a past life long buried?

'Where is he now?' Thomas raised his eyebrows.

'In the lobby, sir.' John shrugged. 'I thought it best.'

'Bid him enter and let him warm himself at the fire in the hall. It is only Christian to offer him some token of hospitality, especially at this time of year.'

Thomas did not welcome the intrusion. In recent years few had come to see him for social reasons, still less send him an invitation to a masque or banquet. He usually treated unexpected visitors as an irritant, something he could deal with swiftly and then ignore. He felt a terrible weariness in his bones and did not wish to be disturbed now that he had settled by his fire for the evening. If this man, Philippe de Nanterre, had come with an offer of military service then he would leave disappointed. Thomas had made his peace with the world, and with his enemies, and wanted to be left alone. He stroked his neatly cut beard and stared at his servant.

'Did you divine anything of his business with me?'

'I did.' John smiled. 'He has a letter for you, master. I saw it in his saddlebag while I led his horse to the stable yard. It has now been safely returned to him.'

Thomas could not help a small smile of his own. 'His bag just happened to be open, no doubt.'

'It is no fault of mine if the buckle was not adequately fastened, sir. I merely sought to bring you more information.'

'Then you have done well. And what of his letter that you just happened to see?'

'It is a folded parchment, sealed. The sender left no name on the outside.'

'So, did you recognise the seal?'

'No, sir.'

'Then describe it.'

'It is a cross, sir. A cross with an indent at each end.'

Thomas felt a ripple of lightness in his head and he closed his eyes briefly and fought down the tide of memories and images that swelled up unbidden and unwanted. Yet there was also a spark of hope in his chest, fanned by his curiosity. He drew a deep breath before he opened his eyes and regarded his servant. 'Take him to the kitchen and feed him.'

'Sir?' John raised his eyebrows. 'But he's a foreigner, sir. Not to be trusted. I'd send him on his way, if I were you, sir.'

'Then it is as well that you are not. It will be dark soon and the track to Bishops Stortford is icy. It wouldn't be right. It wouldn't be safe. If he chooses, he can stay here for the night. Feed him and offer him a bed. And tell him I will speak with him shortly.'

John grunted but knew better than to provoke his master.

Thomas smiled faintly. 'He must have come a long way to find me. The least we can do is offer him the hospitality of the house. Now go and see to his needs.'

John bowed his head and left the study, closing the door behind him. As his footsteps echoed down the oak-panelled hall, Thomas stroked his beard thoughtfully. He recognised John's description of the seal only too well. It was the emblem of the Knights Hospitaller. After all the long years of waiting, the Order had at last broken its silence.

As soon as Thomas opened the door and entered the kitchen he knew that all the routine and isolation of recent years was over. Sitting with his back to the cooking fire, the messenger was stooped over a steaming bowl. His eyes flickered up as the master of the hall entered, and he quickly rose, wiping his lips on the back of his hand. He had a swarthy complexion, with a livid white scar across his brow. His face was weathered and his expression firm but polite and yet Thomas saw that he could not have been much more than twenty. A soldier old before his time, as were all novices who survived their first few years in the Order. The messenger still wore a thick dark riding cloak. At the shoulder was a stained and bespattered white cross whose arms broadened out and then divided into two points, one for each of the languages of the Order.

'Sir Thomas Barrett? I have a message for you. From the Grand Master.' The English was good but the accent was thick – from the southern region of France, he guessed. Thomas nodded and gestured for the man to sit down.

He spoke in French. 'We'll use the language of the Order, if you don't mind.'

'It would please me,' the messenger replied in the same tongue.

Thomas nodded towards the two servants. 'They know little of my previous life. I would not have them spread any gossip down in the local village. Things are hard enough for those who keep faith with the Church of Rome.'

'I understand.'

Thomas turned to John. 'You may leave us. And you too, Hannah.'

Once the door closed behind them, Thomas stood on the far side of the table and stared down at the messenger. 'So?'

'The Grand Master—'

'Who is he?' Thomas interrupted.

'Who?'

The younger man was caught off guard. 'I'm sorry,' Thomas explained. 'I have been somewhat removed from the affairs of the Order. I have no idea who leads it at present.'

'Oh . . .' The messenger did not hide his surprise. 'I serve Grand Master Jean de La Valette.'

'La Valette.' Thomas nodded. 'I remember him . . . He must be an old man.'

The messenger stared back, frowning, and Thomas smiled. 'He always had an old head on his shoulders. And the hardest constitution of any man I have ever met. Tell me, does he still lead the first endurance march of the novices?'

The messenger grimaced. 'Oh yes. And still he marches us into the ground.'

They both laughed and some of the tension between them was eased. Thomas pulled a stool out from under the table and sat down, smiling at the memory of a slender man in his forties, striding out ahead of a straggling column of youngsters gasping to keep pace with the veteran knight. Then the smile faded as Thomas's gaze fixed itself on the cross on the messenger's cloak again.

'Where are you from, brother?'

'My family have an estate near Nîmes.'

'Ah, I thought I recognised your accent, Philippe de Nanterre. You have a message for me.'

'Yes, sir.'

Thomas felt his heart quicken inside his chest. 'They've finally made a ruling then. Am I to continue to be excluded from the Order or am I to be recalled, I wonder.'

'I don't understand, sir.'

Thomas stared at him, to see if the youth was foolish enough to make fun of him. But the messenger's confusion seemed genuine enough and Thomas waved a hand. 'It doesn't matter. Just give me the message.'

'Yes, sir.' The youth reached down to the small leather satchel resting on the flagstones by his riding boots. He placed it on the worn cross-hatching of the kitchen table and then paused to examine the buckle suspiciously. He glanced at the door leading out of the kitchen and shook his head before undoing the buckle. He reached inside and withdrew a folded parchment bearing a wax seal. He handed it across to Thomas who took it from his hand after the slightest hesitation. Thomas held it up to his eyes and turned slightly so that the kitchen fire could illuminate the seal of the Order and the words inscribed close by. *To Sir Thomas Barrett, Knight of the Order of St John*. His heart quickened as he read the last phrase a second time.

'How did you find me?'

'Sir Oliver Stokely gave me directions, sir.'

'Sir Oliver must have won himself a high position by now. Assuming he is still the same man I once knew.'

Philippe nodded and replied evenly, 'Sir Oliver is secretary to the Grand Master.'

'Quite something, isn't he?' Thomas laughed. 'For an Englishman, that is.'

'Sir?'

'Never mind. Finish your gruel.' Thomas turned his gaze back to the parchment. He slipped a finger under the fold and broke the seal. The parchment crackled as he unfolded it and flattened it out on the table. Then he began to read.

CHAPTER EIGHT

The opening of the message was crisp enough and the distaste and disdain of Sir Oliver Stokely were immediately apparent.

Sir Thomas,

I am required by the Grand Master, Jean Parisot de La Valette, to write this message to you by virtue of our common language. You will be aware, as am I, that under normal circumstances your suspension from the Order cannot be reversed. Given the grievous nature of your conduct some twenty years ago it has always been my view that exclusion from the Order was the very least penalty that you deserved. However, the current crisis requires that the Grand Master now rescind your exile. Furthermore, in accordance with the oath you swore when you entered the Order, you are herewith summoned to Malta and shall make your passage as expeditiously as possible or suffer pain of disgrace in the eyes of your peers and before God.

I need hardly convey to you the depth of the shame you brought to our English brothers. The peril in which the Order and, indeed, the whole of

Christendom currently stands presents you with the chance to redeem yourself and your countrymen. Having known you, I hold out little hope that you will honour your oath and think that your contribution to our defence would be little enough in any event. Nevertheless, I am under instruction from the Grand Master to issue this summons and hereby do so in accordance with his wishes.

The bearer of this message will provide further information about the situation here in Malta. You may question him for details it would be imprudent to commit to writing.

Yours,

Sir Oliver Stokely, Knight of Justice of the Order of St John Hospitallers, on this day, November 6th.

Thomas looked up at the messenger. 'This was written in November. You've made good time.'

Philippe shrugged. 'Time is not a luxury the Order can afford.'

'So it would seem. Are you familiar with the contents of this letter?'

'No, sir. The messengers were briefed on the danger and then handed letters to distribute to our brother knights. You are the fifth on my list. After you, there are two more. One in York and the last in Denmark. Godwilling I shall return to Malta before the enemy arrives.'

'I see. How many knights are being recalled?'

Philippe stared at him for an instant, and a look of despair flickered across his face before he replied, 'All of them.'

Thomas laughed. 'All of them? Come now, don't humour me, boy.'

'Sir Thomas, I said we could not afford to waste time. Within the next six months, a year at the most, the Order may be utterly erased from God's earth by the infidel.'

Thomas was more than familiar with young men who had a passion for rhetorical flights of fancy, but out of politeness to his guest he kept his opinion to himself.

'The letter says you can tell me the full details. So out with it.'

Philippe pushed his bowl away. 'Last October our spies reported that Sultan Suleiman had called a meeting of his advisers to discuss strategy for the coming campaign season. Although the spies weren't able to penetrate the meeting, they saw a great many viziers, admirals and generals arrive at the palace. They came from every corner of the Ottoman empire. There were even envoys from Dragut and the other corsairs and Barbary pirates. It was clear that the Turks were planning something on a vast scale for the coming year. Later, we began to receive reports from other agents telling of vast stockpiles of weapons, gun-powder and supplies of grain and salted meat. Scores of new artillery pieces have been cast in the Sultan's foundries, and his best gunners and engineers have arrived in Constantinople. Then there was news of shipping massing in harbours all along the Aegean coast, and the arrival of columns of soldiers into camps close by.' Philippe leaned slightly across the table. 'It is clear enough. They mean to attack the Order. To wipe us out.'

Thomas smiled. 'It is clear they intend to attack someone. But why Malta? Why now? Surely Suleiman has more pressing business elsewhere. I fear that our friend the Grand Master is jumping to conclusions.'

'No.' Philippe slapped his hand down heavily. 'How dare you question his word!'

Thomas stared at him and lowered his voice. 'Careful, lad. I will not be spoken to in that manner, least of all in my own home.'

For a moment the messenger glared back at him, brazenly challenging Thomas. But then he saw the cold, ruthless glint in the older man's eyes and recalled the few words he had heard back in Malta concerning the reputation of Sir Thomas. His gaze wavered and fell back to the worn surface of the kitchen table.

'Sir, I apologise. It has been a long journey and my mind is weary. I meant no disrespect to you. I only sought to defend the honour of my master . . . and yours.'

Thomas nodded. 'I understand well enough. It's good to see that La Valette still has the power to inspire such fierce devotion amongst his men. But why is he so certain that Suleiman is turning his sword on the Order? And why now, when he is poised to strike at Christendom through the Balkans?' He frowned. 'I cannot see the sense of an attack on Malta.'

'It is clear enough, sir. From the beginning of his reign, over forty years ago, Suleiman has claimed the titles "King of Kings" and "Supreme Lord of Europe and Asia". It has always been his plan to bring every kingdom of Christendom under his sway and impose Islam on all his subjects. Now he grows old and fears that he may die before his ambition is fulfilled.'

Thomas smiled. 'That is the stuff of fantasy. I have been

a soldier long enough to know that such a plan is beyond even the reach of the Sultan.'

'Fantasy or no, it is his plan, sir. The spies of the Grand Master heard it from Suleiman's lips. And it begins with Malta, and our Order of knights. We have been a thorn in his side these long years and now he is minded to destroy us.' The young knight collected his thoughts and continued. 'The immediate cause of the Sultan's resolve to take Malta was born from our seizing one of his most prized trading carracks last summer. Commander Romegas took the ship off the coast of Egypt. She was carrying a lady of high rank, and the Sanjak of Alexandria. In the ship's hold was a vast fortune in silk and precious metals. The value was estimated to be the equivalent of eighty thousands ducats . . .'

Thomas shook his head in wonder that so much treasure could possibly be contained within the wooden confines of even the greatest of ships.

Philippe smiled briefly. 'Exactly my response, sir. And one can only imagine how the Sultan reacted at the news. The Order has been raiding Suleiman's commerce for decades. We have been growing ever bolder and now he is determined to crush us.'

'For revenge?' Thomas raised an eyebrow. 'The Suleiman I recall would not let his mind be ruled by his heart.'

'Nor has he,' agreed Philippe. 'It is not for revenge alone that he seeks to add Malta to his empire. Once Malta is his, Sicily will be next. From Sicily he can strike into Italy and seize Rome, the very heart of our faith. Even then his appetite will not be slaked. Not until he has

crossed the Alps and killed or enslaved every last Christian.'
Philippe leaned forward again and he tapped a finger on
the table. 'Do you think even this far island is safe from the
jaws of his ambition?'

Thomas chuckled. 'Fine words. I think I can hear the
voice of Sir Oliver in them.'

Philippe leaned back with a wry smile. 'Well, I tried.
And you are clearly as wily a fox as they say.'

'They?'

'Those brothers who remember you from the time of
your service in the Order.'

'There can't be that many of them,' Thomas mused.

'No.'

'And those who truly remember me will recall the
manner of my departure from the Order.'

'That is true, sir. But now past grievances must be
put aside.'

Thomas wagged a finger at the messenger. 'Clearly you
have little understanding of the depth of feeling that divides
the Order's nationalities. In my day we were at each
other's throats almost as often as we were at the throats of
the infidels.'

'Then I think you will notice that not much has
changed when you reach Malta, sir.'

'Reach Malta?' Thomas looked up sharply. 'Do not
presume, boy. What makes you think I will come running
back to the service of those who exiled me? If they've
been honest with you, Philippe, then you must know the
circumstances of my departure from Malta.'

Philippe shook his head. 'I've only heard that you were
responsible for some scandal. That's all they will say.'

'Then they are as tight-lipped and as stiffly righteous as ever. I owe them nothing.'

'You swore an oath. There is no release from the oath, sir . . . The only release is death.'

Thomas glanced into the shadows in the corner of the kitchen for a moment and then smiled bitterly. 'It seems that everyone in the Order may be granted release from that oath very soon.'

'We won't be alone, sir. The Grand Master has sent for help to every Christian kingdom. If they answer, then we must triumph over the infidel.'

The young man's simple-minded faith filled Thomas with great sadness. Philippe, and hundreds like him, would go to their deaths clutching such idealistic notions to their hearts like the holy relics they fought and died for. Thomas had hoped that he would never be a part of such foolishness again, and out of compassion for his guest he tried to explain.

'Tell me, Philippe, since you left Malta to come here, did you not once cross a Christian kingdom locked in some conflict or other with its neighbour? Are you ignorant of the fate suffered by thousands of Catholics in this country? While we Christians are so determined to destroy each other, what chance is there of us joining ranks to resist the infidel? There will be no more crusades. We have forsaken the true church of God and Suleiman is our punishment. Our judgement.'

Philippe opened his mouth to protest but Thomas raised a hand to silence him, and after a moment continued in a quiet, weary tone. 'Go back to the Grand Master and tell him I will come. I will not die for those who cast me out. I will not die for the faith. But I will come for reasons of my own.' He stood up. 'Now, I'm to bed. My servant will find you quarters for the night. I imagine that you wish to leave for York at first light.'

Philippe nodded, and as Thomas strode towards the door, the young messenger cleared his throat. 'Sir Thomas. You have my gratitude, and that of our brothers in Malta.'

Thomas paused at the door but he did not turn back. Instead his shoulders sagged and he sighed deeply. 'Gratitude? I have nothing here to keep me, and I would see Malta one more time before I am done. That is all.'

He left the kitchen and saw John rise stiffly from a bench against the wall of the corridor. Thomas gestured towards the kitchen as he strode past. 'See to his needs. He intends to leave the hall before I rise on the morrow.'

'Yes, master.'

Thomas went straight to bed, consumed by a swirling host of memories that the messenger had reawakened. Beneath the covers Hannah had earlier placed a warming pan but even with that comfort, Thomas remained restless and sleep eluded him, chased away by a succession of images and emotions that would not be banished from his mind. At length he gave up and stared at the ceiling of his bedchamber, while a light moaning came from the fireplace as the wind rose outside. The prospect of a return to Malta was bittersweet. That was where he had once been certain that he belonged. That was where he had loved Maria. Perhaps, by some miracle, she lived there still, and nursed the same love that he had over all the years they had been apart. Then he cursed himself for being an old fool and turned on his side and eventually fell asleep.

When he woke, the wind had died down and bright sunlight beamed into his room through a gap in the curtains. The fire in the grate had long since died and the leaded glass on the windows was laced with frost. Thomas rose stiffly and sat on the edge of his bed for a moment, recalling the details of the previous evening. He was convinced of the rightness of his decision. In any case, the messenger would have left by now and would carry his reply back to Malta. It was too late to change his mind. He would need to prepare for war yet again. Grasping that conviction, he dressed himself and made for his study where John would bring him his breakfast the moment he heard the heavy tread of his master's boots descending the stairs.

John confirmed that the young knight had left at first light, with a small basket of pies and cheese to sustain him for his next day's ride.

After a bowl of porridge, Thomas pulled on a thick hooded cloak and set off on foot across the fields of his estate to the farm of one of his tenants. There were trees that needed felling in one of the copses that grew on his land and he had arranged to join the farmer and his burly sons to cut them down. It was hard labour that Thomas might easily have left to them, but he relished the exercise and the warm glow of satisfaction at seeing the pile of logs that had been amassed by noon. After bidding the others farewell, Thomas strode back to the hall, feeling purged of the thoughts that had troubled him the previous night. He resolved to leave for Malta within the week.

It was at that moment that the second messenger arrived.

The rider came through the arched gateway just as Thomas was kicking the snow from his boots by the porch of the main entrance to the hall. The hooves of the messenger's horse had been muffled by the snow so there was no warning of his approach. Thomas looked up quickly as he sensed movement and saw the rider jerk the reins to direct the horse across the courtyard towards him. He wore a blue cloak and the new breeches that had become fashionable in London. The blue of the cloak marked him out as the servant of a wealthy household. As he approached he raised a gloved hand and pointed at Thomas.

'You there! A word with you.'

Thomas straightened up and folded his arms as the rider's mount trotted across the snow, the hooves of the horse kicking up little sprays of white crystals in their wake. He stopped a dozen yards from Thomas and plumes of breath swirled from the muzzle of the horse.

'Can you tell me if this is Barrett Hall?'

'It is.'

The rider nodded with relief and then swung himself down from the saddle and landed softly in the snow, still holding the reins in one hand. He offered Thomas a smile. 'Been on the road from London since dawn. Turned off at Bishops Stortford on to some forsaken track. It's taken me hours to find this place. Hardly anyone on the road had ever heard of it.'

'We like to keep to ourselves,' said Thomas. 'The fewer visitors the better.' His tone was not hostile yet the rider's expression hardened at the presumed insult and he addressed Thomas with a haughty look.

'Fellow, is your master at home? I am told he rarely ventures far from this place in recent years.'

'That is true.' Thomas nodded.

'Is he within?' the rider asked tersely. 'I have no time for games. I must away to London as soon as my duty is done.'

'The master is not yet within. What is your will with him?'

'That is for me to say directly to his face, not to his servant.'

'Then speak it.'

The other man's irritable expression darkened for an instant before realisation struck him and at once his demeanour changed and he bowed his head. 'My apologies, sir. I did not know.'

'Then why presume to treat me as an inferior?'

The man raised his head and gestured towards Thomas. 'Sir, your apparel is not that of a gentleman. I assumed—'

'Assumed? Presumed? Do you always judge a man by his appearance?'

'Sir, I . . . I . . . I can only apologise.'

Thomas stared hard at him, until the rider looked down. The man had made an honest mistake and no ill will had been meant, yet it rankled with Thomas. The rider was typical of the society that filled the royal court and those lesser circles that clung to its periphery. The appearance of a person was everything, while the substance of their character was largely ignored. It offended Thomas's understanding of men and the world, and he felt a sour resentment settle on his spirit over the fact that his privacy had been invaded twice in so many days.

'Very well, what news for me?'

'A summons, if you please, sir.' The rider looked up again, and spoke in a respectful tone this time. 'From my master, Sir William Cecil. He requests that you attend him at his house on Drury Lane in London tomorrow, at six of the clock.'

'He requests? And if I say no?'

The servant's jaw slackened momentarily, as if he had not understood, as if there was no question of an alternative to simple acquiescence to his master's will. He swallowed nervously before he replied. 'I have no instructions concerning your refusal of his request, sir.'

'A pity.' Thomas shrugged. 'Then it is a command that you bring me. In which case I am compelled to attend. Very well, tell your master that I will be there at the appointed time.'

'Yes, sir.'

Thomas looked at him for a moment. The servant had been in the saddle for over half the day and would not return to the capital before dark. The gates would be shut and like as not he would be compelled to find a place to sleep outside the walls of London. It would be a kindness to offer him refreshment and rest before he left the hall, as he had done for the Frenchman. But then he had not had to endure such haughtiness from his other guest. For that reason Thomas did not move from his place in front of his door.

'I have your message and you may go.'

'Aye, sir.' The servant nodded, willing enough to quit his presence. He grasped the pommel of his saddle in one hand and placed his boot in the stirrup. He made to rise into the saddle but the cold had made his joints stiff and he slipped back on to the ground. With an irritable grunt Thomas stepped up, bent down and hoisted the servant up into the saddle.

'My thanks, sir.'

Thomas nodded and the servant took in the reins and wheeled his mount round, spurring it into a trot back across the courtyard and out through the arch, the soft thump of the hooves fading swiftly away. Thomas stared at the gateway for a while, and then turned and strode into his home, calling out loudly, 'John! John! Damn you, man! Where are you?'

'I'm coming, sir!' came the reply from the kitchen. A moment later the door opened and the old retainer came hurrying out, wiping crumbs from his chin.

'I shall need my saddlebags, riding cloak, boots and sword for the morrow. See that they are cleaned and ready for the morning. I ride to London.'

'Yes, sir.' John tilted his head slightly to one side. 'Might I ask how long you will be gone?'

'Who knows?' Thomas smiled faintly. 'It would appear that it is not in my power to say when I will return.'

CHAPTER NINE

London

Dusk was gathering as Thomas approached the capital which sprawled across the landscape like a dark stain some miles ahead. The Great North Road had frozen hard and the heavily rutted surface had forced Thomas to slow his horse to a walk as he settled in behind a wool merchant's cart in the long column of wagons, riders and travellers on foot making their way to London before the gates closed for the night. Thomas had been content to ride at the pace of the column, unlike the handful of post riders who had hurried past during the day. On either side of the trampled snow and exposed streaks of frozen earth a blanket of white lay over the fields and copses. The sky was overcast and there had been brief flurries since noon and a fresh fall of snow looked likely. Thin skeins of smoke trailed into the sky from the chimneys of isolated farmhouses and villages that dotted the landscape. Here and there a rosy glow shone through a window and made the travellers long for the comfort of a warm hearth.

Even though the day had been long and the cold had seeped into his flesh so that he hunched into his thick cloak, Thomas's thoughts were elsewhere. Only a small amount of his attention, as much as was needed, was fixed on guiding his mount and paying occasional attention to his surroundings. For the rest, he was concerned with the reason behind this summons to the home of Sir William Cecil, the Queen's Secretary of State. Thomas knew that Cecil had been a firm supporter of Elizabeth in the difficult years before she had succeeded to the throne. Like her, Cecil was a devout Protestant and the prime mover behind efforts to suppress the influence of Catholics in England. He wielded great power and was the foremost statesman in the country, so what could he possibly want with an obscure knight who had not shown his face in London these last three years?

Since his return from the wars in Europe Thomas had mostly remained on his small estate and overseen the planting of crops and the raising of his sheep and tending to the welfare of his tenants. On the rare visits he had made to London he had attended the royal court on a handful of occasions and, with the one exception during the reign of Catholic Queen Mary, he had not drawn any attention to himself. Even then, when he had shed a small amount of blood for which the penalty was the severing of a hand, he had not made any claim on his religion to assuage his punishment. In the event, he had been given only a small fine which some might well attribute to Mary's preferment of a fellow Catholic. Thomas could hardly believe that his summons several years later could be due to any settling of such an old score.

He had not made common cause with any of those who protested for the rights of Catholics in public, or who plotted in private. That was a very dangerous game. Sir

William Cecil's spies were numerous and the rewards for those who informed against Catholics most tempting for anyone who bore a grudge or whose greed ruled them. There were some aristocrats whose faith had been used to justify the confiscation of their estates, and even their condemnation for treason. Many men had acquired great fortunes as a result of persecuting Catholics, just as many men had become rich during the earlier dissolution of the monasteries by King Henry. The same men now supported Elizabeth, as long as she guaranteed their rights over their recently acquired fortunes.

It was hard for Thomas to credit that his modest wealth had attracted the attention of Cecil or one of his faction. The only motive William Cecil could have for requesting his presence in London must concern the visit of the young knight from the Order. Thomas felt a shiver trace its way down his spine. If that was the reason then he had been deluding himself if he had thought that his quiet retreat in the depths of the countryside had removed him from scrutiny. It seemed that little escaped the far-seeing eyes of Cecil and his men, Thomas reflected irritably, and muttered a curse at the knights who had forced him to leave the Order. Long after he had resigned himself to spending his remaining days living a quiet life, they had grudgingly asked for his help. No doubt they would cast him out the moment the crisis passed and they felt able to dispense with his services.

The tolling of a distant bell announcing the fourth hour of the afternoon sounded and broke into Thomas's train of thought. He stretched himself up in the saddle and eased his horse to the side of the road to see the way ahead more clearly. The loose column of travellers and wagons had just crested a low ridge which afforded a view of the capital beneath a thick pall of wood smoke. The snow resting on the rooftops already looked dirty. Half a mile away stood the great market of Smithfield where the meat traders brought in their flocks from across the country to be sold and butchered. A short distance from the pens and long rows of stalls was an open patch of ground where several thick charred timbers rose up above small mounds of compacted ash. In one place the ash was fresh and still smouldered, melting any snow that fell on it.

This was where heretics were put to death by being burned alive, Thomas knew. Once, ten years before, he had been in a vast crowd that witnessed the execution of three Protestant priests who had defied Queen Mary's edicts by preaching in public after their licences had been revoked. The Queen had inflicted the spectacle on her entire court and had watched with prim satisfaction from an ornately padded chair set up on a dais erected for the event. Thomas could well recall the piercing screams of the men. The priests had writhed amid the flames spreading rapidly through the faggots piled below the small plinth on which their feet rested. In minutes a whirling torrent of brilliant yellow and red engulfed the bodies, which could yet be seen – blackened figures squirming against the chains that bound them as their cries of torment rose above the crackle of burning wood. The memory, still vivid even now, chilled Thomas's heart. He averted his gaze from the stakes and clicked his tongue to urge his horse into a trot.

Beyond Smithfield was the city wall. Once it had been a formidable line of defence but had long since fallen into neglect. There were gaps in its length where sections had collapsed, and the ditch that had once surrounded the city was now filled in with generations of rubbish and human waste. A powerful stench filled the chilly air as Thomas passed through the wide arch at Newgate and entered London. The sounds of the great city assaulted him from all sides. The cries of street traders, the bawling of infants and the shouts of those striving to be heard above the din filled his ears, just as the odours of baking bread, cooked and rancid meat, and the stink of sewage filled his nostrils. The main thoroughfares of London were crowded by the buildings pressing in from each side and looming overhead where each storey of a building projected out above the one beneath, lending the streets a murky gloom that depressed Thomas's soul.

It was with some relief as the light faded beyond the jagged lines of the rooftops and cast London into the realm of shadows that he turned on to the wider road along Holborn. Thomas ignored the hawkers who hurried alongside his horse trying to sell him snacks or handkerchiefs, and he kept a close eye on his saddlebags to ensure that no cutpurse attempted to snatch anything as he rode by. At length, he saw the entrance to Drury Lane and turned his mount into a somewhat quieter street. The shops on either side were well appointed and neatly painted signs advertised a variety of expensive goods: fine cloth, wines and cheeses, silverware and glassware imported from Europe. In between the shops were large houses, increasing in size and opulence as the lane approached Aldwych and the Thames a short distance beyond.

As the last of the daylight faded, Thomas stopped a boy

running an errand with a small parcel tucked securely under his arm. He asked for Cecil's house and was directed to an imposing property occupying the corner that Drury Lane shared with another street. The façade fronted Drury Lane with finely carved timbers and geometric patterns of brickwork. A gate to the side led into a small courtyard with stables and a pair of burly servants barred Thomas's way until he announced his appointment with their master, having dismounted and handed the reins of his horse to a groom. He was led through a door into the rear of the house and handed over to one of the neatly dressed house servants wearing the same blue as the messenger who had arrived at Thomas's estate the day before. Once more Thomas explained the purpose of his visit and was taken through the main hall of the house and up a flight of stairs and along a corridor illuminated by candles that dimly revealed paintings hanging on the panelled walls, almost every one of them depicting a hunting scene or a dour-looking family member. There was only one painting depicting a religious scene, Thomas noted, before he was led into a small waiting room lined with wooden benches and warmed and illuminated by a fire. A slender young man was busy adding several fresh logs to the modest blaze. He looked over his shoulder as Thomas was shown into the room. His features were dark and delicate-looking, and his eyes were brown and lent his gaze a piercing aspect that Thomas found vaguely unsettling.

'I will inform the master's secretary that you have arrived, sir,' the servant announced. 'Do you wish me to bring you any refreshment while you wait?'

'I would be grateful for a cup of warmed mead.'

'Mead?' The servant's eyebrows rose a fraction and Thomas could not help being amused by the man's inability to place him neatly in some niche on the hierarchy of London's social classes. His clothes were well made but unadorned and his hair was close cut, like his beard, with no attempt at the precise styling of the more fashionable type of gentleman. Thomas could have passed for a well-to-do tradesman or a country yeoman, but his business with Sir William Cecil hinted at something more and the servant bowed his head. 'As you wish, sir. Mead it is.'

He closed the door behind him while the man by the hearth looked Thomas over with keen eyes before he nodded a respectful greeting and turned his attention back to building up the fire. When he had finished he brushed his hands together and eased himself down on to a small bench next to the fireplace. To his side was the room's only other door. Thomas removed his cloak, gloves and hat and set them down beside him as he settled on a bench opposite. For a moment he relished the rosy atmosphere and let the warmth gradually penetrate his garments and take the chill off his flesh.

At length he looked up to examine the young man more closely and was surprised to find him staring back at him. Far from being discomforted by having this scrutiny discovered and lowering his gaze, the man continued to study Thomas in a manner he found overfamiliar.

'Do I know you?' asked Thomas.

'No.'

'Then do you know me?'

'This is the first time I have ever seen you.' His voice was cultured and Thomas could not quite place the accent.

But before he could pursue the conversation, the door beside the young man opened and a frail-looking clerk in blue livery stepped into the room. He cleared his throat and looked towards Thomas.

'Sir Thomas Barrett?'

'Yes.'

'The master will see you now.'

'So early? I was supposed to see him after six.'

'He is ready for you now, sir.'

'Very well.' Thomas rose from his bench and cast a final glance towards the young man, who inclined his head slightly in response.

The door gave way to a small room with a window overlooking the courtyard at the back of the house. A desk and stool stood beneath the window, with a large document chest on either side. The clerk scurried past Thomas and rapped lightly on a door on the far side of his office. There was a brief pause before he reached for the latch and gently pushed the door open and stepped across the threshold.

'Sir Thomas, master.'

'Pray show him in,' a deep voice responded.

The clerk backed out and gestured to Thomas to enter. The Secretary of State's domestic office was in proportion to his importance. The room stretched from the courtyard at the back of the house to Drury Lane, which a series of leaded windows overlooked. The walls were lined with filled bookcases, more books than Thomas had ever seen in one place. He estimated there must be at least four or five hundred of them. A truly magnificent private library, he marvelled with a touch of envy. There were two fire-places in the study to heat each end, and chairs were positioned between the bookcases, enough of them to seat perhaps thirty or forty guests. Between the two fireplaces was a large desk upon which rested a wooden tray with documents piled within it. A pair of inkwells and a handful of pens lay neatly beside them. Behind the desk sat a large man with a silk cap. His hair was trimmed in a neat line about his scalp and his beard formed a tidy point above a double chin. He appeared to be a few years younger than Thomas. There was only one other man in the room, thin and clothed in a black gown that reached almost to the floor. He stood close to one of the fires, warming his back. Both of them regarded Thomas briefly before the man seated behind the desk gestured to him impatiently.

'Come, sit down, Sir Thomas. There.' He indicated one of a handful of cushioned chairs on the other side of his desk, arranged in a shallow arc. 'You too, my dear Francis.'

Thomas did as he was bid and sat in the middle of the chairs so that the other man would be displaced from the centre, the implicit position of most importance. Once they were settled Sir William leaned forward and fixed Thomas with a steady gaze. His expression was good-natured and he spoke in a pleasant tone. 'I trust your journey was not too troubling?'

'Not at all, sir. The roads were safe and the snow was only light. I made good time.'

'So I see. You reached London earlier than I thought you would.'

Thomas smiled faintly. 'A man who is summoned by the Secretary of State does not tarry a moment longer than he can help it, Sir William. And so here I am, at your pleasure.'

'Indeed, and I dare say that the cause of my request is uppermost in your mind.'

'Of course.'

'Then let me say that your being here is due to the delicacy of the task I have in mind for you. Even though our blessed sovereign has been on the throne for five years, there are still many who take exception to her elevation to the throne and not just because of her espousal of the Protestant faith. I take it you know of John Knox?'

'I have heard the name.'

'And you are no doubt aware that he cries out against the very principle of a woman succeeding to the throne. Perhaps you have read some of his pamphlets on the matter.'

'It would be a foolish man who dared to read his arguments, Sir William. His pamphlets are banned. It is a capital offence to be discovered in possession of them, I believe.'

'Quite so. But you are familiar with his thoughts.'

'I have heard of them,' Thomas replied carefully, aware that he was being watched closely by the other man in the room, who no doubt served as a witness. 'Though I cannot recall who was speaking at the time.'

'Naturally.' Sir William smiled. 'And it would be point-less for me to press you on the matter, still less to subject you to the pains in order to encourage your memory of the names of those involved.' He chuckled as if to under-score the levity of the comment, but Thomas understood the threat of torture well enough. He was completely in this man's power, regardless of his views of Knox or any of those who opposed Queen Elizabeth. As a Catholic his jeopardy was doubled. He returned Sir William's gaze without expression. There was an uncomfortable silence before Sir William eased himself back a short distance and raised his hands slightly.

'Ah! Pardon me, I forget my manners. I should have introduced you two gentlemen. Sir Thomas, it is my pleasure to acquaint you with Sir Francis Walsingham, the partner of my labours in the service of our sovereign. I trust him implicitly,' Sir William added with emphasis.

Thomas turned towards him and nodded. 'Walsingham.'

The other man stared back and responded coldly, 'It is a pleasure to meet you, Sir Thomas.'

'You must forgive Sir Francis,' the host laughed. 'He is no lover of the Church of Rome and sometimes that causes him to forget certain social niceties. But come now, let us not dance about the point any longer. I can assure you, Sir Thomas, that you have not been asked here for the sake of persecution. I have a task for you. One that will be an opportunity to serve your sovereign and your country and put the question of your loyalty to both beyond reproach.'

'I do not consider my loyalty to either to be in doubt,' Thomas countered evenly.

'Of course not. You know your own heart and I would not have asked you here if I had any doubts. Let us take that as settled. Agreed?' He shot Walsingham a warning glance. The latter nodded.

'There. Which brings us to the first question I have to put to you, Sir Thomas. I believe that you were visited two days ago by a French knight who belongs to the rather select Holy Order of the Hospitaller Knights of

St John.' He turned to Walsingham. 'That is their title, is it not?'

'More or less.'

Cecil's eyes fixed on Thomas and the good-natured wrinkles that spread out at their corners eased into a cold, heartless stare. 'Would you be so good as to tell us why a French knight from a Catholic military order might travel across Europe to pay a visit to you, Sir Thomas?'

CHAPTER TEN

So, as he had suspected, Philippe de Nanterre's visit was the reason he was here, Thomas thought wryly. For twenty years he had done all that was in his power to avoid attention or attract suspicion and now it was all undone by the young knight and his masters on Malta. His abiding feeling was resentment rather than fear and he returned Cecil's gaze without flinching as he replied.

'He came to deliver a letter.'

'What letter?' Walsingham cut in. 'Where is it?'

'At home. In my study.'

'And what did it say?'

'The letter was addressed to me, Sir Francis. I do not see why I should share its contents with you.'

'Really?' For the first time Walsingham smiled, his thin lips parting to reveal neat but stained teeth. 'I wonder what you have to hide.'

'Nothing.'

'Then tell us.'

Thomas gritted his teeth and felt the first surge of anger ripple through his veins as he stared at Walsingham. The man was perhaps ten years his junior and in the prime of life, but he had lived in London too long and the pallor of his complexion told of lack of fitness and strength. In a fight, Thomas knew that he could break the man into pieces and the mere thought of it fired the taste for violence he had long suppressed. There was the true danger and he forced himself to edge back from the temptation. He closed his eyes for a moment and drew a steady breath. There was nothing to be gained from this confrontation.

'The letter was from Sir Oliver Stokely, in Malta,' he began. 'He has requested that I honour my oath to the Order and return to defend the island against the host that the Turkish Sultan is gathering to hurl upon Malta. That is the substance of it.'

'Sir Oliver Stokely,' Cecil mused with a faint smile. 'A distant cousin of mine, as it happens. We were close as children, until he let his faith lead him astray. More than a little astray in the end, as his presence in Malta eloquently demonstrates. But I digress. I assume your guest required a response from you before continuing with his travels.'

'He did.'

'And what did you say?'

'I accepted.'

Cecil and Walsingham exchanged a brief glance and Thomas thought he sensed their disappointment with his reply. The former returned his gaze to Thomas.

'Why did you accept?'

'I swore an oath that is still binding. The Grand Master has summoned me and I must go.'

'You still consider you are bound by an oath taken so many years ago?'

'A man is only as good as his word,' Thomas replied. 'Even so, it is a long time since I shared the aims and beliefs of the Order.'

'Then you disagree with defending Christendom from the Turks?'

'No. I believe in self-defence. I have lived long and seen enough to know that only a fool turns the other cheek. What I wish for is peace between men and their faiths. What has the war with Islam ever given us but bloodshed, sorrow and destruction? Do you know how many years the Order has been waging its war against the enemy? Over five centuries.' For a brief moment Thomas sensed the terrible burden of such a length of time devoted to unremitting hatred and violence. Generation upon generation steeped in the gore of innocents. He shook his head slowly. 'I would rather the struggle came to an end and there was peace between Christendom and the Sultan.'

'Peace with the Sultan?' Walsingham laughed harshly. 'Did you ever hear of such a thing?'

Thomas looked at him. 'If I have to kill again then it will not be in the name of religion.'

'Yet you were happy to become a mercenary and to kill for money for many years,' Walsingham sneered, and was about to speak again when his superior raised a hand to stop him.

Cecil folded his hands together and regarded Thomas thoughtfully. 'It is an admirable sentiment, Sir Thomas, truly. In a better world than this I would share your convictions. However, the world is filled with sinners going about their mischief and we must do what we can to obstruct them. The Sultan is one such man who must be stopped. Your former comrade, Sir Oliver, was correct to write that your Order is in peril on Malta. We have heard the same from our own sources.'

Thomas's eyes narrowed. 'Pardon me, Sir William, but how would you know what Sir Oliver wrote to me?'

'Ah.' A pained look crossed Cecil's face. 'I had hoped to return this to you a bit later on.' He fished a hand into his robe and extracted a folded piece of paper with a familiar broken seal, and slid it across the table towards Thomas. He stared at the letter in frank surprise.

'How did you get this?'

'Do you imagine that we would permit a foreign soldier free passage across England without ensuring that his every movement was observed?'

'You had him followed to my house?'

'Of course.'

Then it struck Thomas. 'But this letter was in my study this morning. I placed it there, in my desk. I am certain of it.'

'Yes, you did. But one of my agents called at your house after you had left. He managed to persuade a servant to relate all that had passed and it was a simple matter to search your study. The letter was found and brought to me as swiftly as possible. Sir Francis and I were able to read it a good two hours before you arrived.'

'Did your man harm any of my servants in order to get your information?' Thomas asked quietly.

'He didn't have to.' Cecil smiled. 'Your servants are Catholics, like yourself. It was a simple matter to remind them of the fate that befalls those accused of heresy, and a somewhat lower standard of proof is required to charge a servant than a man of status like yourself, Sir Thomas.'

'Although that can be arranged,' Walsingham added darkly.

'Sir Francis, if you please, there's no need to threaten our guest.' Cecil turned back to Thomas. 'There, the letter is your property. Please take it. I regret that we had to read it, but in my position I have to guard against any potential threat to Her Majesty. You must understand that.'

'I understand perfectly,' Thomas replied as he retrieved the letter, holding it by the tips of his fingers as if it had been sullied. 'There is no base behaviour or abuse of common law that you will not use to bend people to your will.'

Cecil shrugged easily. 'I do what I must.'

'And was it necessary to steal this letter? Why ask me about the purpose of Sir Philippe's mission if you knew all this from reading the message?'

'We had to know that you were telling the truth. We had to know if you were hiding anything from us. As it is you have passed the test.'

'How gratifying,' Thomas replied sourly. 'Then I think it is time for you to explain this task which you mentioned earlier. Although you should know that I will not help you to persecute my fellow Catholics here in England.'

'I would hardly expect a man of your integrity to do that, Sir Thomas. Well then, let us get down to brass tacks. As you know, the Turks are preparing to strike a blow against one of the cornerstones of Christian influence in the Mediterranean. If they take Malta, Sicily will be next. Then Italy and Rome itself. If Rome falls then it will be as if the death knell of our faith, Protestant as well as Catholic, has sounded. Suleiman has made no secret of his aim to be master of the known world and impose Islam on all his subjects. He has chosen a good time to unleash his forces against us. Europe is divided by war and religious faction. Spain and France are snapping at each other's throats and the great fleet that Venice might have sent against the Turks has been decommissioned following the cowardly alliance they signed with Suleiman to safeguard their interests. So you see, your brothers in the Order can expect little help from outside in their stand against the Turks. Only Spain has promised to send what aid she can.' Cecil paused to lend his next words emphasis. 'If you agree to return to Malta you will be in the vanguard of the fight to save Europe from the infidel. Save Malta and save us all.'

Thomas could not resist a cynical smile. 'So you have called me here to ask me to join the fight against Islam.'

'That, and for one other purpose.' Cecil sat back and wagged a finger at Walsingham. 'You explain, Sir Francis.'

The other man collected his thoughts before he addressed Thomas. 'Since you have elected to return to Malta you will have a chance to serve England's interests in a more direct fashion. Earlier, you upbraided Sir William and myself over the measures we are obliged to pursue in order to preserve order in England.'

'Order is one word for it,' Thomas countered. 'Another word would be tyranny.'

'Either way, our actions prevent a far greater evil, namely that of civil war. Ever since King Henry denied the supremacy of the Church of Rome, our country has been riven by the tensions between Catholic and Protestant. It is a miracle that this has not flared up into open civil conflict. I need not remind you of the horrors that have taken place in the Netherlands and France. John Foxe has written extensively about them.'

'You should not give credence to all that you read in *The Book of Martyrs*,' said Thomas.

'Maybe,' said Cecil. 'But you will not deny such atrocities took place. After all, you must have seen them with your own eyes when you served there. Even allowing for Foxe's sensationalism there is enough truth in his words to point the way to what might happen here in England if religious differences were to be expressed through violence. The streets of our cities would run with blood. So far that has been prevented because Protestants have largely been united in their opposition to Catholicism. But what if a wedge were to be driven between English nobles and the Queen? Such a division would embolden the Catholics and it would not take long before we were at each other's throats.'

'Perhaps,' Thomas reflected. 'But what would cause such a division?'

Cecil exchanged a brief glance with Walsingham before he continued. 'There is a document in the possession of the knights in Malta that, if it were made public, could tear this country apart. The aristocrats would turn on the Queen and the common people would turn on the aristocrats, before they turned on each other. That is what we seek to prevent.'

'You said it *could* tear this country apart. Why would it, pray? I find it hard to credit that a simple document might be the cause of such strife as you describe. Besides, what has such a document got to do with me, or the Order?'

'The contents of the document are known to only a handful of men. It is best that it remains so. Such knowledge is dangerous. I can tell you that it was in the possession of an English knight from the Order some eighteen years ago. He died in Malta before he could carry the document to its ultimate destination. As far as we know, it is still in Malta. It is best for you to know only that the document exists and that it must be retrieved and brought back to me, or destroyed if that is not possible.'

'What is to stop me reading it if I find it?'

'There is a seal upon it. I would know if it had been tampered with. However, it will not be your job to find the document we seek. That will be the task of another man. You will take a squire with you to Malta. The man in question will be our agent. Because he will be attached to you, his presence there will not attract attention to him. His mission is to find the document. If either of you survive the coming siege then you are to return to England with the document. In the event that Malta is taken then it will be the duty of the last of the two still alive to destroy the document before it falls into the enemy's hands. I will not disguise the grave peril attached to this mission, Sir Thomas,' Cecil concluded. 'But we are playing for high stakes and you will have the chance to serve your country and your faith and to save many lives. Now, I imagine you may have some questions for us.'

'Indeed I have, Sir William,' Thomas replied. 'Firstly, if this document is so important, why has it not been revealed to the world? The Order is answerable to the King of Spain. I cannot believe that Philip would not have used it if it would harm the interests of England, as you claim.'

'Fairly stated.' Cecil nodded. 'We have to assume that the document has not been put to such use because the Order is ignorant of what it has in its possession.'

'How can that be?'

'The document left England in the hands of an English knight, Sir Peter de Launcey.'

Thomas frowned. 'I remember him. A good man.'

'Indeed he was. A few years after you left Malta, Sir Peter was given leave to visit his family in England when his father was dying. Soon after he returned to Malta he fell from the deck of a galley and drowned. What is not known is that King Henry entrusted him with this document, which Sir Peter was to guard for him. Henry was ill at the time and did not know if he would survive. In the event that he recovered, Sir Peter was to bring the document back to him. If Henry died, which he did, then Sir Peter was to take the document to Rome and present it to the Pope. But Sir Peter died on Malta, and Henry died at almost the same time. A small handful of his closest advisers knew of the document and were only prepared to reveal this under duress.'

'You mean, under torture.'

'Yes,' Cecil admitted freely. 'And the document remains in Malta, where Sir Peter must have secreted it. You must find it if you can. You, or rather, our agent. Are there further questions, Sir Thomas?'

'Yes. You seem certain that I will accept your mission. Why should I not refuse?'

'Because you are a knight, both of this realm and of the Order of St John and that places certain obligations upon you. You are a man of honour, and principle. If you can be instrumental in averting the catastrophe that threatens your country you will seize the chance to do so, unless I have utterly mistaken your character. Furthermore, you are a Catholic, and live at the whim of a Protestant Queen and her ministers, of whom I am the foremost. I need not point out the implications of your situation. Suffice to say that you have my word that I will protect you upon completion of the mission. If you refuse . . .'

Thomas shook his head. 'I do not need to be threatened.'

'Perhaps not, but it is as well that you know that there is no real choice in the matter. That should be of some small comfort to you in the hard times ahead.'

'My thanks for your solicitude,' Thomas responded acidly. 'I have one more question. Who is this agent of yours, the one who is to be my squire? I presume he is the man waiting in the anteroom.'

Cecil smiled. 'Then you have met already. Young Richard is one of the most accomplished men in my service. I put it down to the fact that I took him on as an orphan. He did not know his parents and so he owes his loyalty to me. He shows great promise and this will be the first big test of his skills. He speaks French, Spanish and Italian like a native and has fluency in Maltese.'

'And yet he is not quite English,' said Thomas. 'There is an accent and a certain Latin look about him.'

'He is as English as you or I, and I have complete faith in him. As must you if you are to see this mission through.'

'Trust has to be earned, Sir William. It is not a commodity to be freely given.'

'Then you had better get to know Richard as soon as possible. Sir Francis, fetch him in.'

Walsingham's eyes flashed with a glint of irritation at his superior's peremptory manner but he rose swiftly and crossed the room. As Thomas watched, the soft tread and fluid movement reminded him of a cat, an apt demeanour for the man who stalked and killed his prey with no compassion.

When Walsingham had disappeared through the door there was a brief silence until Thomas leaned forward and spoke quietly.

'I have no need of a squire. It would be better to entrust this matter to me alone. If I give you my word to return the document without reading it then your spy can remain here, out of danger.'

There was an amused look on Cecil's face as he shook his head. 'A considerate offer, but while you may have no real need for a squire, my need for a trusted pair of eyes and ears on the spot is very real to me. You must take Richard with you and that is an end to it.'

Before Thomas could reply there came the sound of footsteps and a moment later Walsingham re-entered the room, followed by the young man Thomas had seen earlier. They approached the table and Walsingham resumed his seat while Cecil's agent stood to one side.

'Richard, I gather you have already met our guest,' said Cecil.

'We only exchanged a few words, master.'

'Then it is time for a formal introduction. Sir Thomas, I give you Richard Hughes, your squire.'

Thomas rose and walked over to the young man, stopping at arm's length to look him over thoroughly for the first time. Hughes was tall and broad-shouldered. His doublet fitted him well and there was no unnecessary adornment to the sleeves, no ruff collar, and his hair was neatly cut and free of the oils and pomades that were fashionable amongst young men of a certain social status in London. Thomas approved of that, then looked straight into the man's eyes. His gaze was met unflinchingly, and yet there was something else there besides boldness, Thomas sensed. A coldness, and a simmering degree of resentment.

'Whatever the true nature of your orders may be, you are to be my squire first and foremost. Is that understood?'

'Yes, sir.'

'When I give an order you will obey it without question, just as would be expected of any squire.'

'Yes, sir. Provided it does not conflict with my instructions from Sir William.'

'I have little idea what your instructions are, but if we are to succeed in convincing the knights of the Order that we are what we purport to be then it must be as second nature for you to do my bidding. I take it you have been instructed in the duties of a squire?'

'Yes, sir.'

Thomas arched an eyebrow. 'Really? And when exactly did Sir William inform you of your mission?'

The young man's gaze wavered and he glanced over Thomas's shoulder towards his master. Cecil nodded. 'Speak the truth.'

'Two days ago, sir.'

'I see. And you have learned all the elements of this new position in that time?'

'I have been extensively briefed by the squire of the Queen's champion, sir. The rest I can learn on the road to Malta. If you will instruct me.'

Thomas shook his head and turned to the others. 'It is folly to use this man.'

'Nevertheless, you will take him,' Walsingham replied firmly. 'You will train him in what he needs to know and do. I grow weary of your truculence. Were you not the only individual with a chance of serving our needs then I would readily pick another. You will go to Malta, with Richard as your squire. The matter is settled.'

Anger flared in Thomas's heart and for a moment he was tempted to confront Walsingham and refuse the mission, whatever consequences followed. The satisfaction of denying him, and perhaps challenging him to back his arrogance up with his blade was almost too tempting for Thomas.

'He has agreed to our request,' Cecil intervened. 'There is no more to be said. Come now, we are all on the same side. There is no call for ire. All that remains is for Sir Thomas to settle his affairs and arrange for the good management of his estate in his absence. Such is the nature of his mission that he need not spend an undue amount of time preparing whatever baggage he requires for the coming campaign.'

'How long do I have to prepare?'

'Two days.' Sir Francis smiled faintly. 'There is a Danish galleon loading at Greenwich. She sails for Spain in two days' time. You and Richard will be on that ship.'

'Good luck,' Cecil added, and then, with more feeling, 'God be with you . . .'

CHAPTER ELEVEN

Bilbao, Spain
New Year's Eve, 1565

Thomas looked on in frustration as his squire engaged in a fraught conversation with the port master. It had been many years since he had spoken the tongue, albeit imperfectly even then, and he was only able to catch a few words that passed between Richard and the official, and little sense of what was being said. Meanwhile he stood on the glistening stones of the quay as a chilling drizzle beaded his cloak. They had disembarked from the Danish vessel at midday and were immediately confronted by a patrol. The Spanish sergeant in charge of the men had demanded to know his business and refused to let him proceed unless he could provide documentation that proved Thomas had leave to travel across Spain. The letter from Sir Oliver had been brushed aside and a man had been sent to find the port master.

Thomas, Richard and the soldiers of the patrol had been forced to wait on the blustery quay while behind them the fishing boats and cargo ships bobbed and swayed on the grey swell rolling into the harbour from the Bay of Biscay. After a while the sergeant had retired to a nearby inn and left orders that the two Englishmen were to remain under guard and no one was to move until the port master's will was known. So the small party had settled down to wait, Thomas and his squire sitting on their bags hunched in their capes while the Spaniards leaned against the mooring posts, the rain dripping steadily from the rims of their morion helmets.

As it was winter, there was little activity in the port and the cargo of glassware from Denmark and wool from London was quickly unloaded into a warehouse before the crew hurried below deck to the relative comfort of their hammocks. All was quiet along the quay, except for the hiss of rain and the sweep and swirl of the wind when it picked up. A handful of locals passed by, casting suspicious glances at the two Englishmen under guard. For his part, Thomas was glad to be ashore. In the years that he had served on the Order's galleys he had rarely been to sea in winter, and never in waters exposed to the seasonal fury of the Atlantic Ocean.

The Danish galleon had emerged from the mouth of the Thames and crossed the Channel before hugging the French coastline. A violent storm had blown them out to sea and for five days the crew had had little sleep as they battled the heavy sea, losing the main spar and sail in the struggle. Icy sea water sluiced across the deck and soaked through their clothes as the vessel shuddered under the impact of each wave and soared and swooped from swell to swell. The seasickness was the worst that Thomas had ever experienced and after he and his fellow passengers – Richard and three priests returning to Spain from Amsterdam – had thrown up the last contents of their stomachs, they had retreated to the tiny communal cabin they shared. Thomas sat with his back to one of the thick compass timbers and hugged his knees to try and keep warm. Richard did the same a short distance away, head tucked down, while the priests clutched their rosaries and prayed until their voices gave out and then fell to muttering as they beseeched the Lord for mercy.

It was in that moment of greatest vulnerability that Thomas took careful stock of his companion, watching him closely over his folded arms. Despite his youth, no more than twenty years, Thomas estimated, he seemed to have a cool, detached maturity, frequently looking about him, at his surroundings and at those he came into contact with. So far he had said little to Thomas beyond what was absolutely necessary and civil. Only when the galleon had broached the heavy seas in the Channel did the implacable façade slip for an instant. They had been standing on deck when a wave had crashed over the bows. Richard had been caught unawares and was swept off his feet. As the water carried him several feet along the deck he had cried out in alarm and then looked at Thomas with an instinctive appeal for help. Thomas had braced himself, legs spread to retain his balance, and with one hand clasping the bulwark he had grasped Richard's hand with the other and hauled him off the deck. A small roller following in the wake of the wave pitched them together, as if they were friends embracing. At once Richard had pushed himself free and his expression returned to its usual coldness, his dark eyes narrowing as he nodded his gratitude before making his way down to the cabin to change into dry clothes. It had been only the briefest of moments, but he had revealed a very human aspect to his character and at the time Thomas could not help smiling at his squire's shame for having done so.

As soon as the storm had subsided the captain turned his ship towards land and they made for La Rochelle to rest and make repairs before continuing the voyage. The galleon picked its way along the coast of the Bay of Biscay and passed the border between France and Spain on a cheerless Christmas Day. It had been Thomas's intention to land at San Sebastian, but the port was being besieged by the French and the captain had continued to Bilbao instead, over the protests of the priests who had demanded to be set ashore at San Sebastian.

As Thomas had sat brooding on the quay the soldier finally returned with the port master who launched into a tirade when Richard attempted to explain the purpose of their journey. Behind them the sergeant crept out of the door of the inn and rejoined his men before he was missed. Thomas listened to the angry exchange for a while before he stirred and rose stiffly to his feet. His body was no longer as keen a hound to its master and did not respond willingly. His muscles trembled from the cold and wet and felt heavy as he walked across to interrupt the two men locked in argument.

'What is the problem with our friend?'

Richard glanced round. 'He says that all Spanish ports are closed to travellers from England, on the orders of King Philip, in reprisal for the Queen's continued persecution of Catholics.'

'Really? Then tell him that I am a Catholic.'

Richard translated and the port master replied shortly and tilted his nose up.

'He says that you are still an Englishman.'

'That is true, and it is no cause for apology. Tell him it is he who should be apologising for detaining us here.'

Richard hesitated. 'We are supposed to pass through Spain as discreetly as possible, sir.'

'Discretion is one thing, humiliation is quite another. I am an English knight, marching to serve the Order of St John, and defend all Christendom against the Turk. If this man impedes me then he will not only answer to his King, but also to his God.' He reached into his cloak and took out the leather tube in which he kept the letter from Sir Oliver. He extracted the letter and held it up for the port master to see. 'This is the seal of the Order, and this letter is my call to arms. Tell him.'

Richard nodded and addressed the Spanish official. The latter's expression turned to one of alarm as he leaned forward to inspect the seal. He waved the document away and began speaking hurriedly. Then he bowed to Thomas, nodded to Richard and turned away to issue his orders to the sergeant in command of the patrol before striding back into the town.

Thomas carefully replaced the letter and stopped up the tube before he spoke. 'Well?'

'He says that we are welcome to stay in the officers' quarters of the customs house. The sergeant will escort us there. The port master says he will arrange for us to have a warrant to travel across Spain to Barcelona. That is where a fleet, under the command of Don Garcia de Toledo, is being readied to send against the Turks. He will also provide us with two horses for the journey.'

Thomas pursed his lips appreciatively. 'It is amazing

what the threat of a little divine vengeance will do to the motivation of a minor official.'

The corners of the squire's mouth flickered briefly into a smile. 'I confess that I embellished the tale a little.'

'Oh?'

'I said that the letter was co-signed by the Viceroy of Catalonia.'

Now it was Thomas's turn to smile. 'Ah, so it was earthly rather than divine authority that swayed his will.'

'As is always the case with petty officials.'

The sergeant beckoned to them and gave a curt order to two of his men to pick up the baggage. Finally they left the rainswept quay and made their way up a narrow street into the port.

The customs house was a square building with offices downstairs where merchants were obliged to bring their cargo manifestos and pay the duty owing on them. Few ships ventured on the seas during the winter months and the sole clerk had closed his ledger and was cleaning his quills with an old rag when the two Englishmen arrived. They were led upstairs to a modest room with four simple beds, a few chairs and a small fireplace with logs and kindling in a basket to one side. The clerk brought them up a lamp and some bread, cheese and a jug of wine before bidding them a good night. They heard the door downstairs close and then the rattle of a lock.

'That's that, then.' Thomas let out a sigh as he looked round the room. 'I'll take the bed nearest the fire.'

'As you wish.'

Now that they were alone Thomas noticed that his

companion had dropped the deference due from a squire to his knight.

'And you can get the fire lit before we eat. We need to get warm and dry our clothes.'

Richard frowned at him but before he could speak, Thomas raised a warning finger. 'I know what you're thinking.'

'Then why don't you tell me?'

'You were sent on a mission on behalf of Sir William Cecil, not to be my squire, and you're starting to resent it.'

'I wonder why I might do that? After all, I am an educated man. I have studied at Cambridge, I speak a number of languages, I have performed valuable services for the Secretary of State. All of which is perfect preparation for being the dogsbody of a knight long past his prime.' He paused and gritted his teeth before saying apologetically, 'Pardon me, I am cold and exhausted. I spoke out of turn.'

Thomas laughed and shook his head in wonder. 'That is the most you have said to me since we left England. Truly.'

Richard shrugged, and undid the clasp of his cloak and let the sodden garment drop to the floor.

'Well, it's good to know a little of your background,' Thomas continued in an amused tone. 'And that you consider that my best years are long behind me.'

'I apologise.'

'No need. You are right, I am no longer the warrior of my youth. But I assure you, when I was your age my body was as well-shaped as yours. Better perhaps. Even now, who knows?'

The young man had removed his leather jerkin and struggled out of his woollen shirt before he stared at Thomas with an amused expression. 'You would try your strength against me?'

'You think I would be afraid to?'

'No. Not from what I know of you, Sir Thomas. But I think you would be unwise to.'

Thomas cocked an eyebrow but kept his silence as he also removed his wet garments until he was standing in his boots and breeches and his powerful torso was revealed. The knotted white flesh of old scars was clearly visible by the pale glow of the lamp and he saw Richard staring at him curiously, before he looked away in embarrassment.

'I'll light the fire,' said Thomas. 'There's another lamp over there. Take it, and go and see if you can find some more blankets. I want to be warm tonight at least, before we continue on our way.'

Richard nodded. Using a length of straw from a tear in one of the mattresses as a taper, he lit the lamp's wick and left the room. Alone, Thomas eased himself down on to the floor beside the fireplace. His damp skin felt colder still in the chill air and he shivered as he built up the kindling over a small bed of straw and then applied a small flame. It caught readily and Thomas leaned forward, blowing gently to encourage it. Soon there was a soft hiss and crackle as the small flames licked up around the kindling. By the time Richard returned, the room was lit by the rosy glow of the fire and shadows danced on the plaster walls of the room.

'Here.' Richard had some folded blankets balanced against his chest and he held one out. 'Found them in a cupboard. Spare bolsters too if you need one.'

'I'll be comfortable enough without.' Thomas nodded his thanks and took the blanket, quickly shaking it out and then draping it around his shoulders before he added some of the smaller split logs to the growing blaze.

Richard took a blanket for himself and sat on the edge of the bed that Thomas had chosen for himself, leaning forward slightly to get closer to the warmth of the fire. There was a brief silence before he spoke.

'Those scars. Did you get them in the service of the Order?'

'Some. Others came from my service elsewhere.' Thomas eased himself back and round so that he could face the younger man. He touched his left shoulder. 'An arrow cut through me there while I was in Flanders. 'Twas a flesh wound, but I bled like a stuck pig, as I recall.' He moved his hand down to his left breast. 'This is where a dagger cut me deeply. This other I got on an expedition in the harbour at Algiers. La Valette did not want us to be hampered by armour. There was a skirmish aboard the galleon we seized and a corsair leaped out of the shadows in front of me and struck. I'd have been cut down with his second blow if La Valette had not come between us and killed the fellow.' Thomas looked down into the fire, his brow creasing at the memories. He tapped the inside of his left elbow. 'The scar there was from a burn, when we attacked a corsair fort near Tripoli. The enemy were using incendiary pots. One burst on the wall beside the ladder I was climbing and the naphtha burned through the chain mail and the gambison beneath and on to my flesh.' He winced at the memory of the terrible, intense pain that he had endured during the long night it took to capture the fort.

'What about that one, on your forehead?' Richard asked quietly.

'This?' Thomas raised his hand and traced the thin scar an inch below the hairline. He was silent for a moment as he slowly ran the finger backwards and forwards along the scar and Richard watched him expectantly, eyes glinting with reflection from the fire that was warming the room. Thomas cleared his throat. 'This one I got when I slipped on some ice and hit my head on the door of an inn.'

Richard's jaw sagged and then he burst into laughter and Thomas joined in, filling the room with a hearty sound. The laughter continued for longer than it might have done now that the tension between the two men had eased for the first time since meeting. And then, as it died away, Richard became self-conscious and stood up and pulled two chairs over towards the fire and hung his clothes over them to dry, hesitating a moment before he did the same for Thomas's cloak, jerkin and shirt. Meanwhile, Thomas took out the small knife he carried in a sheath at his back and cut the bread into hunks and sliced the cheese and offered half to Richard.

'Thank you.' The young man stood up and gestured to the bed. 'Yours, I think.'

Thomas shook his head. 'Have it.' He thumped the sleeping mat beneath him. 'This will serve well enough.'

Richard sat and they both began to eat. It was the first meal in weeks that Thomas had eaten that was not infused by the salty tang of the sea, nor spoiled by the nauseating roll of the galleon as it clawed its way across murky waves under a grey sky. Consequently, simple bread and cheese as it was, the taste was unrivalled and as his stomach filled and his body was warmed Thomas felt content. Partly, he realised, because now there was a prospect of some companionship where before there had been only a frosty tolerance between himself and Richard. Thomas wanted to find out more about Cecil's agent, partly out of a desire to learn what he could about the document and the precise nature of Richard's orders but also out of simple curiosity and a wish to know the man better. Yet he knew that to presume too much too quickly might risk having Richard raise his guard once again. He reached for the jug of wine and poured them each a cup. He handed one across to Richard. The clothes had begun to steam and a musty aroma filled the room.

'You were well chosen for this mission,' said Thomas. 'If you speak your other languages as well as you do Spanish then you will be very useful indeed.'

Richard gave a quirky smile. 'Useful? Perhaps a man of my social station should consider that a compliment.'

Thomas was tempted to ask more but there was a touch of anger and, more, shame in the young man's voice and he decided not to pursue the matter for the present.

'You have played your part well enough,' Thomas continued. 'But we will both be called upon to perform like the best players in London if we are to convince the other members of the Order when we reach Malta. It is not enough that you behave like a squire. You must begin to think like one. You must do whatever I ask of you without hesitation and without any of the resentment you occasionally show. You will keep my armour, equipment and wardrobe clean. You will behave with due courtesy to everyone you encounter, no matter what their class. You must, at all times, deport yourself as a gentleman who aspires to become a knight. And not just any knight, but one of the Order. If you can do that then you will pass for a squire.'

Richard's expression became bitter. 'Then I shall pass for what I shall never become, nor ever a knight.'

'How so?'

'Nobility is the preserve of those with no stain on their past. It matters not what the worth of a man is if there is a blemish against his name which nothing can erase.'

'But you are of gentle birth,' Thomas replied. 'That is self-evident. You are as much a gentleman as I am, I can see that.'

'Save for the fact that I was born on the wrong side of the sheet, Sir Thomas. That is something that no one can change. I am a bastard, known as such by those who raised me. That is why I have chosen this course in life. Now, if you will excuse me, I am tired and would sleep well before we journey on the morrow.' He drained his cup and lay down on the bed, turned on his side, so that his back was towards Thomas and the fire.

For a while Thomas gazed at him, wondering about his origins. What must it be like to bear the burden of such a stigma in a world in which such things counted so deeply, despite the manifold wickedness and immorality of many who laid claim to the mantle of nobility? No wonder the young man was bitter. Nature had clearly blessed him with a fine mind, fair body and sound constitution. Society had cursed him with a label which would blight him until the day he died. For a moment Thomas began to feel pity for his companion, and then he caught himself. There was no need to add to Richard's difficulties with such an unworthy sentiment.

He sighed softly and then built up the fire. Turning the clothes drying on the backs of the chairs, he placed the boots beside them and then climbed into his own bed and lay on his back staring up at the ceiling. Sleep no longer came to him as easily as it once did and a church bell in the port sounded midnight before Thomas closed his eyes and drifted off.

CHAPTER TWELVE

The road across the north of Spain passed through the rocky terrain of Navarra and Aragon before reaching Catalonia. It rained frequently and the high passes over the hills were laden with snow and ice that slowed their pace. Most nights Thomas and Richard stopped in small villages, paying to sleep in barns when they could not find a room. Twice they had to sleep in the open, horses tethered to stunted trees while the two men huddled round a fire in the shelter of a rocky outcrop. They took it in turns to sleep, wary of the small bands of robbers who preyed on passing travellers. Once they were followed for half a day by a group of men on small unkempt ponies. Thomas and Richard stopped briefly to strap on their swords and made sure that the weapons were clearly visible. Shortly after, the men reined in and watched them ride out of sight.

The two Englishmen attracted attention in every village and town they passed through. The King and Church had been assiduous in their efforts to ensure that their people considered the island ruled by the Protestant Queen Elizabeth a godless realm of evil and depravity. As such the knight and his squire excited a degree of suspicion and fear and while they were never threatened or turned away, thanks to the travel warrant issued by the port master of

Bilbao, there was no warmth or hospitality in the way they were received.

The conversation that they had enjoyed on their first night in Spain was not repeated; Richard had once again retreated into a quietly hostile demeanour, even though he did as Thomas had asked and made sure that he fulfilled his role as a squire faultlessly. After a few attempts to return to the warm moment of companionship they had shared, Thomas gave up trying and they rode on, exchanging a handful of words only when necessary and eating in silence each night as they sat by a fire or hunched in the shelter of a barn.

At noon on the fifth day of the new year they crested the last ridge in the hills that overlooked the narrow plain where Barcelona nestled against the Mediterranean. The clouds had cleared that morning and the sun shone down from a brilliant blue sky. Even though it was the depth of winter the sea somehow looked bright and inviting and Thomas felt a warm ache in his heart for the island in the very centre of the Mediterranean, a place he had once believed to be his home for life, amongst a band of brothers in arms fighting for God against impossible odds. It had all seemed so clear and noble back then, before Maria had stepped into his life and the realisation had slowly dawned that there was little nobility to be won in a never-ending war where progress consisted in visiting new horrors upon the enemy. For all its sparkling beauty, this sea was a battlefield as old as history. Long before the present conflict had begun, the Mediterranean had been fought over by Romans, Egyptians, Carthaginians, Greeks and Persians. Who knew how many thousands of warships lay rotting in the deeps? This was a sea watered by the tears and blood of generation upon generation of human beings, Thomas reflected with a shudder.

He clicked his tongue and nudged his heels into the flanks of his horse. 'Come on, let's not tarry.'

Richard took in the view for a moment longer before he followed and they picked their way along the track that looped back and forth down the side of the hill. Below them the city of Barcelona lay in the shadow of the fortified citadel. In the harbour some thirty or forty galleys lay at anchor and two more rested on timber rollers in front of the royal shipyards, a series of long sheds with high roofs that dominated the shoreline. On the parade ground outside the fortress several companies of pikemen were drilling beneath the billowing colours of their standards. Preparations were clearly in hand to confront the threat rising at the other end of the Mediterranean. But would it be enough? Thomas wondered. From experience he well knew how the Turks could field vast forces of men and ships. They had the finest gunners and siege engineers in the world in their ranks and the size and destructiveness of their cannon were without equal.

As they approached the city walls the track joined a coastal road. A short distance ahead the two horsemen passed a trundling line of wagons laden with kegs of gunpowder and cast-iron shot. Thomas spurred his horse on so that they were in front of the convoy by the time they reached the city's main gateway. Gesturing to Richard to come to his side, Thomas drew out his travel warrant and handed it to one of the soldiers on duty. The Catalan stared uncomprehendingly at the document before he

ordered them curtly to wait and then turned away to find
his officer, disappearing through an arched doorway into
the gate's guardroom. Thomas eased himself out of the
saddle and slipped on to the ground with a weary grunt. A
moment later Richard followed suit and took the reins of
both horses, as any squire would have done, Thomas noted
with satisfaction.

The guard emerged a short time later with a portly man
dabbing at his mouth with one hand as he looked at the
warrant in the other. He glanced at the two Englishmen
before addressing Thomas, who gestured to his squire.

'Richard, if you please.'

As the two conversed, Thomas tried to follow the sense
of what was being said, but the Catalan language was
strange to his ears. It made him feel uncomfortable and
even vulnerable; he did not yet trust the young man who
had been foisted on him by Cecil and Walsingham.
Richard knew a good deal more about the purpose of this
mission and the nature of the sensitive document at the
heart of it. If the document was located and recovered
then what, Thomas wondered, were his companion's
orders at that point? He himself would be of no more use
to Cecil; perhaps Richard's orders included the quiet
elimination of a man whose knowledge of the mission,
limited as it was, might prove to be an embarrassment at a
later date. He must be on his guard against such treachery,
even as he faced the Turk in battle. The thought made
him feel bitter towards Richard and his spymasters back in
London.

Richard interrupted his thoughts. 'Sir, I have explained
our purpose to the captain. He says that since we are to

voyage to Malta then it would be best to announce our arrival at the citadel. That is where we will find Don Garcia de Toledo. His army is making ready to embark for Sicily and we may be able to travel with the fleet.'

'Sicily?'

'It is where King Philip is gathering his forces to face the Turk. The Spaniards will be joined by mercenaries from Italy, including the galleys of the Doria clan. The captain here says that he has heard it will be the largest army ever amassed to fight in the name of Christ. And Don Garcia is the finest general in all Europe. The Turks, he says, will be utterly crushed.'

Thomas looked at the Catalan officer, fat and too used to good living. He would not last long in any strenuous campaign. 'Tell him that I pray to God that he is right. We will go to the citadel now.'

'He says that he will have his men take us there.' Richard glanced warily at the Spaniard before he continued. 'There have been rumours that the enemy have spies in Barcelona. I don't think he trusts us.'

'Spies?' Thomas laughed. 'Do we look like Turks?'

'We are English, sir. It seems that there are many here who think that their enemies share a common cause. It is understandable. They have never forgiven the French for fighting alongside the Turks twenty years ago.'

Thomas nodded with feeling. It had been an alliance that had scandalised the rest of Christendom as little more than a pact with the devil. It had endured only briefly. The French had been shamed by the massacres carried out by their new allies against the Christians along the coast of Italy. Thomas could imagine the horror that it would have brought to the French knights of the Order, and La Valette most of all.

'Very well, thank the captain for providing us with an escort.'

With two men leading the way and another pair following on behind, Thomas and his squire walked their horses through the sturdy walls and into a wide thoroughfare. The towers of the cathedral of Santa Eulalia rose up above the roofs of the closely packed buildings lining the route. The recent rains had washed away much of the filth that covered the streets and the more offensive smells of the city were mild in comparison to the stench of London. It had been many years since Thomas had last seen Barcelona but for Richard it was clearly the first time, judging from the way he gazed at his surroundings with frank curiosity. With his dark looks he might have passed for a local if not for his lack of a Catalan accent. Cecil and Walsingham had chosen their man wisely, Thomas mused.

As they entered the square in front of the cathedral, Thomas's attention shifted to the ornate façade with the three towers constructed from a sturdy latticework of stone. So different from the cathedrals back in England, he thought. Craning his head, he squinted at the crosses thrusting up towards the azure heavens. A handful of seagulls circled above, black against the glare. For a moment Thomas felt his heart lift at the sight, before he was struck by the thought that at the other side of this sea, in Constantinople, the great city that the Turks had renamed Istanbul, a man like him, a warrior, might be standing in front of the great mosque, staring up at a golden crescent – a man he might face in battle one day soon. The thought sent a cold tremor down his spine. It was not fear, just a brooding sense that he was fated to be consumed by the coming clash of faiths and empires.

The small party crossed the square and soon they had left the confines of the city behind and were making their way up the steep hill to the citadel. A fresh breeze was blowing in off the sea, carrying a salty tang with it. When they reached the entrance to the citadel, once again they had to explain their business. While the escort was sent back to the city wall, the knight and his squire were admitted to the outer courtyard where they tethered their horses and sat down on a bench to wait.

They were not kept long. An officer dressed in red velvet hurried out of the governor's headquarters and approached them.

'Sir Thomas Barrett? It is an honour to meet you, sir,' he announced in good French and bowed deeply. Thomas and Richard rose to their feet and inclined their heads in return.

'May I introduce myself?' He flashed a pleasant smile. 'I am Fadrique Garcia de Toledo, and I am at the service of you and your squire, Sir Thomas.'

The young man looked to be in his early twenties at most and Thomas exchanged a brief glance with Richard before clearing his throat and replying in French.

'Are you the commander of the force that King Philip is sending against the Turks?'

'Me?' The Spaniard's eyebrows rose in amusement. 'Decidedly not, sir. That would be my father. I have sent him word of your arrival. He will be pleased to greet another member of the Order who is answering the call to arms.'

'Have there been many of us?' asked Thomas.

Fadrique's smile faded. 'Not as many have passed through Barcelona as we had expected, sir. You are, in fact, only the fifth knight we have seen. Of course many will have taken ship from other ports. I am sure that no member of your Order will deny himself the chance to partake in the glorious victory we shall celebrate over the Turk.'

'Let us hope that you are right.'

'I am sure of it, sir. This is the great battle of our age. The decisive test of arms between our faith and the false faith of Islam.'

Thomas pursed his lips but held his peace.

The Spaniard gestured towards the entrance. 'If you follow me I shall provide you with refreshment while you wait on my father's pleasure.'

Thomas smiled faintly as he recalled the fine manners of those Spaniards he had once fought alongside. He bowed his head. 'Thank you.'

Inside the building they passed through a tiled hall with arches leading off into gloomy corridors on either side. Other than a handful of guards on duty, there was little sign of activity. The three men's footsteps echoed off the walls.

'It seems very quiet here,' Thomas commented. 'I had assumed your father's staff would be busy planning for the campaign.'

'It is all in hand, I assure you,' Fadrique said lightly. 'Most of his staff officers are down at the shipyard overseeing the loading of our galleys. We sail for Sicily in a matter of days. Once we have joined forces with our allies we shall confront the Turk.'

They entered a modest chamber with a long table stretching down the centre. Comfortable chairs stood on each side and two, more ostentatious, stood one at each end. Fadrique waved them towards the table.

'Please sit. I have given orders for food and wine to be brought to you. Now, if you will excuse me I shall attend my father until he is ready to meet you.' He bowed again and left them alone. Once the door had shut, Richard let out a sigh. 'Just five knights . . . There should be more than that making for Barcelona. Many more.'

'There is time yet,' Thomas countered. 'And, as he says, they might be taking other routes.'

Richard stared at him. 'Do you really believe that?'

Thomas shrugged. 'It does no harm to hope for the best and accept the worst.'

'That is a fool's philosophy.'

Thomas was not disheartened. 'The greater the odds we are required to face, the more our share of the glory.'

'Glory, that's what you knights live for. I understand that. But whereas your glorious deeds will be entered, by name, in the record, that is not the case for those in the lower orders. Our heroes are faceless. I have little desire to add to the sum of obscurity, Sir Thomas.'

They were interrupted by a servant who entered the room carrying a tray. He crossed to the table without meeting their eyes and set the tray down. Then with a deep bow of his head he retreated a few steps before turning and hurrying out.

'There,' said Richard. 'That is what becomes of those who have no place in history.'

Thomas did not respond for a moment but silently took

a plate from the tray, placed the other in front of his companion and poured them both a cup of wine. Then he looked at Richard and spoke in a quiet, weary tone.

'I cannot help the way that history marks the passage of a man's life, Richard. Nor can I mend the accident of your birth. So it achieves nothing to lay your troubles before me with such poor grace. All that matters is that we do our duty. I, to the Order I have pledged my life to defend. You, to your masters in London, for the sake of whatever task they have placed in your hands. You must help me in my duty, in so far as you can. For my part, I would be better placed to assist you if I knew more of your purpose in Malta.'

Richard's dark eyes stared back. 'I can tell no more than you already know.'

'And what happens if any ill fate should befall you?'

'In that event, I dare say Walsingham will send another agent to complete the mission.'

'I see. And your master has a ready supply of men who speak as many languages as you do?'

Richard looked down at his plate and delicately picked up a lamb chop. He took a small bite and began to chew.

'I thought not.' Thomas smiled to himself. 'So if you are lost, the mission is over. Unless you can tell me more about the document.'

Richard swallowed. 'No.'

'Why not? Surely you can see the sense of it?'

'I have my orders.'

'I understand. But if the stakes are as high as Sir William said, then it is vital that one or other of us retrieves the document and returns with it to England.'

'Assuming that either of us survives the attack on Malta,' Richard replied wryly.

Thomas pursed his lips. 'Granted.'

'I'm sorry, sir, but my orders are clear. I am to tell you nothing about it.'

'Why not?'

'Because Walsingham does not trust you.'

'I see. Then what about Cecil?'

'Sir William respects Walsingham's judgement in nearly all things.'

Thomas folded his fingers together and rested them against his chin as he felt the anger rise in him. This was a wound to his honour. 'I take it that their suspicions arise from my religious convictions – because I am a Catholic. Is there some aspect of the document that would make it dangerous if I was to know its content?'

'I cannot say,' Richard replied before he took another bite of meat.

'Cannot, or will not?'

'I have already said more than is wise. If it helps to put your mind at rest then know that Cecil trusts that you consider yourself an Englishman first and a Catholic second. But enough. I will speak no more on it. Talk of something else, if you must.'

'Very well. Tell me, are you a Protestant, like your masters, or of the Church of Rome?'

Richard stopped eating as he considered the question. 'Surely you must know. Do you really think Cecil would employ a Catholic in his service? That is no question.'

'And were you always a Protestant?' Thomas persisted.

'Why do you want to know?'

'I am curious to know you better. In the conflict that lies before us I would prefer to know what manner of man will be fighting at my side.'

'And knowing if I have been a Catholic will make a difference?' Richard chuckled briefly. 'It would be better to know if I have ever killed a man.'

'And have you?' Thomas watched him closely.

'No. But I am sure that I will have done before I return to England.'

Before Thomas was able to probe any further the door opened and a heavily built man in his fifties entered. His hair was grey and thinning and his beard clipped close on his ponderous jowls. The eyes, however, were lively and alert and he scrutinised the two Englishmen rising from their chairs. Fadrique entered behind him and made the introductions.

'His Excellency Captain General at Sea of his most Catholic Majesty King Philip of Spain and Viceroy of Sicily, Don Garcia Alvarez de Toledo.'

Don Garcia advanced towards them and stopped just out of reach as Thomas made to reply with a dignified bow. 'It is an honour to meet you, sir. Sir Thomas Barrett, and his squire Richard Hughes, at your service.'

'Fadrique tells me that you are travelling to Malta.' Don Garcia spoke softly with a faint lisp. 'You are answering La Valette's call to arms.'

'That is so.' Thomas nodded.

'Then you are most welcome, Sir Thomas. Particularly given your hard-won reputation on the battlefields of Europe.' Don Garcia smiled warmly.

Thomas was mildly surprised that his reputation was

known in Barcelona. He smiled modestly. 'That was some years ago.'

'Experience is everything in warfare.'

'Almost. But numbers play their part.'

Don Garcia patted Thomas on the arm. 'I trust your journey has been untroubled thus far.'

Visions of the storms that they had battled on the voyage to Spain passed fleetingly before Thomas's mind's eye but he suppressed them and nodded. 'We have made good time, sir, given the season.'

Don Garcia looked at him shrewdly. 'The Atlantic in winter can be like a wild beast. You have done well to reach us. And it is good that you have. Every man will be needed to bolster the defences of Malta. But pardon me, you must be weary.' He waved a hand towards the chairs. 'Sit, please. I did not mean to interrupt your meal.'

Once the four men were seated, Thomas pushed aside his plate, the food upon it untouched. He indicated to Richard to do the same, as it would be unseemly for the squire to eat alone in front of his superiors.

'Sir Thomas, forgive me if I avoid the usual niceties and come directly to the point. I have little time before I sail for Malta. What do you know of the situation?'

'Only what I was told by the knight who brought the summons to me in England, sir. He said that the Grand Master had intelligence of the Sultan's plan to take Malta and eradicate the Order of St John once and for all.'

'That is so.' Don Garcia nodded. 'He must secure Malta to protect his supply line. And that is where we must hold him. I have no doubt about his wider strategy. For many years Suleiman, and his corsair allies, have been extending their influence throughout the western Mediterranean. Every spring we have been watching the eastern horizon, waiting for the assault, but they have been content merely to probe the coasts of Italy, France and Spain, seizing our ships, or raiding coastal villages and small towns for slaves. There has been little that we could do to prevent it. By the time we receive a report and despatch a fleet to the scene, the enemy has slipped away. Meanwhile, I have been doing all in my power to ready our defences and prepare our galleys for the onslaught when it comes, as it must. Now that time is upon us. There is no question of it. Our spy in Istanbul has seen the enemy's preparations at first hand. Galleys and galleons are massing in the Golden Horn, while daily wagons enter the city with powder, shot, siege tools and rations. Outside the walls, tens of thousands of soldiers have gathered to await the order to embark.' He sat back and rested his hands on the arms of the chair. 'There is no question that the Turks are coming. This is the moment I have long dreaded. This is the year when our faith must make a stand or fall under the shadow of the crescent.'

'Then we shall make our stand,' Thomas said firmly, 'and if the Order is wiped out, then the manner in which we face our destruction will inspire the rest of Christendom to match our example.'

'I pray that you are right, Sir Thomas. If the rulers of Europe do not make common cause against the greater threat then we are lost. Our people will be forced to kneel before the false religion. It is a small mercy that none of us at this table will live to see that day. I swear before you that I will die with a sword in my hand, and Jesu's blessed name on my bloodied lips, ere I kiss the foot of Suleiman.'

'So swear we all,' Thomas replied and crossed himself.

There was a brief stillness before Don Garcia spoke again. 'I have chosen to concentrate my forces on Sicily. His Majesty has informed the other powers of Europe that if they wish to be allied to our great cause they must send their men and their ships to join us in Sicily. With good fortune I shall have enough galleys at my disposal to face Suleiman's fleet. I will also be able to sail south if he strikes at Malta first, and north if he lands in Italy.'

'A wise plan, sir,' Thomas agreed.

'Wise? Yes.' Don Garcia smiled. 'But unless I receive all the forces that I have been promised, we can have little hope of victory.'

Fadrique cleared his throat. 'However few our numbers, we shall always have God on our side. We cannot be defeated. Our Lord is all-powerful and would not permit it.'

His father looked at him indulgently. 'Of course you are right.' Then he turned back to Thomas. 'I leave for Sicily tomorrow with six galleys, escorting four galleons carrying the first two thousand men to establish my base of operations. I will go from there to Malta to confer with La Valette. I would be pleased to offer you and your squire a place on my flagship.'

'That is most generous of you, sir.'

'Then be aboard by first light. We sail at dawn.' Don Garcia rose from his chair and the others followed suit. 'Now you will have to excuse me. There are still many details to attend to. Fadrique will see to it that you are provided with quarters here in the citadel, and stabling for your horses.'

'They are not mine, but the property of your King, loaned to us by the port master in Bilbao.'

'Then they can be impressed into my army. Now, I bid you good day, gentlemen. Please, finish your meal and rest. Come, Fadrique!'

Despite his bulk Don Garcia moved with great energy and strode swiftly from the room, his son hurrying after him. The door closed behind them and their footsteps faded. Richard drew his plate back across the table and continued eating for a moment before he spoke quietly. 'The odds against us are not encouraging.'

Thomas shrugged. 'That has always been the case as far as the Order is concerned. Throughout its history.'

'The heroic ideal,' Richard mused. 'Or perhaps a way to add glory to a suicidal compulsion.'

'Still your tongue. You know not of what you speak. The men of the Order are sworn to fight for the glory of God, and no other purpose. Suicide is a sin, and well you know it.' Thomas restrained his irritation and continued in a wry tone. 'Besides, as Don Garcia's son said, God will be on our side.'

'Yes, a divine change of heart would be welcome. He did not seem to be in evidence when Suleiman took Rhodes from the Order. And where was he when the Order was almost wiped out at the fall of Acre? What makes you think he will stand behind you, behind us, at Malta?'

'It can do our cause no harm to put faith in the Lord,' Thomas replied, though he shared Richard's doubts. He looked up to see the younger man watching him closely.

'I wonder, if it is God's will to heap such sorrow on

those who worship him, I cannot help but question His purpose.'

'Be careful, Richard. That is blasphemous.'

'It is only philosophy. My point is that both sides in the coming conflict are fighting in the name of their faiths. If the Turks win, does that mean that God has forsaken us, or that their faith is the more potent? If the faith of both sides is equally strong then this fight will be decided by men alone.'

Thomas could not disagree but if he could no longer kill in the name of Christ, he would still fight to prevent being killed in the name of Allah. 'If it is to be settled by men, then so be it. I am ready to play my part.' He stood up. 'I need to take a walk.'

'Shall I—'

'No. You stay here. Finish your meal, then fetch our bags and rest. Get as much rest as you can. All too soon it will be a luxury you will crave as no other.'

'Save the final rest.'

Thomas thought a moment and shook his head. 'Even that you may come to welcome before this is over.'

CHAPTER THIRTEEN

The flotilla was only half a day out of the harbour at Palma on the island of Mallorca, and Thomas and Richard were enjoying the cool morning breeze, when the first sail was sighted. A sailor in the small crow's nest at the top of the main mast shaded his eyes with one hand while the other stretched out, pointing towards the northern horizon, into the wind blowing from the direction of France.

The flagship's captain stepped towards the stern deck rail and cupped a hand to his mouth. 'What do you see?'

There was a short pause as the sailor scanned the horizon, straining his eyes to pick up as much detail as he could. On the main deck of the galley everyone stood and waited on his word.

'I see two lateen sails, sir.'

'More than likely it's a galley,' said Thomas.

'How do you know?' asked Richard as he craned his neck and stared across the slight swell. 'I can't even see it.'

'And you won't for a while yet. They'll be hull down for an hour or so.'

'Hull down?'

Thomas grinned as he recalled that his squire had spent most of the trip from London curled up in misery in the galleon's cabin. 'You know little of the ways of the sea.'

'Yes, and I have no intention of boarding a ship ever again when this is over,' Richard added with feeling.

'Since you are an educated man, you must have heard that the world is round.'

Richard shot him an irritated look. 'Of course.'

'Then it should be self-evident why the sails of a ship are visible before the hull, given that the horizon is curved.'

Richard ground his teeth. 'I knew that.'

'Deck there!' the lookout shouted. 'I see more sails. Three . . . five, more. They look like galleys . . . Yes, I'm sure of it.'

'Come.' Thomas tugged his squire's sleeve and they climbed the short flight of steps and joined the group of officers clustered around Don Garcia.

The captain turned away from the rail and sought out his commander. 'Corsairs, sir.'

'Surely not,' Fadrique protested. 'If they are corsairs, then why are they approaching from the north? Their lairs are on the African coast to the south.'

'They are to windward, sir,' explained the captain. Thomas had once spoken Spanish well and it was swiftly coming back to him; he found he could follow the exchange without difficulty. The captain continued, 'They have the advantage over us. It is more than likely they have been following us for days and have worked their way round to the north to gain the weatherly advantage.' He turned his attention to Don Garcia. 'What are your orders, my lord?'

The Spanish commander looked out over the ships of his flotilla. The galleys formed a loose cordon around the galleons wallowing in their midst. The decks of the ponderous vessels were packed with soldiers and their arms and other equipment. They would be easy prey for any corsair galley that managed to evade the escort vessels.

'At all costs we must protect the galleons,' Don Garcia announced, 'assuming that those are enemy ships. I will take no risks. Give the signal to send the men to their battle stations, Captain, and signal the other galleys to do the same, if you please.'

'Aye, sir.'

A moment later the drummer on the main deck was beating out a shrill rattle and the soldiers hurriedly strapped on their breastplates and helmets and readied their weapons while the sailors climbed aloft and spread out along the spars to wait for the order to take the sails in. Below deck came the sound of a whip cracking and the rumble of timbers as the oars were unshipped and eased out of the ports along the sides of Don Garcia's flagship. Thomas felt his heartbeat quicken at the sounds and the movement, even the stink wafting up from below. Old memories and sensations welled up inside him as the galley prepared for battle. He turned to Richard.

'Bring me my cuirass, helmet and sword. And arm yourself.'

Richard nodded and hurried below to the hold where their baggage had been stored for the voyage.

Overhead a long red and gold pennant climbed up a halyard and rippled out with a faint crackle. Moments later the other galleys raised their pennants and the sound of drums carried faintly across the waves as they made ready for battle.

'Deck there!'

The officers at the stern looked up at the cry and saw that this time the lookout was pointing to the south.

'More sails! At least five galleys.'

'How many to the north?' bellowed the captain.

The lookout quickly turned, staring hard for a moment before he replied. 'Six, sir! I can see 'em clearly now. Hull up.'

'Can you see any of their colours?'

'Not yet, sir.'

'Could they be our allies?' asked Fadrique. 'Genoese, perhaps?'

His father shook his head. 'Not this far to the west. The rendezvous is at Sicily. It is almost certainly the enemy. Corsairs from the Barbary coast.'

'I agree,' said Thomas. 'It is a classic ambush, Don Garcia. I have seen it many times before.'

'From the point of view of the hunter, no doubt.'

'That is true. When the galleys of the Order operated together, this is how we would hunt. I suspect that our enemy has learned the technique from us. Indeed, in many ways the corsairs and the men of the Order are alike.'

'Except that the Order is blessed by the Church of Rome.'

'Just as the Muslim pirates are blessed by the imams of their faith, sir. In the end we are all holy warriors, or we are all pirates.'

Don Garcia frowned. 'That is a troubling pronouncement, Sir Thomas. I do not care to think of my enemy, and the enemy of the one true God, in such a light. I'd prefer that you did not speak in such terms before me again.'

'As you wish, Don Garcia.'

'What I do wish to hear more of is their tactics. You have more experience of them than I do. How will they seek to defeat us?'

Thomas paused a moment to think, mentally positioning the three forces and taking into account the wind direction. 'Their target will be the galleons. They are your most vulnerable vessels, sir. The corsairs will know that is where the most valuable cargo will be. But they will soon realise that the galleons are filled with soldiers. So they will either stand off and blast the decks with grapeshot before they board, or they will attempt to sink the galleons in a bid to kill as many of your soldiers as possible. For that they can expect to be handsomely rewarded by the Sultan.'

'Then what is to be done to frustrate them? Is it too late to turn back to Palma?'

'That is what they will have calculated. Even now they are on converging courses. If you order the flotilla to turn about, they will follow suit and continue to close in on us. We will be engaged long before we could hope to lie under the protection of Palma's cannon, sir.'

'Then what would you advise me to do, Sir Thomas?'

'Keep the galleys as close to the galleons as possible. The enemy must not be permitted to break through the protective cordon. Have one galley to the front of the formation, one to the stern and two on either side. The galleons will need to sail side by side in pairs for mutual support in the event that the enemy attempts to board them. The biggest danger is that the enemy will try to draw our galleys away from their positions. That must not be permitted, sir. We must hold the formation, whatever happens. Given that their galleys outnumber us two to one, that is our only hope.'

'Very well.' Don Garcia nodded. 'Captain, we'll need to pass close to each of our warships to give the orders. See to it.'

'Aye, sir,' the captain acknowledged before advancing to the rail to bellow orders for the oars to be lowered.

Richard returned from the hold laden with Thomas's weapons and armour. He placed the bundle on the deck and stood behind Thomas to assist him in fastening the breast- and back-plates of his cuirass.

As the flagship pulled past each of the other vessels in the flotilla, the captain relayed the orders via speaking trumpet. By the time the galleys had taken in their sails, unshipped their oars and formed a protective screen, the sails of the two groups of corsairs closing in from either beam were visible from the deck. A short time later the lookout finally confirmed their identity beyond any doubt.

'They're flying green pennants.'

Richard edged towards Thomas and muttered, 'Green?'

'It is the colour of Islam.' Thomas inspected his squire, tugging on his helmet. Richard wore a burgonet design, with the visor raised, as did Thomas. 'Your helmet is too loose. Tighten the chinstrap.'

'If I fasten it any tighter I'll choke.'

'And if you wear it as loose as that it will twist on your skull at the first blow and your view will be impaired. You'll fall victim to the first corsair who can move quickly enough to catch you on your blind side.'

Gritting his teeth, Richard undid the buckle and tightened the strap a notch.

'That's better,' said Thomas. He grasped the helmet and gave it an experimental twist. 'And make certain you wear mantlets if you want to keep your fingers.'

'Yes, sir.' Richard bowed his head. 'As you command.'

Thomas turned back to track the progress of the enemy. The two formations of galleys were in clear view, just over a mile off each beam. Their green pennants flickered like snakes' tongues in the gentle wind blowing across the sea. Flashes of polished metal glinted amid the distant figures packed on to the decks of the corsair galleys. For the first time since they had been sighted Thomas felt some small relief as he realised that the enemy vessels were smaller than the galleys of Don Garcia's flotilla. The slender hulls would not carry the same weight in cannon, nor would they have sufficient impetus to significantly damage the Spanish galleys in the event of a collision. But they still posed a considerable danger to the galleons and would have the advantage in speed and manoeuvrability. It would be a contest between swiftness and strength, and Thomas was reminded of the bear fights he had seen back in London. But here at least the bears, though ponderous in comparison to their tormentors, would not be chained.

'Here they come,' announced the captain.

A puff of smoke rapidly dispersed from the bows of the leading corsair to the south and a moment later the dull thud of a cannon reached those standing on the stern deck of the flagship. The corsair altered course towards the Spanish flotilla and the other galleys followed suit. As the sound of the signal gun reached the other galleys to the north, they too changed course and bore down on Don Garcia's force. The Spanish commander watched them briefly and then turned to Thomas with an anxious expression. 'What will they try to do? What would you do in their place?'

Thomas pressed his lips together and turned to view the oncoming enemy. They would be upon the Spanish ships within the half hour. There was no time to waste. He did not like being placed in this position by Don Garcia, yet the Spaniard was right. There were few Christians in the Mediterranean who knew the enemy's way of waging war better than the knights of the Order. He quickly assessed the converging courses and cleared his throat.

'They will try to break the formation, sir. If they can lure the galleys out of position they will be able to pass through them and wreak destruction on the galleons. As we are, each of our galleys can cover the gap between them and the galley ahead of them. The corsairs cannot pass between the galleys without coming under the guns mounted in the bows of our warships. Their vessels are small enough for a well-placed shot to hole them and force them to withdraw from the fight, or sink them. The only position we will not be able to cover with our guns is the stern of this galley. But as long as we hold the formation we can offer the galleons the best protection.'

Don Garcia weighed up his words and nodded. 'I understand. Thank you. Captain!'

The ship's commander turned smartly towards him. 'Sir?'

'You heard Sir Thomas. Steer straight and keep your station. Tell the gun crews they may fire at will on any enemy ships that pass in front of our bows.'

'Aye, sir.'

Don Garcia turned back to Thomas. 'Now we wait and see if you are right about our enemy's intentions.'

The corsairs were still under sail and the vessels were handled with skill so that they began to pull ahead of the Spanish force even as they converged on it. Then, when they had gained a lead of perhaps a quarter of a mile, they turned towards the flotilla and hurriedly took in their sails and unshipped their oars for their final approach, on a perpendicular course to the direction of Don Garcia's vessels.

'Now we shall be put to the test,' Thomas said quietly. At his side Richard shot him a questioning glance and Thomas nodded towards the nearest of the corsairs. 'Look at the bows.'

Richard saw the dark muzzle and long barrel of a cannon protruding from the small gun port at the front of the galley. Having stolen a lead on the Spanish convoy, the corsairs now steadily closed on the leading ships. There was a jet of flame and billowing cloud of dirty grey smoke from one of the galleys and Thomas saw fragments of wood explode into the air as the iron ball tore through the bulwark of the leading Spanish galley. The boom of the shot reached the flagship just as more shots flashed out from the bows of the other corsairs and two further shots struck home on the galley, while a water spout showed where a ball missed. A fresh shot came from a cannon loaded with iron nails and lengths of chain, and several men were swept off the foredeck of the galley as if swatted away by a giant hand.

'Hold your course,' Thomas whispered to himself as he watched. 'Hold on.'

The captain of the leading galley steered straight and continued to endure the enemy's fire until he had passed through their arc of fire. Next to come under the guns of the corsairs were the two galleys flanking the galleons. The corsairs were firing at close range this time, and backed their oars to keep a safe distance from the arquebusiers on the decks of the Spanish galleys. Thomas reflected that the last time he had taken part in a sea battle, the soldiers of the Order had only just begun to use the arquebus. At the time he had disliked the weapons because they were loud, took far longer to load than a crossbow and were cumbersome. Now they were prevalent.

Even though the corsairs were three hundred paces away from the Spanish galleys the arquebusiers could not endure the fire of the corsair guns without trying to strike back. Small spouts of water lifted from the sea around the bows of the enemy ships, and a handful of shots struck home as a figure pitched from the deck of one of the corsair galleys and splashed into the sea close to the bows. The damage done in reply was murderous, as each corsair gun belched flame and smoke and flayed the sides of the Spanish ships with a hail of iron. Several men were cut down at a time, sheets parted, their trailing ends whipping through the air like enraged serpents, and splinters slashed across the decks, cutting down yet more of the crew.

The bow of the galley to the left began to swing towards the enemy, faster as the oars on the port side hung in the water and the forward momentum dragged the galley round to face its tormentors.

'The fool!' Thomas growled as his fingers gripped the wooden rail tightly. 'The fool.'

The galley fired on the corsairs as soon as its two bow guns came to bear. There was no attempt to wait for the vessel to settle and take the best shot. Even so, one of the balls crashed through the gun port under the forecastle of the nearest enemy galley and then tore down the length of the ship, smashing through the rowers, their benches and several of the oars which jerked savagely along the side of the galley. The other shot plunged harmlessly into the sea a short distance in front of the galley, throwing spray over the corsairs brandishing their weapons in the forecastle.

As soon as the Spanish galley had begun to turn, the other corsairs surged forward again, heading either side of the galley to take full advantage of the gap that opened up between the warships escorting the galleons. The damaged corsair could not move until the casualties amongst the rowers had been cut free and dropped into the bilge, and then the survivors redistributed amongst the remaining oars. As the vessel wallowed on the swell, the Spanish galley continued to pound it, cutting down the foremast and smashing the bows into a splintered ruin. As Thomas watched he could see that the corsair would not be able to take any further part in the battle even if the vessel was lucky enough not to sink. But that was small comfort since the way was now open for the remaining five corsairs to sweep past the Spaniard and fall on the galleons. A crackle of musket fire sounded as the corsairs exchanged shots with the crew of the galley, then the crash of cannon from the galley ahead and to the left of the flagship. The shot struck the stern of the foremost corsair, striking down the officers gathered there.

'Sir.' Thomas turned to Don Garcia. 'We have to stop the corsairs reaching the galleons.'

'I can see that, thank you. We must move closer to them.'

Thomas took another look at the scene before he saw that one of the corsairs was flying a much larger pennant than the others. He pointed it out. 'That must be their leader, there.'

Don Garcia followed the direction he indicated.

'If we can take or sink him, then we might discourage the others, sir.'

'What of the formation? If we take after that ship we will no longer be able to cover the rear of our other galleys.'

'It's already too late for that. The formation was only good for as long as every ship held its station.' Thomas gestured towards the galley still firing at the dismasted corsair, which had started to settle by the bows. 'Now it's every ship for itself, sir.'

CHAPTER FOURTEEN

'Captain!' Don Garcia called out as he strode to the rail that overlooked the main deck. 'Alter course towards that corsair with the long pennant. Do you see him?'

'Yes, sir.'

'Have your gunners make ready. We must destroy him as swiftly as possible.'

As the captain passed the orders on, Thomas watched the corsairs' attack unfolding. Five galleys had slipped between the Spanish escorts and were closing on the galleons to open fire at point-blank range. One of the enemy vessels had heaved to, and there were figures running across the stern deck as they looked for survivors amongst the officers who had been scythed down by a blast of grapeshot. Beyond the corsairs the leading Spanish ship was starting to turn back to rejoin the battle. To the south the two galleys tasked with protecting that flank were still keeping station even though they were under fire from the second group of corsairs.

'What will the enemy do now?' asked Richard.

Thomas considered the situation briefly before he replied. 'If they follow usual practice they'll try to shred the rigging and sails to stop the galleons and then clear the decks with grapeshot before they attempt to board. But there isn't time for that. I believe they will fire on to the decks first and cause as many casualties as possible before they are forced to retreat. Then they'll repeat the same pattern of attack. As long as the corsairs handle their ships well and avoid a melee they can continue their running attacks on the galleons.' He sucked air through his teeth. 'The soldiers on board are going to suffer grievous losses unless we can drive the corsairs off.'

The pace setter's drum quickened and the flagship turned towards the enemy leader who was backwatering as he approached the nearest of the galleons. There was a flash and puff of smoke from the bows as the gun fired on the galleon. Just as Thomas had feared, the shot was aimed low and cut a swathe through the soldiers trapped on the deck. Small puffs of fire and smoke blossomed along the side of the galleon as some of the arquebusiers fired back. The other corsair galleys took up positions abeam of the galleon and added their fire and the officers on the deck of the flagship could only look on in despair as the Spanish soldiers were steadily cut down.

'Can't this damned ship move any faster?' Richard hissed in frustration. 'And why doesn't anyone give the order for our guns to open fire? Surely we're in range.'

They were little more than a quarter of a mile from the leader of the enemy fleet, whose galley was in direct line with the galleon.

'We can't fire,' Thomas realised. 'We'd risk hitting our own men.'

The captain of the flagship had also seen the danger and steered wide for long enough to ensure that the galleon would be clear of the line of fire when the flagship resumed its original course. The other Spanish galleys on the northern flank were turning to bear down on the enemy, their crews crying out battle cries as they saw their comrades being cut down on the galleon. The corsairs were alert to the danger and their oars dipped into the swell as they turned swiftly and made towards the next galleon, leaving the first with shattered bulwarks and thin trails of blood running down from the scuppers. The pale dots of the faces of the men on the high stern of the second galleon looked back towards the oncoming corsairs and Thomas could imagine the sick fear welling up in the pits of their stomachs as they prepared to endure the same fate their comrades had moments before.

The pursuit of the clumsy galleons had turned into a one-sided stern chase as the sleek vessels of the corsairs rapidly advanced on their prey. The enemy slowed as they closed up on the second galleon and the first shots struck the stern quarter, shattering the painted wooden shutters and tearing ragged holes in the ship's side.

'Are we in range yet, Captain?' asked Don Garcia, his fist clenched tightly over the pommel of his sword so that his knuckles were white.

The captain silently judged the distance before he replied. 'The range is still long, sir. But we might get a lucky shot in.'

'Then give the order. At once.'

The deck shuddered as the first gun roared and a thick cloud of smoke briefly obscured the target. The wind stripped the smoke away as the men on the stern deck strained their eyes to see if the shot had struck home. The flagship rose on the swell and Thomas and the others saw a foaming white circle and ripples on the water close to the stern of the ship of the corsair leader.

'Near enough,' Don Garcia nodded. 'Fire at will.'

The second gun blasted out and a fluke of the breeze swept the smoke aside swiftly enough for those on the flagship to see a section of the stern explode into a shower of splinters. A cheer tore from the throats of the crew and some waved their fists triumphantly.

'Have your men load with chain shot,' Thomas suggested. 'Aim for the oars. If we can cripple them then we can put alongside them, board their ship and end this quickly.'

Don Garcia nodded and gave the order to the captain to pass on. The gun crews hurriedly swabbed out their weapons and loaded the next charges as the flagship closed the distance. The guns roared out again at a range of two hundred paces. The first shot tore up the surface of the sea behind the oar blades on the port side and sheared through the rearmost of the oars. A moment later the second shot struck home. Several of the oars shivered and splintered as the weighted lengths of chain ripped through the wooden shafts. At once the corsair slewed round to port and exposed its beam, providing an easy target for the gunners on the Spanish flagship.

'Pound 'em!' Fadrique called out, his voice high-pitched with excitement.

His father gave him a disapproving glance before he fixed his attention on the enemy ship. The guns boomed out in a steady rhythm as their crews reloaded and fired as swiftly as possible. The flagship bore down on the corsair and as the range diminished every shot struck home, shattering oars, smashing gaps in the bulwarks and tearing men to crimson tatters on the main deck. Even so, the tiny flames of musket fire stabbed back towards the flagship and some shots were finding their targets. Thomas saw one of the gunners' chests bloodily explode as a lead ball tore through his body.

'Come with me, Richard,' he commanded and led the way down on to the main deck and forward towards the armed men clustered between the two masts. The soldiers wore breastplates and helmets and their arms and hips were protected by studded gambisons. Some carried shields and heavy swords, and iron-headed clubs hung from their belts. Others held short pikes, ready to wield them double-handed. Thomas turned to his squire and looked him over, testing his straps and the buckle under his chin before he nodded with satisfaction. 'You'll do.'

Richard nodded too quickly and Thomas saw the fear in his eyes. A familiar fear – the terror of a man who is facing battle for the first time, his head filled with dreadful expectation of being wounded, or failing to acquit himself with honour. Thomas placed his hand on the young man's shoulder and spoke just loudly enough to be heard over the crackle of musket fire and the beating of the drum below deck.

'Stay close to me. I need you to protect my back. Are you ready?'

'Yes . . . Of course . . . Why are we doing this?'

Thomas frowned. 'What do you mean?'

Richard gestured at the men around them. 'Fighting. That is surely the job of these soldiers. We are merely passengers.'

'I am a knight. It is my duty to fight. As it is yours, as the man who calls himself my squire.'

'Yes, yes, you are right. But our place is there on the aft deck and our duty is to defend Don Garcia with our lives. That's where we should make our stand.'

As Thomas looked at his companion he felt no anger or contempt at the young man's reluctance to fight, only an ache of disappointment that Richard was resisting the chance to put himself to the test. Unless the young man could suppress his fears and face this peril, he would be crippled by self-doubt through the rest of his life. It was not through love of violence that Thomas had moved forward to join the men about to board the corsair lying directly ahead. It was, as he had said, a duty. But there was more. Regardless of his wider moral concerns about the endless war of the faiths, circumstance had placed him in this conflict and perforce he would fight and kill without reservation.

'Don Garcia is surrounded by his officers. He is safe. Our place is here, where we can have a more immediate effect on the outcome of the fight. We will fight alongside these men.'

Richard's mouth opened to protest but Thomas cut him off before he could utter a sound. 'No more words. Steel your heart and take a firm grip of your sword handle.'

The young man swallowed anxiously. 'Should I pray?'

'If you wish. Many men pray before a battle but I never saw that it protected them from either bullet or blade.' Then Thomas smiled reassuringly. 'Fix your mind on surviving and do all you can to ensure it. That is the only right and proper thought for a soldier to have before battle. Ready?'

Richard breathed deeply. 'I am ready, Sir Thomas.'

Ahead, the masts and slender yards of the corsair galley loomed up against the sky. The Spanish gunners fired their last shots across the enemy deck and then the order was given for the flagship to turn to port. The oars on that side dug into the sea while those to starboard made one last powerful stroke before the timekeeper shouted at the rowers to ship their oars. There was a dull rumble from below the deck as the lengths of timber were slid in through their ports and heaved across the width of the galley. Then the stern of the corsair passed down the side of the warship and the vessels closed beam to beam. Thomas could see the enemy fighters lining the galley's rail, screaming their war cries and insults as the gap closed.

'Boarding hooks away!' the captain bellowed through his cupped hands. The sailors who stood ready with the hooks tied to coils of rope swirled the iron prongs above their head before releasing them up and over the narrow gap. The grappling hooks arced over the sea, trailing snaking ropes, and then plunged out of sight amid the robed figures crowding the deck of the other galley. At once, several Spaniards took up the ropes and braced their bare feet on the deck, straining to draw the two vessels closer together. The air was filled with the staccato crash of arquebuses and the frenzied cries of the men waiting for the chance to launch themselves into battle.

The swell lifted Don Garcia's flagship and it crashed violently against the corsair so that the men on both vessels struggled to keep their footing. At once the captain shouted the order: 'Fasten the lines!'

The men assigned to the grappling hooks pulled the ropes taut and looped them round the belaying pins to secure the two vessels together. About them the Spanish soldiers ran planks across the narrow gap between the two galleys and clambered up on to the bulwarks, yelling defiantly at the waiting corsairs. Thomas pushed his way through the soldiers and grasped a shroud and pulled himself up on to the wide wooden rail running along the side of the galley. He drew his sword and glanced back to see Richard right behind him. To his right a huge sergeant with an artfully patterned morion punched his sword towards the enemy and bellowed.

'With me, boys! Death to the heathen!'

The sergeant leaped over the gap and landed on the rail before his impetus carried him on, falling amid the robes, dark-skinned faces and limbs, and curved gleaming blades beyond. Scrambling back on to his feet with a savage roar he began to lay about him with his sword, savagely hacking at the men scrambling to get clear of his reach. Blood arced across the deck. More men leaped after the sergeant while some dashed across the boarding planks.

Thomas sucked in a deep breath and leaped forward. For an instant he saw the gleam of the narrow strip of sea between the two galleys then he fell against one of the enemy, a slender man in dirty cotton robes, his head tightly wrapped in a turban. Both men thudded down on to the deck and at once Thomas thrust out his left arm to push himself back up as his feet found their grip. He felt a waft of warm breath and realised that the man he had landed on was screaming at him in rage as he lay pinned down under Thomas's weight. He slammed the guard of his sword down into the corsair's face, cutting off his shouts. He struck again, harder, and felt bone break and give way under the blow. Then he rose into a crouch and swung his blade in an arc to his front. Another Spaniard landed to his right before the corsairs surged forward, desperate to cut down the attackers before they could gain a foothold on the deck.

There was a glint to the left of his field of vision and Thomas saw a blade slicing through the air towards his shoulder. The blow rang in his ear as the edge glanced off his shoulder guard. The padded jacket beneath absorbed most of the energy and Thomas slapped the blade away with his forearm and then cut at the corsair's bare arm with his sword, the muscled flesh giving way beneath the finely honed steel edge. The corsair's sword clattered on to the deck and blood spattered down on to it as the injured man drew back, gritting his teeth in agony. Thomas looked quickly from side to side and saw the Spaniard to his right double over as a large Moor with a chain-mail vest and spiked helmet drove a pike into his stomach, carrying him back hard against the bulwark so the deadly point burst through his body and lodged in the timbers at his back.

As the Moor wrenched the shaft back, Thomas thrust his point into the man's side but the chain links did not give way. The man grunted in pain and turned the bloodied point of his pike towards Thomas's body. Then, seeing the breastplate, the Moor dropped the point and stabbed at Thomas's groin. Twenty years before, Thomas would have nimbly dodged the blow but now he had to throw himself to the side against the mortally wounded Spaniard who had dropped his weapons and stood mouth agape as he stared down at the ragged tear in his quilted jacket and greasy grey length of gut that had been torn out as the Moor wrenched the pike free.

Thomas recovered his balance and struck back, cutting towards the side of the Moor's head. The edge of the blade struck the cheekguard, bending it in half, and the Moor's jaw shattered under the impact. Blood and teeth spurted from his gaping mouth. For an instant the Moor was dazed and Thomas snatched his blade back and thrust deep into the man's throat, then ripped the blade free in a rush of bright crimson. Stepping back into a crouch, Thomas held the dripping tip of his blade up and glanced to both sides. The Spaniards were swarming over the bulwark and leaping into the fight. A thud to his left caused Thomas to twist round sharply and he saw Richard, wide-eyed as he held up a hand to ward off the point of Thomas's sword.

'Keep close,' Thomas commanded, then moved cautiously across the deck. A sprawling melee extended on each side as the Spaniards pressed forward, cutting wildly about them as they struggled to create more space for their comrades to follow them. Towards the stern Thomas saw a richly robed man in a braided green jacket leading a party of armoured men down from the aft deck, and realised it must be the enemy commander and his officers. Strike him down and the rest of the crew might surrender, Thomas decided. Without their leader the rest of the corsair ships might also lose heart and break off their attack.

'This way!' Thomas gestured towards the man and beckoned to Richard to follow him. They had advanced no more than a few paces before a knot of corsairs blocked their path – five men, unarmoured but equipped with shields and heavy scimitars. They had been hanging back from the fight but now, seeing the two Christians before them, their confidence flowed back and they surged forward with enraged cries. Thomas parried the first blow before a second weapon glanced off the reinforced crest of his helmet. He blinked and struck back, hacking at a shield and driving it down, then grasping the rim and wrenching it away as he punched the guard into the man's face.

He was dimly aware of a blur of action to his left and he heard Richard hiss a curse, before the savage scrape and clatter of blades that ensued. Then Thomas was dealing with his next foe, an older man, ten years or more older than Thomas himself. He held back as they briefly weighed each other up. Then the corsair feinted, testing Thomas's reactions. He did not flinch, but stood poised as he stared back. The second attack was followed through and Thomas parried three cuts before he made a riposte that was knocked aside at the last moment by the corsair's shield. As he drew back his sword and lunged again, aiming for the man's face this time, Thomas's boot caught on the limb of a body sprawled on the deck and he pitched forward and fell heavily, at the mercy of the corsair standing over him. He rolled on to his side and raised his left arm to protect his head, willing to risk it in order to save his life. The corsair raised his scimitar and his expression gleamed with bloodthirsty triumph as he swung the fatal blow. Then there was a blur and a sharp metallic ring as another blade blocked the scimitar, a swift arcing movement and then a deep grunt.

For a brief moment all was still and then Thomas felt several warm drops spatter across his face. He blinked them aside as a hand reached under his arm and hauled him up on to his feet. Richard glanced over his body.

'Are you wounded, sir?'

'No . . . I think not.' Thomas shook his head, and then saw the two bodies to one side, each mortally wounded by a thrust to the heart. Richard was holding a rapier in one hand. He drew a broad-bladed dagger from its sheath with his other hand. The man Thomas had just been fighting lay on his back, legs working feebly as he clutched his hands to his throat and tried to stem the blood pulsing from a ragged wound beneath his chin. Richard pushed in front of him, leaning slightly forward, his arms held loosely to each side, both weapons poised. A heavily built African with a studded club had stepped forward and with a loud roar he leaped forward and swung the club in a diagonal arc. Thomas watched as his squire ducked nimbly under the attack and then stabbed the dagger into the corsair's powerful bicep and ripped it free, tearing the muscle apart. The African howled in agony but managed to hold on to his club and aimed a fresh blow at the squire's head. Once again Richard moved neatly aside and this time swung his sword up and punched the tip under the corsair's ribcage. The man's momentum did the rest; the sword blade sliced up into his vital organs and cut through blood vessels. Stepping back, Richard twisted the blade and yanked it free before he resumed his en garde position.

Thomas was breathing heavily and nodded his thanks. 'I thank you, young Richard,' he said hoarsely.

'There will be time later,' he replied curtly, then stepped forward between two corsairs standing back to back. Both men were despatched with carefully executed blows that they never saw coming, and Richard took another couple of paces before he stopped long enough to allow Thomas to catch up and resume the lead.

'Now do as I said and stay at my side,' he said.

'As you will.'

Around them the fight was clearly going the Spaniards' way. The corsairs had already suffered heavy losses from blasts of chain shot that had scourged the deck of the galley, and now they had been pushed back to the bows and stern of their vessel and only a handful of men continued to fight along the deck between the masts. Thomas and Richard were only ten or so paces from where the corsair leader and his officers were fighting the Spaniards pressing around them, anxious for the honour of killing the enemy commander and looting his body. Yet several of their comrades had already fallen under the bejewelled scimitars of the corsairs and as Thomas watched, another was struck down, the blade of the leader cleaving through his collarbone and deep into his chest so that his right shoulder and sword arm slumped to the side as the Spaniard collapsed on to his knees. Thomas was close enough now to see the deep lines on the enemy commander's face and the scar across his brow and cheek. He had lost one eye. The other glittered, as did his teeth, within the dark weathered skin of his fierce expression.

'Make way!' Thomas called out to the Spaniards facing

the enemy officers. 'Move aside there!'

He roughly shoved one of the soldiers from his path and then thrust between two more before he stood a short distance from the enemy commander. Raising his sword, Thomas bellowed, 'Hold fast! Hold fast!'

The Spaniards looked at him and then as reason mastered their fury they backed off a pace and regarded their opponents warily.

Thomas raised his left hand and thrust his finger at the corsair commander. 'Surrender your ship.'

The corsair needed no familiarity with English to understand the instruction and his lips twisted into a sneer before he spat on to the deck at Thomas's feet. Ignoring the insult, Thomas turned his head slightly towards his squire, while keeping his eyes fixed on the corsair.

'Tell him the fight is over. His ship is ours. If he surrenders now, he and his men will be spared. If not, they will surely die.' Thomas lowered his voice. 'I already have enough blood on my hands and wish no more. Tell him.'

Richard did so. The corsair chuckled and shook his head. He snarled a reply and raised his head haughtily and glared down his nose at Thomas with his remaining eye.

'He says he would sooner die a thousand times than accept mercy from the son of a jackal,' Richard translated.

CHAPTER FIFTEEN

There was no sadness or regret in Thomas's heart as he stared back, just anger at the needless loss of life the corsair had inflicted on his followers. He felt fire flow in the sinews of his muscles as he locked his fingers round the handle of his sword and nodded sombrely. 'If that is his wish, then so be it.' He cleared his throat and drew a deep breath that all might hear him. 'No quarter! Strike the dogs down!'

On either side, the Spaniards surged forward, swords and pikes thrusting at the corsair officers. Thomas swept his arms wide and shouted, 'Not him! Not the one in green. Their captain is mine!'

The men on either side drew back and a small space opened out for the corsair and Thomas as they paused to size each other up. Then the instant was past and Thomas lunged forward with all his strength. There was no attempt to feint, the blow was intended to finish the fight at a stroke. The corsair nimbly stepped to the side and parried the blow, and Thomas could sense the considerable strength of his opponent through the contact between their blades. The parry, having done its work, continued into a glittering swing upwards and then a slash at Thomas's face. He just had time to throw up his sword hand and block the blow with the guard. Sparks flickered into the air between the two men. He stepped in, close to the corsair and inside the sweep of his sword. His left hand grasped the corsair's throat and he clenched his fingers in the silk cloth wound round the other man's neck. The corsair dropped his scimitar and snatched at Thomas's hand, struggling to wrench it away. At the same time the fingers of his other hand locked round Thomas's sword to thrust it away. They stood there straining for advantage, staring into each other's faces. A sweet musty scent filled Thomas's nostrils, vying with the stink of the rowers below deck and the tang of the sea. Then he felt his left hand drawn back a fraction and he knew that the corsair was stronger than he was. It was only the thought of an instant but it was enough for the first chill of dread to trickle down his spine.

'No,' Thomas hissed, and dipped his head and smashed it forward. The curved peak of the morion helmet caught the corsair on the forehead, tearing a flap of skin from his skull. He howled with pain and rage, and his grip slackened enough for Thomas to free his left arm. He splayed his fingers and thrust them against the other man's chest with all the force he could muster. The corsair staggered back, then stumbled and fell heavily on to the deck. Even before the impact drove the air from his lungs, the tip of Thomas's sword took him low in the stomach, under the breastplate he wore beneath his green jacket, the point driving deep into his guts before Thomas was at the end of his reach. The corsair let out a deep groan and sagged back, mouth agape as his single eye rolled up and fixed on the blue heavens above.

Thomas pulled his blade free and turned to Richard. 'Tell his men to surrender. Tell them their captain has fallen. Do it!'

Richard cupped a hand to his mouth and cried out, above the sounds of fighting. At his words the corsairs closest risked a glance in his direction and saw the body. They broke away from the engagement as best they could and stood by the steps leading up to the aft deck. A handful of Spaniards pressed forward until Thomas commanded them to stop. Richard continued to shout, and turned to repeat the call towards the men still engaged towards the bows. The clash and clatter of weapons died away and the two sides drew apart and watched each other anxiously.

'Order the corsairs to drop their weapons,' Thomas instructed.

As the swords and pikes fell to the deck, Thomas turned his attention back to the enemy commander. He lay writhing on the deck, his hands clasped over his stomach. Blood oozed from between the dark skin of his fingers and he groaned through clenched teeth.

The sergeants amongst the Spanish soldiers began to bellow orders for their men to gather the prisoners around the foremast. Those corsair officers still standing looked down at their stricken leader before they were roughly shoved towards the bows. Thomas turned to look at Richard who was standing a short distance away. The young man was looking down at the blood smeared on the weapons in his hands and Thomas could see the telltale tremor of one who had survived his first experience of battle. He sheathed his sword and gently rested a hand on his squire's shoulder.

'You fought very well.'

Richard pressed his lips together and nodded.

'A credit to whoever trained you in the use of rapier and dagger,' Thomas continued. There was no reaction and Thomas stepped closer and spoke in an undertone. 'Richard, you are alive and you have triumphed over your fears. You have passed the test. You are one of us, a fighter.'

Richard looked up. 'I was afraid, sir. More than I ever thought I would be.'

'I understand.' Thomas offered a kindly smile. 'Do you not think it was the same for me? For all those who enter battle?'

Then something caught Thomas's eye and he glanced down to see a small puddle of blood at Richard's feet, and another drop fell from a dark rent in the sleeve of his sword arm. 'You are wounded.'

The young man looked confused. 'Wounded? I–I don't recall.'

'Look there.' Thomas gestured towards the bloody sleeve. 'Your arm. Put your weapons up and see to the wound. There will be time to talk of your thoughts later, when the danger has passed.'

Thomas left his squire to sheath his weapons with trembling hands, and made his way over to the side of the galley. The crews of the nearest corsair vessels were looking on, as yet unsure of the outcome of the duel between the two galleys. Any doubt was extinguished as one of the Spaniards freed the halyard attached to the broad green pennant billowing above the deck. A moment later the pennant came fluttering down towards the deck and came to rest in an untidy heap amid the bodies of the dead and wounded. Thomas watched anxiously as the other corsair vessels held their positions for a while, before one of the other Spanish vessels opened fire, the chain shot shredding the foresail of the nearest corsair vessel and shearing off the end of one of the spars. Before the escort could fire again the galley began to turn away, towards the open sea. The neat line of oars swept forward, dipped down and thrust the corsair vessel away from the battle. One by one the other corsairs broke away and retreated to the north. Their comrades to the south continued their attack for a little longer before they ceased fire and drew back out of range in case the escort vessels turned on them.

The sound of boots thudding on to the deck caused Thomas to turn and he saw Don Garcia and his officers crossing one of the boarding planks on to the corsair galley and jumping down. The relief in the Spaniard's face was clear to see and he grinned as he caught sight of the English knight.

'We have them on the run, Sir Thomas! They flee like whipped curs now that we have their commander. Where is he?'

'There, sir.' Thomas gestured towards the figure lying on his back, the soft leather of his boots scraping the deck as he continued to writhe in his agony. To one side, Richard unbuttoned his gambison and laid it down on top of his breastplate. The sleeve of his white shirt was slick with blood and he peeled it back cautiously to reveal a deep gash on his forearm.

Thomas lifted Richard's arm to examine the wound. 'It's a clean cut. Have it sewn up and bandaged.'

Richard nodded, his face drained of blood as he stared at the torn flesh. Fearing that his squire might faint, Thomas steered him over to a small chest on the deck. 'Sit there. I'll see to the wound myself directly.'

Don Garcia and his entourage picked their way over the bodies and discarded weapons on the deck and approached the stern. Don Garcia nodded with gratification.

'There's one less of the vermin to trouble our people. Well done, Sir Thomas. I saw you strike him down.'

Thomas bowed his head in acknowledgement.

Don Garcia's officers grasped the corsair by the arms and dragged him over to the steps leading to the stern deck and propped him up. The corsair's face contorted in agony for a while before he fixed his eye on the Spanish aristocrat and spoke through gritted teeth in Spanish.

'You have . . . your small victory today, infidel . . . I am dead. Paradise awaits me . . .'

'So, you speak my tongue.' Don Garcia smiled faintly. 'I assume then that you are a Morisco, or some such traitor.'

'I am no traitor . . . but a martyr, ready to ascend to heaven.'

'There is no heaven for you, only eternal torment for what soul you may have,' Don Garcia replied coldly. 'That is all that awaits you, and all other followers of the false prophet. It is God's will.'

The corsair's lips flickered into a smile. 'We shall see the truth of it . . . soon enough, Christian. Your days are . . . numbered. Soon you will be as I am . . . You and all these about you . . . A great power is rising. One that shall sweep before it . . . all the enemies of the Sultan . . . and the true faith.'

Don Garcia leaned forward and grasped the corsair's beard, pulling his head closer. 'Where will the Sultan strike first? Speak, you dog.'

He released the beard and the corsair's head thudded back against the steps. He winced and then smiled again.

'Is it Malta?' demanded Don Garcia. 'Or Sicily? Tell us.'

'Go to the devil.'

'No. It is you who will go to the devil!' He turned to his officers. 'Chain his feet together.'

Thomas stepped between Don Garcia and the dying corsair. 'What do you intend to do, sir?'

'I intend to teach these scum a lesson, Sir Thomas. Now, out of the way, if you please.'

One of the officers retrieved a length of chain from the hold and thrust the corsair's booted feet into the iron hoops before sliding the locking bar through the eyelets and forcing the locking spindle into place. Then he wound the rest of the length of chain round the corsair's ankles. The man groaned in agony at his rough treatment. When the order had been carried out, Don Garcia addressed the corsair again.

'Your wound is mortal. I can make the end painless, if you tell us where the Sultan intends to strike first. Otherwise I will cast you into the deeps.'

Thomas shook his head. 'Sir, this is without purpose. He will not tell you.'

'Then he will drown, in the darkness, alone.' Don Garcia kicked the man in his side, close to the wound, and he cried out in torment. 'I give you one last chance. Tell me.'

For a moment the corsair clenched his remaining eye shut and sweat pricked from his brow until the wave of agony had passed. Then he looked up, his chest rising and falling swiftly as he gasped for breath. There was blood on his lips now, and a faint gurgling as he spoke again. 'You will die . . . all die . . . Your women and children too . . . Your bodies will be carrion for the dogs.'

'Enough!' Don Garcia turned to the nearest of his officers and snapped, 'Get rid of this vermin!'

Fadrique and another officer bent down and reached under the corsair's arms to wrench him on to his feet. Then they dragged him to the bulwark. Spaniards lined the side to get a good view of his end, and began to jeer. By the foredeck the prisoners cried out, some in protest and grief. But others cried in terror and fell to their knees, praying for salvation.

Fadrique was holding the corsair tightly by the arm and he looked towards his father. Don Garcia nodded and Fadrique released his grip and gave the corsair a firm push that sent him tumbling over the rail. Thomas was close by and saw the tranquil blue of the sea explode into white spray and flailing green cloth. Then through the disturbed surface of the water he watched as the corsair swiftly sank into the depths, his robes billowing gracefully like reeds in the flow of a river. Then, with a last dull waver of colour, there was nothing to see, just the blue of the ocean.

'One less unbeliever to deal with.' Don Garcia nodded with satisfaction, before he turned to the captain of the flagship. 'Send some men below to free any Christians at the oars. Have them brought on deck to be fed and watered. The prisoners can take their place. The wounded who will recover will be chained in the hold. The others can be disposed of.'

'Yes, sir,' the captain nodded.

Don Garcia paused to look around the galley. 'A fine-looking vessel. His Majesty's navy can always use a new addition.'

As the first of the wretched creatures was helped up on to the sunlit deck from the living hell of the rowing benches, Thomas paused from his cleaning of Richard's wound. The sight of the emaciated figures, stooped from having to bend below the low deck of the corsair galley, filthy and covered in sores, awoke a painful chain of memories in Thomas.

'It's hard to believe those creatures are men,' Richard muttered. The rowers that had been marched down to Don Garcia's flagship from the dungeons of the citadel in Barcelona had been pitiful enough but at least they had been rested, fed and given a chance to scrub themselves clean over the winter. The men stumbling on to the deck had endured far greater privation and degradation. They tore into the bread and cheese that was brought to them. Some of the Spanish soldiers looked on in pity while others stripped the robes off the prisoners and handed them to the freed men. Then, when the last of the Christians had been brought up, the corsairs were forced below and put in chains, destined to be worked to death in the vessel that had so recently been their own.

'Such reversals of fortune are commonplace in this sea,'

said Thomas. 'You'll grow accustomed to it, I'll warrant, if you live long enough. Now hold still, this will hurt.'

He had taken some thread and a needle from the well-stocked medical chest in the cabin that had belonged to the galley's captain. Squinting, Thomas threaded the needle and tied the ends into a knot. 'Hold your arm up and keep it still.'

Richard did as he was told and took one last look at the puckered lips of his wound before he turned and fixed his gaze on the nearest of the galleons where the crew were busy splicing some of the sheets that had been severed by the corsairs' chain shot. Thomas gently pinched the sides of the wound together with his left hand and then pressed the needle through the skin, across the wound and out through the flesh on the far side of the cut. He pulled the thread through until the knot pressed lightly against the skin and then began the second stitch. Richard clenched his teeth and fought against the pain.

'For a moment I thought you might not follow me into the fight,' said Thomas, trying to take the young man's mind off the stitching. 'Back there, before we boarded. You were afraid?'

Richard shot him a quick glance. 'You know I was.'

'And yet you fought like a lion.'

'I have been trained to fight.'

'And right well. Who was your teacher?'

'Another of Walsingham's men.'

'A soldier?'

'Hardly.' Richard smiled thinly. 'He used to be a leader of a London gang. He was due to hang for murder but Walsingham offered him the chance to live if he was prepared to serve and obey orders without question. When he wasn't questioning those Walsingham suspected of treachery, he was tasked with training the rest of the agents in the use of blades and street fighting.'

'I see. Chivalry was not a part of the curriculum, I imagine.'

'Far from it. We were trained to kill quickly and quietly.'

Thomas nodded, and then concentrated on making the next stitch before he continued. 'But you have never had cause to kill a man before this day, I think.'

The young man was silent and then looked down at the deck. 'No.'

'It is not a step taken lightly, Richard. The real tragedy is that now you have killed, it will weigh less on your conscience the next time. The greatest challenge you will face is trying to remember the man you were before your soul was stained with the blood of another. The more you kill, the harder it is to remember.'

'Is that what you think?'

'It is what I know. What I endure,' Thomas added quietly.

'Is that why you left the Order?'

'That is my business, not yours. But I will admit to it being one reason why I could not continue in its service. Killing was so commonplace to us that it lost all meaning. And so it is with the enemy. It is all either side has come to know and the only profit on it is that we have perfected the very idea of hatred and revenge.'

The squire thought for a moment, until the prick of a fresh stitch made him wince. 'Then how is it that you are here again? You could have refused Sir William and Sir Francis. They would have found another man.'

Thomas glanced up and chuckled. 'I was summoned by my Order, to which I am bound by oath. As for your masters finding another man, there are few as well suited to their needs as I am. They need a man who is of the Order of St John yet does not carry its credo in his heart. Your masters are shrewd men, young Richard. They read me as easily as the pages of a book.' He paused and reflected briefly on the other reason he had been ready to return to Malta: the need to know what had become of Maria. Had the Queen's spymasters understood that too? He looked at Richard. 'And perhaps even more shrewd than I give them credit for.'

'Sir?'

''Tis nothing. Now, the last stitch and we are done here.'

Richard gritted his teeth again as Thomas pierced the skin and drew the last of the thread through. He carefully used Richard's dagger to cut the needle free, and then tied off another knot. He inspected his handiwork and then took a strip of linen from the chest and covered the wound with a bandage.

'There. That will heal within the month, provided you rest the arm and don't disturb the stitches.'

Richard looked at his arm and then lowered it. 'Thank you, sir.'

Thomas rose to his full height and rubbed the small of his back as he looked round the deck. The bodies had been removed, thrown over the side, and water sluiced across the deck to wash the worst of the blood away. The parted sheets had been repaired and the galley was ready to get under way. Already the other galleys had resumed their formation around the galleons and only the prize crew were now on board the captured vessel.

Thomas wiped his hands on a rag and patted Richard on the shoulder. 'Come, we must return to the flagship.'

The squire picked up his gambison and armour and then stared at Thomas for a moment. 'It seems that we both have our secrets, sir.'

Richard nodded. 'And perhaps on Malta the truth will out.'

CHAPTER SIXTEEN

Ten days later, after the soldiers aboard the galleons had been safely landed on Sicily, Don Garcia's small squadron of galleys reached Malta. The sun was setting in the western sky, half hidden by a thin veil of sea mist, as the slim warships entered the mouth of the natural harbour that Malta had been blessed with. Or cursed, Thomas mused. The sheltered waters stretched deep into the heart of the small island and were separated by a peninsula with a rocky ridge running along its spine. To the north of the peninsula was the Marsamxett harbour, and to the south the Grand Harbour that had become home to the Order of St John. Such a fine harbour and the location of the island at the centre of the Mediterranean had drawn the attention of every naval power across the centuries, even back to the ancient empires of Rome and Carthage.

Over twenty years had passed since Thomas had last seen the vista of the Grand Harbour and much had changed. A new fort had been constructed at the end of the peninsula to command the entrances of the two harbours, and additional defence works had been added to St Angelo, the fort that was the headquarters of the Order. The red standard bearing a white cross floated above the highest towers of each fort. Beyond St Angelo lay the village of Birgu, which had steadily grown to serve the needs of the knights and their soldiers in their eternal war against the hordes of Islam. As he gazed at the thick limestone walls and squat towers of St Angelo, Thomas felt a slight ache in his heart as he recalled the years he had served there and the men he had counted as brothers, some of whom had died before his eyes and whom he had mourned. And those others he had known, like La Valette, who had inspired devotion and fanatical zeal.

And then there had been Maria. He had tried to put off thinking of her but there had never been a moment in all the years he had since spent in England when memory of her had not been lodged in his heart like a splinter, a constant reminder of what he had lost. If she still lived, he prayed that she would be here. There was little reason to suppose that she had chosen to remain on this dry rock in the middle of a war-torn sea, but Thomas could not help hoping. Many times he had allowed himself to imagine seeing her again, untarnished by the passage of time, still slender, dark and with the serious expression that belied her fiery spirit. Such fantasies always left him feeling vulnerable for fear that she would reject him, as he had once been forced to abandon her.

'A formidable prospect.'

Thomas thrust his troubled reverie aside and turned to see Richard standing a short distance further along the galley's rail, gazing at the defences of St Angelo. The sun had been lost behind the high ground beyond the harbour and to Thomas's eyes both St Angelo and the fort at the mouth of the harbours seemed somehow diminished by the gloom of the gathering dusk.

'Formidable?' Thomas pursed his lips. 'Not so formidable to our Turkish friends, I think. There is not a fortress in all Christendom that can stand before the great cannons of the Turks. And when the walls come down, the outcome will be decided by the quality and quantity of the men who face each other.'

'The quality is spoken for.' Richard smiled. 'There are no better warriors in this world than the knights of the Order of St John.'

'That may be true, but the Sultan has quantity on his side,' Thomas replied wearily. 'Tell me, Richard, which is more important, quality or quantity? From your experience, as a warrior?'

It was a barbed question, and Thomas regretted it at once. Richard had only intended an amiable exchange but Thomas was irritated by his complacent comment.

Richard frowned and his lips set into a tight line as he stared fixedly at St Angelo. Thomas decided that the most practical form of apology would be to change the subject.

'How is your arm today?'

'The worst of the pain has passed,' Richard replied tersely, without shifting his gaze.

'And you have changed the dressing each day?'

'Just as you ordered.'

'And there was no sign of putrefaction?'

'None.'

'Good.' Thomas nodded.

There was a long silence in which neither man showed any sign of being willing to move from the galley's rail and be the first to give way in their tacit confrontation. Thomas could sense the tension, anger and even hatred seething in the breast of his companion, but there was no question of assuaging it with an open apology and so he said nothing and acted as if he was alone as he watched the harbour open up on either side of Don Garcia's flagship. The remaining galleys of the squadron were in line astern and glided across the quiet waters of the harbour as the oars stroked the surface with graceful symmetry. From St Angelo a gun boomed out in salute as the flagship drew level and there was a brief pause before one of the galley's guns replied, the deep rumble echoing back from the limestone walls of the fort as a host of gulls swirled into the air, disturbed by the noise.

The flagship rounded the end of the promontory and steered into the creek between Birgu and the twin promontory of Senglea where a handful of windmills stood on its highest point. Ahead lay the masts of dozens of cargo ships and fishing boats, packed close to the quay lined with the warehouses of Birgu. The walls of St Angelo continued along the creek a hundred yards before reaching the channel that had been painstakingly cut across the promontory to provide a last line of defence before the fort. Thomas's eyes were drawn to a large galleon riding at anchor in the channel. The forecastle, sides and high poop deck were painted green and decorated in gold leaf and the figurehead was a veiled woman in black robes picked out with stars and moons in gold and silver. There was no mistaking the origins of the vessel and Thomas realised that this must be the galleon that Philippe had told him of, the loss of which had provoked the Sultan's rage.

'Ship oars!' ordered the captain and the dripping blades were raised clear of the sea and rumbled into the hull.

'Port the helm!'

The flagship slowly swung in towards the length of quay closest to the fort. Thomas could see a small party of men waiting there, several wearing the cloaks of the Order, adorned with the distinctive cross motif. To one side a servant held the leashes of two magnificently conditioned hunting dogs. Standing alone a short distance in front of the others was a tall figure with silver hair and beard who was dressed in a plain black doublet, breeches and half-cloak. He watched the approaching galley without expression as the last of the steerage way carried it towards the quay.

Thomas felt his pulse quicken and an old affection stirred in his breast. He recognised the man, even though the passage of twenty years and the burden of command had wrought their changes on the weathered features.

'Jean Parisot de La Valette,' he said softly.

'Him? The old man?' Richard stared, comparing the man's appearance with the more richly finished attire of the men behind him. 'I would not have taken him for the Grand Master of the Order of St John.'

'Clothes do not make the man.'

'Nor does great age. I hope his mind is sound.'

'The High Council of the Order would not permit him to remain in office if it wasn't.'

Sailors tossed coils of rope towards men on the quay and the galley was hauled in until it bumped softly against the tarred rope buffers. A section of the bulwark swung open and the gangway was extended to the quay as Don Garcia and his entourage approached. The Spaniard saw Thomas a short distance further along the deck and beckoned to him.

'It would please me if you and your squire joined us.'

Thomas bowed his head. 'As you will, sir.'

Four of Don Garcia's soldiers hurried ashore and formed a small guard on either side of the gangway. When they were standing to attention, Don Garcia led his entourage ashore, followed by Thomas and Richard. Glancing over the faces of the men at La Valette's back Thomas could only recognise Romegas, the foremost of the galley captains when Thomas had campaigned with the Order. He, too, had grown old, but no doubt his bitter feelings towards Thomas endured.

Don Garcia and La Valette exchanged a bow and brief greetings in French before they took turns to introduce their subordinates. When he waved Thomas forward, Don Garcia could not suppress a small smile.

'Grand Master, I think you may have heard of my English companion, Sir Thomas Barrett.'

La Valette's eyes were still clear and piercing, even though they had set deeper into his countenance. He strained them a little as Thomas approached and bowed his head respectfully.

'Thomas . . . I hoped that you would answer the call.'

'I have been waiting for twenty years, sir.'

A brief look of pain flitted across the old man's expression before he continued. 'Due to the circumstances there was not much I could do, you understand. But you are here now. Back at my side, where your talents are most needed.'

The kindly tone affected Thomas deeply and memories of their comradeship flooded back. 'I will do my duty, sir.'

'I am sure you will. Tell me, are you still as fierce and

deadly a fighter as you were when you last served the Order?'

'In truth? No, sir. But I can still wield a sword as well as most men.'

'That is good.' La Valette smiled and gestured to his retinue, none of whom seemed any younger than Thomas. 'As you see, few of us are men in the prime of life, but we are unequalled in experience and wisdom, the more so since you have rejoined us. For which I give thanks to God.'

'I suspect that some in the Order will not be as grateful, sir,' Thomas replied, avoiding the temptation to glance at Romegas.

'Only a handful survive that still remember, Thomas, and now they are answerable to me and obey my will.' He paused and then clasped Thomas's hand gently. His skin was dry and the bones beneath the mottled flesh were pronounced. 'Your place will not be questioned. It does my heart good to see you again.' He looked beyond Thomas and his gaze rested on Richard for the first time. 'And who is your young companion?'

'My squire, sir. Richard Hughes.'

'You, too, are welcome.'

'Thank you, sir.' Richard bowed.

'Sir Thomas, I will have my servants fetch your baggage. You can retire to the English auberge once you have eaten.' La Valette turned back to Don Garcia who had been following the brief exchange with a curious expression.

'I had no idea that my passenger was held in such regard by the Order,' the Spaniard remarked.

La Valette's expression was strained for a moment before he responded. 'Sir Thomas was one of our most promising knights, before his . . . absence. He has proved himself before, and I do not doubt that he will perform valuable service for the Order again in the great trial that we face. Now the light is dying and we have much to discuss. A meal is being prepared in my lodge for you and your officers, Don Garcia. Some of the senior officers of the Order will arrive later. They were not present in Birgu when your ships were sighted. I have sent for them. There is much to discuss.'

'Indeed.'

La Valette glanced towards the last of the Spanish galleys approaching the quay. 'Only six galleys? The main body of your reinforcements is following on behind, I take it?'

Don Garcia looked round at the faces of the local people who had gathered behind the Grand Master and his retinue. He took a step closer and lowered his voice. 'It is best that we talk about such matters in more . . . private surroundings. If you would lead the way?'

La Valette's expression had hardened. He and Don Garcia were seated together at the head of a long table running down the centre of Fort St Angelo's banqueting hall, but every man present had sat in silence and listened intently as Don Garcia outlined the instructions he had received from King Philip. The pair of hunting dogs lay asleep by the modest fire burning in the iron grate along one wall, a luxury on an island where wood was scarce enough to be sold by the pound weight. Thomas was halfway down the table and had eaten lightly of the first good meal he had

had since leaving Barcelona – honeyed chops of mutton and freshly baked bread. The tension between Don Garcia and La Valette had been palpable and the sour mood had spoiled the appetite of those in the hall. For a moment Thomas envied his squire who was eating at the lower table with the other junior officers of Don Garcia's small force.

La Valette pushed his platter aside and shifted in his chair so that he might face his guest more directly as he spoke.

'Last year I sent warning to His Majesty about the Sultan's plan to strike west, and that Malta would be the Turks' first target. I said that if Malta was to be held I would need five thousand fresh men, cannon, powder and supplies of food. So far he has sent me nothing but messages of support.'

'His Majesty shares your concerns,' Don Garcia countered calmly. 'However, Malta is just one of the territories he is obliged to defend. While it is true that you present the most obvious line of attack, the enemy may yet mean to surprise us by striking elsewhere – Sicily, the coast of Italy or even Spain itself.'

'And thereby leave Malta sitting astride their supply lines?' La Valette replied acidly. 'His Majesty appears to be in need of a lesson in strategy.'

'His Majesty is my sovereign lord, just as he is yours, Grand Master. Your Order was given this island in return for your fealty to the King. His Majesty has appointed me as his Captain of the Sea and placed all his forces, including yours, under my command. I would therefore request that you temper your opinions accordingly.' Don Garcia met the Grand Master's bitter glare steadily before he continued. 'I, in my turn, am obliged to follow the instructions laid down by King Philip. He has stated that I am to meet the enemy in battle only when I enjoy numerical advantage, at sea and on land.'

'Then you will never fight them. The ships and men of the Sultan will always outnumber those of Spain.'

Don Garcia shrugged. 'I cannot help that. But I am doing all in my power to gather support from our allies and concentrate our forces on Sicily, from where I will be best placed to counter the enemy, wherever he chooses to strike. I agree that it is likely that the Sultan casts his gaze towards Malta and I will do what I can to provide you with the wherewithal to counter the blow if it falls here. At the moment I can do little but provide you with some companies of Spanish soldiers and Italian mercenaries. In time, as my strength grows, I will send you more men.'

'By then it may be too late.' La Valette took a breath and calmed his voice before he spoke on. 'There are but six hundred knights in the Order. I have nearly five hundred here and pray that the others answer the summons, as Sir Thomas did. In addition we have a thousand soldiers, and I have sent men from the Order to Italy to recruit more.'

'And you have the local people. The Maltese will fight with you.'

'The Maltese . . .' La Valette could not hide his scorn. 'It is true that there are some militia but they are of poor quality. I dare say that they will break and run the first time they see any Janissary point a weapon at them.'

'I think not. It is true that they are not professional

fighters but a man may fight like a lion to defend his home and family. You have but to train them to use weapons and lead them by good example and they will fight well.'

'Even so, I can expect to raise little more than three thousand men from the local population. So we are no more than five thousand in all to face the horde that will descend on us from the east. Our last report from our agent in Istanbul is that a vast fleet is gathering to carry fifty thousand men, together with their arms and supplies for the entire campaign. No one can withstand such odds, Don Garcia.'

There was a pause and Thomas watched as Don Garcia folded his hands together and rested his forehead against them.

'The hour is late, and our voyage has been tiring,' he said. 'Let us talk of our preparations to face the Turks tomorrow. I would see the defences at first hand, Grand Master, if you would take me over them.'

'It would be a pleasure,' La Valette replied curtly.

'Then I will eat some more, drink and then sleep.' Don Garcia smiled politely. 'As will my officers.'

Their exchange was interrupted as the main door into the hall was opened by one of the servants and a small group of men entered. Thomas looked over his shoulder. They wore plain cloaks with the badge of the Order over their hearts and Thomas realised that these must be the knights La Valette had summoned from the interior of the island earlier on. Some were young but looked tough enough. The rest were veterans, scarred by wounds and the passage of the years. As they made for the chairs and spaces on the benches that were still untaken, Thomas's eye was caught by one of the older knights, a man roughly his own age, tall and sinewy with dark hair receding towards his crown. At almost the same moment the new arrival spied Thomas and he paused mid-stride, and then slowly approached.

Thomas eased himself on to his feet and advanced a few paces towards the man. The other knight looked him over and then breathed in sharply through his nose before he spoke.

'Sir Thomas. So you got the message.'

'As you see. It's been a long time, Oliver. A very long time.'

'I had hoped you would stay away. The Order does not need you.'

'The Grand Master thinks otherwise.'

Sir Oliver Stokely glanced towards the head of the table. 'The chevalier has a short memory. He forgets the damage that you did to us.'

Thomas felt another pang as the tendrils of past sins tightened round his heart again. 'I was a different man then. So were you. I have suffered and repented every day since. Can you not forgive me?'

'Never.'

Thomas shook his head sadly. 'I am sorry to hear you say that.'

'Why? Did you think that I would forget all just because you were willing to answer La Valette's call?'

'Oliver, there are greater matters that should concern us both. I cannot change the past, but I pledge that I will do whatever I can to preserve the future of our Order.'

Sir Oliver shook his head. 'Do what you will. Just stay

away from me. Or I will not answer for my actions.'

Thomas nodded, a weariness settling on him like a heavy shroud. 'I would it were otherwise between us. You were once my friend.'

'Until I discovered your true nature. I have said all I wish to say to you. You are here. Fight for the Order, then when it is over, leave and never return.'

'Very well . . . But I would know one thing more.'

Sir Oliver's lips pressed into a thin smile. 'I thought you might ask.'

'Then tell me.' Thomas hesitated before he continued, eager to finally know yet afraid of the answer. 'Does Maria still live?'

'She is dead.'

'Dead?'

For an instant there was a flicker of emotion in Sir Oliver's features, then his expression hardened. 'Yes, Maria is dead. She has been dead to you, Thomas, ever since that time. Do not ask me about her again or as God is my witness, I shall strike you down and kill you with my bare hands.'

CHAPTER SEVENTEEN

After the meal was over, Thomas and Richard were escorted by one of the Grand Master's clerks to the auberge of the English knights. The house had belonged to a wine merchant before the Order had arrived on Malta and commandeered the property. The clerk set down their bags and rapped on the door and waited. Presently they heard the sound of footsteps within and then the door opened. As Thomas entered the hall which he had once known so well, he turned to look at the servant – a stooped man in a cotton shirt and black breeches and boots. He held a brass candleholder aloft and his face was illuminated by the pale flame.

'What is your business, sir?' he asked in a thin voice.

'I am an English knight of the Order. I need quarters for myself and my squire.'

'English?' The old man started. 'You're the first English knight to arrive at the auberge for . . . nearly ten years. There's only one knight left here now.'

As the old man had been speaking Thomas recognised him and smiled. 'The saints be blessed! Is that you, Jenkins?'

'Aye, Jenkins is the name.' The old man squinted and he leaned closer to inspect the late arrival. 'How is it that you know my name, sir?'

'Come now, surely you remember me.'

The old man raised his candle up and scrutinised Thomas's face. Then his eyes widened. 'No . . . surely not. Sir Thomas . . . Sir Thomas Barrett! Good Lord above. I, I had never thought to see you again, sir.'

'And yet here I am.' Thomas laughed. 'But what of the other servants? Harris? Chapman?'

The gap-toothed smile that had formed on the old servant's face faded. 'They have all gone, sir. I am the last of the retainers.'

'But you must be nearly seventy if you are a day.'

'Sixty-eight in December, sir.' He frowned briefly.

'Then why are you still in service, Jenkins?'

'Where else would I be, sir? There is nowhere for me to go. Not while there is still an English knight to serve at the auberge.'

'What the devil's all that noise?' a voice shouted from the shadows. 'Jenkins, what is it? Speak up, man! Who are those fellows?'

A shadow emerged from a corridor leading off the hall and a powerfully built man with a bull neck – if the transition between his close-cropped head and muscled shoulders could be described as a neck – strode into the pale loom cast by the servant's candle. He looked to be some ten years younger than Thomas and in need of a close shave about the jowls. He scowled at the new arrivals and Thomas caught a waft of acid wine on his breath as he introduced himself.

'Sir Thomas Barrett, eh?' the man repeated. 'I've heard the name. Can't recall when. Well then, I'm Sir Martin Le Grange, from Wickle Bridge, near Hereford. Ever hear of it?'

'Alas not.'

'That's a great pity – for you. Anyway, make yourself at home. Jenkins will see to your needs. I'm off to bed. I was about to go before you arrived. Speak to you in the morning, eh?' He nodded and turned, disappearing back into the corridor.

'Not the most charming salutation I've ever received,' Richard muttered. 'Is he always so . . . hospitable?'

'Only when he's in his cups,' Jenkins replied.

Thomas coughed. 'Would you be kind enough to show us to our quarters?'

'Yes, Sir Thomas. My apologies. If you would follow me, sir.'

Jenkins made to pick up the bags in one hand while he held the candle aloft with the other. Thomas took his arm and gently eased him away from the cumbersome bags.

'Richard can see to those. He is young and strong.'

'And tired,' Richard added.

'Besides, you should not strain yourself at your age, Jenkins.'

The old man straightened his back and raised his chin proudly. 'But I am a servant of the English auberge, sir. It is my duty.'

'Quite so, and how would you carry out your duties if you were to injure yourself by carrying too heavy a burden?' Thomas asked with a grin.

Jenkins opened his mouth to protest, then shrugged and turned away. 'Please follow me, sirs.'

Thomas followed while Richard muttered bitterly and picked up the baggage and strode as quickly as he could to catch up and stay within the small pool of light provided by the wavering candle flame. The servant led them to the accommodation corridor leading off the hall. Glancing up to the rafters, Thomas could see the small wooden shields fixed to the cross-beams, each one bearing the coat of arms of an English knight who had served the Order. There were a handful of gaps where the icons had been removed when the knight in question was judged to have brought dishonour upon the Order. His eyes hurriedly sought out the position where the Barrett icon had once hung. Now there was just a wooden peg and he looked away with a heavy sense of guilt, and shame.

'Are you and Sir Martin the only men living here?' asked Richard.

'Yes, young master. There is one other who keeps quarters here, Sir Oliver Stokely, but he rarely visits the auberge. I haven't seen him here for several months. He has a house near the base of the Sciberras peninsula. That's where he lives these days. Here we are, sir.' Jenkins stopped outside a door and lifted the latch and led them inside. 'It's not the cell you used to have, sir. After you left, that became a storeroom. I hope this will suit you.'

He raised the candleholder up and Thomas saw that the chamber was perhaps ten feet wide by fifteen long. There was a bed, a chest, a small table and chair, and pegs for his clothes. High up on the rear wall was a shuttered window.

Thomas nodded. 'This will do. Richard, you may leave my bags here.'

The young man glanced round. 'And where do I sleep . . . sir?'

The servant chuckled. 'Rest easy, young master. It's not the floor for you. There's a squire's cell next door. In the old days you'd share that with three others but you'll have it to yourself.'

'Does Sir Martin not have a squire?' asked Thomas.

'He can't afford one, sir. His family lost everything when King Henry took their lands many years ago. That's why Sir Martin joined the Order in the first place. He looks after his own weapons and armour. Insists on it. I just feed him, tend to his fire and cook his food. Of course, now that we have another squire at the auberge, perhaps young Master Richard could serve some of Sir Martin's needs.'

Richard looked sharply at Thomas and gave a barely perceptible shake of his head.

'Of course.' Thomas smiled. 'I will see what can be arranged.'

Richard glared at him before he spoke. 'If you will excuse me, sir, I'll take the other bags to my cell.'

Thomas nodded.

'Just a moment.' Jenkins crossed to the table where a stout candle stood in a hardened pool of wax on top of a small platter. He lit the wick and it sputtered a moment before growing into a steady flame that added to the illumination of the cell. 'There, young master. Follow me.'

'When my squire is settled, bring me a jar of heated wine,' said Thomas. 'There is much I would know about what has happened during the years of my absence.'

Jenkins nodded. 'Aye, sir. I'd be pleased to tell you, and hear the news from England.'

The servant gestured to the squire to leave the room and then followed him out and shut the door quietly behind them. Thomas looked around the cell, dimly recalling that it had once been occupied by Sir Anthony Thorpe, a surly older knight from some obscure village in Norfolk who had insisted on sleeping with the door open. His loud snoring had echoed down the corridor, disturbing the sleep of his comrades.

Once he had removed his cloak and hung it on a peg Thomas picked up the plate holding the candle and trod quietly towards the door. The muffled sounds of conversation came from the next cell as Jenkins attempted to engage Richard in conversation. Thomas eased the latch up and stepped into the corridor, raising the candle so that he might see better. To one side the corridor led off towards the kitchen, with doors on either side for the cells of the knights and their squires. A dim glow under the door opposite revealed where Sir Martin had his quarters. Turning the other way, Thomas retraced his steps to the hall.

Despite his careful pace the sound of his footsteps was clearly audible as he made his way across to the hearth opposite the entrance and only served to make the hall seem more empty and still. He stopped to look round slowly, and remember. There was a hint of roast meat in the air, a common enough smell in England but in this place it suddenly evoked in the most tangible way a memory of his first feast day at the auberge. He had been knighted at seventeen and joined the Order a year later and his heart had swelled with pride as he sat at the table to one side of the fire, together with a score of English knights, eating and drinking while the warm fug of the hall was filled with the sound of their loud conversation and laughter. He could even recall their faces. Sir Harry Beltham, whose red-blotched complexion matched the fiery red hair and beard on his round face. His laughter had been deep and infectious, and when he had slapped Thomas on the back, the young knight had been shot halfway across the hall. Sir Matthew Smollett, a Welshman, tall, sinewy and so darkly featured that rumours were spread that he surely must have Moor blood in him. He had been quiet and content to observe his companions with a wry smile and make the occasional dry quip that served to remind the others of his superior intelligence. There were others Thomas recalled with affection. And finally Sir Oliver Stokely, the comrade he had once considered a friend and who had become a bitter enemy by the time they had parted. The earlier icy encounter with his former comrade had shaken Thomas.

The memories faded and then there was only the cold and the dark shadows around him. For a moment Thomas tried to draw the memory of his feasting comrades back before his mind's eye, but the desire seemed false and he gave up. With an aching heart Thomas returned to his cell and opened his bag. In it were a few changes of clothes and a handful of personal effects. He took out his brushes and the silver crucifix – a family heirloom – he had once prayed before every day, at dawn and dusk. He held it in his hands and regarded it thoughtfully for a moment before placing it on the small table, against the wall. He deliberately left the leather pouch until last. He eased open the drawstrings and tenderly took out the gold locket. After a brief hesitation he opened the lid and stared at the dark lock of hair inside.

He was still for a moment and then he pressed his lips together and lightly touched the hair with his little finger, slowly stroking the silky strands.

'Maria . . .'

There was a knock at the door. Thomas snapped the locket shut and hastily replaced it in the pouch and put that in the table's one drawer.

'Come.'

Jenkins entered, carrying a tray bearing the candleholder, a small stoppered jar and two brass cups. He turned and nudged the door closed before he crossed the cell and set the tray down. Thomas sat on the bed and gestured to the chair. Jenkins nodded his thanks and eased himself down with a sigh and then pulled out the stopper and poured the first cup which he handed to the knight before pouring his own. Thomas raised the cup and smiled.

'To old comrades and absent friends.'

The wine was warm and pleasant to the palate and felt comforting in the stomach as Thomas drank. Then he lowered the cup to his lap and held it in both hands as he gazed fondly at the auberge's remaining servant. Jenkins drained his cup and set it down with a sharp rap before he wiped his lips on the back of his bony hand.

'A good drop, that.'

'Drop?' Thomas arched an eyebrow. 'Rather more than a drop, I'd say.'

The servant shrugged. 'When you're on your own, sir, the lack of conversation leaves nothing but drink to occupy a man.'

Thomas nodded, knowingly.

Jenkins leaned forward and spoke in a low voice. 'Your

squire doesn't seem very content with his lot, if I may say so, sir.'

'Oh?'

'I showed him his cell, tried to talk to the fellow, but he was in sour spirits. Didn't seem to know much about looking after your kit either. The leather of your boots was too dry and there was rust on the blade of your sword and his. Would have been unthinkable in the old days. He'd have been soundly beaten for less. He's no boy, he's old enough to know better.'

'That may be but he was the best I could find before setting out from England. There are not many young men willing to jeopardise any future they might have at home by serving the Order.'

'Really?' Jenkins pursed his lips. 'Things must be bad for the true faith then. That's to be expected with one of them heretics on the throne.'

'I'd hardly call Queen Bess a heretic.' Thomas chuckled. 'Especially not to her face, or in front of anyone who is likely to report the remark.'

'It is of no concern to me, sir. I shall not return to England. I will die here, in Malta. One way or another. So I am free to say what I like about a Protestant queen.'

Thomas considered Richard in the next room, and the masters in London he served. The young man had been trained to kill and this was his first important mission and he was anxious to succeed, and no one would be allowed to get in the way of that, the elderly servant least of all.

He took another sip from his cup and spoke thoughtfully. 'Protestant she may be but the Queen has avoided executing quite as many of her religious opponents as Mary did before her. She is taking steps to draw our people together again and may well prove to be as good a monarch as any.'

'Pfftt!' Jenkins sniffed with contempt. 'Her mind has been poisoned against the Church of Rome. She will be damned to a well-deserved eternity of torment alongside all those who embrace heresy. Her Majesty is as much our enemy as the Sultan.'

'Even though she is a Christian?'

'Even so.' Jenkins nodded resolutely.

Thomas looked at the old man with a heavy heart. 'I see that those who serve the Order have not lost any of their zeal since I was last here.'

'Zeal is our strength, sir. It is all that has sustained the Order in the centuries since we last held the Holy Land. We need it now more than ever.' Jenkins stroked his chin wearily. 'The truth is that the Order is in poor shape to make its stand against the Turks. Thanks to the wars in Europe, there has been little fresh blood to fill out the ranks of the knights. Captain Romegas has barely enough fighting men and sailors to man half of the Order's galleys. Too many of the knights are past their prime, sir. Oh, their faith and their courage are as strong as ever but their poor bodies are worn out. The Grand Master most of all. He is older than I am, and his sight and strength are starting to fade, according to one of my friends who serves in his private quarters.'

'That's just gossip,' Thomas retorted. 'He appeared to be fit and sound of mind when I saw him earlier this evening.'

Jenkins smiled faintly. 'Of course he did, sir. The Grand Master knows that everyone looks to him to lead them through the coming peril, his knights and soldiers most of all. But he cannot hide the true condition of his age from those closest to him.' He shrugged. 'Powerful men never seem to take account of their servants.'

Thomas was struck by the harm that could be done to the morale of the Order, and those who depended on it, if they came to see La Valette as his servants did. 'It would be best if you did not repeat what you have heard about the Grand Master.'

'Yes, sir. I did not mean to speak out of turn.'

'In the normal course of events I would not mind, Jenkins. But we are all in the gravest of dangers, and La Valette is the rock upon which all hope is placed. It is a cruel burden to be laid upon the shoulders of an old man who has given his life to the service of the Order. This is the hour of his greatest challenge and even if his body is a shadow of what it once was, his heart, mind and spirit are as keen as they ever were, and tempered by his vast experience. If anyone can lead us to victory over the Turk then it is surely Jean Parisot de La Valette.'

Jenkins stared at him for a moment before he responded. 'Fine words, sir. But do you truly believe them? It would be better if the Order elected a younger man to replace the Grand Master and let La Valette retire in peace.'

Thomas shook his head. 'Who would not want to be at the heart of such a moment in history? If the Order triumphs then none shall forget his name, and if they are crushed then he will have won the glory of fighting to the last in the name of our faith.'

'For my part, sir, I'd rather he won his glory some other

way. I've no desire to be put to the sword by the Turks if they take Birgu. None of us common folk have.'

'I am sure that some of the knights share your point of view. As for me, I would rather survive than be butchered. I am not yet convinced that God has determined a hopeless heroic end for me.'

There was an awkward silence and then Thomas drained his cup quickly and reached for the jar. 'But enough of that. If it happens, it happens. I want to know more of what has passed in the years since I left the Order.'

Jenkins's expression hardened and he looked down, refusing to meet the knight's eyes. When he spoke again his voice was low and strained. 'Must we talk of that, sir? I feared you would ask.'

'I would know what happened.'

'Perhaps it would be best if you sought out Sir Oliver, sir. He can tell you more than I can.'

'I met Sir Oliver earlier,' Thomas replied coldly. 'He does not want to speak to me. That is why I ask you, Jenkins. There are questions I must ask. Answers I must have.'

'Sir, please, ask me not. It does my heart good to see you again. You were always one of my favourites amongst the knights before . . . you were made to leave. I pray you, do not open old wounds. What was done is over with. Nothing can be changed. It is best to forget.'

'Yet I cannot forget!' The anguish in his voice caused Jenkins to start and he looked up with a fearful expression.

Thomas leaned closer, his eyes blazing. 'When I was banished, I lost everything that counted with me, everything. My comrades, my honour, my faith and . . . my love.' The last word was uttered through clenched teeth. 'Twenty years I have endured this. At first I tried to set my heart like stone and exile emotion.' And he had failed pitifully in the attempt. 'Then, when I knew I could not, I turned to the service of the warlords of Europe and yet still endured the memories that filled the void between work and sleep. Time, finally, assuaged the worst of the burden, and then I am summoned back here. Jenkins, I cannot tell you how the very sight and scent of this island have torn at my heart. To walk the streets of Birgu and enter the auberge once again has wounded my soul. Here I was once happy. That which I had prized above all else in life is gone. Maria is dead.'

'Who says so?'

'Sir Oliver.' Thomas eased himself back and rubbed his brow slowly. 'In England I had considered it, and tried to make myself believe it. What else could I do? I had no way of knowing what happened here. Every member of the Order was forbidden to communicate with me, and it would have been death for me to set foot on the island. I had come to accept that Maria was gone from my life, if never from my heart, and now I am returned and discover she is dead and it is as if I must learn to live without her all over again. Forgive me.' Thomas looked up at the joists and took a deep breath. He had never intended for his feelings to find such expression, only to ask for the bare details of the knowledge he sought. But now it was too late and the cold, hard face he had presented to the world had melted like late snow in spring.

'My poor master,' said Jenkins. 'I did not know that

she, that Maria, was dead. Only that after you were banished she left Birgu.'

Thomas felt his heart lurch. 'Where? Where did she go?'

'I do not know, sir. All I knew was that she had gone into confinement, until the child was born. After that I heard nothing for several months. It was the following winter, when Sir Oliver was entertaining La Valette in his quarters here at the auberge. As I brought them more wine I overheard them speak of the matter. Sir Oliver said that the child, a boy, had been born, but had been sickly and died shortly afterwards.'

'I had a son . . .' Thomas felt an ache in his heart at the news. A son. Maria had borne his son. He was caught between the pain of knowing what he had lost and anger over never having known of it until now. It was a while before he could control his thoughts enough to speak again. 'And Maria? What became of her?'

'I know not, sir. There was a rumour that she had left Malta for a convent at Naples. I have not seen her since she left Birgu. If she is dead then it will have been in Naples.' He paused and continued in a cautious tone, 'Sir Oliver knows more than I. Ask him.'

'I would ask but he will not speak to me of her. He hates me.'

'Are you surprised? It was well known that he, too, had lost his heart to the lady. She chose to love you.' Jenkins shook his head sadly. 'It is a hard thing for a man to accept without growing bitter and hateful. I have lived long enough to see more than enough of it. Envy is a cruel master.'

'Even so, she left our lives a long time ago, long enough, surely, to heal the wound in Sir Oliver's heart.'

Jenkins eyed the knight warily. '*Your* heart is not yet healed.'

'That is true,' Thomas admitted.

'And your arrival has reopened Sir Oliver's wound.'

Thomas nodded his understanding and felt a great weariness settle upon him. He was tired of this life with its ceaseless burdens of suffering and memory. He craved to forget and begin anew, or simply to have an end to it all. He closed his eyes and lowered his head into his hands.

'Leave me, old friend. I must rest.'

'Yes, sir. I know.' Jenkins rose stiffly from the chair and made to pick up the cups and jar, hesitated a moment and then left them alone and quietly made his way towards the door. He glanced back at the knight wrapped in his inner torment, and then closed the door behind him.

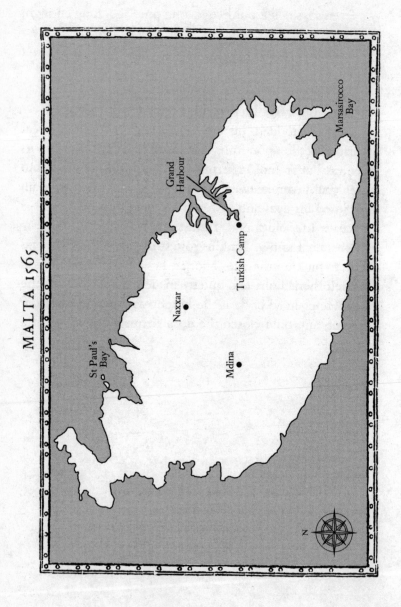

MALTA 1565

St Paul's
Bay

Naxxar

Mdina

Grand
Harbour

Turkish Camp

Marsasirocco
Bay

N

CHAPTER EIGHTEEN

Shortly after first light the next morning Thomas and Richard were roused by a servant of La Valette with an order to attend the Grand Master at his headquarters. Sir Martin was still snoring as they hurriedly left the auberge and made their way through the quiet streets and across the drawbridge into the fort of St Angelo. Don Garcia was with the Grand Master, impatient to begin his inspection of the defences. While La Valette's expertise lay in naval warfare, Don Garcia had considerable experience of the battlefield and siegecraft.

They started with the fortifications of St Angelo which commanded the harbour approaches to the Birgu promontory. Don Garcia had insisted on climbing every tower, and then descending into the bowels of the fort to examine the store chambers and cisterns before he announced his satisfaction.

'A well-founded structure. If the Turks break into Birgu, then the remaining knights can fall back here and hold out until relieved.'

'Or until they – we – are pounded to pieces by the enemy's cannon,' the Grand Master responded.

Don Garcia ignored the comment and requested to be shown the defences of Birgu. These he was much less satisfied with. Work parties of galley slaves, chained to-gether, were labouring to raise the height and depth of the walls and bastions that protected the base of the promontory. More slaves, under the watchful eyes of soldiers, were busy breaking up the rocky ground outside the wall to deepen the ditch that lay in front of Birgu.

A short walk to the south brought the party to the defences that protected the Senglea promontory. The fort of St Michael guarded the bare finger of land that stretched out beside the creek where the galleons, fishing boats and the Order's seven galleys lay at anchor. Once again, Don Garcia thoroughly explored the fort and made his observations about the defences from the tower that afforded the best view.

'The weak point is that shore facing those heights over there.' He pointed across the strip of water known to the locals as French Creek. Beyond the water the ground was level for a short distance before it rose steeply a quarter of a mile from the fort. 'The Turks could mount heavy guns there to enfilade the outer defences. There's not much that we can do about that.'

Thomas cleared his throat. 'There's a rather bigger danger, sir.'

Don Garcia turned to look at him with a slight frown. 'What's that?' asked the Spanish commander.

Thomas pointed towards the shore of the Senglea promontory facing the heights. A few small redoubts constructed from rock were spread along the water's edge. 'There's not much to stop a landing there. If the Turks seize the point then they can land cannon and bombard St Michael from the rear. They will also be able to destroy the ships in Dockyard Creek and fire on Birgu.'

'You're right.' Don Garcia stroked his beard. 'It would be a disaster.'

'The threat has already been taken in hand,' La Valette intervened. 'I have given orders for a line of stakes to be driven into the seabed ten paces from the shore. There will be an iron loop on each stake for a chain to pass through. Any boats attempting a landing there will run up on the chain and those on board will have to swim ashore.'

'That's good, very good,' Don Garcia said. 'Though you will still need to defend the shore. Even if your chains prevent them landing, you must be able to contain them on the beach so that they can be cut down by fire from your cannon. You will need to construct a parapet there.'

The Grand Master gestured to his clerk to make a note.

Don Garcia looked slowly round to survey the Grand Harbour and the surrounding landscape. 'The trouble with the entire position is that every fort is overlooked by higher ground. You may have a fine base for your galleys, Grand Master, but it is a poor situation to defend in a siege where the enemy will have cannon, and no doubt plenty of them. The main aspect in your favour is that the Turks will be obliged to attack on narrow fronts, whichever fort they attempt to take.'

'Which is just as well, given how few men I have.'

Don Garcia pursed his lips thoughtfully. 'The question is, which will they attack first? If I was the Turkish commander I would begin there.' He raised his hand and pointed at St Elmo. 'It is the smallest of the forts and it is isolated from the rest of your defences. It should be the easiest one to capture. If St Elmo falls then the enemy commands the approaches to both harbours and can safely anchor his ships in the Marsamxett. Moreover he will be able to fire across the Grand Harbour and bombard both these promontories. It will also deliver a blow to your morale while raising the spirits of his own men.' Don Garcia weighed up his observations and then nodded. 'Yes, that is where he will attack first, I am certain of it. Therefore it is vital that St Elmo holds out for as long as possible. Let us see that fort now . . .'

Even though it was early in spring and the air was still fresh, Thomas, Richard and the other officers in the small party were perspiring freely as they climbed the stairs of the cavalier tower rising to one side of Fort St Elmo and looking north-east out to sea. Thomas emerged at the top and stood to one side for a moment to catch his breath. The Grand Master stood by the parapet, leaning against the cut limestone to recover. Don Garcia's face was also flushed with the effort and for a moment no one spoke on the platform of the tower. Beyond the parapet the cavalier tower dropped down towards the rocky end of the peninsula where the sea began. There was no wind and the surface of the sea looked smooth and grey as it stretched out towards the horizon like a sheet of cold steel.

Richard looked at the other officers around him calculatingly before he muttered, 'There are too many old men here, Sir Thomas.'

The knight shot him a black look but did not trust himself to reply without gasping and proving his squire's point.

'Look at them,' Richard continued. 'The Grand Master is a relic from an old war, and so are most of the other senior knights. How can they hope to hold Malta with a band of greybeards and the natives of the island? Even if they can find some mercenaries foolish enough to take their coin, it would still be a hopeless situation.'

Thomas licked his dry lips and sucked in a deep breath. 'Never underestimate the value of . . . experience. These men, and I, were fighting the Turk long before you were born. When the time comes, the value of such experience will be clear to all. If the enemy make the same mistake as you and misjudge the quality of the knights of the Order,' Thomas smiled grimly, 'both you and the Turks will be in for a surprise. Mark my words.'

He turned and walked steadily across the platform to join the other men clustered around Don Garcia and La Valette. The Spaniard was tutting to himself as he looked down on the rest of the fort. The tower afforded a clear view into the heart of St Elmo where a Maltese militia company was being drilled by a Spanish sergeant, bellowing out his orders for a swarthy local to translate in a pale imitation of the sergeant's ferocity and volume.

'Who gave the order to build the fort here?' he asked La Valette. 'You?'

'The Grand Master before me.'

'And who advised him, if anyone?'

'There was an Italian siege engineer commissioned to oversee the work but he died shortly after reaching Malta.'

'That is a shame, since he might have prevented your predecessor from making such a catalogue of mistakes.'

'Oh?'

'To begin with, this fort is in the wrong location.' Don Garcia pointed towards the ridge running along the peninsula dividing the harbours. 'Up there it could command every approach. As it is, the enemy will be able to occupy the high ground and dominate the fort. Furthermore, there is no shelter along the parapet. As soon as a man shows his head above the wall he will be clearly outlined against the sky, making an easy target for any arquebusiers concealed in front of the fort. And there's too little space on the walls to mount more than a handful of cannon. You will have to use the towers. There's another thing. Look down there.' Don Garcia pointed to the nearest corner of the star-shaped fort. 'If the Turks can work round the front face they'll be able to scale that corner easily. It's too low. You'll need to construct a ravelin there.'

As La Valette nodded, Richard leaned towards Thomas and whispered, 'Ravelin?'

'It's a fortification that's constructed in front of a weak spot,' Thomas explained calmly. 'Usually in the form of a chevron.'

Don Garcia was quiet for a moment as he collected his thoughts. 'Every day that the flag of the Order flies over St Elmo is a day that you can use to improve the defences of Birgu and Senglea. If you can only buy enough time for the relief force to gather, or for the campaigning season to come to an end in October, then there's a chance Malta will remain in our hands.'

'I will ensure that Malta holds out,' La Valette said firmly. 'The Order of St John was cast out of the Holy Land, and then Rhodes. Whatever the odds, we will hold

Malta. If not then the Order will perish here. Every one of us is resolved to that end.'

Don Garcia looked at the old knight. 'A glorious death, eh? Is that what you want?'

'I am not afraid to die in the service of Christ. I never have been.'

'Laudable as your devotion to your cause may be, I would strongly advise you to keep yourself from harm's way as much as possible if the Turks come to Malta.'

La Valette frowned. 'I will do no such thing.'

'You must. You are a proud man, I know that. But you must consider the morale of those you command. You are their figurehead, not just their commander. They will look to you and you must appear strong and resolute at all times. If you were wounded, or killed, then the spirit of your men would be greatly harmed. I have been a soldier long enough to know the truth of this. The will to fight is a fickle thing. You know what is riding on the successful defence of this island and I beseech you to put the interests of others before your pride. The Order already faces the gravest of challenges.'

'Then perhaps you should consider sending me the soldiers I requested from His Majesty. Five thousand men would make a most valuable contribution to the safety of Malta.'

'I do not have five thousand to spare you. I have little more than that in Sicily as it is. More men are being recruited in Spain and will soon be joining my army. As I said last night, I will send you reinforcements the moment they can be spared, but you must be patient.'

'Patient?' La Valette repeated bitterly. 'For months I

have been sending you and the King details of what our spies have observed in the shipyards and arsenals of the enemy and you have done nothing but make ships and sit in your castles in Spain and wait for the enemy to come. I tell you, he is coming here, and it is here that the fate of the Order and the rest of Christendom will be decided.'

'You may well be right, but I have my orders and my own responsibilities. However, I will request the King's permission to send you a thousand of my best soldiers from Sicily, and I will do what I can to send further reinforcements as soon as possible.'

La Valette looked directly at the Spanish commander. 'And I have your word on this?'

Don Garcia's expression darkened at this attack on his honour. He bit back on his anger and replied in a flat voice, 'Better, I will leave my son here with you as a token of my promise.'

'Your son?'

Don Garcia looked round and called Fadrique forward. He rested his hand on his son's shoulder. 'Do you agree to this?'

The young Spaniard could hardly do otherwise but it was clear from his expression that he welcomed the prospect of making his stand before the enemy onslaught.

He cleared his throat. 'It would be an honour to fight with the knights of the Order of St John, sir.'

'There.' Don Garcia turned his attention back to the Grand Master. 'You can see, I place the highest value on this fortress holding out against the Turks. I invest my own blood in this island, alongside you and your men.'

La Valette nodded and Thomas saw the respect in his

expression. 'Very well. I am certain that your son will do honour to your family. I am pleased to have him fight at my side.'

'Good.' Don Garcia regarded his son for a moment and then patted his cheek tenderly before he let his hand drop. 'Grand Master, there are two other matters I would raise with you before I am done here and must leave. Firstly, you will need a council of advisers to help you plan your defence of the island. I know that the Order has a ruling body, under your command. But it is too large, too unwieldy and too prone to dissent. You must keep your council as small as possible and there must never be any sign of division amongst you. If anything happens to you, then a member of the council must take over at once. Therefore you must choose men whose leadership will be accepted by your soldiers as willingly as they accept yours.'

The Grand Master pursed his lips briefly and nodded. 'Very well. And what is the other matter?'

Don Garcia turned and pointed across the harbour to the Order's galleys riding at anchor below the battlements of St Angelo. 'Your ships will be vulnerable if they remain here. They will not be able to serve you if the Turks lay siege to Malta. It would be better if you were to place them under my command. The Turks have a powerful fleet and I need every galley I can find if I am to confront them.'

'My galleys are staying here,' La Valette said firmly.

'Why?'

'We need them.'

'For what purpose? What good are they to you if Malta is besieged?'

'I need them to guard the supply ships that are bringing food, arms and men in, and evacuating those who wish to leave before the Turks arrive. There are still plenty of corsairs hunting for prey. If you take my galleys you will leave the cargo vessels without protection.'

'I can provide you with galleys to patrol the seaways for as long as possible.'

'Why would I need your patrols if I can use my own warships?'

Don Garcia's eyes narrowed. 'This would have nothing to do with the fact that the two finest galleys happen to be your personal property, would it?' He lowered his voice. 'We must all make sacrifices for the common good. We cannot allow personal interests to stand in the way of reason, Grand Master.'

'It is with reason that I speak,' La Valette protested. 'Without our galleys the Order is powerless. But if you think my argument is partial, then let us seek a more detached opinion.' The Grand Master turned. 'What is your opinion, Sir Thomas?'

'Why ask him?' objected Don Garcia. 'He is a member of your Order. His opinion is prejudiced.'

'He has not served the Order for twenty years and he is not a subject of the King of Spain. His views are those of an outsider. Well, Sir Thomas, what say you?'

Thomas's mind raced as he considered his reply. Don Garcia's request made sense, given the immediate threat, but he knew how the Order prized its galleys. If he supported the Spaniard then he risked the enmity of the Grand Master and most of the other knights. It would only result in bitterness and division. Besides, this was a fine chance to win La Valette's approval. Without that he could not hope to further Richard's mission or discover more about the fate of Maria. He cleared his throat.

'Without the galleys the knights cannot take the war to the enemy. The warriors of the Order would be stranded on this rock. Once the siege is lifted, they will continue to wage war against the Turks and their corsair allies. For that the knights must have the galleys. If you take them, what guarantee can you give the Grand Master that they will be returned to us? In any case, what difference will seven galleys make, given the odds? Sir, you are under orders not to risk your ships or your men unnecessarily. In which case, it does not matter if the galleys join your fleet or stay here.'

Don Garcia glared at the Englishman. 'Is this how you repay my confidences?'

'I did not know that you spoke in confidence at the time, sir.'

The Spaniard turned his gaze to the Grand Master. 'So much for detached opinion. Very well, keep your damned galleys. Just promise one thing. If there is any danger that they might fall into enemy hands, you will destroy them.'

'I guarantee it. I will burn them down to the keel with my own hand rather than see them taken by the Turks or, worse, those corsair devils.'

'Then the matter is settled, though I think you have ill served our cause. As for the defences, you have my opinions and I pray that you act on them while there is still time. Now I must return to my command on Sicily. I bid you farewell, and good fortune. Come, gentlemen!' Don Garcia gestured to his officers to follow him.

As the Spaniards descended the staircase into the tower, La Valette watched until the last had disappeared from sight before he approached Thomas and smiled warmly.

'I hoped that I could count on you. Only a knight could understand what the galleys mean to the Order.'

Thomas bowed his head. 'I am your servant, sir, and my loyalty is to the Order, but I pray that my words were wise. Don Garcia may turn out to be right after all and those galleys could tip the balance against the enemy.'

'Now the decision is made we shall never know, Thomas. Put the matter aside and do not let it burden your thoughts.' He patted him on the shoulder and then turned to descend the staircase.

Thomas lingered behind for a moment and Richard leaned towards him and muttered, 'Good work, Sir Thomas. You have La Valette's trust. We can make good use of that.'

'If you say so.' Thomas rested his elbows on the parapet of the tower and stared across the Grand Harbour towards Birgu. All morning he had been trying to avoid thinking about the brief encounter with Sir Oliver the previous evening. Sleep had not come to his troubled mind and for the moment he wanted to thrust aside all thought of the secret purpose behind his presence here. There was a more urgent, more personal, purpose that needed satisfying. Only then could he face the enemy with an untroubled mind.

That night, after the two knights had taken their supper, Jenkins and Richard were tasked with cleaning Thomas's armour. They carried it through to the hall along with a box containing rags and stoppered pots of polish and wax. Settling on stools by the hearth, they set to work. Jenkins quietly instructed the squire to work the polish on to the surface of the armour then rub it in with a fresh cloth until there was only a faint smear on the metal, after which he used a clean rag to buff it to a shine. Richard worked in silence for a while before he cleared his throat. 'Jenkins, do you recall a knight by the name of Sir Peter de Launcey?'

'Of course, sir,' Jenkins replied as he dabbed some more polish on to the rag that covered his finger, and then rubbed it into the crest of the helmet. 'It's not as if there have been many knights joining the Order from England since King Henry took on the Pope. I remember Sir Peter, though he was not with us for long. He joined two years before the King died. Quiet man, and very devout. More so than most of the others. He took his vows seriously. It was a sad day when I heard he had lost his life. He'd only just come back from a voyage to England. Called back for some family affair, as I recall.' Jenkins shook his head sadly. 'To have travelled all that way, only to drown here in the harbour. Tragic accident.'

'Yes. More than you know,' said Richard. 'Sir Peter was a cousin of mine.'

Jenkins paused in his polishing and looked up. 'Really, sir? I'm sorry to hear that.'

'Oh, we weren't close. But he was family.' Richard paused for a moment as he put down the breastplate and reached for the gorget. 'I met his brother before we left London.'

'Brother? I didn't know he had a brother.'

'Well, a half-brother in fact. He was an infant when Peter left England. I doubt he would have mentioned him. Anyway, when I told him where I was bound he asked me if I might look into a small matter for him.'

Jenkins kept his attention on his work. 'Mmm?'

'Sir Peter's personal effects were never returned to the family. They'd written to Sir Oliver Stokely but received no reply.'

'He's a busy man. I'm not surprised.'

'Still, it would have been a small kindness to at least have answered the letter and arrange for the return of his property, such as it was.'

'Well, he didn't leave much behind.' Jenkins hawked up some phlegm and spat on to the crest of the helmet and rubbed furiously. 'A small wardrobe of clothes, a Bible, a writing case and a few other oddments. Just enough to fill a small chest. His armour was added to the Order's stores.'

'I see . . . I don't suppose you could show me his chest? There might be time to arrange for it to be sent back to his family before the Turks arrive. I know they'd appreciate it. They took the news of his death badly.'

Jenkins lowered the helmet and flexed his gnarled fingers. 'The chest isn't here any longer.'

'It isn't?'

Jenkins shook his head. 'We had it in the cellar for a while. Then a cistern in the next building started leaking so we had to move the lot out. As far as I recall, anything of value was removed to St Angelo. That's the last time I saw it. The chest was taken up to the fort in a cart with some other boxes and caskets. I remember it well enough as it was a handsome lacquered piece. Anyway, the chest is still up there as far as I know.'

'Good.' Richard smiled. 'Lacquered, you say? Black, I assume.'

'Black as coal. With brass strappings. And his coat of arms set in a crest on the lid.'

'Coat of arms? What device would that be?'

Jenkins looked up at the crests fixed along the beams above. 'There. That one. The field of red with the boar's head beneath a gold chevron. See?'

Richard tilted his head back, stared a moment and nodded. 'It should be easy enough to find if I go and look for it.'

Jenkins chuckled. 'Not so easy as that, Master Richard. They put it in the dungeon beneath the keep, where they store the archive and treasury of the Order. You don't just walk in. You have to get written permission from the Grand Master himself to enter the dungeon. There's a fortune in gold, silver, gemstones and silks in there. The proceeds from the galleys' raids on enemy ships and ports.'

'No wonder he keeps it under lock and key.' Richard laughed. 'Out of temptation's way. And under heavy guard, I'll warrant.'

'Of course.'

''Tis a pity. I would have liked to send Peter's belongings home to his family.'

Jenkins cracked his knuckles and nodded towards the greaves and mantlets. 'Just those to do now. Should be done in time to see to the gentlemen's supper.'

Richard heaved a sigh, reached for the nearest greave and began to apply the first blob of polish. He glanced sidelong at the servant whose concentration was fixed on the tricky overlapping plates of the mantlet, and he allowed himself a smile of satisfaction now that he knew what to look for and where to find it. The smile faded as he contemplated the challenge of getting into the dungeon – in the very heart of the Order's headquarters, and under heavy guard.

CHAPTER NINETEEN

The pace of the work being carried out on the island's defences increased feverishly following the departure of Don Garcia and his squadron of galleys. True to the Spaniard's advice the Grand Master gave orders for the construction of a ravelin to protect the most vulnerable corner of Fort St Elmo. The bare rock of the peninsula provided a firm foundation but there would only be time to cut enough stone for the outer facing before the Turks could arrive. Behind the stone façade the defenders would have to pile up and pack down rubble and earth. From the outside the new fortification would look formidable enough but the moment it was subjected to the penetrating power of iron cannonballs it would soon be battered down.

Meanwhile St Elmo was fully provisioned and the modest cistern that lay beneath the keep was filled to the brim. Gunpowder and shot was placed in the storerooms, ready to feed the small complement of artillery that was mounted on the fort's gun platforms. Stout boxes filled with shot for the arquebusiers were positioned along the parapet and hessian sacks were filled with soil and piled in the courtyard, ready to fill any breaches in the walls.

Each day ships entered the harbour with cargoes of

grain, wine, cheeses and salted meats. There were also tools and building materials needed to prepare the defences and ensure that damage could be repaired. Some of the vessels had been intercepted at sea by Captain Romegas and his galleys and summarily requisitioned since the Order's needs overrode any notions of legality. The owners and crews were promised compensation in due course, though that depended upon Malta surviving the Turkish onslaught.

In the first days of spring the companies of Spanish and Italian mercenaries hired by the Grand Master began to arrive and were assigned billets in the towns of Birgu and Mdina. They were hardened professionals and had been lured by generous payments from the Order's coffers, and the prospect of loot. It was well known that the Sultan's elite corps, the Janissaries, were richly dressed and paid handsomely in gold and silver. Their corpses would provide rich pickings for the mercenaries. There were also small groups of adventurers who travelled to Malta to offer their services to the Order, motivated by religious fervour and the desire for glory. Amid the new arrivals were a handful of knights who had received and honoured the request to return to Malta and fight alongside their brothers.

Throughout April the defenders laboured hard to raise the height and depth of the walls and bastions that protected the promontories of Senglea and Birgu. In front of the wall, slaves and Maltese work gangs swung picks to break up the rocky ground and excavate a defensive ditch deep enough to hamper attempts to scale the walls. So short was the time and so desperate the need to bolster the defences that none was spared the duty of toil. The Grand Master, despite his advanced years, appeared every morning in a plain tunic and a strip of dark cloth tied about his brow, ready to work for two hours, breaking ground with a pick or joining the long chain of workers carrying baskets of rubble inside the walls of Birgu. All the knights and soldiers were required to do the same and the grudging indifference of the local people gave way to surprise and then respect as they found the sons of Europe's noblest families working alongside them. Within days they had taken to cheering La Valette when he appeared each morning and took up his pick or basket.

Buildings close to the walls that might be used by the enemy for shelter were demolished and the timbers and rubble taken into Birgu to add to the material set aside for repairs. Those made homeless by the destruction of their houses were given billets in the town. There was little problem accommodating them as a steady stream of the town's inhabitants with sufficient wealth to fund their temporary exile took ship for Sicily, Italy and Spain, there to await news of Malta's fate.

As April drew to an end all knew that the Turkish fleet would already be at sea, heading west. Orders were given for the farmers and villagers across the island to prepare to abandon their homes and seek shelter in Mdina, a fortified hill town that had once been the capital of the island, or within the walls of Birgu. No crops, cattle, goats, grain or fruit was to be left for the enemy to forage and preparations were made to foul the wells and cisterns with rotting animal carcasses and slurry. The Turks would find a waste-land waiting for them when they landed and would be forced to ship in their sustenance, or starve before the lines of the Christian defences.

At first Thomas, Richard and Sir Martin had been assigned to training the Maltese militiamen in the most basic of fighting skills. It had long been the policy of the Order to discourage the islanders from using weapons out of fear that the local people might be emboldened to rebel against the Order of knights that had been imposed on them. As a result the majority of them were strangers to swords, pikes and arquebuses and only a handful had ever worn any armour. There were some who had been selected to serve as soldiers of the Order and these assisted with the training and translated the commands into the local tongue that sounded more like Arabic than any European language to an unfamiliar ear. Indeed, the islanders, with their dark features and skin, looked more like Moors and Turks than Christians. Yet they were fanatic in their loyalty to the Church of Rome and hatred of the enemy who been preying on the Maltese for over a hundred years. They were keen to learn and were soon handling their weapons like experienced soldiers. Thomas had insisted that they should also be taught to use the arquebus, but such was the shortage of gunpowder that only three live firings were permitted once the militiamen had learned how to load the weapons.

Once the hurried training was complete, the English knights and their squires were allocated to the work party under Colonel Mas, one of the mercenaries recruited by the Grand Master. They were tasked with constructing the ravelin and rose at dawn to take a hurried breakfast before heading through the narrow streets to the quay. There they waited with the other soldiers and civilians for places on the boats ferrying the workers across the harbour to the landing stage below the fort. Outside the wall they were issued with picks and joined the slaves already at work cutting a ditch into the rock in front of the ravelin.

For most of the morning they worked in the shade, but as the rays of the sun reached down into the ditch, the heat added to the discomfort of the constant chinking of the picks, the swirling dust and the ache of tired limbs. The glare of the sun was harsh enough to make the men squint, and it steadily burned exposed skin as the workers swung their picks under the burden of their sweat-soaked tunics. At noon they climbed out of the ditch and slumped in the shade of the awnings. They took their midday meal from the boys who had emerged from the fort carrying pitchers of watered wine and baskets of bread and roundels of a hard goat's cheese made locally. These were handed to the soldiers and the Maltese while the slaves sat in the open and were fed warm gruel from a tureen, one ladle per man, slopped into battered leather cups. These were thrust into the soiled hands of each slave and, still chained in pairs, they squatted down to savour the paltry rations that kept them alive and able to work, and no more. They were barefoot and dressed in rags stained with their own filth. Unkempt hair hung in knotted locks about their bearded faces and their features were gaunt.

On the first day Richard had regarded the slaves with abject pity and when they had settled to eat he chewed slowly at his bread for a while before he spoke to Thomas.

'Those slaves, they look more like animals than men.'

Sir Martin chuckled as he chewed on a strip of salted

beef. He swallowed and cleared his throat. 'They're worse than animals, young Dick.'

He spoke loudly so that the nearest of the slaves would hear him. One of them, fairer skinned than the others, looked up at the insult and glared fiercely from beneath his matted locks of dust-grey hair but kept his silence.

'They're still humans,' said Richard.

Sir Martin shrugged. 'Whatever they are, they're the enemy, the enemy of our faith, and they would slaughter us without mercy had they the chance. And you, Dick, are a squire and you will treat me with due deference.'

'I am Sir Thomas's squire,' Richard replied.

'That is as may be, but you still call me "sir" when you address me.' Sir Martin turned to Thomas. 'You need to tame your squire, he lacks the necessary humility.'

Richard glanced at Thomas and the knight sighed.

'He's right, Richard. Remember your place and act accordingly. Else I will not be so tolerant. Understood?'

The squire nodded reluctantly.

'That said, a knight is required to show charity, even to his enemies.' Thomas rose stiffly and walked over to the nearest pair of slaves and stood over them. 'You understand some of our tongue, I think.'

The Muslim who had reacted to Sir Martin's insult looked up warily and then nodded.

Thomas held out the remains of the bread he had been eating. 'Here. Take it.'

The slave stared at the bread and chewed his chapped lips. Then, hesitantly, he reached a hand out and delicately plucked the hunk from Thomas's fingers. At once he began to tear at it, watching Thomas anxiously as if the knight might snatch the bread back without warning. The slave chained to him was a thin dark-skinned Moor who seemed to be in pain as his companion fed, and he began to make a pitiful keening noise. The other man paused for a moment and then tore what was left in half and gave a piece to his companion. The act surprised Thomas who had often witnessed the selfish levels to which slaves were driven by the need to survive. Compassion was a weakness that could kill a man.

'I gave you the bread, not him. Why did you share it?'

The slave looked up. 'Because I chose to . . . master. That is one freedom I still have.'

His accent was familiar and Thomas was curious to discover more about a slave who spoke like a native of England yet was a Muslim slave.

'Where are you from?'

'Tripoli, master. I was the bodyguard of a merchant, until his ship was captured by one of your galleys.'

'And how does a slave from Tripoli come to speak English?'

'I was born in Devon, master. On the coast.'

'Devon?' Thomas raised his eyebrows. 'Then what the devil are you doing here?'

The slave lowered his gaze as he spoke. 'I was nine when a corsair ship raided our village, master. They killed my father and several other men, and took the women and children to sell in the slave market at Algiers. I never saw my mother again. I was kept by the corsair captain. He raised me, trained me to fight and then sold me to the merchant.'

'And converted you to Islam?'

The slave nodded. 'It is my faith.'

Sir Martin spat with disgust. 'A traitor to your own kind is what you are!'

The slave flinched and seemed to shrink under the harsh rebuke.

Thomas squatted down in front of him. 'What is your name?'

'Abdul, master.'

'I meant your real name. Your Christian name?'

'My name is Abdul,' the slave said firmly. 'Abdul-Ghafur. I am no Christian. I am a Muslim.'

Thomas met his gaze and for a moment the slave stared back as a man, defiant and proud, before he wavered and slumped back into himself.

'Is there no part of you that remains from your previous life? After all, you still speak your mother tongue.'

The slave shrugged his bony shoulders. 'There are memories, but that was another life. Before I was shown the truth through the teachings of Mohammed, peace be upon him.'

'And yet this is the reward won by your faith.' Thomas gestured at the other wretched creatures hunched nearby. 'You have become a slave. Renounce Islam and you could be free, and return to your home in Devon.'

'There is no home for me there. The boy I was then is no more, Hospitaller. I am now Abdul. In due course I will be the master and you will be the slave. Then perhaps I might return your kindness and offer you a crust.'

Thomas smiled mildly. 'You think that the Sultan will take this island?'

'How can he not? He has God on his side. The faith of

226

his soldiers is stronger than yours, and those who fight with you. The outcome is certain and only a fool would doubt it. I, and the other Muslim slaves, will be set free. Those Christians who still live will be put in chains and sold in the markets of the Sultan. The leader of your Order will be executed and his head will be thrust upon a spear and mounted high enough for all in Istanbul to see and know that God is great.' The slave's eyes glittered with fanaticism as he spoke and there was a harsh, cruel edge to his voice. Then his expression softened and he addressed Thomas earnestly.

'Save yourself, while there is still time. Leave this place, master. What does it profit an Englishman to fight and die so far from home? Get out, before the iron fist of the Sultan closes around this rock and crushes it to dust.'

'You might ask yourself the same question. In any case . . .' Thomas scooped up a stone the size of a plum and held it up in front of the slave's eyes. Then he placed his other hand over the stone and clasped his hands together with all his strength, grimacing as the hard edges pressed into his palms. He held his hands there for a while before he relaxed with a gasp and eased them apart. The stone lay as before, and the skin of Thomas's hands was impressed with marks of its edges. 'There. The rock is unbroken and your Sultan shall be no more successful than I, when his fleet descends on Malta. Think on that.'

Thomas stood up and returned to his comrades. Sir Martin let out a deep laugh and clapped his hands together. 'Oh, that showed him. You put the cocky little beggar in his place, Sir Thomas. Well done!' He picked up a pebble and lobbed it at the slave who flinched as it bounced off his shoulder. 'You'll rue the day you ever betrayed England! *Mal si le das la fe falsa del Islam*, as they say in Spain.'

The slave who called himself Abdul-Ghafur glared back with cold loathing and muttered something under his breath before he looked down at his feet again. Sir Martin smiled with satisfaction and chewed another mouthful of cheese and bread before washing it down with a gulp of the watered wine. He regarded Thomas out of the corner of his eye for a moment before he cleared his throat.

'There's something I've been meaning to ask you, Sir Thomas. For some weeks now.'

'Oh?'

'Yes, well, it's about the, uh, circumstances relating to your leaving the Order a while back . . . some years before my time, you understand.'

'Really,' Thomas said evenly. 'What would you ask of me that you don't already know? I assume you have approached some of the other knights about my personal business.'

Sir Martin puffed his cheeks and tilted his head to one side. 'I have spoken to a few, yes. Of course there aren't that many fellows who were around in your day.'

'But enough to give you the necessary details, I'll be bound.'

'They were fairly tight-lipped, as it happens. All I got from them was that a woman was involved and there was something of a scandal and that you had brought dishonour on the Order.'

'Then you have it all. There is no more that needs to be said.' Thomas gestured towards the open sea. 'I think we have more pressing problems, Sir Martin. The Turks could be upon us at any moment. That is surely what we should be fixing our minds on. Not events from many years ago.'

The other knight opened his mouth to reply, paused briefly, then let out an exasperated breath and rose to his feet. 'Need to relieve myself. Back soon.' He turned and strode off across the stony terrain towards the shallow latrine ditch that had been dug a hundred paces beyond the ravelin's defence ditch. Thomas bit into what was left of his cheese ration and chewed on its woody texture. Opposite him Richard swept the crumbs off his tunic and glanced round quickly before he spoke in an undertone.

'I think it's time that you told me the whole story.'

'Why?'

'Because I need to know. If my mission here is to succeed then I have to be aware of any potential dangers, or advantages, that might affect the outcome.'

'And I suppose you might make good use of any information that might help you to have some kind of hold over me?'

'Of course,' Richard replied flatly. 'That is the nature of my employment.'

'Then have you ever questioned the ethics of that employment? Perhaps you should.'

'I serve Sir Francis, who serves Cecil, and both serve our Queen and country. Therefore my ethics are beyond reproach. And nothing will stand between me and my purpose here.'

'Come now, Richard. You are not quite the iron man you pretend to be. You are well trained, but your feeling for others has not been trained out of you. I saw that clear enough in the fight on the galley. And again just now when you considered the plight of that slave.' Thomas leaned over and tapped his squire's breast. 'You have a heart. Don't try and starve it of nourishment, else you will cease to be a man and become a mere device.'

Richard glanced over towards the latrine ditch where Sir Martin was already squatting down.

'Tell me exactly what happened, before he comes back,' he demanded.

'If I refuse?'

'Then you compromise my mission.'

'And what if I don't care about that?'

Richard smiled shrewdly. 'But you do care. I, too, can peer into another man's heart. If we fail to fulfil our task then many others will suffer. That is something you, Sir Thomas, will not conscience. So tell me what I want to know.'

There was a tense silence before Thomas bowed his head and thought. Little needed to be kept secret and in any case, he could surely find out the details if he was diligent in his enquiries. Thomas ordered his memories before he began. 'Very well. Some twenty years ago I was serving with one of the Order's galleys off the coast of Crete. La Valette was the captain. It was clear that he was destined for one of the senior posts in the Order and it was considered an honour to be chosen to serve on his galley. It had been an uneventful voyage, we had had no luck in finding any Turkish shipping. Then we put into a port on the south coast and discovered that a galleon had passed by the day before so La Valette set off in pursuit. By the time we tracked them down to an isolated bay further along the coast they had been joined by two corsair galleys. As you have seen, the Grand Master is not the kind of man who is discouraged by unfavourable odds, so he launched a surprise attack just before sunrise. We sank one galley and captured the galleon and the other galley. I was placed in command of the galley and ordered to return to Malta. It was as we were searching the hold that we came across a captive, a woman.' Thomas paused as he felt the familiar longing in his breast. 'Maria was the daughter of a Neapolitan noble and betrothed to the son of an aristocratic family on Sardinia. Her ship had been taken by the corsairs and she was to be held for ransom.'

Thomas looked at Richard, feeling foolish as he continued. 'I tell you I had never seen such a woman in my life. She was slight and darkly featured with the most beautiful brown eyes. It would not be honest to say that my first thought was of love. I was just flesh and blood, despite my vows to the Order – not that many knights strictly observed their vows. Indeed, I was not the only one captured by her charms. However, there was some spark of deeper affection between us from the outset. If you had a cynical nature you would no doubt be smiling at what you consider to be my naive feelings, scoffing at the folly of youth, but I tell you, with all my heart and experience of life, that she is the one real love I have ever known. I had never felt the fierceness of such feeling before then, and the barely endurable ache of it ever since. I tell you, Richard, love is forever balanced between a paradise of passion and infernal torment. That is its price . . . and it is the price I freely paid at the time and have regretted ever since.' Thomas winced and shook his head. 'No. That is not my regret. My regret is that I was not stronger.'

He was silent for a moment, struggling to restrain the rage and self-loathing that threatened to consume him.

'Go on,' Richard coaxed coldly. 'Tell all.'

Thomas gritted his teeth and snatched a deep breath with a soft hiss. 'We loved unwisely, and without restraint, during the summer months, while word was sent to her family that she had been found and was safe. We both knew the danger of what we did but could not master our desires. So we met in secret, or so I thought, until La Valette ordered me to cease contact with her. Of course I did not. And the inevitable happened. We were discovered together one night. I say discovered, but we were not. Maria had been spied upon and followed, by Sir Oliver Stokely, who had thought himself a rival for her affections because she had shown him kindness. But that had been her nature. She was kind to all. He considered it a token of something more, something he would have had, were it not for me. So he gathered some men at arms as witnesses and caught us together. We were arrested and taken before the Grand Master of the time.'

'And then?'

Thomas rubbed his brow. 'The fault is mine. I should have obeyed orders, and I should have been aware of the danger Maria faced as a consequence of our affections. Even La Valette could not save me from expulsion, and I would not save myself. I did not deserve any form of clemency, and I did not deserve her love. Because of me her life was ruined. Her family disowned her. I never saw her again. I was put on a galleon and taken to Spain and ordered never to set foot on Malta, nor attempt to find Maria. La Valette sent me one last private message, that he would attempt to have me recalled when the time was right. And so I waited. Year after year. Wondering if Maria lived, if I would ever be permitted to rejoin my comrades. My hopes dying by a tiny but incremental measure each day. Until the summons arrived.' Thomas breathed in deeply to release the tension in his chest. 'This is my chance for redemption. It is too late for me to make good what I did to Maria, but I might yet prove worthy of the life that has been given to me.'

Thomas glanced up and saw that Sir Martin was making his way back from the latrine ditch. There was little time left to say any more for the present. He turned back towards his squire but before he could speak the sharp blast of a trumpet cut through the still air. Up on the wall of the fort Colonel Mas leaned forward on his hands and bellowed, 'The break's over! Back to work!'

The slave overseers picked up their whips made from the dried penises of bulls and set about driving the slaves back on to their feet and down into the ditch. The other members of the work party stirred with weary groans, some still hurriedly finishing off their rations. Thomas placed his hand firmly on Richard's arm.

'Whatever happens here, do not dishonour yourself as I did. Whatever your masters have ordered you to do, only do what is right.'

'And how will I know that?'

'Trust your heart. Not your ambition.'

Richard shook his head with a look of pity and pulled

himself free of Thomas's hand and reached for his pick. 'I need neither heart nor ambition. I just do my duty. That is all that should concern a man. Perhaps if you had thought the same, you might have saved yourself from a life of torment, Sir Thomas.'

'Upon my soul!' Sir Martin puffed as he trotted up to them. 'A fellow needs a break long enough to eat and perform his ablutions, eh? This won't do.'

He glanced at them both, noting the sullen expression on the squire's face and the anxiety etched in Thomas's features.

'What? What's happened?'

'Nothing,' Thomas replied, forcing himself to tame his emotions. 'Nothing at all. Let's to work. We live in the shadow of the Turk and there's still much to be done.'

He took up his pick and set off after Richard. Sir Martin watched them for a moment, and quietly tutted to himself.

'What irks them so? By God, there's enough peril already without having private conflicts to settle.'

CHAPTER TWENTY

There was a surprise for them when they returned to the auberge that evening. Seated at the head of the long table in the hall was Sir Oliver Stokely, waited on by Jenkins. He looked up sourly from his platter of goat chops as the three men entered, faces streaked with grime and their clothes covered in dust from the ditch they had been cutting in front of the ravelin. There was a tense pause before Sir Martin broke the silence with a cheerful laugh.

'Sir Oliver, you've not been to the auberge in months! I had thought you had abandoned me forever.'

'I fear we may be obliged to endure each other's company a good deal more in the days to come. When the Turks arrive I will have to quit my estate near Mdina.' Sir Oliver gestured round the hall with his fork. 'Birgu will be my home for the duration of any siege, though it lacks the comforts I am used to.'

'It suits me well enough,' Sir Martin replied as he untied the cords of his tunic and pulled it over his head and tossed the garment to Jenkins who caught it deftly. 'Some food for the rest of us.'

'Yes, master.' Jenkins bowed his head then took the dusty tunics of the other two and retreated down the corridor towards the kitchen.

'Needless to say,' Sir Oliver continued, 'I am not overjoyed at the prospect of sharing accommodation with a knight who brought lasting shame upon the Order. But there is no helping it.'

Thomas shrugged. 'The past cannot be undone, no matter how much we both wish it.' He sat on the bench halfway down the table. 'Whatever once divided us should be set aside given the threat that faces us all, Sir Oliver.'

'It is no easy matter to overlook the shame that hangs upon you like a shroud,' the other knight replied coldly. 'As we both know, those who stand too close to you are bound to suffer. Perhaps it would be best if you left the island for good, Sir Thomas. Go now, while you still have the chance, and never return to plague us again.'

'Go?' Thomas cocked an eyebrow in mock surprise at the suggestion. 'I came in answer to a summons from the Grand Master himself. I was recalled to the Order. It is fit and proper that I am here. You talk of my past dishonour, but that would be nothing compared to abandoning my comrades at this dark hour.'

Sir Oliver's lips lifted in a sneer. 'I think we might do just as well, or as badly, without you. One knight and his squire cannot affect the outcome and will surely not be missed for more than a moment should they quit the island and return to England.'

'We are not leaving,' Richard intervened. 'Not me, nor the noble knight I serve.'

'Silence, whelp!' Sir Oliver's eyes widened angrily. 'Your squire speaks out of turn. He knows his place and his obligations as poorly as you know your own, Sir Thomas.'

'He is intemperate and foolish,' Thomas replied. 'But though he lacks some of the required obeisance before his betters, I value his courage and skill at arms. I believe that the present conflict will be the making of him and I would not deprive him of the honour of being here, any more than I would deprive myself, or you, or any of the few who stand their ground in the face of the many. However, he spoke out when he should have kept his silence and I apologise for his outburst. As will he.'

'Apologise?' Richard looked astonished. 'I will not.'

'You will!' Thomas rounded on him. 'Or I will have you flogged for insubordination, as I would have any squire flogged. Apologise. Now. I will not ask again.'

Sir Martin watched the exchange with a slight smile of amusement. 'A good squire needs regular beatings, I say.'

Richard flinched slightly at his master's anger and glared back defiantly, then lowered his eyes as he slowly turned towards Sir Oliver in silence. When he did not speak the knight tapped his fingers on the table.

'You have something to say to me, young man?'

The squire's shoulders dropped slightly as he answered in a strained voice, 'If it please you, sir, I beg to apologise for my intemperate manner. I have done you wrong in presuming to speak freely before my superior. For that I apologise, humbly.'

'Apology accepted. Now take your place at the bottom of the table and do not interrupt your betters again or, as Sir Thomas said, you will be flogged.'

'Yes, Sir Oliver,' Richard replied in as meek a manner as he could affect. He bowed his head and made his way to the bench at the far end of the long table and sat down.

Sir Oliver turned his attention back to Thomas. He was about to speak when Jenkins returned with three silver plates in one hand and a platter of cold meat and bread in the other. He set the plates down in front of the two knights and the squire, heaping each one with cuts of meat and hunks of bread. From a cupboard by the wall he fetched them a goblet each, together with a jug of watered wine, before making his way back towards the kitchen to await further instructions. As his footsteps receded, Sir Oliver gestured towards Sir Martin.

'I wonder what you would do in this situation.'

'Me?' Sir Martin looked puzzled. 'What situation?'

'I assume you know what it is necessary to know about the guilty past of Sir Thomas?'

Sir Martin glanced sidelong at Thomas but the latter's expression was fixed and unfathomable.

'Well now, I have heard a thing or two, yes. But I have known many knights who have sought the comfort of a wench.'

'The daughter of a Neapolitan noble is hardly a wench,' Sir Oliver replied coldly. 'As any decent gentleman would know. The Order is prepared to look the other way when a knight forsakes his vows to take his pleasure of a common slattern, but the despoiling of a woman of noble blood is another matter entirely and is intolerable. A man who did that is without honour and is unfit for the company of the other members of our sacred Order. If I were such a man I could not endure the shame of what I had done. I would quit Malta at once and take myself off into exile for what was left of my pitiful life. The question stands, Sir Martin, what would you do in the place of Sir Thomas?'

The knight shook his head warily and shrugged. 'It is not for me to say.'

'But it is,' Sir Oliver insisted. 'I am asking you quite directly.'

'I . . . I . . .'

'There is no need to ask Sir Martin,' Thomas interrupted. 'As a knight whose morals are not in question here, Sir Martin is not answerable to you, or for me. The matter ends there,' Thomas concluded firmly.

'Not for my part,' Sir Oliver replied through clenched teeth. 'I will not rest until you are exposed for the scoundrel you still are and punished in a fitting manner, or forced to quit this island.'

'Then you are condemning yourself to exhaustion, for I will not leave. Not until the Order has passed through the hour of its greatest peril or the Grand Master tells me to go.'

'Which he may, if I can persuade him to see reason.'

'La Valette sees well enough. The question is, does he see what you really are – a traitor to friends?'

Sir Oliver opened his mouth to reply, then clamped it shut as he struggled to contain his anger. At length he slumped back in his chair and swept his plate to one side dismissively.

'Very well. You have set your mind to staying. I wish it were not so with all my heart. I shall watch you closely, Sir Thomas, and pray that you find reason to disappoint the Grand Master.'

'It would be better to pray for salvation from the enemy.'

'If God wills it, we will be saved.'

'Then what is the point of prayer?' asked Thomas. 'And if I am to disappoint La Valette, then that is a matter for God to resolve, not you.'

For a moment the two knights stared at each other while Sir Martin quietly chewed on a morsel of meat, gazing fixedly at the surface of the table a short distance beyond his plate. Richard sat hunched forward, his jaw resting on his intertwined fingers. He was listening intently but did not dare to look up and risk catching anyone's eye.

'One day,' said Sir Oliver, 'you will finally reap what you have sown . . .' He breathed deeply. 'As I have not been able to persuade you to leave, I come to the purpose of my present visit to the auberge. It appears that Don Garcia offered the Grand Master some advice concerning the manner in which he conducts the defence of Malta.'

'That's right.' Thomas paused and nodded towards Richard. 'We were there.'

'Then you will recall that the Grand Master was advised to set up a war council, limited to a handful of men. It seems that you are to be one of this august body,' Sir Oliver concluded with thinly disguised scorn.

'Me?' Thomas raised his eyebrows. It was true that he had served five years in the Order, and several more as a mercenary fighting on the battlefields of Europe. He had also witnessed many sieges, in two of which he had been besieged. But there were bound to be many senior knights of the Order who would take offence at his preferment by the Grand Master. La Valette was taking a risk in offering the appointment. 'This is something of a surprise.'

'Quite. Naturally I advised against it. At present he has not told anyone else, in case you declined the offer.' Sir

Oliver leaned forward and stared intently at Thomas. 'You do not have to accept. In fact, it would be far better if you didn't. Better for all of us. Your appointment would be a divisive influence on the Order. This is your chance to go some way towards redemption, Thomas. You know that no good can come of it.'

'I still don't understand. Why does La Valette want me?'

'Aside from your considerable martial experience there are two reasons, one of which he explained. It is the Grand Master's view that the senior ranks of the Order are filled with ambitious men who might seek to use the present emergency to put their interests before the common good. They in turn are supported by factions within the Order. Such men cannot be permitted to indulge their political temptations. Whereas you have no constituency here. You are an outsider and therefore your opinions will not be guided by anything other than the need to defeat the Turks. In addition, as you will be serving alongside the more junior knights, you will be able to inform the Grand Master and the other members of the war council of the concerns and state of morale of the rank and file. That sums up the arguments he gave for choosing you.'

'That makes sense,' Thomas responded, then asked, 'What of the other reason?'

'It's simple enough. You always were one of his favourites. A protégé. When you were compelled to leave the Order, it greatly disappointed La Valette. It is my belief that he viewed you as a man views his son. And like any father, he was, and no doubt still is, blind to your most significant faults. In the years of your absence he frequently spoke of you with fondness,' Sir Oliver said bitterly. 'Now, at precisely the time when he needs sound judgement, he is giving rein to an old man's sentimental attachment to a prodigal son. It is foolish self-indulgence that speaks to him.'

'Yet the words he spoke to you are reasonable enough. I think you judge him on his age too severely.'

Sir Oliver pursed his lips. 'Maybe. But we shall see. The coming conflict will try us all to the utmost. Do you think a man of his years will long endure the demands heaped on his shoulders? And when the burden is too great and he buckles, then perhaps we shall require a new leader.'

'You perhaps?'

'Possibly. And if it should be me, then you can be sure that your special status here will come to an end and you will be treated no better than a common soldier. There will be many in the Order who will seek to punish you for your preferment at the whim of the Grand Master.' He smiled thinly. 'So what am I to tell him? Do you accept or decline his offer?'

'I accept.' There was no doubt in Thomas's mind about his answer. He was determined to serve his old mentor as well as possible and vindicate the faith La Valette had placed in him. Besides, the position might well help him and Richard locate the prize that Walsingham had sent them here to retrieve.

'I feared you would say that,' said Stokely. 'As ever you are prepared to put personal desires above the needs of others, and above the requirements of duty and honour. So be it. I tried my best to dissuade you and my conscience is clear. I will inform the Grand Master of your decision. That concludes my business here tonight.' Stokely stood up and bowed his head briefly to Sir Martin. 'Take care that you do not associate yourself too closely with this man. You may regret it, as others have had cause to.'

He picked up the cape hanging over the back of his chair and strode to the door. He stepped out into the street and a moment later there was the dull thud and clatter of the latch as the door closed.

Sir Martin let out a deep sigh of relief. 'Thought he was never going to go. The fellow was putting me off my food. Never have found him easy company, even on those few occasions when he has deigned to spend a night in the auberge.' He looked at Thomas. 'He doesn't seem to have much love for you, Sir Thomas.'

'It seems not.' Thomas picked up a thick slice of cured sausage from his plate and chewed slowly. In truth, La Valette's offer made him anxious. It was a great responsibility and he was determined not to betray the Grand Master's trust. In all aspects but one. Thomas glanced down the table and saw that Richard was watching him with a triumphant gleam in his eye. No doubt he was already scheming to turn the situation to his advantage.

Sir Martin concluded his meal speedily and noisily and wiped his mouth on the back of his hand before stretching his neck and sighed contentedly. He drained the last of his wine and smacked his lips.

'Ah, that's a good feeling. A decent meal after a hard day's labour. And now, sleep!' He rose stiffly, rubbing the small of his back. 'I bid you good night, gentlemen.'

Thomas nodded his response and Richard stood up and

bowed his head in dutiful respect. At the sound of Sir Martin's cell door closing behind him, Richard turned to Thomas with an intent expression.

'I had begun to fear that we might never find a way to gain entry to St Angelo without arousing suspicion. Now you have access to the Grand Master's lair you can get me into that dungeon. I have the description of De Launcey's chest, and the prize is sure to be inside. If it's done quickly we can quit this death trap before the Turks arrive.'

'Quit?' Thomas raised his eyebrows. 'I have no intention of leaving. Not now. I am needed here. Every man is.'

Richard stared at him. 'Are you mad? When the enemy lands on the island no one will be spared. They will pound all the forts into rubble and cut the throats of any survivors.'

'That is one possibility.' A smile passed fleetingly across Thomas's face. 'Or we make our stand and hold out until the Turks give up the attempt to reduce the island. That, or we are relieved by Don Garcia and the army he is gathering on Sicily.'

'You might as well wish for the moon.' Richard gave a hollow laugh. 'Don Garcia's force is only ever going to be a paper army. His king will not let him take any risks with what men he has, and I would wager my soul that less than half of the men and ships promised to him by the other powers will be forthcoming. There is no chance of the Turks turning tail. If Suleiman has ordered that Malta be reduced, then do you think for one instant that those to whom the command is given would dare risk his wrath if they failed?' Richard paused to see if his words had struck home but Thomas kept his silence and the younger man hissed with exasperation before he continued.

'Sir Thomas, I have been with you long enough to see that you are a good man. There is sure to be a place for you within Walsingham's service when we return to England having carried out our mission successfully. Don't throw your life away in some futile gesture.'

Thomas stirred. 'Firstly, this was never really *our* mission, just yours. I was simply the pretext to get you inside the Order. Secondly, this is no simple gesture, Richard. Whatever that precious document may turn out to be, there are times in a man's life when he must stand for something. When I was forced to leave the Order I lost my place in the world, as well as the woman I loved. Now she is gone, and all that I have left is the chance to do something right.'

'I thought you had grown tired of the Order's endless war.'

'And so I had. But the situation has changed. The very existence of these knights and the islanders who stand with them is under threat. If the Order is annihilated and Malta falls, you know well enough the danger posed to every Christian kingdom in Europe. Even England may fall under the sway of the Sultan. The coming battle is the very fulcrum upon which the fates of two civilisations are balanced. Even one man might make a difference to the outcome.'

'One man?' Richard shook his head. 'You have drunk too deeply at the well of the Order's fanaticism, Sir Thomas. That, or . . . perhaps I see a more simple truth. It is the Grand Master's offer to take you into his confidence that has clouded your judgement. You feel flattered by his request, and now you cannot face letting him down. Is that it?'

'There is some truth in that. But it matters not.' Thomas splayed his hand over his heart. 'All I know is that I must make my stand along with the rest of the Order. There is no reason to it. Just a certainty that brooks no doubt. I will stay and fight, and die, if that is my fate.'

'Then you disappoint me. I had taken you for a wiser, more rational man than that.'

'Well, I am content to disappoint you. But I will do what I can to help you complete your mission and escape before it is too late to flee, if you do not choose to fight at my side.'

Richard thought for a moment before he replied in a world-weary manner, 'I would count it an honour to fight at your side. Believe me. But I would not share a certain death without good purpose. I must let you have your glorious death alone, or at least in the ranks of your precious band of brothers.' He scraped the bench back and stood up. 'There is nothing more to be said. We can talk in greater detail on the morrow and plan our next step. Good night, sir.'

They exchanged a brief nod and Richard turned and strode off towards his cell, leaving Thomas alone in the hall decked with the mementos of the English knights who had devoted their lives to the Order. He stared up at the heraldic devices on the small wooden shields and the faded banners that hung from the beams. In his heart he knew, as surely as a man can know, that his decision to remain and fight with his comrades was the right and only path for him.

CHAPTER TWENTY-ONE

18 May

When he had listened to the strength returns of each of the garrison posts, and the report on the output of the gunpowder mills, the Grand Master rose from his chair and walked over to the window. His favourite hunting dogs, Apollo and Achilles, jumped up from beneath the table and padded over to their master. He reached down and stroked their silky ears as he stared out at the view from the keep of St Angelo, gazing over the thick walls and across the glittering blue water of the harbour towards the peninsula where the ridge of Sciberras dominated the small fort of St Elmo. It was a clear morning, the sky was a deep blue and the low rays of the sun washed the stone of the fort with a brilliant yellow hue. A light air lifted the flag of the Order flying from the mast above St Elmo so that the white cross on the red background fluttered lazily. The faint chink of picks from those working to deepen the ditches in front of the fort carried across the harbour. Despite the continuing preparations, the scene looked peaceful enough and the fair weather heralded the arrival of summer, and the dreadful heat that came with it.

From his chair Thomas scrutinised La Valette and saw that the hard work of the previous months, far from exhausting the Grand Master, had given him renewed strength and energy. He stood erect, and moved with purpose. Only the white curls of his hair gave indication of his true age, for his face, though weathered and creased, seemed to belong to a man fully ten or fifteen years younger, and his grey eyes gleamed beneath his heavy brows. Glancing to his side, along the line of chairs where the other members of the war council sat, Thomas noted that Romegas and Sir Oliver Stokely looked tired and tense. Only Colonel Mas seemed at ease. That could be misleading, though; the colonel was a professional soldier to his core and rarely showed any emotion except anger at any sign of inefficiency or laziness in the men under his command.

With a sigh La Valette turned away from the window and faced those he had chosen as his closest advisers, his eyes flicking over each man in turn before he spoke.

'I cannot accept that it will take at least another month before the defences of Birgu and St Michael are complete.'

Colonel Mas tipped his head slightly to one side. 'They would have been completed by now if you had given the order to start when I first arrived, sir. As I advised.'

'Thank you, Colonel, I remember. However, we cannot go back and change that. We must work the people harder. Add another hour to each shift. That applies to everyone, including me. Starting from this afternoon.'

'Yes, sir. I'll have my clerk draft the declaration after the meeting.'

'And what of the harbour chain?'

Romegas folded his hands together. 'It is set in place between the points of Senglea and Birgu. The ring bolts were secured to the sturdiest posts we could find to drive into the seabed and they in turn have been chained to the rocks on each shore. There is a small section in the centre where the chain can be slackened to allow for the passage of a galley, if that becomes necessary. Otherwise nothing but the smallest of boats will be able to get across the chain. The enemy's galleys will not be able to penetrate Dockyard Creek, sir.'

'Very good. That at least is one line of defence we can count on.' La Valette turned his attention back to Colonel Mas. 'Assuming that the enemy does decide to attack St Elmo first, there should be enough time to prepare the defences of Birgu and St Michael. With the unfinished condition of the fortifications on this side of the harbour it is essential that we delay the enemy at St Elmo. How long can the fort hold out?'

Mas thought for a moment before he responded. 'From the time the enemy invests the fort? Say ten days to cut approach trenches, then another two days to construct gun batteries. After that it's a question of how much weight their guns can throw against the walls before they create a breach large enough to risk an assault. With the poor design of the fort and the weakness of the ravelin, I'd say that the Turks will reduce St Elmo within three weeks.'

The Grand Master sighed with frustration. 'That's not long enough. If we need a month to complete the defences on this side of the harbour now, then that will only take longer once the enemy can harass our work parties. St Elmo must hold for longer than three weeks, whatever it costs.'

Mas puffed his cheeks. 'We can pack the fort with troops and should be able to ferry reinforcements over and evacuate the wounded under cover of darkness, and keep our men supplied with gunpowder and food if they run short. That's assuming that they hold out long enough to exhaust the thirty days of provisions we've already placed there.' The colonel paused. 'Of course, we must recognise that every man we feed into the fight for St Elmo is one man less to defend this side of the harbour when the enemy throw their weight against Birgu and Senglea. There will come a point where sending reinforcements will not affect the outcome.'

'Then what happens?' asked Sir Oliver.

'Then we must decide whether to evacuate the remaining defenders or permit them to surrender or order them to fight to the last.'

'I see.'

No man spoke for a moment as they considered the desperate nature of the coming struggle. It was the colonel who broke the silence. 'Given the importance of holding St Elmo for as long as possible, it would be prudent to place the fort under the command of one of our most experienced officers.'

La Valette returned to his chair and sat down, clicking his fingers and pointing to the floor. His dogs obediently hurried back beneath the table and lay down. 'I take it that you are volunteering for the position.'

'Yes, sir.'

'Even though you know the inevitable outcome? It will be a most desperate struggle, Colonel.'

'It is what you pay me for.' Mas gave one of his rare

smiles. 'And most generously, compared to some of my previous employers.'

'I knew that I needed to recruit the best for this battle,' La Valette replied with a gracious nod. 'But I would not care to risk losing you so early in the struggle. I would rather you remain here where your experience will be needed. We can settle the matter of the command of the fort later.'

'As you wish, sir.'

'There is something that occurs to me, sir,' Thomas intervened, immediately aware of the disdainful looks shot at him from Romegas and Stokely. He had soon grown used to their scorn for the junior member of the war council.

'Well?'

'We are assuming that the enemy will attack St Elmo first. What if they don't? What is our plan if they decide to assault Birgu or Senglea first?'

Romegas half turned towards him. 'That possibility was considered and discounted by Don Garcia when he inspected the defences and gave his advice to the Grand Master. The Turks will make it a priority to secure a safe anchorage in the Marsamxett harbour, and complete the encirclement of Birgu and Senglea. As I recall we all accepted his reasoning and have planned accordingly.'

'That is so,' Thomas conceded. 'But the question remains, what do we do if the Turks strike at the fortifications on this side of the harbour first?'

'And why would they do that?' Romegas asked scathingly. 'It makes sound tactical sense to take St Elmo first.'

Stokely cleared his throat and interjected, 'Grand Master, this kind of comment is further proof of Sir Thomas's ineptitude in military matters and, again, I question his fitness for membership of this council.'

'I second that,' Romegas added.

'Enough!' La Valette slapped his hand down on the table. 'I will not have you question my decision over the inclusion of Sir Thomas. Do not raise the matter again.'

'In any case, Sir Thomas is right,' said Colonel Mas. 'Just because it makes sense for your enemy to proceed in a certain manner does not mean that he will do so. We need to be ready to respond to any contingency, sir. However unlikely.'

La Valette thought for a moment and then nodded. 'Very well, Colonel. Then I want you to draft a plan for us to meet such a threat. You can present it at tomorrow's meeting.'

'Yes, sir.'

The Grand Master turned to Stokely. 'Which brings me to our final matter. The preparedness of the rest of the island.'

Stokely bowed his head in acknowledgement and quickly glanced over the list of notes on the sheet in his lap before he responded. 'The Mdina garrison reports that all is prepared. Most of our cavalry has transferred into the stables of the citadel. There's enough fodder for six months. The cisterns are almost full and the town is provisioned for the same period. The knight you appointed to take command, Pedro Mesquita, has moved into the citadel with his staff and has orders to use his cavalry to harry the Turks whenever the opportunity arises.' Stokely looked at

Thomas. 'Assuming that the enemy does not decide to attack Mdina first, that is.'

'They will be coming to take the harbour and destroy the Order,' Thomas replied patiently. 'Mdina lies in the heart of the island. It is irrelevant to the enemy's main purpose.'

'Sir Thomas is right,' La Valette cut in. 'Please continue.'

Stokely frowned briefly before he turned to his notes again. 'I have managed to evacuate some of the population of Mdina but most refuse to leave their homes and farms. Some even within my own household have been adamant that they will not leave, even when encouraged in the strongest terms.' He glanced quickly at Thomas. 'Those that remain have yet to obey the directive to harvest their crops early and move their grain and animals into the city. The same is true of the farmers close to the harbours. And so far no steps have been taken to make the wells unusable.'

As he had been speaking, the Grand Master's expression had darkened and now he raised a hand to stop Stokely.

'This is not acceptable. The people mistake my instructions for advice. My directives are not to be flouted. This is your responsibility, Sir Oliver. See to it that those peasant fools are made to do as I command. I want the last of them safely billeted within our walls before the week is out. Then their farms are to be torched and their wells poisoned and not a living thing or a handful of grain is to be left in place to offer shelter or food to the Turks. Is that clear? Use force to ensure that it happens if that becomes necessary. I will have complete discipline over the islanders as well as my soldiers. It is the only way we shall all survive what is to come. Tell them that, and brook no protests. If you can't enforce my orders then I shall have to find a knight who can.'

Stokely nodded, his face flushed with shame at having been so roundly criticised in front of the others. 'I will do as you command, Grand Master. At once.'

La Valette's stern expression gradually softened and when he spoke again his voice was gentle. 'Sir Oliver, you are a fine administrator. I have known no equal in all my years in the service of the Order. But we are no longer waging war against the enemy's trade routes – they are bringing the war to us. Your skills are needed as never before but the people you command will need a firm hand. They will look to you for orders and inspiration and you must assume a steadfast countenance. From now on, everyone is a combatant under my direct command, and military discipline will be applied. There are no longer any civilians on Malta. Every man, woman and child must play their part in defending the island. Do you understand?'

'Yes, Grand Master. I apologise, sir. I will not disappoint you again.'

La Valette smiled warmly and was about to speak when the flat roar of a cannon sounded in the distance, then again, and a third time. Before the sound had died away, every man in the room was on his feet and hurried across to the window.

'Where did the shots come from?' La Valette demanded, straining his eyes as he looked towards the open sea. Beside him Thomas was also scanning the strip of horizon that was visible between Gallows Point and the tip of the Sciberras peninsula. As yet there was nothing to see, just the flat line separating the sea from the sky.

'It came from beyond St Elmo,' decided Colonel Mas. 'The signal guns at one of the observation stations.'

Even as he spoke there was a flash from the keep of St Elmo, and a jet of smoke and flame ripped through the morning air. A second cannon was fired and a moment later the sound of the first echoed off the walls of St Angelo. As the third gun fired, there was no longer any doubt about the reason for the firing of the signal guns. La Valette drew a deep breath and continued to stare out across the harbour as he addressed the members of the war council. 'The enemy has arrived . . .'

THE TWO MAIN HARBOURS OF MALTA SHOWING
THE LOCATION OF THE ORDER'S DEFENCES

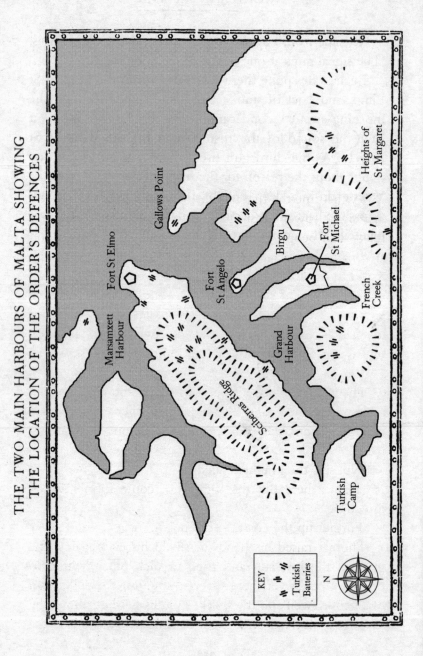

CHAPTER TWENTY-TWO

By the time the five men had climbed to the top of the signal tower of St Angelo, the streets of Birgu were filled with people running for the walls of the town and any natural vantage point to see the approach of the Turkish fleet for themselves. Thomas was the first to reach the platform and saw one of the younger knights in the company of an elderly-looking soldier staring intently towards the eastern horizon. A faint dawn haze still lingered out to sea, concealing the separation of sea from sky.

'Do you see them?' asked Thomas.

The two men looked round and then stood to attention as they spied the Grand Master and the other senior officers emerging from the staircase behind Thomas, breathing hard.

'No, sir,' the knight replied.

'Then where did the signal fire come from? Which direction?'

'Further up the coast, to the north.'

Thomas raised his hands to shield his eyes against the glare of the low sun and tried to pick out anything in the haze, but as yet there was nothing, just the dull gleam of a gentle swell and the specks of gulls swirling above the surface as they fed on a shoal of fish. La Valette and the others joined him along the waist-high wall and stared into the distance. In the background the same pattern of signal guns rumbled as the warning spread along the coast and inland. Besides the occasional sound of cannon, a hush had descended on the island. The usual hubbub rising from the narrow streets and the faint sound of picks had died away and there was a stillness as the men of the Order and the islanders waited for the first sight of the enemy. It felt to Thomas as if the world around him was holding its breath, waiting for the sign that would forever change the lives of those caught in the thrall of that moment.

Sir Oliver hissed, 'If some fool has raised a false alarm I'll have him flogged . . .'

'There!' The old soldier thrust his arm out and pointed to the north-east. At once the other men's heads turned to stare in the direction indicated, trying to pierce the haze for a sign of the enemy ships.

'Where?' La Valette growled. 'I see nothing.'

'I see it now,' said Thomas. 'There, just beyond the end of Gallows Point. A sail.'

Stokely muttered, 'Just as long as it isn't a single ship, or even a flotilla of corsairs setting out on a raid.'

'We'll know soon enough,' Romegas said, then looked towards the old soldier with an openly impressed look. 'Your eyes are keen. Especially for one of your age. What is your name?'

'Balbi, sir.' The man bowed his head. 'Francisco Balbi.'

'Italian, eh?' Romegas sized him up. 'One of the mercenaries recruited by the colonel then?'

Mas glanced over at Balbi. 'Yes, you were the one claiming to be a poet as well as a soldier of fortune.'

'That's right, sir.'

'A poet?' Romegas chuckled. 'Well then, Balbi, I'll wager you'll find enough material for an epic in the days to come. Make us all famous, eh?'

'Enough!' the Grand Master snapped. 'I can't see any damned ships. Where are they?'

Thomas was surprised by the anxious tone in La Valette's voice and deliberately responded as calmly as he could. He raised his hand and pointed directly towards the single vessel that was visible. 'There, sir . . . And there . . . Oh . . .'

As if a fine silk veil had been stealthily drawn aside, the first sail was suddenly joined by others, one by one, until scores of them appeared on either side, spreading out along the edge of the fading haze.

'Good Lord,' Sir Oliver muttered.

The others kept their silence, as did the knights, soldiers and civilians pressed together along the walls of St Angelo and every vantage point of Birgu. Across the harbour Thomas could see the heads and shoulders of men lining the walls of the fort. Several had climbed up on the parapet for a better view.

It was La Valette who broke the spell on the tower. He lowered the hand that had been shielding his eyes and turned abruptly towards his advisers. 'There's no question of it. That's the invasion fleet. It's too big for anything else. We must not tarry. The first enemy troops could be ashore well before nightfall. Every civilian has to be safely behind walls before then. Sir Oliver, you will take charge of that with respect to Birgu and Senglea.' He turned to Romegas. 'You will ride to Mdina and inform Mesquita of the situation and ensure he clears the centre of the island. Colonel Mas, take a party of horsemen and see to it that as many of the wells are spoiled as possible. And fire any farms or buildings you encounter, anything that can provide shelter to the enemy. Be back here by nightfall.'

'What of the estates?' asked Sir Oliver. 'Surely you can't mean to destroy them as well?'

'The estates particularly. Would you want to return to your home after it had been despoiled by some Turkish officer and his companions?' La Valette did not wait for a reply and turned to Thomas. 'You will take a boat across to St Elmo and ensure that the garrison is ready to fight. Also, there are bound to be many islanders who make straight for the fort. I gave orders for all to make for Mdina, Senglea and Birgu, but some will panic and make for the closest shelter. There's no space for them at St Elmo and they will need to be ferried across the harbour before the Turks make that impossible. See to it.'

'Yes, sir.' Thomas nodded.

La Valette took a last look at the horizon, squinting as he struggled to make out the vast force bearing down on the coast. Hundreds of vessels were now visible: galleys, galleons and many smaller cargo vessels, a clear sign of the Sultan's determination to take the island and obliterate the Order of St John that had plagued the Islamic world for the past three centuries. The Grand Master took a deep breath.

'You have your instructions, gentlemen. May God have mercy on us all. Now go.'

★ ★ ★

The garrison of the fort were still standing watching the approaching fleet when Thomas and Richard entered St Elmo. The small courtyard was piled with baskets of apples and oranges, sacks of flour, roundels of cheese and kegs of gunpowder just arrived from the powder mills on Senglea. Thomas's brow furrowed as he beheld the disorganised scene and he stopped a small party of Spanish troops crossing the courtyard to get a better view of the enemy from the keep.

'You there! Why are all these supplies still left out? Get them into the storerooms at once! Where is your commander?'

One of the sergeants who was with the party pointed towards the keep. 'Up there, sir. I saw Don Miguel on the tower.'

'Right.' Thomas gestured towards the kegs of gunpowder. 'Start with that before some panicky fool sets the lot off.'

Thomas left the sergeant to bark out his orders and strode across the courtyard to the entrance of the keep. There was a large hall beyond the door where several long tables were still littered with the meals abandoned when the signal guns had sounded across the island. A serving boy was busy filling his pockets with bread rolls and looked up guiltily as the knight and his squire entered.

They hurried past him, through the arch, and found a short passage ending where the stairs climbed up in a series of flights. At the top, fully a hundred men were crowded along the parapet, gazing out to sea. Some wore the red surcoats with the white cross of the knights of the Order. There was no time to single out the commander and

Thomas cupped a hand to his mouth and bellowed, 'Don Juan de La Cerda! Don Juan!'

Faces swivelled round towards the shout, some with startled expressions. A knight stepped back from the parapet and approached Thomas.

'I am Don Juan de La Cerda.'

He was one of the older knights, thin and gaunt with a fringe of grey-streaked hair around a bald crown. He frowned as he looked Thomas over. 'Who are you? I've not seen your face before.'

'Sir Thomas Barrett.'

The knight's eyes widened as he recognised the name. 'The English knight.'

'One of them.'

'The one who has been much on everyone's lips since he arrived.'

Thomas ignored the comment. 'I am here on the authority of the Grand Master to take charge and ensure that the fort is ready for action.'

There was a brief look of surprise before La Cerda responded with a haughty air. 'My garrison is ready. We don't need you.'

'Ready?' Thomas shook his head. 'The courtyard is in chaos, and soon a small horde of terrified locals are going to come pouring through your gate seeking shelter – while you and your men sit here and take in the scenery.' He spoke loudly so that all might hear his words and the scorn in his tone. 'Ready? If this is what you consider ready then the battle is already as good as lost. The Grand Master needs you and your men brought to order at once, Don Juan. I want half your men clearing the courtyard. Everything must be placed in the storerooms before the Turks land. The other half of the garrison is to form into parties and leave the fort and gather in every civilian between here and the approaches to Mdina. If they are too old, or infirm, then your men will carry them. They are to bring back any useful tools and portable stocks of food that they find. Anything else is to be destroyed. Leave nothing that will be of use to the Turks. Understood?'

La Cerda hesitated. 'By what authority do you give such orders?'

'I told you. The Grand Master sent me.'

'You say.'

'There is no time to lose.' Thomas stepped closer to the knight. 'If you waste another moment then I assure you that the Grand Master will strip you of command of this fort and find you a post worthy of your indolence. I suggest you obey my orders without further delay. I will not warn you again.'

Don Juan stared back briefly and then his gaze wavered. Abruptly he turned round and shouted the necessary orders. The sergeants drove the men down the staircases at each end of the platform, leaving a handful on watch duty and the two knights and squire.

'You had no right to speak to me in such a manner in front of my men,' La Cerda hissed furiously.

'And you have no right to be in command of your men if you can't do what is required of you. Now, while the orders are carried out I want you to accompany me while I inspect the fort. Provide my squire with paper and a pen to take notes. Richard?'

'Sir?'

'You will record my findings and recommendations for each post in the fort.'

'Yes, sir.'

'Then show us to your quarters, Don Juan. As soon as my squire has his materials we can begin.'

The last shred of La Cerda's defiance melted away and he nodded and turned to lead them down the nearest staircase. Thomas strode after him, too angry to feel much satisfaction at having faced the other man down. Before they reached the head of the stairs, he paused to take one last look at the Turkish fleet. The sun had risen high enough to bathe the island in its warm rays and out to sea the last of the haze had disappeared to reveal the full scale of the invasion force. It seemed as if the entire horizon was covered with the sails and hulls of vessels, now little more than five miles from the coast, arragned in a giant crescent across the surface of the sea. Thomas's lips lifted in a brief smile at the appropriateness of the enemy's formation, and then he hurried down the stairs.

For the rest of the day the garrison laboured to clear the courtyard. La Cerda followed meekly as Thomas toured the fort and dictated notes about the number of men allocated to each position, the siting of the fort's cannon and the ground covered by each weapon's firing arc. He questioned La Cerda on where the ammunition would be stored and what arrangements had been made for its replenishment once the siege began. He also demanded to know the arrangements for the treatment of the wounded and their evacuation to Birgu if communication with the other side of the harbour could be kept open.

At noon the first of the civilians began to enter the fort and Thomas and Richard stood above the gate and watched as an extended stream of humanity anxiously hurried along the dusty track that ran along the peninsula, just below the crest of the ridge of Sciberras. In the distance thin trails of smoke billowed into the air above glittering flames as buildings and stocks of food were fired by the parties sent out from the fort.

The people were ushered into the courtyard, their expressions anxious. Some of the children were crying as they clung to their parents. They had been raised on stories of the terrifying raids that the corsairs had made on the island and how families had been captured and sold as slaves, torn from each other's arms forever. Only those too young to understand the danger wore smiles and laughed cheerfully at the exciting break from the usual routines of daily life. Older members of the family were helped by their kinfolk while some were bodily carried. A few brought livestock with them: a handful of goats, mules and large cane cages with chickens inside. The smaller animals were permitted to enter the fort, but Thomas knew that there would be no space within for the larger beasts, and in any case the garrison could not afford to feed them. They were taken from their owners at the gate and led round the corner of the fort and killed. Many animals were hurriedly butchered and chunks of meat tossed into barrels of brine ready to be added to the garrison's stores. But the carcasses of the dogs and mules were thrown into the sea.

Early in the afternoon Thomas's attention was drawn to a small party approaching along the track on foot. Their clothes were of good quality and he realised that this must be the household of one of the island's estates. The party was led by a stout figure carrying a staff. Behind him came a handful of women in headscarves, led by a tall figure in a green cloak.

Richard chuckled. 'There's nothing like fleeing from an enemy to erode the most obvious distinctions between the common people and their betters.'

'Oh, they'll do well enough for themselves, you can be sure,' Thomas responded.

Both men continued to watch for a moment, and Thomas found his gaze drawn to the tallest of the women who carried herself with an air of authority, slightly apart from the rest. As they came within a hundred paces of the gate he felt some memory stir deep within his mind. The detail eluded him for a moment, and he was aware of a vague, unsettling feeling in the pit of his stomach. He strained his eyes but the distance was too great. Yet there was a growing sense of recognition and he felt a cold shiver ripple down his spine, even as his pulse quickened. His fingers clutched the edge of the parapet tightly and he craned his neck forward, staring.

Beside him Richard turned to him with a puzzled look. 'What is it, Sir Thomas?'

Thomas opened his mouth to reply but his jaw just hung slackly. Then the woman raised her face, framed by dark, unadorned tresses of hair, to look over the fort as she approached, and Thomas shuddered in a turmoil of denial and hope.

'It's her . . . Sweet Jesus, it's her . . . Maria.'

CHAPTER TWENTY-THREE

'Maria?' Richard started. 'Impossible. She's dead. Stokely said so. How can she be alive?'

'That's her,' Thomas replied simply. 'As sure as I live.'

'Where?'

Thomas raised his hand and pointed. 'The woman in the green.'

The finery of her clothes marked her out from the procession of frightened islanders and Richard picked her out at once. She was still some fifty yards away. 'You must be mistaken.'

Thomas did not reply at once, fearing that Richard was right, and that he had allowed his deepest desire to see her again trick him. He stared hard, and his certainty that this was Maria grew with every step she made towards the gate. There was only one way to tell for certain and before he knew what he was doing, Thomas turned away from the parapet and strode across to the stairs leading down into the passage behind the gate.

'Sir Thomas!' Richard called after him. 'Wait.'

He ignored the squire and quickened his pace, his boots echoing off the stone walls of the staircase. A hand grasped his shoulder. It was Richard.

Thomas shook him off and continued down the steps.

'What are you going to do?' Richard called after him but made no attempt to follow.

Thomas did not know, only that he had to be certain. Already the doubt was creeping back in and he dreaded the deadening blow to his heart should he be wrong. He emerged into the gloomy passage at the bottom of the stairs and saw that it was filled with people streaming past from the main gate. The woman and her retinue could not yet have reached the gate, Thomas reasoned. He stepped to one side of the passage and waited, his heart beating swiftly and a light, almost giddy feeling filling his head.

Then the man carrying the staff came out of the shadow of the passage. A moment later there was the woman and now he could see the fine patterns of green lace sewn on to her cloak. Her hair hung down over her shoulders, showing faint streaks of grey. She paused, not more than five paces from him, and looked around the interior of the fort. Her eyes, dark and piercing, passed over Thomas and the parties of soldiers carrying off the last of the supplies that had been heaped in the courtyard that morning. Lastly she looked with pity on the frightened huddles of civilians squatting on the flagstones, some openly crying with despair. The small group of servants who had been following her caught up and were pressed on by those behind, and their mistress stepped forward into the courtyard.

The image of Maria that Thomas had carried in his mind for over twenty years was not that of this woman, yet there were enough similarities to feed his burning desire for it to be her. He felt the urge to call out her name, but he could not bring himself to and thereby shatter the possibility that this was her. The woman took several more paces, each one slower than the last, until she stopped and stood quite still. Despite the people filing past either side of her, including those of her household, a sense of stillness bound her to Thomas and he was blind to the swirl of detail that surrounded them both, and deaf to the voices of the soldiers and the sobs of the civilians. Slowly she turned round and then, as if not quite daring to meet his gaze, her eyes tracked across the flagstones that separated them and up his body towards his face. Her lips moved slightly as she stared at Thomas.

All doubt was banished now and Thomas slowly paced towards her and stopped at arm's length, not knowing what to say. What words could express twenty years of longing that had warred with the need to accept that the past could never be revisited?

'Thomas . . .' she said softly.

He half smiled, then caught himself and nodded. 'Yes.' Then he smiled again. 'Yes . . . Maria.'

Her expression was filled with shock and bewilderment. 'How can it be? How is it possible?'

He wanted to hold her, felt that he should, yet it was so long since they had last touched that it seemed he had forgotten how to and did not dare do the wrong thing and risk a rebuff. But he must say something.

'I have been recalled. La Valette sent for me. I came back, from England. I had hoped, prayed, to see you again.'

At once there was a frightened look in her eyes, as if she had suddenly discovered herself to be standing on the edge of a precipice. For an instant Thomas dreaded that she was going to recoil from him, turn away and flee. But the expression swiftly faded from her face and she smiled uncertainly.

'Now you see me.' She held out her hands.

Thomas glanced at the fingers, still slender as he remembered them but now there were small creases and a slight waxiness to the skin that told of her age. Nonetheless, he took a half pace towards her and took her hands in his, and felt a tremor run through him at the cool softness of her flesh.

'I was told you had died,' he said without thought.

'Dead?' She laughed. 'No. Quite alive. For the present. And you? I have often wondered what became of you once you left. I imagined that you had returned to that estate you spoke of. Found yourself a wife perhaps, and had a family.' She spoke with forced cheerfulness.

'No wife and no family. But I have my estate at least.'

The stilted conversation was like a dam holding back a deluge of questions, declarations and things that demanded to be said.

'I thought of you often,' said Thomas. 'Every day.'

She smiled, then the smile faded and she released her light hold on his fingers and let her hands fall back to her sides and shook her head. 'I tried to forget you. I tried . . .'

'Sir Thomas!'

The shout instantly drew him back from the seething turmoil of emotions and he turned to see La Cerda hurrying across the courtyard towards them. A servant in a dark tunic with the white star of the Order on his breast followed at his heels. Thomas was torn between his need to hold on to this fragile link with Maria and his duty. He glanced at her pleadingly.

'Stay there, just a moment, I beg you.'

Maria nodded and Thomas turned to La Cerda. 'What is it?'

'A message from Birgu.' La Cerda indicated the servant. 'Speak.'

'Yes, sir.' The servant drew a breath as he tried to stand erect and deliver his instructions. 'The Grand Master sends his compliments and requests that you return to St Angelo at once, sir.'

'At once?' Thomas frowned. He glanced anxiously at Maria. 'But I am not finished here. There is still work to be done.'

'Sir, the Grand Master demands your presence,' the servant insisted.

La Cerda could not help a thin smile. 'You have your orders, Englishman. I think I can take charge of my own command again. I thank you for your assistance. Now, you'd better go.'

Thomas gritted his teeth and then nodded. 'A moment.'

He turned away and stepped towards Maria. 'You heard. I have to go. But I must see you again as soon as possible. We need to talk.'

'Talk?'

'Of course, there is so much I want to say, so much I want to hear. Say you will speak to me.'

'Very well.'

Thomas glanced round the courtyard and saw the door to the small chapel. 'Take shelter in there. I will come and find you as soon as I can. I swear it.'

He took her hand and pressed it tenderly, feeling the tremor in her flesh and the flush of heat in his breast.

'Sir Thomas, please,' the servant said. 'We must go.'

He released her hand and spoke softly so that only she might hear. 'I will be back.'

She nodded and turned away, gesturing to her small retinue to accompany her to the chapel. Thomas watched her briefly and a moment later Richard appeared from the entrance to the tower. He stood to one side, a short distance away, and glanced at Maria's back with a calculating expression.

As the boat crossed the harbour, Thomas willed himself not to turn and look back, as if in the hope of seeing Maria standing at the parapet gazing after him. Despite his stillness, his mind was a chaos of memories and wild hopes. It shocked him that even at his age, with all that he had experienced and the hardened outlook to the world that he had made himself adopt, he was still so easily filled with the wild emotions and unrealistic ambitions of youth. It seemed that the old adage was true: a man only grew older, not wiser.

Beside him Richard also sat in silence, unnaturally still, no doubt marshalling his thoughts at this unexpected turn of events. When the younger man finally spoke, as the boat drew close to the looming mass of St Angelo, Thomas could not help a weary resentment at the inevitable probing into his past, and his heart.

'Why did Sir Oliver lie about her?'

Thomas shrugged. 'Revenge perhaps. He knew that I would grieve at the news of her death.'

Richard reflected a moment. 'The question is, does her presence in any way affect our real purpose in being here?'

'Why should it?'

'It has made the situation more complicated for you, and I need your help in getting into the archives. I do not welcome any distractions.'

'I will hold to my part,' Thomas replied.

'Just promise me that you will not be reckless with your life before I have secured what I came for.'

'That rather depends on the Grand Master. We shall know his will soon enough.' Thomas turned and pointed out to sea. The white sails and dark hulls of the Turkish fleet were only a few miles off the coast and they had altered course to the south and were sailing slowly past the mouth of the harbour, well beyond the range of any of the cannons mounted on the walls of the Order's forts. 'And it depends on them.'

Richard placed the tip of his thumb between his teeth and thought on. The boat rounded the rocks of St Angelo and the oarsman pulled towards the small jetty at the foot of the fort.

'What do you intend to do about the woman?'

Thomas shook his head. 'I have no idea. It is hard enough to countenance the fact that she is alive and she is here. I must speak to her and find out what is in her heart. It has been many years, and our parting was not on happy terms. For all I know her affections for me may have dimmed long ago. I can only see her again and discover the truth.'

'And if the truth is that she still . . . loves you?'

Thomas frowned. 'I honestly don't know. If I have been given a chance to put right those wrongs that I have carried on my conscience then I will, with full heart.'

'And if her affections are no longer yours to have, what then?'

Thomas turned to him with a wry expression. 'Do you think I would lose the will to live? You forget, I have long since grown used to the idea of merely living. And now I have things to live for. The Order and Maria. I pray that I may save them both and live to enjoy the satisfaction of having done so. Does that put your concerns to rest, Richard?'

'For now.' Richard turned his gaze towards the open sea. ''Tis a pity that I failed to complete my mission before the trap closed.'

The oarsman backwatered one blade and pulled hard with the other and the small craft turned beam on at the last moment and rubbed gently against the tarred ropes alongside the jetty. The servant sent to fetch Thomas leaped on to the jetty, mooring rope in hand, and tied it securely to a post before helping the knight and his squire ashore. Thomas brushed down the creases in his cloak and gestured to Richard to follow him up the narrow flight of stairs leading up into the fort.

The Grand Master was in his study with several other knights, clustered about the window as they watched the main body of the Turkish fleet inching across the calm sea. The rearguard was still some miles to the north and would not pass the harbour for some hours yet. Thomas indicated to Richard to remain with the handful of squires and servants waiting outside the office.

'There must be at least three hundred ships,' Thomas heard one of the knights estimate as he approached.

'At the very least,' a taller man replied, whom Thomas recognised as Marshal de Robles, the senior military officer of the Order and one of the men who had been a rival to La Valette before the latter had been elected to the post of Grand Master. Thomas had expected to see Stokely in attendance as well but there was no sign of him. When La Valette caught sight of Thomas he nodded discreetly and then turned to address them all.

'The enemy is making for the south of the island. It is clear that they intend to land in Marsaxlokk Bay, or some of the smaller inlets along the adjoining coast. We can't hope to prevent them gaining the shore but we can try to delay them. Accordingly, I have given the order for Marshal de Robles to take a thousand men and shadow the enemy fleet as it passes along the coast.' He faced the marshal. 'You may fall on any attempt to land but you are not to risk a general engagement. Strike quickly, kill as many as you can, and then fall back before they can be reinforced. Is that clear?'

'Yes, sir. But the men's blood is up,' de Robles added. 'They will want to test themselves against the enemy as soon as they can.'

'Then it is your duty to restrain them. They will have their chance to prove their valour soon enough.'

'Yes, sir. I will keep them firmly in hand.'

'See that you do.' La Valette indicated another of his knights, a striking-looking man with shoulder-length blond hair. He looked to be no more than thirty and wore a neatly clipped moustache. He smiled as the Grand Master singled him out.

'Chevalier La Rivière. You have been tasked with

commanding a smaller, separate force of mounted men. It will be your job to ambush and harass the enemy once they have come ashore and the marshal falls back to Birgu. You, too, must take no unnecessary risks. I just want the enemy to think that we have men waiting behind every rock and wall on the island to fall on them and cut their throats. This contest will be as much a battle of nerves as it is a conventional siege, and subterfuge and trickery will have as much a part to play as courage and skill at arms.' He paused and looked round at his officers. 'This will be a fight to the death. Outnumbered as we are, the only route to victory is to maintain the will to resist longer than the Turks can maintain the will to conquer. Make no mistake, this struggle will be as bitter, savage and brutal as any in history.'

He let his words sink into the minds of the other men before he turned his attention back to La Rivière. 'There is one other purpose you and your men must achieve besides unnerving the enemy's scouts. We need some prisoners to interrogate. Capture a handful and bring them back here for questioning. We need detailed intelligence on the strength and intentions of our enemy as soon as possible.'

'It will be my pleasure, sir.' La Rivière grinned.

'I am sure. You will take Sir Thomas Barrett as your second-in-command. He once showed a useful disposition for this kind of work in the past. I am sure his old instincts will reawaken with such an opportunity. Listen to his advice, La Rivière. There are few knights better than you on horseback, and your men would follow you into the jaws of death itself if you asked them to. However, you have an impetuous side to your nature and require a moderating influence, and that is the role of Sir Thomas. You both understand?'

Thomas and La Rivière nodded.

'Are there any questions, gentlemen?'

Thomas spoke up. 'Yes, sir. When do we leave?'

'Hah!' La Valette laughed deeply. 'Can't wait to test yourself against the Turk, eh? Marshal de Robles will be leading his men out of the gates of Birgu within the hour. You and La Rivière will move out three hours before dawn so that you can set your ambush under cover of darkness.' He looked at each of them in turn. There were no more questions. 'Good luck, gentlemen, and God be with you.'

Marshal de Robles led his men out of the office and La Rivière and Thomas followed. He introduced the French knight to Richard and explained their mission.

'Return to the auberge and prepare our armour and weapons. I take it that we will be provided with mounts?' Thomas asked La Rivière.

'Of course. It would not do to have a knight walk into battle. There'll be horses provided for both of you.'

'I thank you.' Thomas bowed his head and turned to address Richard. 'Then there is nothing for me to do for the present. I'll return to the auberge at midnight before we join the force inside the main gate of Birgu.'

'Yes, sir. And where will you be until then?'

'I have something I must attend to.'

'Oh?' La Rivière cocked an eyebrow. 'What could be so important? Or perhaps I should ask, *who* could be so important?'

Thomas stared at him, concerned that his motives were so apparent. He faced the French knight with a firm expression. 'It is personal business, and any knight who values his sense of honour should know better than to pry into it.'

The oarsman was about to settle down for a rest in the bottom of his boat when Thomas returned to the quay and ordered him to row back across the harbour. A handful of other craft were making the crossing as the late-afternoon sun dipped towards the horizon. Some were carrying supplies out to St Elmo and returning laden with civilians anxious to reach the greater safety of Birgu. His heart felt light at the prospect of seeing Maria, and sharing a few hours with her before he had to return and prepare for La Rivière's raid. The earlier awkwardness had been caused by his shock at finding her alive, and not knowing what he wanted to say to her. Now he felt confident that they would be able to talk more freely and he would discover what had become of Maria during the intervening years and whether she still held true to the intense feeling they had once shared.

As the boat reached the tiny strip of shingle below the fort, Thomas did not wait for it to beach but leaped over the bows and splashed into the shallows. He surged ashore and ran to the path that wound up the rocky cliff to the fort. The courtyard was already in shadow and there were hundreds of Maltese crammed within, and more were arriving through the passage from the main gate. There was fear in the expressions of all gathered there; some were weeping and many others were on their knees praying earnestly to be delivered from the wrath of the Turks.

Thomas threaded his way through them as he made his way across the courtyard to the chapel. The large door was open and the glitter of many candles was visible inside. The benches of the chapel were filled with more of the devout, praying fervently. Thomas's eyes searched for Maria but could not see the green of her cloak anywhere. He walked slowly down the aisle, looking closely to each side, but there was no sign of her. With a growing sense of anxiety he approached a priest who had just emerged from the confession box.

'Father, I'm looking for a woman. She should have been here, where I told her to wait for me.'

'A woman?'

Thomas nodded. 'She was wearing a green cloak. She arrived not long after midday, with her household staff. I told her to wait here for me. Did you see her?'

'Oh, yes. In fact she came to confession.'

'Then where is she?'

'She left.'

'What?' Thomas felt a stab of anxiety. 'Where did she go?'

'I don't know. She didn't say. All I know is that she seemed greatly disturbed, but then who wouldn't be in the circumstances? She ordered those with her to gather up their belongings and then they left the chapel. That's the last I saw of her.'

'Did she leave any message for me?'

The priest looked at him. 'And you are?'

'Sir Thomas Barrett. A . . . friend of the lady.'

'I see. No, there was no message.'

'Nothing?'

279

'Nothing. I'm sorry.'

'And you have no idea where she went? Could she still be in the fort perhaps?'

'I doubt it. I saw her party making for the main gate. My best guess is that they were making for the landing, to find some boats to take them across to Birgu. If you want to find her I suggest you look there. Now, if that's all, I have to offer comfort to the refugees. Do you mind, sir?'

Thomas stood aside and let the priest pass. He felt sick in the pit of his stomach. Why had Maria not waited for him? Why had she left in a hurry? He could not think of any reason that did not carry the possibility that she did not want to see him. That was too dreadful a prospect to face and Thomas clung to the hope that there was a sound reason why she had felt compelled to leave the fort. Very well, then he must track her down. He would not be satisfied until he heard the truth about her feelings, either way, from her lips. One thing was certain. A fortress under siege was a small world. It would only be a matter of time before he found her.

CHAPTER TWENTY-FOUR

'This will do.' La Rivière held up his hand to halt the small column. It was still dark and the barely discernible shapes of the knights and foot soldiers were strung out behind them so that they did not stumble into each other. The knight behind the two leaders drew a breath to relay the command. 'Column! Halt!'

Thomas turned swiftly in his saddle and hissed fiercely, 'Quiet, you fool!'

'Sorry, sir.'

Thomas turned his mount towards him. Peter Von Harsteiner was a tall big-boned German with cropped dark hair. He had been keen to volunteer for the ambush party and clearly idolised La Rivière, which was why Thomas had been doubtful about including him. He would have preferred more seasoned soldiers who had experience in such work, but La Rivière had already chosen his men and cheerfully brushed aside the Englishman's concerns. Thomas reined in close to the German and spoke gently.

'Look here, Von Harsteiner, the Turks have already landed advance parties. Do you want to give us away?'

The German shook his head vigorously. 'No, sir.'

'The question was rhetorical,' Thomas said wearily.

'Just keep calm and keep quiet. Move slowly and carefully and do not speak unless you have to. I know your blood is up, but this work needs careful timing and self-control. Do you understand? That question *wasn't* rhetorical.'

In the gloom Thomas saw the German's amused smile. 'I understand.'

'Good lad.' He pulled the reins and walked the horse back alongside La Rivière and spoke in an undertone. 'Impetuous, but willing to learn. Be sure to position him where he can't do us any harm.'

'Oh, he'll be no problem,' the French knight replied dismissively as he surveyed the surrounding landscape. The column had been advancing along a narrow lane bordered by the waist-high stone walls that were a common feature of the island. On either side the ground was broken by outcrops of rock and stunted bushes. A small farm building loomed ahead and the odour of swine carried on the night air. Beyond, the lane rose to a low ridge that overlooked one of the bays on the southern coast.

'We'll deploy on either side of the lane,' La Rivière decided. 'Let the Turks wander into the trap and then attack them from the flanks. The arquebusiers can open fire and then the mounted men can charge home. Should be over very quickly.'

'If we deploy on both sides, isn't there a risk that our men might fire on each other by mistake?' Thomas said patiently.

'You think so?'

'I've heard of it happening.'

'Hmmm. In that case we'll deploy to the left. Arquebusiers in the centre and the mounted men on each flank. Once I give the signal, the men will open fire and we will charge on to the lane in front and behind the enemy and turn in to crush them like a vice. That should do the trick, eh?'

Thomas nodded.

While the men armed with arquebuses clambered over the wall and found positions with a good view over the road, the knights and their squires, eight in number, dismounted and led their horses into concealment. Once La Rivière and Thomas were satisfied that their small force was well deployed, they handed their mounts to Richard to hold for them and continued cautiously along the lane towards the crest half a mile beyond the ambush point. As they passed the farm they saw a small heap of pig carcasses hurriedly burned to leave as little as possible for the enemy. The acrid stench of charred meat filled the air and they hurried on. From their left came the occasional crackle of musket fire and the rattle of drums in the distance as Marshal de Robles and his men engaged the first of the Turks to land on the island near Marsaxlokk Bay. The surrounding countryside seemed still and quiet and Thomas was conscious of the noise that their footsteps made on the dry and dusty surface of the lane. They slowed down as they reached the crest and turned off the road, making for a jumble of rocks fifty yards away where they would be concealed while they watched for the enemy. As they rounded the largest boulder, the small bays of the southern coast came into view and La Rivière caught his breath and muttered a curse.

Even though the coming dawn was no more than a hint of lighter sky along the eastern horizon, the stars and the thin sliver of a crescent moon provided enough illumination to reveal at least a hundred ships hove to in the small bay directly before them. The dark blots of several small houses less than a mile away marked the location of the tiny fishing village at the end of the lane. Straining his eyes, Thomas could just make out movement on the shore to one side of the village.

'There, they've already started landing to the west of Marsaxlokk.'

They squatted in silence, keeping watch on the enemy in the village, and as the dawn crept over the horizon it gradually revealed the full spectacle of the enemy's invasion of the island. The ships anchored in the bay seemed so tightly packed that they merged into a confused mass whose masts looked like the bare trees of a forest in winter. Between the ships and the shore scores of smaller craft were ferrying soldiers and their stores ashore. A number of galleys had beached and men were picking their way carefully down the gangplanks into the surf and wading ashore. It had been a long time since Thomas had last seen the Muslim warriors he had fought in his youth and as he looked on, memories of past battles stirred.

Already a screen of men with conical helmets, round spiked shields and light flowing robes had spread out ahead of the main force and advanced cautiously. Behind them, other bands of men were forming up into their units. Warriors from every corner of the Turkish empire had been gathered for the invasion. Armoured horsemen with chain-mail veils protecting their faces, archers who had trained to shoot from horseback but were to fight this campaign on foot, men from the mountains of Kurdistan, with wild hair and dressed in animal skins. By far the most impressive body of men was landing from the galleys. Tall, fair-skinned soldiers with high white hats, above which long ostrich feathers bobbed. Each man carried the long-barrelled arquebuses favoured by the Turks. Although more cumbersome than those used by the armies of Europe, they were more accurate and quite deadly in the hands of men who had trained for years to use them. Besides their firearms, each man carried a scimitar and a shield on the pack slung across their shoulders. As soon as they reached the shore they quickly formed up in their companies and waited for their turbaned officers to issue orders.

'Janissaries,' Thomas muttered.

'So I can see,' said La Rivière. 'Have you ever fought them before?'

'Once.' Thomas recalled the event as he replied. 'La Valette raided an enemy outpost on Rhodes. We didn't know that a company of Janissaries was in the fort until we scaled the gatehouse and surprised the sentries on duty. Once the gates were open, La Valette charged in at the head of our crew. That's when we discovered what we were up against.' He shook his head. 'They fought like furies, even though few of them had the chance to put on any armour. We cut them down and still they came on, using their fists and even their teeth if they had lost their weapons. I've never see such fanatics, and hoped I never would again.' He turned to the Frenchman. 'It looks like the odds against us have just lengthened.'

La Rivière grinned. 'I am a gambler by nature. I've always played by the principle that the longer the odds, the greater the pay-off.'

Thomas sighed. 'I take it that you haven't made your fortune at the gambling tables.'

'I've never lost more than I can afford.'

'That may be about to change.' Thomas turned his attention back to the enemy forces landing on the beach. The first of the Janissary companies was moving forward, towards the lane leading back towards the site of the ambush. Half a mile ahead of them the Turkish scouts edged forward, picking their way across the broken ground towards the ridge. 'They're starting their advance.'

'Then I hope de Robles has the sense to fall back on Birgu before he is in danger of being outflanked.'

'He knows his business,' Thomas responded.

There was a brief silence before the Frenchman turned to him. 'Of course, you must have fought alongside him, before . . .'

'Before I was obliged to leave the Order. Yes. I knew him then. A fine soldier. He won't take any unnecessary risks.'

'Unlike you.'

Thomas turned abruptly. 'Is there something you want to ask me? If so, let's attend to it before we have to deal with the enemy.'

La Rivière chuckled. 'Ah, I think I have found a chink in your armour. But you don't have to worry about me, Sir Thomas. I am not as preoccupied with the code of honour as some of the other members of the Order. I joined so that I might have a chance to fight. That is my calling. As far as I am concerned, the only mistake you made over that affair with the Italian noblewoman was not getting away with it.'

'Really?' Thomas replied coldly. 'I thought my mistake was in not holding to the values expected of a knight.'

'Those values have become more flexible in recent years. It is a pity that your, ah, indiscretion did not happen ten years later. I doubt whether there would be any question of you being asked to leave the Order.'

'You think so?'

'I know. There's a little more to your unfortunate tale than you know.'

Thomas wondered what the Frenchman meant but he did not like his mocking tone and would not rise to the bait. There was no time anyway, the enemy was drawing closer and they had to return to the rest of the men.

'Come on, we have to go.'

They stayed low as they crept away from the rocks and hurried back to the ambush site. A pale glow was spreading along the eastern horizon and by the time the enemy reached the position, the first rays of the sun would be in their eyes, making it harder for them to detect any signs of danger. Thomas was pleased there was no sign or sound of the men as they approached and it was only at the last moment that the bullish head of Von Harsteiner rose up from behind the wall of a pen close to the farm.

'Are they coming?' the German asked eagerly.

'They are.' La Rivière smiled. 'And there will be plenty to go round.'

A brief look of anxiety flitted across Thomas's expression. The Frenchman seemed to have a reckless streak that might jeopardise the success of the ambush. He was too keen to fight the enemy. The task that La Valette had set them depended upon patience, stealth and a willingness to retreat the moment any skirmish threatened to get out of hand. They were to take prisoners, not supply them.

Once they had retrieved their mounts Thomas and La Rivière joined the party of squires on the left of the line. The knights at the other end, beyond the line of footsoldiers, were under the command of Von Harsteiner. The men stood ready and waiting, senses alert for the approach of the enemy. Thomas spared a quick glance at Richard; he was a few yards away, crouching behind a boulder, one hand resting on the pommel of his sword.

They did not have long to wait. A single figure appeared at the top of the ridge and cautiously advanced along the lane, peering right and left. He wore a conical helmet rising in a spike and carried a spear. As he reached the farm, he paused and looked over his surroundings carefully. At one point Thomas was certain that the Turk was looking directly at him and he kept perfectly still, waiting for the man to raise the alarm. Then he turned away and Thomas let out a soft sigh of relief. In the distance the sounds of battle from the direction of de Robles's force intensified and helped to cover up any whinny from the horses, or the scrape of a hoof on rock. The Turkish scout suddenly left the track and entered the farm. They heard the sound of furniture being moved and then he emerged from the back of the farm with a couple of stools. Moving a short distance from the building he smashed one of the stools on a rock and started to build a fire.

Thomas looked over his shoulder and saw the golden hue along the horizon. He edged towards the French knight and whispered, 'If he remains there, he'll see us as the sun rises. We have to get rid of him.'

'We could take him prisoner,' Richard suggested. 'And return to Birgu.'

'We need an officer,' La Rivière countered. 'And the enemy needs a sharp lesson. But first we must deal with him.'

'I'll go,' Richard said softly.

Thomas shook his head. 'No. You stay here. I'll do it.'

For an instant La Rivière looked surprised and then he gestured towards the abandoned farmhouse. 'All right then, be my guest, Englishman.'

Drawing his dagger, Thomas crept forward, picking his way carefully through the stunted undergrowth which concealed the knights on the left flank of the line. Ahead of him the scout continued to arrange the splintered lengths of timber in a crude cone, and then tore apart some rags he had taken from the farm and pressed them into the gaps he had left between the lengths of wood. As he worked he frequently looked up, scanning the ground in the direction of the main harbour and occasionally looking back towards the ridge as he waited for his comrades to arrive. Thomas reached the small barn, little more than a shed, and moved slowly along its length until he reached the corner and could peer round to spy on the enemy soldier.

Once the fire was complete the Turk stood up, stretched his shoulders and then crossed the farmyard and leaned on the low stone wall that bordered the lane, presenting his back. Thomas waited a moment to see if he moved, but the scout remained where he was. He glanced both ways down the lane, and then settled on staring towards Mdina, where the spire of the church stood dark against the pink smear of the dawn. Thomas drew his dagger in an underhand grip and hunched lower as he paced towards the Turk, easing each foot down so as not to crunch any gravel under his boots. The sound of gunfire to the east was diminishing to a handful of parting shots as de Robles and his men broke contact and fell back towards Birgu. Then, when Thomas was no more than ten feet from the scout, a flicker of movement to his left drew his eyes and he saw a standard edging up over the ridge. The Turk noticed it too an instant later and half turned in that direction. The moment he saw Thomas his eyes widened in alarm.

CHAPTER TWENTY-FIVE

There was no time to think. Thomas launched himself forward, drawing the dagger back a fraction as his arm muscles tensed, ready to deliver the blow. The scout turned quickly and his surprise caused only the briefest of hesitations. He threw up his left arm to protect his face as his right hand snatched at the ivory handle of his dagger. The thin curved blade was out of its sheath at the moment Thomas struck.

There was no finesse in his attack, no attempt to duel with his adversary, just a headlong charge intended to smash into the scout and knock him down. The other man was slightly built and the impact drove him back against the wall. Thomas thrust his dagger in hard and the blade tore through cloth and flesh and the scout gasped in pain. But the blow glanced off his ribs; the wound bled freely but it was not disabling. With a growl of anger the scout swung his knife arm round and the blade clattered off Thomas's shoulder plate and deflected up, the point grazing through his hair and tearing his scalp with a searing pain. Thomas struck again, and this time buried the blade in the soft tissue of the other man's stomach. He let out a deep groan and then smashed his fist into Thomas's face. Instantly his vision blurred and he stumbled back, out of range of the Turk's knife. His heel caught on a small rock and he stumbled and fell heavily on his back, driving the breath from his lungs.

Thomas gasped softly and cursed himself for failing to make a clean kill. Now he was at his enemy's mercy and at any moment he expected to feel the sharp, lethal blow of the scout's dagger. Then, as his vision began to clear, he raised himself up on his elbows and drew up his legs to get back on his feet. He saw the scout, ten feet away, on hands and knees as he desperately tried to scramble away and flee towards his comrades. Glancing back, he saw Thomas. He struggled on to his feet, one hand clutching at his stomach, the other, still holding the dagger, braced on top of the wall. He began to move towards the lane, towards his comrades, trying to shout, but the effort was too much agony and he gritted his teeth and concentrated on making his escape instead.

Still struggling to breathe, Thomas went after him, staggering across the farmyard. His chest felt as if it was being pressed by a great weight and he began to feel dizzy. He paused and shook his head to try and shake the nausea off and then saw that the scout had increased his lead, even with his wound. He might yet escape. The Turk glanced back and came to the same realisation and his lips parted in a brief grin before his features twisted in agony. With a muttered curse he stumbled on.

'No . . .' Thomas whispered in furious despair. He clenched his spare fist and forced himself to step out after the scout, and drew up gasping after only a few paces. Then he was aware of movement and someone ran past him. There was a blur as his arm swept back and then forwards and a soft thud from the direction of the Turk who had just reached the lane. With a moan he dropped to his knees and his left hand groped up his back towards the dark haft of the knife that had struck him just under the shoulder blade.

Richard turned to Thomas. 'Are you injured?'

Thomas shook his head. 'Winded . . .'

Satisfied, Richard turned to the scout and trotted up behind him. He raised his boot and kicked the man savagely behind the knee so that he collapsed. Reaching down, Richard braced his boot on the scout's back and pulled the knife from his back. In one quick movement he grasped the Turk's helmet and jerked his head up before cutting his throat. His body shuddered and his boots flailed on the dry track. Richard did not wait for his movements to cease before wiping his blade on his enemy's robes and then returning it to its sheath. Then he grabbed one of the Turk's sandalled feet and dragged him back into the farmyard.

'Help me,' he hissed to Thomas.

Still recovering, Thomas sheathed his dagger and took the other foot. Together they hauled the body towards the small barn.

'What happened?'

Thomas looked up to see La Rivière half crouching by the corner of the barn.

'It's all right, sir,' Richard answered. 'We dealt with the scout.'

'So I can see. What are you doing?'

'We'll hide the body in the barn, then get back to our positions.'

'Wait.' La Rivière straightened up and turned to look at the lane. He pointed to a gap in the wall, where some stones had collapsed opposite the men waiting to launch the ambush. 'Put the body over there, leaning up against the wall on the far side of the lane.'

'What?' Richard frowned. 'They'll see him.'

'Precisely!' La Rivière smiled. 'Do it. I'll be with you in a moment.'

Richard glanced at Thomas who nodded and they dragged the body out and sat it up against the wall. La Rivière went over to the scorched remains of the pigs and drew his dagger. He worked briefly and then hurried over to the others.

'Here. The finishing touch to our little trap.'

The French knight leaned over the body and forced open the jaws with one hand and then stuffed something into the mouth. A moment later he straightened up with a satisfied nod. 'That should do.'

Thomas looked down and saw the snout of a pig protruding from the stretched lips of the dead Turk and he understood La Rivière's purpose at once.

'Why have you done that?' Richard asked softly, in a revolted tone.

La Rivière chuckled. 'Explain it to him, Sir Thomas.'

'To the Muslims the pig is a dirty animal. They will not eat its flesh. When the comrades of this man see him, they'll be outraged. The first thing they will do is drop their guard while they seek to remove this effrontery from their sight.'

'Quite so,' La Rivière nodded, then looked round towards the ridge. The others followed the direction of his gaze and Thomas could clearly see the head of the approaching column cresting the ridge, burnished by the first rays of the rising sun.

'They're looking into the light,' Richard said. 'With luck they haven't seen anything to cause them any alarm.'

'Then let's go,' La Rivière ordered. 'Stay low.'

He led the way out of the lane and hurried across the small field to the boulders where his men were concealed. They took the helmets hanging from their saddle horns and quickly put them on, fastened the chinstraps, and stood by their horses ready to mount and charge as soon as La Rivière gave the command. Thomas had recovered from his winding and his lips set in a thin line of bitter self-reproach. He had made a mess of dispatching the enemy scout. But for Richard, the Turk might have escaped and warned his comrades about the trap that awaited them. It pained Thomas to have had his squire come to his rescue. The days when he was a formidable warrior were gone and this was perhaps his last opportunity to do something of note before he was good for little more than telling tales of past glories to young boys at the fireside.

He shut his eyes tightly and forced the shame from his mind. A soldier must never be distracted before a fight. This was a lesson that his father's sword master had drilled into him from the very first. A soldier, yes, Thomas reflected, but for a knight there were other codes and standards to live by. Chivalry above all. Yet there was no place for such moral strictures in the ageless war between the Order and Islam. All that mattered was the destruction of the enemy wherever and whenever he was encountered.

With sudden insight Thomas knew that this was the real attraction of the Order for men such as himself and La Rivière. The wars that waged within Christendom, the vicious sectionalism and rivalry of kings and princes were all poor shadows of causes worth fighting for, worth killing for . . . worth dying for. The Order alone provided a simple moral clarity. It pitched one world against another. There were no doubts about the cause to trouble a man, or at least a man with religion, Thomas thought wryly. He had long struggled with his faith, felt it slipping from his grasp as he had grown from a boy into a man. Despite all his prayers, there had never come the faintest reply, let alone a holy vision, or miracle. Just an emptiness that grew within, always presenting a stark choice: either this life was all there was and a man came from dust and went to dust and accepted the brevity of his existence, or he chose to perform deeds worthy of preserving in the record of human achievement. This he understood – he was here to give some meaning to his being. He fought not for the glory of God but for the survival of the world of those who believed, and those forced to endure their non-belief in silence, like himself. For them he was prepared to fight and die. He hardened his heart and refocused his mind as he watched the enemy approach.

The Turks came marching down the lane with a carefree boldness, talking and laughing loudly amongst themselves, their hearts and minds filled with the swaggering confidence of men at the start of a campaign whose outcome they did not doubt. They came in strength, possessed of the mightiest cannon in the world and the cleverest siege engineers, at the bidding of Sultan Suleiman the Magnificent, and blessed by Allah. Thomas could well understand their high spirits, and also the shrewd mind of the Grand Master who knew how important it was to strike down this confidence from the very first moment that the Turks set foot upon Maltese soil.

As the enemy approached, Thomas saw that there were no more than a hundred of them, armed with swords and shields and a handful with pikes. They wore no armour and apart from the shields their only protection was a polished brass helmet with a mail curtain to protect their neck and shoulders. Their robes were worn loose to ease movement and limit the discomfort of the summer heat. At their head rode an officer on a grey horse whose reins and saddle were adorned with silver braid. The officer's robes were of dark silk with white stars and crescents sewn on the flowing material. He wore a black turban, and his thin beard and haughty, erect posture in the saddle betrayed his youth. His lack of any watchfulness and failure to send forward a vanguard also betrayed his inexperience.

Thomas looked at La Rivière and saw that the French knight was watching the enemy company intently, all trace of his earlier levity gone. He sensed Thomas's attention and glanced briefly at him without any expression, before turning back to the Turks. The sound of their light-hearted talk filled the dawn air and drowned out the song of a handful of birds in the scattered brush about the farm. As they approached the entrance to the humble collection of buildings, the officer caught sight of the scout's body propped up against the wall that bounded the lane. He drew in his reins sharply, threw up a hand and shouted a command. The column shuffled to a halt and their tongues stilled as they craned their necks to see what had caused them to stop. The officer rattled out an order and the leading four men of the column lowered their packs on to the track and cautiously moved past their officer and approached the body.

La Rivière placed his hand on his saddle pommel and stood poised to place his left foot in the stirrup to mount his horse. But his eyes were still fixed on the enemy.

A moment later there was a cry of horror and then another, but this time enraged. More shouts followed and the young officer spurred his horse forward to join his men. He swung down from the saddle and snatched the severed pig snout from the scout's mouth and hurled it over the wall. Despite having no orders, the column began to edge forward to better see the cause of the outburst.

La Rivière made to mount and Thomas whispered fiercely, 'Wait. Let them fill the gap before we attack.'

The Frenchman hesitated a moment, torn by the desire to charge on his enemy and the good sense of Thomas's advice, then he nodded and kept still. As more of the Turks became aware of what had been done to the scout, their cries of outrage increased and they began to surge around the officer standing over the body. Thomas sensed the tension in the men around him and along the line concealed behind the rocks and stunted scrub.

'Just a moment longer,' he muttered as the column became more disordered.

'Open fire!' a voice cried out from the left.

Thomas's head snapped round, mouth opened to countermand the order before he realised it was pointless.

The air filled with the frizzle of powder in priming

pans and then the deafening explosions as the arquebuses spat flame and smoke. The Turks had turned in alarm at the shouted order and now several of them tumbled back into the closely packed mob as they were struck down by the heavy lead shot.

'Charge!' La Rivière bellowed.

Thomas, Richard and the squires scrambled into their saddles, drew their swords and spurred their horses from cover. To his left Thomas saw Von Harsteiner slapping the flat of his sword against the side of his horse as he led the knights on the other flank. The German was bellowing incoherently as he charged and Thomas realised that it was he who had shouted the order to fire. Between the two flanks the footmen lowered their arquebuses and snatched up their hand weapons and raced towards the Turks who were still too stunned by the attack to react. As they entered the lane, both parties of horsemen swerved their mounts and turned on the Turks and charged home. Grasping the reins tightly in his left hand, Thomas leaned forward and lowered the tip of his sword, arm braced to strike as he bore down on the swirl of robes and terrified faces trapped in the lane. The nearest of the enemy panicked at the sight of the steel-clad riders and turned and tried to flee. Some clambered over the stone wall, others ran into the heart of the mob, causing further confusion. A few stood their ground, shields raised and swords ready to strike.

Thomas picked a man directly ahead and as his mount knocked the man to one side he struck, thrusting through the Turk's shoulder and then savagely wrenching the blade back before he swung at the turbaned head and felt the solid thud of contact before the man dropped to the ground senseless. Thomas's ears filled with the sound of blades clashing, the whinny of horses and the shouts and screams of men fighting, killing and dying. He saw Richard, teeth gritted, urge his mount into the throng of Turks as he slashed savagely to left and right, crimson drops spraying into the air, across the flank of his horse and spattering the polished steel of his breastplate.

Then he glimpsed a flicker of steel to his right and turned just in time to thrust his arm out and block the heavy scimitar arcing diagonally towards his shoulder. A sharp clash of blades filled his ears and the shock of the impact ran down his arm into his shoulder. Thomas gritted his teeth as he pushed the scimitar aside and locked his gaze on a tall, broad warrior in a chain-mail vest and pointed helmet. Dark eyes glared back either side of an ornate nose guard and the Turk snarled with frustration as he snatched his sword back and swept it round behind him to make another attempt to strike Thomas down. Pressing hard on his stirrups Thomas thrust his sword towards the Turk's throat with all his strength. The point stabbed under the man's beard and above the chain-mail and tore through the soft tissue, cartilage and blood vessels before it burst through the muscles at the back of his neck. The Turk's eyes bulged in shock and agony and his lips parted in a grimace as Thomas tore his sword free. As blood pulsed from the wound, the man dropped his sword and clutched his hand to the wound, desperately trying to stem the flow. Then he was swept aside as his comrades surged away from the mounted knights carving their way through the throng.

Even though the Turks outnumbered their attackers, the suddenness and ferocity of the assault had shattered the swaggering confidence of a moment before and now they broke and fled, scrambling over the walls on either side, or desperately trying to get past the horsemen and flee along the lane. A dozen of their comrades already lay sprawled across the rutted track, bleeding into the dust. Only one of La Rivière's men had been wounded, piked in the hip, and he had limped out through the gap in the wall and was clutching a hand tightly to the bloodied cloth of his gambeson. The Turkish officer and a handful of his men still faced their attackers and Thomas pointed the officer out with his sword.

'Take him! Take him and it's all over.'

Richard glanced back and nodded, then spurred his horse, leaning forward, his blade drawn back ready to strike. A handful of the enemy footmen were clustered about their officer, ready to protect him with their lives. Richard's mount barged into them, sending two men reeling while he struck at a third, severing his sword hand and then cutting deeply into his neck to finish the man off. Thomas urged his horse forward, pushing past his squire until he faced the enemy officer.

'Yield!' Thomas called out. 'Yield, or die!'

Whether the Turk spoke French or not, he readily understood the command and spat with derision before driving his spurs in and charging his mount directly at Thomas. The Turk's horse was lighter and barely caused Thomas's charger to stagger back one step as they thudded breast to breast. The enemy officer's blade slashed towards Thomas but glanced off his shoulder guard. Thomas instantly struck back but the officer parried the blow before the horses had passed each other. Both men pulled on their reins and turned to continue the duel. The Turk turned first and swung his sword at Thomas's head. There was no time to block the blow and Thomas threw his body to the side. The blade cut through the air with a low swish and Thomas strained to return to an upright position.

He saw Richard edge forward from the other side of the Turk and called out, 'Leave him! This one's mine!'

Richard hesitated, then drew in his reins. His mount tossed its head as it came to an abrupt halt. Thomas barely had time to raise his sword before the next blow arced towards his helmet. The scimitar struck his sword close to the hilt and Thomas instantly turned his wrist to trap his opponent's sword. With a violent wrench he snatched the scimitar from the officer's hand and shook it to the ground before urging his horse forward and aiming the tip of the blade at the Turk's throat.

'Yield!'

For a moment the Turk's eyes flashed defiantly and Thomas thought he might have to kill the man. Then the officer's shoulders slumped and he bowed his head in defeat.

'Richard, take charge of him. We need him for interrogation, but if he tries to escape, kill him.'

His squire nodded and ordered one of La Rivière's soldiers to bind the officer's hands behind his back while he held his sword up to the Turk's face. Thomas sat erect in his saddle and looked round the ambush site. Over a score of the enemy were now down; some of them were wounded and pleaded desperately before they were finished off by the Italian mercenaries. Further off, the survivors of the column were scattered across the surrounding fields. They were pursued by La Rivière and the other knights and most of the squires, crying out with excitement as they rode down and killed their prey.

'The fools have lost their heads,' Thomas muttered angrily as he sheathed his blade.

A moment later he heard the shrill blast of a horn and looked to the east to see a large party of horsemen, perhaps thirty strong, riding towards the lane. Some of the knights and squires reined in as they heard the sound, and the quick-witted saw at once that they were in danger of being cut off from the direction of Birgu. They turned their horses and galloped back towards the lane. La Rivière and two of the squires were far ahead of their comrades, and slower to react. Thomas realised they were in grave danger. But he had to get the rest of the men safely away. He drew a deep breath and cupped a hand to his mouth.

'Fall back! Back to Birgu! At once!'

The mercenaries and the mounted men heeded the order and quickly abandoned the ambush site, using the broken ground to cover their retreat. Thomas turned to Richard who was guarding the bound officer.

'Get him out of here.'

'What about you?'

'I'll be along directly. Go!'

Richard reluctantly nodded and he sheathed his blade before taking the reins of the Turk's horse and leading him back towards Birgu. They reached the ambush site and the other mounted men followed on. Thomas remained, watching anxiously as La Rivière and his squires, cut off from any hope of escape, made for a small rise and turned to face the approaching Turkish cavalry. The sun had cleared the horizon and its rays burnished the polished armour and weapons of the Turks with a brilliant red hue as they swept up the rise and engulfed the three men. Thomas caught one last glimpse of the French knight before the blades stopped flashing and the dust began to settle.

With a sick feeling Thomas turned his mount away and spurred it back down the lane.

CHAPTER TWENTY-SIX

'Thirty-five thousand men, you say?' La Valette slowly stroked his beard as he digested Colonel Mas's report of the interrogation. The Grand Master was standing with his officers on the bastion assigned to the knights of the langue of Castille, one of the strongest positions in the line of defences that protected Birgu. Thomas had been summoned to the bastion in the early hours. Throughout the night the Turks had been moving into position in a wide arc around Birgu and Senglea, their progress revealed by the torches that flickered across the landscape, and the noise of orders shouted from the darkness. Dawn had revealed the enemy drawn up in formation just beyond the range of the cannon mounted on the bastions along the walls.

As the pale light spilled across the island the enemy had gone down on their knees in response to the wailing cries of their imams and the sound of their chanted prayers carried clearly to the ears of those watching from the walls and bastions defending the two promontories. The spectacle of the horde ranged against them had stilled the tongues of the defenders who looked on in awe and apprehension at the array of coloured cloth and glinting weapons in the dense ranks sprawling across the landscape.

On the high ground behind the enemy formations Thomas could see Turkish engineers labouring to level the ground for the artillery batteries. Each gun had been laboriously drawn by hand from the beaches where they had been landed the previous day. Soon they would be in position, ready to bombard the defenders, although the enemy seemed keen and arrogant enough to attempt to rush the walls without waiting for their cannon to open fire.

'Yes, sir.' Mas nodded sombrely. 'And they are expecting a further force of ten thousand to arrive under the command of Dragut.'

The other men of the inner council stirred uneasily at the mention of the corsair warlord. Dragut's ships had brought terror and destruction to ports and shipping across the Mediterranean. Tens of thousands of people had been seized from their homes by his men and sold into slavery. The corsairs who followed him were all experienced men, ready to fight as fiercely as the most devout Muslim fanatic, but for loot rather than faith.

'With Dragut, that makes some forty-five thousand in all,' Mas continued. 'Together with around a hundred cannon of various calibres, a thousand engineers, and plenty of siege equipment. And of their fleet, no less than two hundred are warships. Not only do the enemy vastly outnumber us, they also outnumber any force that Don Garcia can assemble on Sicily.'

'What is the latest count of our strength?' asked La Valette.

Mas consulted his notes briefly. 'We have less than seven hundred knights, one thousand two hundred Spanish and Italian mercenaries, and the five hundred soldiers from the galleys. There's perhaps two hundred Greek and Sicilian volunteers and ninety squires. And then there's the militia. We've been fortunate there, the latest strength returns show that over five thousand of the local men have taken up arms – far more than we estimated. I know you have reservations about them, sir, but from what I have seen they are determined to defend their homes and their families. I think they may surprise us all before long.'

'We shall see,' the Grand Master responded doubtfully.

'There are also the slaves from the galleys,' Mas concluded. 'They won't fight for us but we can use them to repair the damage to the walls of Birgu and Senglea and work on improving the defences.'

There was a brief silence before Thomas spoke up. 'The odds are only seven to one against. I pity the Turks.'

The other men, save La Valette, smiled.

'There is some good news,' Mas added. 'The officer we captured said that Suleiman has divided the command between Mustafa Pasha and Piyale Pasha. The first is in command of all land forces while the latter commands the ships. Apparently they are already disagreeing over their course of action. When Dragut arrives, that division will be three ways.'

'That is good news,' the Grand Master conceded. 'However, I suspect that the reverence in which Dragut is held will mean that he will take overall command of the siege, which will considerably increase the danger to us. He is the most bitter opponent the Order has ever fought. Dragut is a fine leader, and an inspiration to all who follow him.'

'You admire him?' asked Mas.

'Of course.' La Valette smiled briefly. 'I am not blind to his qualities as a warrior, even if he is little better than a pirate and cleaves to a false faith. But for an accident of birth I would be proud to fight at his side.' His expression hardened. 'But as my enemy I will do all in my power to destroy him, without mercy. Meanwhile, let us pray that the Sultan's decision to split the command contributes to the undoing of his cause. Did the prisoner reveal anything else of value during his interrogation?'

'Not before he died, alas.'

'A pity. At least we have a more precise idea of the forces that confront us.' La Valette turned to Thomas. 'You did well to capture the officer, Sir Thomas.'

'Thank you, sir. Though it was at the cost of one of our own knights. I only hope that La Rivière and those with him fought to the death. If not, then it is likely that the enemy is as well informed about our strengths and weaknesses as we are about theirs.'

'Assuming that La Rivière gives way to their torture,' Stokely intervened. 'I think you may well underestimate his quality. Some knights hold to their oath of service more devoutly than others. La Rivière is such a man.'

Thomas fought to keep his expression fixed at the barbed comment and responded in a calm tone. 'And I think you may underestimate the quality of the enemy's interrogators. The Turks are as skilled in the art of torture as they are in the art of siege craft. No man is immune to torture. It is only a question of finding his weakness, and then breaking him down. Sooner or later La Rivière will talk. Our only hope is that he does not give up too much useful intelligence, if he has been taken alive.'

There was a brief silence amongst the officers as they stared towards the dense ranks of the Turks who completed their prayers at length and rose to their feet, and at once the air filled with the rhythmic sound of their drums and cymbals and the shrill notes of their horns as they raised their weapons and shook them at the walls. The chaotic flicker of the sun's reflections on the weapons of the Turks reminded Thomas of the sparkle of the sea, as if they were a wave about to crash upon a rocky shore.

'They mean to attack without delay,' Thomas decided. He turned to look down the line of the wall. The bastions occupied by the langues of Castille and Auvergne were the only fortifications that had been fully completed. The other bastions were still without embrasures solid enough to withstand the fire of enemy cannon. The same was true for lengths of the wall between the bastions.

'Look there.' Mas pointed towards the Turkish lines. A handful of richly dressed officers with turquoise turbans rode out a short distance ahead of their battle line. Behind them marched a company of Janissaries, their ostrich feathers wafting above their tall hats like a faint haze. The foremost of them was leading a man whose arms were tightly bound behind his back. He stumbled as he was dragged along and Thomas could just make out that he was barefoot and wore only the tattered remains of a red surcoat bearing a white cross, the instantly recognisable garb of the Order. His blond hair hung down to his shoulders and there was no doubt about his identity.

'That's La Rivière,' Stokely muttered. He glanced quickly at Thomas and scowled. 'You were right, it seems.'

The officers watched as the procession began to make its way along the enemy line, parallel to the defences. Every so often the Turkish officers would stop and point towards Birgu as they questioned their prisoner.

Mas shook his head. 'He shouldn't have let himself be taken.'

'Perhaps there was nothing he could do about it,' said Thomas. 'He was overwhelmed, and they would want to take one of our knights alive just as keenly as we desired one of their officers.'

'Still,' the colonel muttered, 'it was his duty not to fall into their hands.'

Thomas shrugged. 'Blame him as you will, there is nothing that can be done now.'

'Obviously,' Stokely sniffed.

Mas turned to La Valette. 'Sir, we should order our guns to fire on them. We must silence La Rivière before the Turks can make any further use of him. We might kill some of their officers at the same time.'

La Valette squinted towards the enemy for a moment and shook his head. 'The range is long and we need to preserve powder. Besides, I think La Rivière might yet provide us with one more useful service.'

'Sir?'

'Just watch him.'

The enemy party continued their examination of the defences. At length they halted opposite the bastions occupied by the knights from Auvergne and Castille and there was a lengthy exchange between the Turkish officers and their prisoner. It was then that Thomas understood what the Grand Master had been alluding to.

'La Rivière's telling the Turks to attack our strongest position.'

La Valette nodded. 'I think so.'

Thomas thought for a moment before he continued in a low voice, 'As soon as they discover the truth, they will take their revenge on him.'

'Then let us hope that their revenge, and his suffering, are swift.' The Grand Master turned to Mas. 'If La Rivière is doing what I think he is, then we must add to his deception. Take five companies of our arquebusiers out of the main gate and send them forward far enough to skirmish with the enemy. They are to exchange fire but avoid any engagement at close quarters. If the enemy advances on them, pull them back at once.'

The colonel hesitated a moment before responding. 'Is that wise, sir? We have few enough men as it is. We're bound to suffer casualties.'

'That can't be helped. We must make the enemy think that the rest of the line is strongly defended, and that there are only a few men holding these two bastions. If they throw their weight against us here, they will suffer grievously and, with luck, they will think all our defences are as strong as this.' He patted the thick masonry of the embrasure. 'Now go and prepare the men, Colonel. And you may lead them. Let them have their first taste of action. See how they stand up to enemy fire. It'll steady their hearts and give them confidence, you'll see.'

'As you command, sir.' Colonel Mas bowed his head.

He strode off and descended the staircase. La Valette and the others turned their attention back to the enemy in time to see the small party move away from the bastions and make their way back through the battle line. There was a short delay before the noise from the enemy's drums, cymbals and horns swelled into a cacophony that echoed off the stone walls of Birgu and the fort of St Michael. In response there was a rattle of drums from the battlements and the main gates opened as Colonel Mas led out the first company of arquebusiers. At their appearance the defenders let out a cheer and the colours of the Order and the banners of the mercenaries swirled in the light breeze as the standard bearers waved them from side to side. Colonel Mas and his small force crossed the drawbridge over the ditch that ran along the front of the wall. The arquebusiers took up position amid the remains of the buildings and low stone walls that had been hurriedly demolished during the previous weeks.

Thomas watched as they loaded and primed their weapons and blew on the smouldering fuses to make sure that they stayed alight, ready for use once the order to open fire was given.

As soon as they saw the arquebusiers emerge from the main gate, the Turks responded in kind. A line of Janissaries advanced from the main battle line, long barrels propped against their shoulders as they strode confidently towards Birgu. Colonel Mas stood on a pile of rubble in full view of the enemy and calmly watched them approach, one hand resting on his hip, the other on the hilt of his sword. Thomas could not help but admire the coolness of the mercenary officer.

The enemy were allowed to get well within the range of the defenders before Colonel Mas bellowed the order to open fire. A rolling crackle of explosions rippled along the line of arquebusiers as they fired from cover along the front of the wall. Tiny tongues of flame darted from the barrels of the weapons and were instantly engulfed in thick greasy-looking clouds of gunpowder smoke. Thomas saw several of the Janissaries tumble as they were struck by the heavy lead balls, while dust and chips of stone burst from the ground where shots missed. At once the arquebusiers began to reload their weapons. The Janissaries hesitated briefly before one of their officers drew his scimitar and waved them on. The advance continued, but now the enemy were hunched forward slightly as they tried to make themselves smaller targets. Colonel Mas gave the order to fire at will and the more handy of the men got their next shots off well in advance of their comrades and then the firing merged into a steady crackle.

A score of the Janissaries were sprawled on the open ground, some writhing feebly or trying to crawl back to the rear. When their comrades had closed to just over a hundred yards from the arquebusiers, their officer gave the order to halt and return fire. It was the last order he ever gave as a moment later a shot struck him in the head and the back of his white headdress exploded in bloody fragments. His body spasmed and he toppled on to his back, spreadeagled, and kicked a few times before lying still. But his men continued to follow his order, setting their long-barrelled weapons up on slim wooden stands and then taking careful aim on the defenders before returning fire.

Even though their weapons were more accurate and they were better trained and could load and fire more quickly than their opponents, the Turks were in open ground and made easy targets. From the bastion it seemed to Thomas that for every one of Mas's men who fell, at least three of the enemy were shot down. The colonel steadily made his way along the rear of the line, encouraging the men while miraculously avoiding the enemy's shots which smashed into stones nearby or kicked up divots of soil and gravel close to his boots.

As the exchange of fire continued, Thomas saw that the Turkish line had edged forward in front of the bastions of Castille and Auvergne and around him the defenders made ready for action. Scores of arquebuses, already loaded, were leaning against the inside of the battlements ready to be taken up and fired. Young Maltese boys who had been trained to reload the weapons stood ready to do their duty. Below, in the body of the bastion, Thomas could hear the rumble of cannon as they were run up to the narrow firing ports in their casemates. More men stood by armed with pikes, ready to rush forward and throw back any attempt to escalade the walls of the bastions, or the curtain wall that linked them.

Looking round, Thomas saw that the Grand Master was watching the enemy's preparations for the attack with grim satisfaction.

Shrill blasts from brass trumpets gave the signal and with a deep roar the Turks swept forward across the open ground towards the bastions. Thomas saw that there were none of the headdresses of the Janissaries in the ranks of those charging towards him. Clearly the enemy commander had decided to spare his crack troops and entrust this first assault to the more expendable Spahis and the religious fanatics dressed in white robes. As they poured forward, the exchange of fire in front of the main gate continued uninterrupted, as if it was a separate battle. Colonel Mas spared the horde one brief look before turning his concentration back to the fight to his front.

On the bastion La Valette watched the oncoming enemy with cool detachment and his closest officers affected the same calm. Ranging posts had been set up a few days earlier and as the Turks reached those furthest from the defences the guns in the casemates opened fire with a deafening explosion that seemed to rip the air apart. Thomas felt the stone shake beneath his boots and his ears filled with the roar of the guns. Smoke billowed up and over the battlements and caught in the throats of the men there, making them choke. As the smoke cleared, Thomas saw that the grapeshot that had been tightly packed into the muzzles of the cannon had torn great lanes through the ranks of the enemy, scything down ten or more men at a time, mangling their bodies into bloody heaps.

The Turks did not waver for an instant but charged on, sweeping over their fallen comrades as they raced towards the counterscarp of the ditch a short distance from the bastions and the wall extending between them. As they passed the second line of marker stakes, the arquebusiers opened fire, adding their weight to the cones of grapeshot blasting out of the casemates. As flame and smoke rippled out from the defences, the Turkish ranks withered before the impact of the defenders' fire. And still they came on, leaping over the bodies of the fallen and screaming their war cries, their robes flying.

'Good God,' Thomas said in disbelief, 'they know no fear.'

The first men reached the counterscarp and slid or scrambled down the steep angle into the ditch in front of the wall. More cannon opened fire from each of the bastions, sited to enfilade the ditch, and heavy shot scourged the Turks as they struggled to clamber up the scarp towards the foot of the wall. Thomas could see only a handful of scaling ladders and shook his head at the foolishness of launching such an assault before more had been constructed. The angle of fire was now so acute that some of the defenders stood on the wall to fire down at the enemy below.

'Order those fools to get down before they are shot!' La Valette snapped.

Stokely ran to the side of the bastion and shouted the order. Only a handful of the nearest men had retained their wits enough to obey. The blood of the others was up and they were shooting down and handing back their weapons for a replacement as fast as they could. Then one of them spun round as he was struck by a bullet fired from the open ground. He tottered on the edge, then lost his balance and pitched over the wall into the ditch. Another man fell before the other soldiers realised the danger and hurriedly ducked back behind cover. Now they began to hurl large rocks over the walls, and the boys who had been loading the guns joined in. The deluge of missiles split open skulls and crushed bones as they crashed on to the Turks.

Only one ladder was raised against the wall and as the Turks began to climb towards the battlements, Thomas saw the barrel of a cannon in the other bastion edge round, and then the muzzle disappeared behind a jet of flame and cloud of smoke and the ladder, and those on it, were obliterated into fragments of wood and flesh.

That was the turning point. For a moment the men in the ditch hesitated, and then the first of them turned away, and then more, and the urge to get clear of the slaughter in the ditch spread like a fierce contagion. Moments later the assault was broken as the Turks turned to stream back across the open ground towards the safety of their original positions. The defenders shouted with excitement, triumph and derision as they watched, while some kept firing until the last of the enemy was out of range. As the main assault fell back, so did the Janissaries engaged with Colonel Mas and his men. They pulled up the supports for their weapons and shouldering both they turned and hurriedly joined the retreat. A handful of Mas's men threw down their arquebuses and drew their knives as they set off after the Janissaries. The colonel bellowed and they stopped and reluctantly returned to their line. The arquebusiers closed up and marched back towards the main gate and across the drawbridge into the shelter of Birgu's defences.

Thomas stared out across the open ground, littered with the enemy's dead and wounded, hundreds of them. In return only a few men had been lost along the wall and perhaps as many as thirty of the men Mas had led out to confront the Janissaries.

'Very good.' La Valette nodded. 'The first round to us, gentlemen. Mustafa Pasha will think twice before he tries anything so rash again.'

He turned to survey the men who were still cheering along the wall. The shouts of triumph were taken up by the civilians in the streets immediately behind the wall, and to the far end of the defences in front of Birgu. And shortly afterwards by the defenders of St Michael who had followed the action from their walls. The bells of the cathedral began to toll and flags were waving above the walls of St Elmo as all savoured the first, small victory over the invaders.

'Let them cheer.' La Valette smiled. 'Indulge them. We will be sorely tested before long, so enjoy this moment. Then, while the Turks make their preparations for the siege, we can complete our defences. Come, we can return to St Angelo now.' He was about to turn and leave the bastion when he stopped and pointed. 'What's happening there?'

Thomas saw that a group of Janissaries had stepped out in front of the shaken ranks of their comrades. They carried a stake with them and pounded it into the ground. When it was in position, two more men came out, dragging La Rivière between them. They tied his hands to an iron ring at the top of the post and then tore the ragged surcoat from his back so that he stood naked. Thomas and the others looked on helplessly.

'What are they going to do to him?' Stokely asked quietly.

The two men who had tied him to the stake took out slender canes tucked into their belts and slashed them through the air a few times before they approached the French knight.

'Bastinado,' said Thomas. 'They're going to beat him to death.'

'With those sticks?' Stokely scoffed.

'Yes, with those sticks,' Thomas replied flatly. 'I've

seen them used in the Balkans. A man can take several hours to die, his agony increasing with each stroke.'

The two Janissaries took up positions either side of La Rivière and began to take turns to lash him with their slender sticks. The knight lurched under the first blows and then hunched against the post and arched his back and endeavoured to keep still and endure his punishment stoically. The Turks sat down to watch the entertainment while those in Birgu looked on in despair and horror. After an hour, La Rivière's knees buckled and he hung limply from the rope, his head lolled back, mouth open in a silent scream of torment.

'Sir.' Stokely turned to La Valette. 'Can we bring one of the cannon to bear and put an end to his suffering?'

La Valette shook his head. 'Look for yourself. They have chosen their ground well. There is no gun that we can aim in that direction. There's nothing we can do – other than spare our men from witnessing it. Only those on sentry duty are to remain. Order all the others to return to their billets. At once.'

As the men filed away into the narrow streets of the town, it was clear from their quiet exchanges that the earlier euphoria had been extinguished by the spectacle of La Rivière's torture. The afternoon wore on and the beating continued under the eyes of those defenders still on watch. On the bastion of Castille, Thomas remained, together with Stokely and Colonel Mas. The Grand Master and the others had retired to St Angelo. In front of Birgu, small parties of Turks gathered their dead for burial. The wounded were carried back to their camp for treatment. When they tried to retrieve those of their comrades who had fallen in the ditch, Thomas ordered one of the sentries to fire a warning shot to keep them away so that they could not examine the wall or bastions at close hand. The bulk of the forces that had made the morning attack had joined the procession of troop columns, wagons and artillery trains passing to the west of Senglea. A covering force remained, busy cutting trenches into the ground ringing Birgu and Senglea.

Despite all the enemy activity the attention of the defenders was irresistibly drawn to the ongoing execution of La Rivière. The first two Janissaries had been relieved early in the afternoon and their replacements continued the beating in a steady rhythm until dusk, when one of their officers strode up to examine the knight. Squatting down, he raised La Rivière's head and examined his face briefly before he drew a dagger and cut the Frenchman's throat.

'At last.' Stokely closed his eyes and bowed his head. 'Poor soul.'

Mas shrugged. 'He should not have allowed himself to be captured. I'll not make the same mistake. Nor will any of our men. It is a lesson well learned and will surely harden the resolve of every man, woman and child on the island. As the Grand Master said, there are no civilians on Malta. And now they know one thing more – there is only victory or death.' Mas stretched his back and turned away from the enemy. 'I'll do the rounds of our sentries before I let the Grand Master know that La Rivière's suffering is over.'

'Very well,' said Stokely. 'I'll see you at the evening briefing.'

The colonel bowed his head and descended the stairs. Only four soldiers remained on the bastion apart from Thomas and Stokely, and they kept a respectful distance from the two knights. For a while neither man spoke as they stared at the naked body still tethered to the post. Then Stokely cleared his throat gently.

'I understand that you have seen Maria.'

Thomas turned his gaze towards Stokely. 'You've spoken to her?'

Stokely's lips momentarily lifted in a mocking smile. 'Oh yes. You gave her quite a surprise, but she has recovered now and come to her senses. She does not want to see you again, ever.'

Thomas felt a cold stab of anxiety in his heart, then it passed as he recalled her expression, her shock in seeing him and then the unmistakable stirrings of the old affection in her eyes. He felt certain that Stokely was lying. 'I must confess, seeing her came as quite a surprise to me too after you told me she had died.'

'I said she was dead *to* you.'

'And now she is very much alive to me. And I am to her. Where is she?'

Stokely stared at him, then said, 'Safe.'

'Safe? From the enemy, or from me?'

'None of us is safe from the enemy. But at least I can save her from you, Thomas. I can spare her that misery.'

'Where is she?' Thomas asked again, this time through gritted teeth. 'Tell me.'

'I will do no such thing. Seeing you again has disturbed her mind enough as it is. Fortunately I was able to talk sense into her and Maria accepts that it would be foolish to even set eyes on you again. As I said before, she is dead to you, Thomas. Do not try to find her.'

'I will find her.' Thomas spoke in a low growl, his hands clenched by his sides to keep him from grabbing Stokely by the throat. 'I swear it. I shall see her again.'

Stokely stared at him for a moment before he spoke with a vehemence that Thomas had never seen in him before. 'May God damn your soul to the eternal fires of hell, Thomas. I pray for that with every fibre of my being. It is what you deserve.'

Thomas frowned. 'Why do you hate me so very much? What have I done to wrong you that you wish such a fate for me?'

'Hate you? Of course I hate you. It was you she loved. Always you.' Stokely gritted his teeth. 'It should have been me. I deserved Maria, not you . . . And you shall never have her. Now get out of my way.'

Thomas met his cold, malevolent gaze, and then slowly eased himself to one side. Stokely swept past and started down the staircase. Thomas listened as the sound of his footsteps faded away, shaken by the venom in his words. After a moment he turned to watch the distant artillery train winding its way around the end of the harbour towards the end of the Sciberras peninsula. One thing was clear. The enemy had swiftly discarded the idea of an assault on Birgu and Senglea. Their full weight would be thrown against St Elmo, just as the Grand Master had hoped. The defenders had won some time to improve the fortifications of the most important positions. Their chances of surviving the siege would improve with every day that St Elmo held out. Thomas turned to look across the harbour at the fort. The setting sun bathed its walls in a warm glow and cast dark shadows where the acute angles of its star-shaped layout cut off the light. The breeze had dropped and the standards flying above the fort hung limply. It was a peaceful scene, Thomas mused. Not something that the eight hundred men garrisoning the fort were likely to see again.

CHAPTER TWENTY-SEVEN

The mood in the auberge that evening was subdued. Jenkins served them a simple barley gruel, explaining that there was no longer any fresh meat to be had in the markets of Birgu. In order to save feed the Grand Master had given instructions for all livestock to be slaughtered and salted and stored in the warehouses by the dock. Only a small number of horses were to be given fodder from now on. With the arrival of a large number of refugees in Birgu, new billets for the soldiers had to be found and so a dozen Italian mercenaries had been assigned to the English auberge and these now joined Thomas, Richard and Sir Martin at the long table in the hall. With the arrival of the mercenaries Jenkins's labours had increased considerably and he treated the Italians with ill-disguised disdain and resentment.

As the men supped they were quiet and reflective and conversation was mainly limited to requests to pass the bread platter, the salt or the jug of watered wine. The mercenaries kept to the end of the table nearest the door and left the three Englishmen to the end nearest the fireplace.

'Where is Sir Oliver?' asked Richard. 'He said he would be accommodated at the auberge once the Turks landed.'

Sir Martin shrugged. 'He has money enough to rent his own quarters. And a sufficiently inflated sense of his own worth not to have to share accommodation with his brother knights.'

Thomas stirred his gruel. 'Do you have any idea where he might have taken up residence?'

'No,' Sir Martin answered and they continued eating.

''Twas a great pity about La Rivière,' Sir Martin said at length. 'He was a good soldier. Never balked at the chance to take the fight to the Turk. One man we could ill afford to lose.'

Thomas nodded.

'He was also reckless,' said Richard. 'He need not have died if he had kept his mind on the purpose of the ambush, which was to take prisoners.'

Sir Martin lowered his spoon and glowered at the squire. 'Once again, you forget your place, young man. Such comments dishonour La Rivière. When you have won your spurs then, and only then, may you pass judgement on the knights of the Order. As it is, he died with honour.'

'I do not dispute that, sir, but the fact is that he need not have died at all.'

Thomas sighed wearily. 'But in death at least he did us all a great service.'

'In what regard?' asked Richard. 'As Sir Martin has pointed out, we need good soldiers, and now we have lost a knight and the two squires who were killed or taken with him.'

Thomas pushed his bowl aside before he half turned towards Richard.

'It was La Rivière who had the presence of mind to convince the Turks to attack the strongest section of our defences. Elsewhere the ditches are far less of an obstacle and they are not yet covered by cannon. If the Turks had launched their assault either side of the main gate it is possible that they would have been able to scale the walls. If they had secured a foothold there and then pushed on into Birgu, our cause would already be as good as lost. As it was, the enemy was bloodily repulsed from the section of our defences they believed to be our weakest. The experience has caused them to choose what they believe to be a less formidable target. That is why they are now marching on St Elmo.'

The younger man lowered his gaze and stared down at his hands. 'I spoke without knowing the full context of his actions, sir.'

'That is the burden of youth,' said Sir Martin. 'You will learn, in time. If we live through this.'

Richard glanced at Thomas. 'I apologise, sir.'

'You owe me no apology,' said Thomas. 'It is the name of a dead man that you have impugned. It may be that La Rivière's courage and presence of mind has altered the outcome of the siege. Think on that, Richard, before you race to judgement on any man in future.' He rose to his feet. 'I am to bed. I bid you good night, gentlemen.' He turned to the lower end of the table and bowed his head. 'And to our guests.'

The Italians looked up as he addressed them and guessed his meaning and bowed their heads in return before turning back to their meal and conversing in low tones.

Thomas made his way to his cell and closed the door

behind him. He sat down on his bed and eased off his boots and breeches before lying down and staring up at the ceiling. A thin beam of moonlight entered from the narrow window above his head and cast a ghostly arch of light on the wall opposite. He folded his arms behind his head and yawned. He had not slept for two days. The strain of the previous night's action and the events of the day had taken their toll and he felt more tired than he had done in many years. He closed his eyes and breathed evenly, yet sleep would not come. Footsteps passed outside his door and then he heard Sir Martin's voice grumbling about Italians before a nearby door closed with a slam.

His weary mind returned to his brief exchange with Stokely on top of the bastion. What was his role in all of this? Had he really nursed his grievance as a spurned lover for twenty years? Perhaps jealousy was just as capable of thriving on the scraps of memory as was love. Was it jealousy that made Stokely refuse to reveal where Maria was or, as he claimed, Maria's wish? He must find Maria. Soon.

There was a light knock at the door and for a moment Thomas considered not responding and feigning sleep. But he welcomed a respite from thoughts of Maria. With a muttered curse, he sat up.

'Come!'

The latch scraped up and the door opened to reveal Richard illuminated by a candle. The sounds of conversation from the hall carried through into the cell, more cheerful and unrestrained now that the Englishmen had left the table.

'I need to speak to you, Sir Thomas,' Richard announced.

Jenkins passed behind him on the way to the kitchen to refill the wine jug.

'Come in, then.'

Richard closed the door and crossed the room. He set the candle down beside the bed and fetched the single chair for himself.

'If this is about earlier,' Thomas began, 'I merely meant to encourage you to think before you pass comment. You are inclined to forget the attitude that is expected of a squire. Even one of the older squires.'

Richard shook his head. 'It's not that. I have a more important matter to discuss.' He glanced back towards the door as if fearful that he might be overheard, and then leaned towards Thomas and continued in an urgent undertone. 'I went to St Angelo on an errand today while you, La Valette and the others were on the bastion.'

'What errand?'

'To see what I could discover about the location of Sir Philip's chest, of course. I told the sentries that you had left your gauntlets in the Grand Master's quarters and sent me to fetch them.'

'Very enterprising of you. Did the sentries let you pass inside?'

'They did. Your name carries some weight these days. I crossed into St Angelo and feigned a search for the gauntlets under the eyes of La Valette's steward, then said that you must have been mistaken and left. It was easy enough to continue down through the keep to the store-rooms. That is where I encountered the first of the problems facing us.'

'Indeed?'

'The Grand Master's hunting dogs. They have their kennels in an arch lining the same corridor as the store-rooms. The entrance to the dungeon is at the far end of the corridor. There is an anteroom to the dungeon and four guards are stationed there. They present a difficulty in their own right but as it was, the dogs began barking the moment I entered the corridor and alerted the guards at once.'

'What happened?'

'I told them that I had lost my way. Two of them marched me out of the keep and sent me away.'

'Let's hope they don't report the encounter. If it excited the curiosity of one of La Valette's staff, it might well make finding that chest somewhat harder.'

'Harder? It's nigh on impossible as it stands. Are you certain there is no other way into the dungeon? Another entrance perhaps, or a drain that passes beneath it or close by?'

'None that I know of.'

Richard frowned. Thomas watched him for a moment and then scratched his chin.

'Isn't this all a little without purpose at present?'

'How so?'

'We are surrounded by the enemy. There will be no escape from Malta unless the siege is lifted. If the Turks succeed then it hardly matters if you retrieve the document or not.'

'It matters a great deal,' Richard replied firmly. 'If it should fall into the enemy's hands they would realise its significance at once and have an immensely strong bargaining counter in any dealings with England.'

Thomas smiled wryly. 'Which enemy? The Turks, the Catholics, or the Order?'

'All of them, as it happens.'

'Ah, a pity. For a moment there I hoped that you might have formed some common bond with La Valette and his followers.'

'Oh, we share a bond all right. Emerging from this trap alive. Until that is achieved, I will do whatever I can to defeat our common foe. But this is not a case of my enemy's enemy is my friend, Sir Thomas. If we are discovered searching for the document, then I doubt there will be any mercy shown to us once La Valette realises the real purpose of our presence here. The Grand Master has a certain ruthless streak and however much he may value your skills and experience, he will not forgive your deception.'

'No. I don't suppose he will,' Thomas agreed. 'Forgiveness seems to be in rather short supply at present.'

Richard looked at him sharply. 'What does that mean?'

'It is nothing that concerns you.'

'Of course it concerns me. I need your help to carry out my mission. I can't afford for you to be distracted. Is it to do with that woman, Maria?'

Thomas was silent for a moment. 'You know it is.'

'Then you had better be careful. She must not be allowed to interfere with our plans.'

Thomas felt a chill enter his heart. 'Is that a threat of some kind?'

'No, I merely meant to remind you of your duty to your country, and your Queen. Keep that in mind.'

Thomas eased himself forward until his face was close

to that of his squire. 'Understand this, Richard. If you ever harm Maria, or act in any way to endanger her, I will kill you.'

Richard stared at him. 'You would kill me to save her? Really?'

Their eyes locked briefly before Thomas slumped back, dispirited. The passion in his heart felt real enough, but Richard's iron resolve to fulfil his mission and duty made his own feelings seem distastefully self-indulgent and his threat empty and ridiculous.

'What would you do in my situation?' he asked.

'I can't imagine.'

'Then I pity you.'

'Save your pity,' Richard hissed. 'Your imagined bond with this woman is a weakness. What do you think you can achieve? Tell me. What are your plans? What could you offer her?'

'A chance to put right the wrong that was done to both of us. Perhaps if we live through this we might yet be joined, as we should have been all along. My plan is to ask her to be my wife and then I would take her home to England where we could grow old in peace.'

Richard shook his head. 'There is no fool like an old fool. And any fool can see that you are presuming upon a degree of affection and forgiveness in this lady that borders on fantasy. You must see that.'

'I see what is in my heart.'

'And it blinds you to all else. Right now, it is my most fervent wish that I could carry out Walsingham's orders by myself but I cannot. You must help me.'

'Must I?' Thomas settled back against the stone wall

before he continued. 'If I help you see your mission through then I expect help from you in turn.'

Richard's eyes narrowed. 'And what is it that you want me to help you with, exactly?'

'For now, I need to know where Maria is. The civilians evacuated from St Elmo were brought here. She has to be somewhere here in Birgu.'

'I have no doubt. It is common knowledge that many of your brother knights have mistresses, and some have even married in secret and live as husband and wife in their homes and estates on the island. Hypocrites!' Richard sneered. 'Like all those whom the Church of Rome holds up as models of rectitude. Hypocrites, all of them.' He raised a clenched fist and his voice was strained with bitter emotion. 'By God, if it was ever in my power I would wipe them all from the face of the earth . . .'

'Them?' Thomas's brow creased. 'Do you speak as a Christian, or a Muslim? For it is impossible for me to tell the difference.'

Richard lowered his fist and opened his fingers. 'I beg your pardon,' he muttered. 'I am very tired. I forgot myself.'

Both men were silent. Thomas stared at his companion with frank curiosity. 'What has been done to you that you should hate these people so terribly?'

'Nothing . . . It's nothing. I lost my temper for an instant. That is all.'

'It is far from all. You revealed your heart for an instant, and I saw a darkness and a rage in you that I had never suspected. Richard, what is it? What torments your soul so badly?'

'Suffice to say that I have no reason to love those who serve the Church of Rome,' Richard replied coldly. 'I am born of Catholics, who abandoned me when I was young. Mine was a hard upbringing, and I knew little kindness until Sir William took me into his service before I joined Walsingham's agents. It was Cecil who taught me that Catholicism is a vile corruption of Christianity and I have dedicated my life to destroying it in England, and wherever it may be found.' He was breathing quickly and it was a while before the rage that burned in him had died down enough for him to talk in a controlled manner.

'If you help me, Sir Thomas, then I shall help you. We will find that letter, and your Maria, and we will take both from this island and return to England, if that is your wish.'

'It is, and I fervently hope that it is hers as well.'

Richard nodded. 'Then we have an agreement. As good as any that is signed in blood.' He offered his hand and Thomas took it.

'I hope your Maria is worth it,' Richard said with a thin smile.

CHAPTER TWENTY-EIGHT

O ver the following days the distant rattle of the iron wheels of the enemy guns carried clearly across the water of the harbour. From the walls of St Angelo the defenders looked on as the ant-like figures toiled on long ropes to haul their artillery along the crude track that meandered down the length of the ridge of Sciberras. Turkish engineers had gone ahead of the guns, improving the track and levelling a large patch of the rocky ground half a mile from St Elmo. Once the ground had been prepared, they constructed the first of the batteries with which to bombard the fort. Then, one by one, the guns were manoeuvred into position and long lines of men carried shot and kegs of gunpowder up to the battery to feed the cannon. As soon as their preparations were complete, the battery opened fire.

The first blast split the late spring afternoon. A puff of smoke spurted from the embrasure and then wafted into the air. Those watching from the keep on the other side of the harbour snapped their eyes towards the fort and an instant later a small explosion of rock and soil erupted a short distance in front of St Elmo, and then again off the stone facing of the outwork. As the roar of the cannon carried across the bay, the ears of La Valette's hunting dogs pricked and they rose, growling, from where they had been lying at his feet. The Grand Master reached down and stroked their velvet heads gently to hush them.

'A lucky shot,' Stokely commented. 'To strike home with the first attempt.'

Colonel Mas shook his head. 'They won't be needing much luck. The ground is hard. Any shot that falls short will ricochet and hit the fort with almost as much force as a direct hit.'

Thomas nodded. He had witnessed a handful of sieges in the boggy conditions of the Netherlands where soft ground swallowed up cannon shot in a welter of mud and damp soil. Only a direct hit had any effect. Here, on Malta, conditions were perfect for the Turkish gunners.

The second gun fired and the hair rose up on the backs of the hunting dogs and they barked ferociously. Other dogs in Birgu joined the chorus with each shot that was fired. La Valette tried to calm his hounds and then with an irritated sigh he gestured to one of his servants and ordered the man to take them down to the kennel in the dungeon corridor. Richard stepped aside to let them pass and eyed them with ill-disguised hostility.

The twelve guns of the battery continued to fire in turn in a rolling bombardment and it was soon clear that the Turks had chosen to concentrate their efforts on the ravelin and the two nearest points of the star-shaped fort. As the guns boomed out, the engineers advanced a short distance beyond the crest of the ridge and began to construct a second battery; further on, a series of green streamers flying from the top of slender posts marked the start of the approach trenches they were cutting into the rocky ground with picks, heavy chisels and hammers.

The handful of cannon mounted on the walls of the fort fired on the engineers each time they advanced the trench and scurried forward to throw up makeshift barricades to screen the men working on the next section. At the same time a company of Janissaries took shelter amid the outcrops of rocks and boulders closer to the defences. They sited their long-barrelled arquebuses on the walls of the fort and sniped at any defenders foolhardy enough to expose themselves too far above the parapet.

Each day, at dawn and towards dusk, the Grand Master and his advisers surveyed the enemy's progress and were disheartened by the speed with which the Turkish trenches zigzagged closer to the fort. The poor quality of the stone used in the construction of St Elmo was evident from the crumbling of the facing of the walls and the rapid pulverisation of the points of the corners of the fort facing the batteries. As darkness fell and all through the night the guns continued to fire in an endless rhythm of detonations that were accompanied by regular outbreaks of barking from all the dogs in Birgu.

The passing days were spent in improving the defences of Senglea and Birgu. As before, La Valette and the senior knights joined the other soldiers and townspeople as they laboured to increase the depth of the walls and construct a second line of defence across the ground where the nearest houses had been torn down to provide building material. Beyond the main wall, gangs of galley slaves and the handful of prisoners that had been taken were chained in pairs and set to work deepening and widening the ditches that cut across the ground at the base of each promontory.

A screen of arquebusiers were sent two hundred paces further out to prevent the Janissary snipers from trying to hinder the work being carried out in front of the walls. The activity only came to an end when the sun set and the slaves were returned to their cells while the rest trudged back to their billets and homes.

There was little time for Thomas and Richard to pursue their respective quests. In any case, they were often too exhausted to do anything more than eat upon returning to the auberge. Then, while Richard fell on his bed and went to sleep, Thomas left the auberge to attend the evening meeting of La Valette's war council in St Angelo. For the present there was little more to discuss than the progress of the work on the defences, and the steady destruction of the fortifications of St Elmo. Stokely made his report on the current levels of rations. There were no more exchanges between Stokely and Thomas outside the meetings; Stokely always contrived to leave first, while the Grand Master engaged Thomas and Colonel Mas in further discussion about the military situation as they gazed out of the window and beheld the ongoing siege of St Elmo.

The dark mass of the fort with its regular lines loomed over the end of the Sciberras peninsula. There was a faint orange loom from the flames of the braziers and cooking fires burning in the courtyard, but no sign of the sentries on duty along the wall. There had been many losses caused by Turkish snipers before the defenders learned to risk only fleeting glances above the parapet, or to find a sheltered place along the wall where they could lie full length on the parapet and keep watch. Even so, there were occasional flashes from the ground in front of the fort as a sniper shot at any movement detected on the wall. Further back, the Turkish engineers continued digging their trenches by the flickering light of torches, behind the cover of their barricades. Up on the ridge, where the two batteries were sited, the guns continued firing through the night. Each round shattered the darkness with a lurid red glare that illuminated a tableau of the men toiling past the batteries with wicker baskets filled with soil and rock to help build up the sides of the trenches, before the night shrouded the scene once more – until the next gun fired.

Thomas could not help admiring the efficiency with which the Turks pressed on with their siege. In the years that he had served the Order he had mostly fought them at sea, and only heard accounts of their wider military prowess from the handful of older knights and soldiers who had faced Suleiman's army at Rhodes. There was no question that their technical skills far exceeded those of most of the armies Thomas had faced on European soil. Only the superior armour of the knights, their long experience of conflict and devotion to their cause weighed against the numerable advantages enjoyed by the Turks.

At the end of May La Valette gathered his advisers at noon to hear grim news. The small council sat round the table in his study. A small scroll of paper lay on the table beside the hollowed-out cow horn into which it had been sealed with wax. La Valette's dogs, as usual, lay at his feet under the table. Trained to run with the Grand Master's hunt, they were used to firearms and no longer barked at the sound of the enemy's cannon, unlike the other dogs in Birgu.

'I have received a despatch from Don Garcia. It came

via Mdina and a local goatherd who swam across the harbour. The Viceroy tells me that the reinforcements he was expecting from Genoa have been delayed,' La Valette said in a voice tinged with bitterness. 'Don Garcia reports that we can expect to be relieved no earlier than the end of July. We are ordered to hold out until then.'

'July?' Colonel Mas let out a sigh of frustration. 'Another two months? I doubt that St Elmo will last another two weeks, and then the Turks will turn on Birgu.' He paused to make a rapid calculation. 'With our defences in the state they are we must expect St Michael and Birgu to fall within a month of the loss of St Elmo. In that event, we will have to make a final stand here, in this fort. With luck we might still hold St Angelo when Don Garcia and the relief force eventually land on Malta.'

'That would be lucky indeed,' La Valette replied. He raised a hand to attract the attention of the servant who had been standing silently by the door. 'Bring in Captain Medrano.'

There was the briefest delay before a tall officer with a neatly clipped beard entered the study and strode towards the table. He was wearing a breastplate tarnished where it had scraped against masonry and Thomas could see that his jerkin was stained with sweat and grime. His eyes had the sunken lustreless look of an exhausted man and his hair was streaked grey with dust.

'A chair for the captain,' La Valette ordered and the servant hurriedly brought one to the table. Medrano sat down stiffly and folded his hands together in his lap as the Grand Master introduced him.

'I doubt that any of you have met the captain before.

He arrived a few days before the Turks and was assigned to the garrison of St Elmo immediately. He is one of La Cerda's senior officers. He has been sent to us to deliver a report on conditions across the harbour. Captain?' La Valette invited him to address the war council.

'Yes, sir.' Medrano nodded. He cleared his throat and began speaking in the clear, direct tones of a professional soldier.

'The commander of the fort begs me to inform you that the situation at St Elmo is critical. The ravelin is close to collapse, as is the south-west corner of the fort. The south-east corner will not endure much longer. The enemy trenches are less than fifty paces from the outer ditch and we can expect them to make their first assault within the next two days. There is nothing that we can do to hamper their progress. The moment any of our men appear above the parapet they are shot down by the Janissaries. We lost twenty men to snipers just yesterday. As a result we are forced to crawl behind the cover of the parapet and try to build up some makeshift battlements with stones taken from the rubble on the corners of the fort. That's a dangerous business, given the continual bombardment. The morale of the men is low. They have had little rest, and stand by their arms at all times in case the enemy attempts a sudden assault on the fort. My commander estimates that the fort can hold out for eight more days. Ten at the outside, sir,' he concluded.

'Ten days is not good enough, Captain,' La Valette responded. 'You and your comrades must buy the rest of us more time. We have heard today that there will be no outside help for two months. Every day that you can hold on increases the chance that our Holy Order will survive. La Cerda must not give up the fight.'

'What does La Cerda want from us?' asked Thomas.

'Sir?'

'I presume that he would not have you risk your life by crossing the harbour in daylight just to report on conditions in the fort. What else did he say? What does he want?'

Medrano lowered his gaze momentarily. 'La Cerda asks for permission to evacuate the fort. He says that the wounded can be loaded into boats sent over from this side of the harbour after nightfall. After that he will gradually thin out the men behind the wall. Any weapons and equipment that cannot be removed will be thrown down the well and the cisterns will be fouled. The last men to leave the fort will fire the fuses to the charges set in the powder store. Nothing of use will be left to fall into enemy hands.'

'I see.' La Valette nodded. 'And when does La Cerda intend to plan to abandon the fort?'

'Tonight, sir – if you give the order.'

'Out of the question! There will be no evacuation. You will tell La Cerda that when you return to the fort. He still has over six hundred men under arms. It is unthinkable that he should abandon his position so early in the siege. It is a shameful request. Shameful! Do you hear?'

'Yes, sir.' Medrano bowed his head. He hesitated a moment before he added, 'I agree.'

La Valette stared at him and then spoke in a gentle tone. 'Thank you, Captain. That is the kind of resolve that is needed. Tell me, in your opinion what can we do to help St Elmo hold out as long as possible?'

Medrano considered for a moment before he replied. 'Fresh men, sir. To steady the nerves of the garrison and to show them that they have not been abandoned. Send them some coin and wine too. There's nothing that soldiers like more than the feel of coins in their purses. There's an empty storeroom where a few gaming tables can be set up, and wine can be sold. That will help to divert thoughts of their predicament.'

'Very well, I shall see that it is done.'

Colonel Mas leaned forward. 'There are other measures we can take to ensure the fort holds out as long as possible. Certain weapons that we have been holding back for the defence of Birgu. It might be better to surprise the enemy with them now, sir.'

'You mean the fire hoops and the naphtha throwers?'

'Yes, sir. If we add those to the incendiaries that La Cerda has at his disposal I am sure we can make the enemy pay a high price for St Elmo, and hold them off for longer than La Cerda's estimate.'

The Grand Master folded his hands together and weighed up the suggestion. At length he nodded. 'Very well, see to it that the fort is supplied. As for men, we will send another hundred and fifty of the mercenaries across. There is one other matter. La Cerda is clearly not fit to retain command. We need to replace him with someone equal to the task that lies ahead. In the meantime I appoint you, Captain Medrano, as commander of the fort. I will have your orders drafted at once so that you can take them with you.' He paused a moment. 'Juan de La Cerda has served the Order faithfully in the past and is a good knight. Relieved of the burden of command I am confident that he will fight well. I will not add to his humiliation unnecessarily. He is to remain with the garrison. Find him a less onerous responsibility, Captain.'

'Yes, sir.'

'Very well, you may leave us. Wait outside while my clerk drafts your orders. Then return to St Elmo at once, before La Cerda undermines the courage of those he commands any further.'

Medrano rose from his chair and left the room. La Valette briefly dictated the details of the new arrangement to his clerk, then signed the order before the clerk left the room to hand the document to the waiting captain.

La Valette sighed. 'I need to find the right man for St Elmo. One who knows he is going to a certain death and does so without hesitation. He must also be determined to make the enemy pay as dearly as possible. He must not be a hothead but a man of cold reason. Not another La Rivière. He must also be a man whom others will follow with the same sense of duty and inevitability about the outcome.'

'Such men are rare, sir,' said Mas. 'I do not count myself among their number, but if you wish it, I will take up the command.'

'I expected no less of you, Colonel. But for now you best serve the interests of the Order on this side of the harbour. Once St Elmo falls, as it must, it will take every effort of the best of us to hold the line here.'

'What about Sir Thomas?' asked Stokely. 'He has the necessary military experience, and he has proved that he has steady enough nerves by capturing that Turkish officer and leading La Rivière's men safely back to Birgu.'

La Valette looked at Thomas questioningly. 'Well? Do you volunteer?'

Thomas shot a bitter glance at Stokely before he faced the Grand Master. There was no question about his response, but he needed a moment to accept the implications. He would never see Maria again. Never make his peace with her and perhaps more. And he might doom Richard's mission to failure, even if his squire was spared the fate of accompanying him to St Elmo. If what he had been told about the document was true, the consequences of failure would be dreadful back in England. There were so many sound reasons to refuse La Valette, and only one reason to accept. One that was all that was ever asked of a knight.

'I would be honoured to volunteer, sir.'

La Valette met his gaze for a moment and then smiled. 'You passed the test, Sir Thomas. Yet I must decline your offer, despite the cogent arguments of Sir Oliver. I have no doubt about your ability to take up the command but for now I need you here. The command must go to another. I will think on it. Captain Medrano will suffice for a few days. He is a good man, but not quite the ruthless martyr that is needed. Now, there is work to be done here in Birgu. I call this meeting to an end.'

'Sir, there is one other matter,' Stokely intervened. 'As we discussed earlier.'

A pained expression briefly crossed the Grand Master's face before he nodded. 'Of course. Thank you for reminding me, Sir Oliver.'

La Valette clicked his fingers and in an instant Apollo and Achilles had leaped to their feet and were nuzzling his fingers, tails wagging. He smiled fondly as he caressed their muzzles and then he drew a heavy breath.

'It's the dogs, they never stop barking at the guns. It is wearing the nerves of those in Birgu and Senglea. Sir Oliver believes it would be best if they were silenced.'

Colonel Mas's brow creased. 'Silenced?'

'Besides disrupting our people's sleep they are consuming rations,' said Stokely. 'It will go hard on those affected but there may come a time when we will have to dispose of them anyway. Better now, and save food that we may need later.'

'It will go hard indeed,' La Valette said gently as he stroked his hounds.

'Of course there is no need to include your dogs, sir,' Stokely cut in quickly. 'Or at least these two, your favourites. It will make little difference if they are spared.'

'Perhaps.' La Valette ran his gnarled fingers across the ears of the nearest hound.

Thomas was watching the Grand Master closely. This was an opportunity to open the route to the chest where a document vital to the safety of England was stored. He cleared his throat and shook his head sadly. 'Sir, it will make a great deal of difference if these two are spared. At present the knights and the people stand side by side. We share the same dangers and privations. That is our strength. That is what binds us. We should not jeopardise that common feeling by being exempted from those edicts the Grand Master imposes upon the generality. If their dogs are to be silenced, then all dogs must share the same fate. Even these two, who are your favourites.'

'Yes, they are . . . .' La Valette said quietly.

The beasts sensed that they were being praised and their tails wagged as they looked up at their master with adoring eyes. La Valette tore his gaze away and clasped his hands together under his chin.

'Take them!' he commanded his servant. 'Take them back to the kennels with the others and see that it is done at once.'

The servant approached the table and took them each by the collar and drew them away from their master. As they reached the door, Apollo twisted his heavy head round and looked one last time at his master before being willingly led from the room for the last time. After the door had closed no one spoke for a moment. Then Thomas coughed lightly.

'I am sorry, sir. It seemed to be for the best. I wish it had been otherwise.'

'Yes, well, it is a necessary evil,' La Valette responded in a matter-of-fact tone. 'And they are only dogs, after all. The smallest of sacrifices to be expected of us in the days to come. The meeting is over, gentlemen. Please leave.'

His advisers rose to their feet and filed out of the study. Thomas was the last to go, and he paused at the door and saw that the old man was staring at the floor where his dogs had been lying shortly before. It had gone hard with him to insist on the destruction of the old man's hounds, yet they had barred the way to the archives and would have to be dealt with one way or another.

'Only dogs,' Thomas said under his breath as he closed the door quietly behind him.

CHAPTER TWENTY-NINE

On the second day of June, at dawn, the lookouts on the towers of St Angelo sighted fresh sails approaching the island. La Valette was holding his morning council on the platform above the keep and they watched thirteen galleys steer towards the entrance to the harbour, before they turned north-west to anchor close to the shore. The lead galley was richly draped with an emerald-green awning embroidered with stars and crescent moons. From the Turks waiting on the shore a cry rose up, repeated over and over.

'Turgut! Turgut!'

Richard had attended with some of the other squires and turned to Thomas with an arched brow. 'Turgut?'

'Their name for the corsair we call Dragut.'

'It is an ill day indeed,' La Valette said. 'Of all the men Suleiman could send against us, this one I fear most of all. He is as much a legend to the enemy as he is a demon to the Christian world. His men revere him and his worth on the battlefield is incalculable. And he brings thirteen galleys laden with his corsairs as well.'

'This will not sit well with our people,' said Stokely. 'Soon every man, woman and child in Birgu will know that Dragut has joined the Turks. Something needs to be done to strengthen the resolve of our people, sir.'

La Valette nodded gravely. 'And now, more than ever, we need to place our faith in the Lord our God and beg for his mercy and salvation.'

Dragut was rowed ashore in his gilded barge, and the cheers of the enemy reached a fresh crescendo as he stepped ashore. His procession around the northern harbour was screened by the bulk of St Elmo and the Sciberras peninsula yet the jubilant welcome of the Turks could clearly be heard from the battlements of St Angelo. The sounds were briefly overwhelmed by the crash of the siege guns as they continued to bombard St Elmo without interruption. The once neat lines of the walls had been broken down by heavy iron shot and rubble partially filled the ditch facing the Turks. Only the cavalier tower to the rear of the fort seemed wholly intact. The steady crash of shot into the walls of the fort filled the air with a brown pall of dust that hung in the air like a shroud when the breeze dropped during the hottest hours of the day. The flags marking the extent of the enemy's trenches were now no more than ten paces from the wall and La Cerda's prediction seemed to be vindicated, Thomas reflected.

The Grand Master had given orders to provide the defenders with as much support as possible. Each night boats slipped across the harbour carrying supplies and returned with the wounded. The Turks, through careless-ness or simple arrogance, had not yet interfered with the passage of the boats. Even though the defenders were under constant bombardment, they were ready to face the assaults that would follow the moment the first breach appeared in the walls.

The man that La Valette had chosen to become the fort's new commander was Captain Miranda, a veteran Spanish soldier. When he had been presented to the war council Thomas had been impressed by Miranda's outline of his plans for the defence of the fort. Colonel Mas had recommended him as a cool-headed and decisive leader, plain-speaking and, most important of all, the kind of man who inspired those he led.

As they waited for the first enemy assault the defenders were huddled below the remains of the parapet, grouped in threes, two arquebusiers to each man armed with a pike. Clay pots filled with incendiary materials were stacked at regular intervals. A handful of the dangerous naphtha bellows were readied for use on the cavalier – terrifying weapons that shot jets of liquid fire that consumed any man in their path. To complete the arsenal of the defenders, fire hoops were ferried across and placed on the walls, ready for use.

This last was a new weapon conceived by La Valette and demonstrated to his advisers only the day before. Barrel hoops were covered with multiple layers of linen which had been soaked in fat and tar and then steeped in boiling water. Thomas and the others had watched as two soldiers held one of the hoops in iron tongs at arm's length while a third soldier set it alight. The fiery hoop was released and flared brilliantly as it ran down the wall of St Angelo and into the narrow channel that had been cut between the fort and Birgu. Thomas could imagine the terrifying effect that such a weapon would have on the Turks as they assaulted the crumbling walls of St Elmo.

As Dragut made his way round the harbour to the main

camp sprawling across the landscape at the base of the Sciberras peninsula, La Valette dismissed his advisers and sent for the archbishop of Malta.

'A penitentiary procession?' Sir Martin scratched the stubble on his chin as Jenkins relayed the brief message that had been given to him by one of the Order's servants a moment earlier. The Englishmen and the Italian mercenaries had only just sat down to their evening meal after labouring throughout the afternoon on the inner wall of the town's defences. 'Tonight?'

'Aye, sir. At eight, from the steps of the cathedral, around the town and then into the market square for the sermon. Everyone in Birgu is to attend. All the civilians, and every soldier who can be spared from his duties.' Jenkins's eyes sparkled with keen expectation. 'Robert of Eboli is to speak.'

Richard exchanged a brief look with Thomas.

'Should I have heard of this Robert of Eboli?' asked Thomas.

'Oh, yes, sir! He is a simple friar but he speaks with such passion and fervour that it is as if the Lord himself has blessed his tongue. I have heard him deliver two sermons in the cathedral and not one of the congregation failed to feel touched by a divine presence. Truly, sir.' Jenkins lifted the wine jug, glanced at the Italians and scowled. 'The other gentlemen appear to have worked up a thirst. At the rate they are working through the cellar, our present stocks may not last much longer.'

'Nor may we,' said Sir Martin. '*Carpe vinum et non postulo credo*, eh? Just refill the jug.'

'Let us hope that the procession and sermon help to bolster morale,' said Thomas. 'With Don Garcia not able to send a relief force for some months, the arrival of Dragut, and the likelihood that St Elmo will fall any day, it is hardly surprising that La Valette is appealing to God for help. Piety may be the only thing that can save us now.'

'Piety, and a sharp sword.' Sir Martin chuckled as he mopped up the last of the stew with a hunk of bread. 'Who would have thought that dog meat could be so tender? Jenkins made a fine job of it.' He popped the bread in his mouth and chewed. When he was done he pushed the bowl away and sat back and stretched. 'Your squire is a sombre fellow tonight.'

Thomas glanced at Richard who was staring fixedly at the table as he mechanically spooned stew into his mouth. Catching his name, Richard glanced up. 'I am tired, sir.'

'As are we all, young man.' Sir Martin swung his legs over the bench and swivelled round. 'And so I shall rest before the procession. Tell Jenkins to rouse me at half past the seventh hour.'

'Yes, sir.'

Sir Martin rose to his feet and walked stiffly towards his cell. Richard waited until he was out of earshot before turning urgently to Thomas.

'This is our chance to get into that dungeon at St Angelo. The dogs have been dealt with and there will be only a handful of men on duty. When are we likely to find a better opportunity?'

Thomas was doubtful. 'There is the drawbridge to

cross, the courtyard and the entrance to the stairwell, and then the sentries outside the dungeon itself. How do you propose to pass through all of that unobserved? Besides, we shall be expected at the procession.'

'The procession, yes. But we could easily slip away before the sermon starts. The streets will be empty and there are ways to deal with sentries. We have to take our chances when we can. Getting into the archive's what we were sent here to do.'

'So you keep reminding me,' Thomas replied flatly. 'Very well, then. Tonight it is.'

The main streets of Birgu were brilliantly illuminated by the torches and candles held aloft by those taking part in the procession. The archbishop paced slowly at the head of the rest of his flock, holding a gilded cross above his head in both hands. Behind him came the Grand Master and the senior knights of the Order, bare-headed and dressed in plain black tunics with no belts or any other adornment. Instead of the usual boots, they wore sandals. Each man had his hands clasped together, head bowed as they chanted the Order's penitent oaths, learned by heart when they had first joined the Order many years before. Behind them came the other knights, soldiers and civilians in a stream of humanity silently offering up prayers to God to forgive them their sins and show them divine mercy and deliverance from their enemy. Thomas and Richard had merged with the tail end of the knights and adopted the same humble posture as they wound their way through Birgu. The boom and rumble of cannon continued in the distance, accompanied by a brief red loom against the night sky above the Sciberras peninsula. While those in Birgu prayed, their comrades in St Elmo still lived under the guns of the Turks and the threat of imminent assault.

The night air was warm and the hooded cloaks that Thomas and Richard wore to conceal their identities were stifling. Even though he accepted his companion's argument that this night presented their best chance to find the document, Thomas had grave doubts about Richard's plan. It lacked detail and depended far too much upon good fortune for Thomas's liking. And they would have to live with the risk of discovery afterwards, until the day when they were able to quit Malta and return to England. Or the day when they perished amid fire and sword along with the rest of the people trapped behind the defences of Malta.

Having paced around the limits of the small town, the archbishop led his people into the open square at the heart of Birgu. As they emerged from the street into the pool of light before the cathedral, Richard gently tugged Thomas's sleeve and edged towards the arched entrance of a bakery on the corner of the square. There they stopped, half concealed by the shadow of the arch, and let the rest of the people flow past and begin to fill up the square in their thousands. The archbishop reached the top of the steps leading up to the cathedral entrance and turned to begin praying. La Valette and the senior knights took up position on either side and then the most affluent and influential of the local people stood on the steps.

'Let's go,' said Richard.

'Not yet. Wait until the last of them have passed by us.

No point in drawing attention to ourselves by heading the wrong way.'

Richard nodded and eased himself back into the shadow of the arch. Glancing down the street, Thomas could see that there were still several hundred more people to come, and he returned his attention to the square. It already seemed to be filled but the crowd steadily pressed forward. Children and young men climbed on to statue pediments and clung to the pillars of the more prestigious buildings fronting the square. By the entrance to the cathedral the archbishop stepped aside to give his place to a tall, thin friar whose angular face was framed by a white beard and tonsure. He gazed steadily round the square and then raised a hand to quell the last of the murmured talk and prayers.

'Brethren! Hear me!' He addressed them in French, the common tongue of those who fought and lived in Malta since the Order had first arrived. His voice was high-pitched and carried clearly across the square. 'Beloved brethren, we are blessed to be here this day. There are amongst us those who feel accursed that they are beset by enemies whose false belief and cruel nature are works of evil. That they are, and it is right that we should fear them. In the place of faith and virtue their hearts are filled with cruelty, lust, avarice and mindless obeisance to the tyrant Suleiman and the false prophet.' Robert of Eboli paused briefly to let his words sink in. 'So much for the character of our enemy. That is why they are not worthy of victory, that is why they shall not triumph. God is merciful to the good and the pious, to those who know their sins and freely and openly repent of them in the loving sight of the Lord. They shall know his love, and his protection through the travails and fortunes of life . . . We few, we devout few are indeed fortunate. This place has been chosen to fight the greatest battle between the light of Christianity, and the darkness of Islam. The great test of the age is upon us, and only complete devotion to our cause can ensure our victory. In the time to come, the Christian world will look on our great feat in wonder, and each of you will hold close to your hearts the inestimable treasure of knowing that you were here, at the side of the Grand Master, fighting in the battle of battles. There are kings and queens in Europe who will hold themselves accursed that they could not be where you now stand.' The friar threw his arms out. 'Who here would shame themselves to change places with such a king or queen? WHO?'

His words echoed round the square and Thomas saw that not a hand was raised against the force of such rhetoric and the fear of being shamed in the eyes of their peers. As his eyes ran over the people on the steps below the friar, they abruptly stopped at a figure standing in the light of a torch. A woman. Though she wore a dark veil over her hair, her face was clearly visible and Thomas felt his heart lurch. He took half a step forward.

'What is it?' Richard demanded. 'What's the matter?'

'It's Maria, there.' Thomas pointed.

She was standing next to a man in a knight's cloak. His head was bowed so that his features were hidden, but his proximity to Maria made it clear that they were not strangers.

'I must speak to her.'

'No!' Richard seized his arm and held it firmly. 'Not now. We have work to do.'

Thomas's eyes were fixed on Maria and he felt his heartbeat quicken.

'You cannot go to her tonight,' Richard hissed. 'This might be the only chance to find what we came here for.'

'*She* is what I came here for.'

'And she will still be here after tonight. Our chance to get the document will not. Sir, be strong. Fail me here and now and thousands may die in England.'

Thomas felt torn between his conscience and his heart. 'I do not know what is in that document you seek but I know that I must speak to Maria.'

'And you will. I swear that I will do all that I can to make it so,' Richard said earnestly. 'Now come, we should leave, at once.'

Thomas was still staring across the square. The man raised his head and the light of the nearby torch revealed his features clearly. Sir Oliver Stokely. He bent his head to whisper something to Maria and she smiled briefly, as if to humour him.

The raw emotion that burned in Thomas's breast twisted violently like a blade and after an instant of confusion, a torrent of thought, of possibilities, coursed through his fevered mind. Recent exchanges and events fell into place and the hope of a moment before crumbled before a tide of anger and a bitter sense of betrayal.

'Sir Thomas. Come. Before the moment is lost.'

He allowed himself to be steered out of the archway and down the darkened, empty street, and a moment later Maria, Stokely, the friar and his rapt audience were lost from sight. As their footsteps echoed lightly off the walls of the buildings lining the street, Robert of Eboli's voice came after them.

'All must ask for forgiveness, or perish in the fires of hell . . .'

CHAPTER THIRTY

They made their way through silent darkened streets where only cats prowled now, no longer keeping a wary eye out for the dogs that used to challenge them. It would be the turn of the cats in due course, Thomas reflected, if the siege endured and food supplies began to be severely rationed. As they neared the channel they entered the poorest quarter of the town, where the fishermen lived in two-storey hovels, a living space above with a room beneath to dry and store their nets, and where fish were salted for winter. Ahead, the narrow street gave out onto a small levelled area of gravel where the men of the garrison drilled. Beyond was the drawbridge that led into the fort. There was only one guard visible at the entrance to the fort, clutching a pike in one hand, his soft cap dipped towards his chin with weariness. There were a handful of others in the bastions of the fort that overlooked the harbour on three sides.

'Time to prepare,' Richard said softly as they crouched beside the last of the fishermen's houses. They removed their boots and pulled the hoods of their cloaks up. Richard reached into the haversack he had been wearing beneath and took out two bleached lengths of rope which they tied about their middles in the manner of friars. Then he hefted the leather cosh he had carefully packed into the bottom of his baggage before leaving England. He slipped the loop over his wrist and gave it an experimental swing to feel its weight and recall the feel of the weapon. He glanced at Thomas. 'Ready?'

'As ready as I can be for such business.'

Richard flashed a grin in the gloom. 'This is the business I am trained for. Trust me and follow my instructions and you will be fine.'

They stood up and with Richard in the lead began to cross the level ground. Thomas was uncomfortable with this reversal of positions but knew that he must trust Richard. He was no longer playing the squire and had reverted to being one of Walsingham's agents, skilled in the dark arts of subterfuge and stealth. The sound of the cannonade was much louder away from the town and the flames spurting from the batteries on the high ground above St Elmo lit up the crest of the ridge brilliantly as each round was fired. As Thomas stepped on to the weathered timbers of the drawbridge he was aware of the dark void on either side. Glancing to the right he saw the looming mass of the Turkish galleon that had been captured the year before and had done much to provoke the Sultan's decision to finally obliterate the Order of St John.

The two men had almost reached the end of the drawbridge before the guard roused from where he had been leaning against the wall beside the gate.

'Who goes there?' he demanded, lowering the point of his pike a fraction and grasping the shaft firmly in both hands.

'Friar Gubert and Friar Henri, from the cathedral,' Thomas called back, as calmly as he could.

'What is your business? You should be at the sermon.'

'We've come from there,' Thomas continued as they approached the man. 'With orders from the Grand Master. He is to entertain Robert of Eboli afterwards and sent us to tell his steward to prepare a meal.'

'His steward is at the sermon,' the guard replied. 'I saw him leave myself.'

'Are you certain, my son?' Thomas stepped closer, and then suddenly shot his arms out and grabbed the wrists of the astonished guard. An instant later Richard stepped round the man and swung his cosh in a savage arc towards the back of his skull. It connected with a solid thud before the man could cry out. He went limp and Thomas took up his weight and then eased him on to the ground, just inside the gate where he would be least visible.

'No, not there.' Richard lifted the guard under the shoulders and dragged him towards the drawbridge.

'What are you doing?' Thomas whispered.

'He might recognise us.'

'Wait.' Thomas stepped between Richard and the drawbridge. 'It's dark, and we're wearing hoods.'

'He heard your voice.'

'Then that's a risk I am willing to take. Leave him,' Thomas said firmly.

Richard was still for a moment. 'What if he comes round? Or he's discovered?'

Thomas knew that Richard's caution was sound, from a cold-hearted point of view, but he was not prepared to see the man killed. 'Leave him, and let's get on with it.'

'You're being foolish,' Richard growled. 'You'll get us killed.'

'Not if we move fast. Now leave him be.'

'Damn you!' Richard let the guard drop then, before Thomas could intervene, viciously hit him again with his cosh. 'There, just to make sure.'

Without waiting for Thomas to respond Richard turned and padded through the arch of the gatehouse. Thomas breathed in deeply to calm his anger and followed. On the far side of the arch they entered a narrow passage overlooked by murder holes. A ramp led up and turned sharply back on itself before they passed through a narrow gate into the fort's courtyard.

All was still and quiet; the enemy guns across the harbour were slightly muffled by the mass of the walls rising up towards the stars overhead. They waited a moment, hearts beating swiftly as their senses strained to detect any sign of movement. Then, satisfied that they had not been noticed, the two men crept round the edge of the courtyard towards the entrance to the storerooms and dungeons cut into the rock beneath St Angelo. Pausing on the threshold, they looked down the staircase and saw that the main guardroom was dimly lit by a handful of candles. There was no sound from below. They descended warily until they stood on the flagstone floor and looked around. The musty air was noticeably cooler and the sweat on Thomas's forehead felt chilly. There were two large tables with benches on either side. A few bare wooden platters remained, together with some brass cups decorated with Islamic verses, part of the loot the Order had taken over the decades following their arrival in Malta. Three corridors led off the guardroom.

'Which way?' whispered Thomas.

Thomas recalled the last time he had stood in the same spot, twenty years before, when he had overseen the soldiers tasked with carrying a chest of silver coins from the hold of La Valette's galley to the security of the dungeons. Then there had only been one corridor opening off the guardroom.

Richard gestured to the left passage. 'Follow me.'

They crossed the room and entered a tunnel. A candle guttered halfway along and dimly illuminated the regularly spaced doors on either side. As Richard led the way, Thomas felt a chill tremor of anxiety ripple down his spine. If they were discovered here, there would be no explaining away their presence. Ahead, the corridor came to a junction with yet more passages leading off to either side. The stale smell of dogs filled Thomas's nostrils.

'We're close now,' said Richard. 'We go right here, then it's perhaps twenty yards to the chamber where the sentries guard the entrance.'

'And then?'

'We'll deal with whatever we find the same way we did with the guard on the gate.'

'Assuming one guard is all there is.'

'That's right.'

'Some plan.' Thomas shook his head. 'And if there are four of them, like you saw before?'

'Then we have to deal with four of them.'

They slipped round the corner and crouched low as they approached the door at the end of the passage where the Grand Master had kept his hounds. The doors to the kennels were open and by the light of another candle

Thomas saw the wooden pegs on which hung the collars and leashes of the animals that had been destroyed on La Valette's orders. Ahead stood an arched doorway. The door was ajar and a brighter light burned within. There was no sound as Richard and Thomas stole silently along the passage. Richard readied the cosh in his right hand and quietly drew out his dagger with the other. Thomas reached into his side bag and took out his own cosh, and slipped the loop over his wrist.

They were perhaps ten feet from the door when there was a light rattle and clack from the room beyond and a brief cry of triumph that was answered by a gruff curse. Thomas and Richard froze. Richard held up his hand to signal Thomas to wait. Then he crept forward towards the door and peered round very slowly. A moment later he backed away and spoke softly into Thomas's ear.

'Two of them, playing at dice. No more than two paces from the door. We'll have to rush them. Ready?'

'Yes, but no killing unless we have to, understand?'

Richard frowned and opened his mouth to reply, but then thought better of it and shrugged instead. 'Very well, on three.'

The two men braced themselves behind the door. In the gloom Richard glanced at Thomas who nodded, then as the dice rattled again he counted softly. 'One . . . two . . . three.'

Springing forward, Richard thrust the door aside and burst into the small chamber, with Thomas right behind him. The two guards were hunched over a table. Their heads turned at the intrusion, eyes wide with surprise.

Richard leaped towards the nearest man, his cosh arcing through the air. The guard tried to throw up his arm to block the blow but he was too slow and the heavy leather bag cracked into his skull and he tumbled off his stool and on to the floor. Thomas ran past and round the end of the table and swung his cosh at the other guard's head. The second guard had time to scramble off the stool and the cosh struck the edge of the table, the shock of the impact sending the cups leaping into the air, spilling their contents over the coins and the dice that had been laid out. The guard snatched a dagger from a small scabbard hanging from his waist and thrust the point at his attacker. Thomas threw himself to the side to avoid the deadly blade. The guard slashed wildly from side to side, forcing Thomas back. Sensing the wall at his back Thomas leaped forward, grasping the man's knife hand and punching his right fist, still clenching the cosh, into the guard's jaw. It was a solid impact and the man's head snapped back. Thomas hit him again, hard, and with a deep grunt he stumbled, tripping over his upturned stool so that he crashed on to the floor. He lay blinking, still holding on to his dagger, and then passed out. Richard stepped round the body and made for the dungeon entrance, a thickly timbered door studded with iron nail heads and with a small grille in its surface.

'We need to find the keys,' Thomas muttered.

Richard shook his head. 'I doubt the guards will be troubled with them.' Reaching into his haversack he felt for something and then pulled out a set of small metal tools on a brass ring. The corners of his mouth lifted slightly as he saw Thomas's enquiring expression. 'Tools of the trade.'

He shifted to one side to allow the light of the candles to illuminate the lock. He chose two of the tools which he inserted into the lock and probed gently, delicately exploring the mechanism. Thomas watched him with the faint admiration of those witnessing an arcane skill. Then his attention shifted from the lock to the rapt concentration on the young man's face.

There was a series of soft clicks from the lock and then Richard withdrew his tools and lifted the latch. The door edged open soundlessly on well-greased hinges and a waft of cooler air came from the dark space beyond.

'Get the candles,' Richard instructed.

Thomas fetched them from the wall brackets of the guardroom and passed one to Richard.

As soon as they stepped through the arch, Thomas sensed the vastness of the space, even before the wavering glow of the candles began to reveal its dimensions. The ceiling arched overhead and the walls were lined with sturdy buttresses to take the weight of the fort above. The ceiling was low but the dungeon was long and wide and interspersed with stout columns that divided the chamber into two. Rows of wooden shelves stretched out before the two men, beyond the loom of the candlelight and on into the darkness. The shelves were laden with baskets of scrolls, ledgers, logs and chests, many of which were sealed with wax to keep the contents safe from dampness. There was a slight movement in the air and little of the musty odour that Thomas had been expecting and he realised that the dungeon must be ventilated to prevent the onset of mould.

'There must be hundreds of chests here . . . thousands,'

Richard muttered. 'We have to search quickly, before the sermon ends and the rest of the garrison returns.'

'Then you take this half of the chamber,' Thomas decided. 'I'll search the other.'

They separated and began to work their way along the narrow space between the shelves, crouching now and then to see what lay on the lowest levels. There were many chests amongst the archives, and Thomas carefully checked each of those that were black or constructed of dark wood with brass fittings, looking for the crest on the lid. All the while he was conscious that time was running out for them. Depending on the passion and stamina of Robert of Eboli, the sermon might last for two or more hours. But given the weariness of the defenders it might well be concluded earlier.

At the end of the first row of shelves was a caged area with thick iron bars that were set into the floor and extended to the ceiling. The door had two locks, with thick bolts and sturdy receivers. Beyond lay dozens of small chests and by the wall were stacked thick bolts of silk that shimmered in the faint glow of Thomas's candle. On a rack to one side hung a collection of scimitars with jewel-encrusted guards and handles of gold and silver. This was the treasury of the Order, Thomas realised, looted from the ships and coastal towns and estates of the Islamic world. A fortune to rival the treasures of any of Europe's monarchs. Paid for with the blood of hundreds of knights and tens of thousands of soldiers and common people, all for the sake of their religion. Thomas felt a tingle of nausea as he beheld the riches and contemplated the centuries of suffering it represented, right up until the present moment, and the weeks and months to come until the siege was resolved. Even then, the conflict would be handed on from generation to generation until the end of time. Or until mankind cured itself of religion.

If there was a divine presence in the world, it would surely look on the works that were carried out in its name in abject horror, Thomas reflected. He had never felt such a presence, never sensed it in the slightest; he was only aware of the heedless elements of a natural world that embraced men, animals and faiths with abiding disinterest. Such thoughts were dangerous, he knew. More than dangerous, lethal. So he tried to keep them at bay, and even prayed along with the faithful as if in an attempt to hide his true thoughts from himself as much as other people.

Something clattered to the floor a short distance away and Thomas flinched and turned towards the sound. A glow amid the shelves revealed Richard's position.

'Richard?' he called out as loudly as he dared.

'I think I've found it. Yes . . . Yes! Over here.'

Thomas hurried round the end of the lines of shelves and saw his companion bent over a chest he was pulling out from the lowest rack in front of him. As Thomas approached, he saw the crest of the ill-fated Sir Peter de Launcey in the light of the candle Richard had placed on the shelf above. It was neatly painted on a shallow relief, carved with some skill. The gleam of the lacquer was visible where Richard's fingers had wiped off the decades of dust that had accumulated in a dull skein across the lid of the chest. Sturdy brass straps bound and protected the fine craftsmanship. A small, delicate-looking lock sat in the front of the chest and Richard fished out his picks again.

'Hold your candle over the lock. And hold it steady. This one's going to be something of a challenge, I fear.' Richard selected one of the finest of his picks and carefully inserted it in the keyhole. His face was frozen in concentration as his fingers made tiny adjustments to the tool. 'Can't quite feel the tumblers . . . It's as fine a piece of work as I have ever encountered . . . Damn.'

He eased the pick out and chose another, the smallest on the ring, and tried again, closing his eyes as he felt for the mechanisms that would release the lock. Thomas watched for a moment and then glanced anxiously in the direction of the entrance to the dungeon.

'How long do you need?'

Richard paused and opened his eyes. 'As long as it takes. Now, please, let me concentrate.'

'Fine. But hurry.'

Richard focused on his work for a while longer, teeth gritted as he tried to build up some picture of the workings inside the lock. At length he extracted the pick and wiped his hand across his brow. 'I can't do it. The locksmith who built this was a better man than I. It's a work of genius . . .'

'Perhaps, but genius is no match for steel, as Archimedes discovered.' Thomas drew his dagger and squatted beside Richard. He set the point into the slight gap between the lid of the chest and main body.

'What are you doing?' Richard demanded.

'This.' Thomas balled his left hand into a fist and pounded the haft of the knife with all his strength. There was a sharp metallic snap and the blade leaped into the gap as the lid suddenly lifted. 'There.'

Richard glared at him. 'Oh, very well done indeed!

Anyone who looks at this will see the lock has been forced.'

'Who's going to notice? From the dust I'd say no one has touched this in years. Now get what we came for, put the chest back in place and let's get out of here.'

Richard bit back on his anger and eased the lid back. The light from the candles revealed a small leather purse, tightly packed with coins. The small opening at the top revealed the warm lustre of gold. Beside it lay a gold cross on a chain, with a ruby set in its centre. There was also a Bible, some letters and a leather tube. Richard picked the latter up and inspected it. A cap at the end of the tube was sealed with wax which had been imprinted with a design. He nodded and muttered, 'This is it. This is what we came here for.'

Thomas's eyes were fixed on the seal. 'That's the royal seal. The Great Seal of England.'

Richard made no reply but quickly and carefully placed the leather tube in his haversack. 'Let's go.'

He closed the lid and eased the chest back on to the shelf. He made a minor adjustment to its position so that it covered the clear area it had screened from long years of settling dust. Then he straightened and retrieved his candle. 'Come.'

After Richard had locked the door behind them they hurried out of the dungeon and past the two men sprawled beside the table. One of the guards moaned feebly for a moment then lapsed into silence. His assailants set down their candles and left the room, padding back along the passage to the main guardroom and then up the steps into the courtyard. They paused to ensure that it was deserted as before and then left by the main gate. The sentry still lay in the shadows by the drawbridge, breathing in faint shallow gasps. Their haste to get away from the fort caused their footsteps to echo dully as they crossed the drawbridge.

'Who's there?' a voice called from the wall above. 'Michel? Is that you?'

Richard froze but Thomas pushed him on. 'It's too late for that. Keep going.'

They crossed the bridge and set off across the parade ground at a brisk pace.

'Michel?' the voice called out again. Then a moment later: 'You there! Stop!'

They ignored the command and broke into a trot, then a dead run, until they reached the cover of the fisherman's hovel where they had left their boots. From the direction of the cathedral the sound of singing carried across the rooftops of Birgu; close by they heard footsteps approaching, and voices muttering. Thomas waved Richard back out of sight against the wall and then pulled a length of fishing net over his body. Several shadows approached along the narrow street.

'Don't care what he says,' one grumbled. 'There ain't no help coming. We're in this alone. Long as we last.'

'Always looking on the bright side, eh, Jules?' another laughed. 'Even after that performance by Robert of Eboli?'

'What, you think the Lord himself, and his cohort of angels, are really going to descend on a wave of celestial light and smite the followers of the false prophet and deliver us from the ambitions of Suleiman and his hordes?'

'They might, if we pray hard for it and perform our Christian duty,' someone responded defensively. 'If we are righteous.'

'Oh, good luck to you!' the first man growled. 'Me? I'm trusting in a sharp pike and dry gunpowder.'

They continued past the two Englishmen and set off across the parade ground towards the drawbridge. Thomas knew that they would come across their unconscious comrade as soon as they reached the far side. He slipped out from under the net and pulled on his boots. As soon as Richard had followed suit, they slipped into the street and hurried away from the fort. They had not gone more than twenty paces when there was a cry of alarm, instantly lost in the boom of a gun as it fired a shot at St Elmo. They increased their pace and soon they came across another party of men and exchanged nods as they passed by. Then they reached the main street leading towards the cathedral. The singing had ended and the street was filling with small groups of townspeople and soldiers returning to their homes and billets. Conscious that they were heading against the flow, at least as far as the side street on which the auberge stood, they kept to the edge of the street and slipped along as unobtrusively as possible. They overheard snatches of conversation, most of which was in praise of Robert of Eboli, and some spoke in confidence about the great army that Don Garcia was mobilising in Sicily to bring to Malta and crush the forces of the Turkish Sultan.

They had almost reached the side street they wanted when Thomas saw Stokely a short distance further along. He was in earnest conversation with Romegas. Walking a pace behind him was Maria, together with a maid. Thomas froze for an instant and then hurriedly turned off the main thoroughfare and stood against the corner.

'What's the matter?' asked Richard.

'I need to find something out. You go back to the auberge. I'll join you later.'

'Why?' Richard glanced round but could see no obvious danger.

'Just go!' Thomas ordered fiercely and pushed him down the street.

Richard stumbled a few paces and turned to stare at Thomas with a concerned expression. Then, touching his haversack to make sure that the leather tube was still safe, he strode away.

Thomas stood still and watched the figures passing by the end of the street. He heard Stokely's voice and a moment later he and Romegas paced by, followed by the tall slender form of Maria, staring fixedly at the ground in front of her. Thomas felt an impulse to step out behind her, speak her name and tell her to follow him into another street but he feared she would refuse, or that she, or her maid, might cry out in alarm and alert Stokely. So he kept his mouth shut and instead slipped into the crowd and followed them at a short distance, making sure that he kept his head bowed enough for the hood to conceal his features in case she turned to look back for any reason. Stokely and Romegas continued for another hundred yards along the wide thoroughfare before Romegas halted, made his farewells and took the street that led to the fort. Stokely took Maria's arm and turned into a side street. Thomas paused at the edge of the junction and then risked a quick look round the corner and saw Stokely approach the gate of a courtyard. Beyond, the walls of a modest town house rose up into the darkness. Stokely paused and looked back to see if they were being followed. Satisfied that there was no one stalking them, he rapped on the door to the courtyard. It was opened a moment later and Stokely led his small party inside and the door closed behind them.

Thomas waited for a moment before entering the narrow street and walking slowly past the gate. The walls were perhaps ten feet high and there were no obvious foot- or handholds. The gate itself was solid-looking and reinforced with lengths of oak. He walked on and then turned back and waited. It did not take long for others to enter the street and make for a neighbouring property. Thomas strode up to a rotund man who, like most of those who had attended the sermon, wore a sombre cloak.

'I beg your pardon, sir,' Thomas addressed him in French. 'But I have a message to deliver to the house of an English knight. I was told he lives in this street but I don't know which house is his.'

'Sir Oliver Stokely?' The neighbour arched an eyebrow. 'Yes, he lives here. That house, next to mine.'

'I thank you, sir. But the message is not for him, but a lady. Maria, I believe she is called.'

'Yes.' The man nodded his head. 'That would be his wife.'

'Wife . . .'

The man tapped his nose. 'What these knights claim to believe and what they do are as different as chalk and cheese, eh?' Thomas was silent for a moment and the man frowned. 'Is that all?'

'Yes.' Thomas forced a smile. 'Thank you, sir. I'll bid

you good night. It's late. I'll deliver my message another time.'

He turned and walked away, back towards the auberge, his heart as heavy as a rock.

CHAPTER THIRTY-ONE

'Thieves, right here in the heart of our defences.' La Valette shook his head in consternation. 'It's an outrage. Whoever it was strolled into the fort and attempted to break into our archives last night. I give thanks to God that they did not account for the quality of the lock or they would have looted the place for whatever they could carry out of the castle. It's a scandal, gentlemen.' He looked round the table at his advisers. 'Not only that but two of our men were injured in the process.'

There was a tense silence before Colonel Mas spoke. 'We were lucky they weren't killed, and lucky the lock held.'

'Luck had nothing to do with it. That lock was made by one of the finest smiths in Paris, as were the locks on the treasury door. Monsieur Berthon assured me that they were impregnable.'

Thomas nodded thoughtfully, along with the others. Despite his apparent calm his heart was beating swiftly and he could feel the clammy sweat on the palms of his hands.

Stokely shot him a curious glance before returning his gaze to the Grand Master, who continued speaking.

'I want these robbers found and made an example of. They will be shown no pity, regardless of what rank they hold. The same penalty will apply for all such crimes from now on. We are all in this together, those who serve the Order as well as the common people of Malta. Colonel, I want a reward posted on every main street in Birgu. A hundred gold pieces for the person who captures these criminals, or who can provide information that leads to their capture.'

'Yes, sir.' Colonel Mas nodded.

'Very well, from now on I want the guard on the archive doubled, and also the main gate. This will not happen again.' La Valette slapped his hand down on the table. He stared round at the other men and then his expression began to soften. 'We must address other matters now. Firstly, Sir Oliver, your report on the water supplies. I gather that we are consuming more water than anticipated.'

'Indeed, sir. But there are additional problems. One of the cisterns under St Michael has been contaminated by seawater. There must be a crack somewhere that has allowed the sea to enter. As a result we have lost approximately one-eighth of our supply. I suggest that we begin rationing the water immediately. I know this will not be a popular—'

'Shhh!' Colonel Mas raised a hand to silence Stokely.

'Colonel, I must protest.'

'Quiet, listen.' Colonel Mas gestured towards the window. 'Something's wrong.'

They had grown so used to the irregular rhythm of the gunfire from across the harbour that they had begun to ignore it. But now it had ceased.

Thomas knew at once the meaning behind the silence of the enemy guns. 'They're attacking St Elmo.'

Chairs scraped as everyone rushed to the windows and stared across the calm waters of the harbour towards the end of the Sciberras peninsula. The sound of drums and horns carried from the enemy trenches and Thomas could just make out the tiny figures of Janissaries rushing forward beneath a green banner, from the top of which flowed a white horsehair tail. They surged out of their trenches and across the broken ground towards the defensive ditch in front of the fort. The defenders appeared along the parapet and the first puffs of smoke from the arquebuses blossomed into the dawn air. Those in St Angelo heard the crackle of fire from the fort, and then the sound intensified as the Turkish snipers began picking off targets along the battered walls of St Elmo.

'Look there.' Colonel Mas raised his arm and pointed towards the end of the ravelin visible beyond the fort. 'Is that an enemy banner flying there? I can't make it out.'

Thomas strained his eyes to pick out the detail through the shimmering air across the harbour. Sure enough, there was a banner flying from the top of the ravelin, but neither it nor the figures swarming about it could be distinguished at that distance. Then, as if in response to their anxiety, the light breeze caused the banner to ripple out and there was no mistaking the colour.

'It's the enemy,' said Stokely. 'They've taken the ravelin.'

La Valette shook his head. 'Impossible! They've only just launched their attack. Quite impossible . . .'

Despite what was clear to his eyes, Thomas shared the Grand Master's disbelief. The Turks would first have had to cross the ditch and deal with the obstacles there, then scale the walls of the ravelin before they even clashed with the defenders. Yet, incredibly, an enemy banner had been planted on the ravelin and now spurts of flame and tiny puffs of smoke showed that the enemy were firing on the fort from the ravelin.

Mas clenched his hands in frustration. 'What the devil is going on over there? What is Miranda playing at?'

'Send a boat across,' La Valette ordered. 'I want a report at once.'

'Yes, sir,' Mas nodded and hurried out of the study. The others continued to watch in growing despair as the enemy emerged from the ditch all along the front of the wall and began to plant their scaling ladders against the scarred exterior of the fort. Sunlight glittered off the armour and weapons of the men defending the parapet until flame and smoke obscured the view. Then only the fierce burst of incendiaries and the swirling blaze of fire hoops were briefly visible through the smoke and dust cloaking the fort.

Below, in the deep blue water of the harbour, Thomas saw a boat striking out across the light swell towards the small landing stage below the fort. The Maltese oarsmen rowed strongly and the boat surged forward. It was over halfway across the placid expanse of water before it drew the attention of the Turks. A handful of Janissary snipers turned their long barrels from the fort and trained them on the boat. Small spurts of water erupted in the sea ahead and to the side of the boat. Those watching from St Angelo shouted their encouragement and willed their comrades on. The enemy's shots grew more accurate as the boat neared the opposite shore. Then one struck the prow of the boat and splinters burst into the air. An oarsman clasped his arm and his oar blade dropped, dragging the boat round until the man on the tiller corrected the course and bellowed at the injured man to take up his oar. Miraculously the small craft passed out of sight of the snipers as it drew close to the landing at the foot of a low cliff. The rowers slumped over their oars as the officer Mas had ordered to report on the attack clambered from the bows and raced up the steps cut into the rock and made for the entrance at the rear of the fort, close to the cavalier tower.

The small drama was over and Thomas puffed his cheeks in relief. La Valette ordered his advisers to follow him and led them out of the study and up on to the tower above the keep from where they would have a better view of the attack on St Elmo. The sun climbed into the sky and a breeze blew in from the north, thinning the dense bank of smoke that clung to the front of the fort. As it cleared, the dreadful struggle for the ravelin and the walls was revealed. Bodies lay heaped in front of the wall, mingled with the wreckage of destroyed ladders. On the walls, more bodies were slumped on the parapet and crimson streaks ran down the pitted stonework. Above the carnage the standard of the Order still flew and the distant figures of the knights gleamed as they urged their men on, defying the enemy as they stood in clear view of the snipers firing from the shelter of their trenches, even though they risked hitting their own men.

Stokely wiped the sweat from his brow and shook his head in wonder. 'How much longer can the Turks endure such punishment?'

'Let them come,' La Valette replied in a cold voice. 'The more men they lose in taking St Elmo, the fewer we shall have to face when they attack Senglea and Birgu. And their morale will have taken a beating as well.'

The words might have been calculating and ruthless, thought Thomas, but the Grand Master was speaking the truth. As long as St Elmo held out, the Turks would throw men against the defences and suffer appalling losses as a result. In between assaults their cannon would use up precious powder and shot from the supplies they had brought with them from Istanbul. Most important of all, Thomas reflected, they would be wasting precious days of the campaign season. When the rain and storms of autumn arrived, there would be little chance of supplies and reinforcements reaching the Turks.

At last, as the bells of the churches in Birgu announced midday, the enemy attack finally began to peter out. They fell back from the walls to their trenches, leaving the ground before the fort carpeted with the bodies of their comrades. The ravelin, however, remained in their hands and the Turkish engineers already seemed to be improving its defences by building up the height. As the last of the enemy withdrew, the guns on the ridge opened fire once more, pounding the defences. Along the walls the defenders disappeared from view as they scurried back into cover.

La Valette turned away from the grisly spectacle and Thomas saw that he looked weary, and yet there was the same unyielding determination in his eyes as he met Thomas's gaze. 'Thanks be to God. We have won ourselves another day.'

At midday Thomas took Richard to one side as they

ate a quick lunch of bread and cheese, washed down by a sharp, vinegary local wine. Thomas quietly related what had been discussed at the morning meeting. Richard listened in silence.

'At least you have what you came for,' Thomas concluded. 'I trust that it is worth risking our lives for.'

'Taking such risks is in the nature of the game,' Richard replied. 'That is why you are not fit for the work that I do.'

Thomas shook his head sadly. 'And it is why you are not fit to serve as a knight, Richard. Such skulduggery is not honourable.'

'Really? You knights kill for your cause, and I do what I must for my country. Would you care to explain – justify – which is the more ethical path?' He gave Thomas a searching look and then smiled thinly. 'I thought not.'

Thomas looked at him with the frustration of one who knows he is in the right but is too weary to explain the matter. For some reason he felt an obligation to guide Richard, as if he was a real squire, or an errant son. At length Thomas sighed. 'I trust that you have put your prize somewhere safe.'

'It's as well hidden as I can manage under the circumstances.'

'Good. Then your mission is all but complete. All that remains is to survive the siege,' he added with an ironic smile. 'Let us bend our efforts towards rendering good service to La Valette and the Order. Until the siege is over, I serve the Grand Master only, and you serve as my squire and set aside your obedience to Walsingham and his schemes. Agreed?'

Richard thought for a moment and nodded. 'Until the siege is over.'

The young man turned his attention back to his food, bit off a chunk of cheese and chewed hard as he gazed across the harbour towards St Elmo.

Dusk was settling over the island by the time the officer Colonel Mas had sent to St Elmo returned to make his report. He entered the Grand Master's study and stood before the table, a bloodied dressing tied about his head. It took a moment before Thomas recognised him as Fadrique, the son of Don Garcia. They exchanged a brief nod of recognition.

'Do you want a chair?' La Valette asked him.

'No, sir.' Fadrique drew himself up proudly. 'I will stand.'

'Very well then. Make your report. What happened at the ravelin?'

'Captain Miranda is not certain, sir. It seems that one of the sentries on duty in the ravelin was shot dead by a sniper. The men on duty on the exposed parts of the wall have taken to lying flat in order not to present the enemy with a clear target. This morning, it appears that the dead man's comrades assumed he was alive and keeping watch. That was why the Turks were able to put a ladder up against his section of the ravelin and get a party of Janissaries on to it before our men were aware of the danger. By the time they reacted, it was too late and the ravelin was seized by the Turks.'

'That is damned careless,' Colonel Mas said bitterly. 'Did Miranda attempt to recapture it?'

'Yes, sir. Twice. The second time I joined the counter-attack. The Turks had fortified the ravelin and packed it full of their men. They shot us down as we tried to force our way back inside. We lost three knights and several men before we even reached the ravelin. Then it was hand-to-hand. Captain Miranda managed to get inside with three men, but was forced back and obliged to retreat into the fort.'

'The ravelin is lost to us, then?' La Valette said.

'Yes, sir. I don't see how we can retake it now the Turks have thoroughly invested the position. They had already started to build up the level inside before I left the fort. Soon they will be able to fire across the walls into the heart of St Elmo.' Fadrique paused briefly before he concluded his report. 'Captain Miranda says that the fort cannot hold out for much longer. A matter of days at most. He has already been approached by a deputation of knights to send you a formal request for permission to evacuate the fort.'

'Evacuate?' La Valette frowned. 'It's out of the question. Captain Miranda and his men know how vital the position is. They must hold on for as long as possible at any cost. Do you hear?' He stabbed a finger at Fadrique.

The Spaniard sighed. 'Sir, I am only repeating what I was told.'

The Grand Master relented. 'Of course. I apologise, young man. You have done well. Now go and have my surgeon see to that wound.'

'It is little more than a scratch, sir.'

'Then it should not take much time to attend to it,' La Valette responded tersely, with a wave towards the door.

Fadrique bowed his head and left the room. Once the door had closed behind the Spaniard, Colonel Mas leaned forward and rested his elbows on the table.

'What are your intentions, sir?'

La Valette thought for a moment. 'Miranda must hold out. We can supply the garrison of St Elmo with more ammunition and reinforcements by night.'

'Not for much longer, sir. This afternoon I saw Turkish engineers marking the ground for more batteries on Gallows Point, and on the headland opposite. Once they have placed guns there they can sweep the harbour between St Elmo and this fort. No boats will be able to cross. The garrison will be cut off. In any case, resupplying Miranda is only part of the problem. The key issue is morale. If his men are already petitioning him to request permission to withdraw, then it is the first step along the road to mutiny.' Mas looked round at the others. 'Gentlemen, I have served in many armies, in many wars, and I have seen enough to know that mutiny unchecked is a disease. It destroys an army just as surely as defeat in battle. We cannot allow the men at St Elmo to withdraw.'

'Why not?' asked Stokely. 'Surely it is better that they add to our strength here than be taken prisoner by the enemy.'

'No. If the Grand Master allows them to quit the fort it will set a precedent. It can only encourage those in Birgu and Senglea who lack the resolve to see the siege through. Better that they stay in St Elmo and buy the rest of us as much time as possible. It is a hard truth, I know. But we have no choice. They must remain at their posts.'

La Valette nodded thoughtfully. 'But there is a risk that

it may spur them to mutiny. And that might be worse than allowing them to quit St Elmo.'

'If they can be persuaded to stay and fight to the end of their own free will,' Thomas intervened, 'they will provide an inspiration to the rest of us defending the island.'

'And how do you propose that we persuade them, exactly?' asked Colonel Mas. 'They appear to have already made up their minds, and every enemy gun that fires on the fort will only add weight to their decision.'

'These men are knights of the Order of St John, the last of the great military orders pledged to fight Islam and recover the Holy Land. There is no higher honour in Christendom than membership of this Order. So what could be more wounding to the hearts of the men defending St Elmo than a sense of shame?'

La Valette stared at him. 'What do you suggest, Sir Thomas?'

'I suggest that you appeal to their sense of honour, remind them of the tradition of which they are a part. Remind them of the oath they took to fight the enemies of Christendom to the last drop of blood. That is one part of the strategy I suggest. The other is to issue a call for volunteers here in Birgu to replace those who no longer have the heart to defend St Elmo. My guess is that those here who know little of the condition in the fort will readily volunteer. If the men of Miranda's garrison try to force the issue of evacuation then you assent, and let them know that for every man who wishes to quit St Elmo, there are three or four in Birgu willing to take his place. Once they know that, they will fear shame and dishonour far more than they fear death. I would wager my life on it.'

'It may come to that.' La Valette smiled, then turned to Colonel Mas. 'What do you think?'

'I think that the devious reputation of the English is well-deserved.' Mas reflected a moment. 'It is the best way to proceed, sir. Despite what I said earlier. In normal circumstances I would insist on, and enforce, discipline. However, our situation is desperate and sometimes men need more than an order to compel them to fight.'

'Very well.' La Valette nodded. 'We shall appeal to their honour. Meanwhile, I shall issue a proclamation asking for volunteers to reinforce St Elmo. And I pray you are right that there will be men with enough heart to answer the call, Sir Thomas.'

Thomas was aware that the other members of the council were all looking at him and there was a fleeting moment of fear before he cleared his throat and spoke as calmly as he could. 'Sir, I request your permission to be the first man to volunteer.'

CHAPTER THIRTY-TWO

A day later, every place in the small force to be sent to St Elmo had been filled, and many more men had been turned away. The friar, Robert of Eboli, had insisted on accompanying the men to offer his spiritual support to their fight. The Grand Master concluded his evening meeting and asked for Colonel Mas and Thomas to remain behind. 'Are you certain about your decision?' La Valette asked. 'I am loath to lose two of my best advisers.'

Colonel Mas nodded. 'It is, as Sir Thomas argued, the only way. It is vital that no one doubts that we all share the same risks, and the same fate, without exception. Save you, sir. You are indispensable. The men of St Elmo are close to breaking point and are beyond the normal codes of obedience and appeals to duty. All they have left is their sense of honour. If Sir Thomas and I return to the fort with fifty volunteers and tell them that you have a thousand more willing to take their place, they will stay the fight to the end. I am sure of it.'

'When will you leave?'

'Tomorrow night, sir. Tonight I will sleep deeply. When I rise early on the morrow I will need time to select my men and to put my affairs in order. There are letters I must write.'

The Grand Master stroked his beard, deep in thought. He turned his gaze to Thomas. 'And you? It is not too late to change your mind.'

'I will go with the colonel, sir.'

'Why?'

Thomas did not reply immediately. There was no one simple reason. Or rather there was, and all other reasons led to it. Maria was now the wife of another man, Sir Oliver Stokely, and must have been for many years. She was lost to him, unless he broke every last code of moral behaviour that was left in him. Even then, the situation was hopeless, for she would never agree to be with him. And there was also the matter of his loss of faith, Thomas reflected. It had been a long, painful road to the belief that there was nothing more than this earthly life. To discover that Maria still lived and might feel for him as he did for her had filled the void and given new purpose and meaning to his life. Now that was gone, and if his life held little meaning, perhaps his death could at least serve a noble purpose.

He cleared his throat and met La Valette's enquiring gaze. 'Because I choose to.'

'And what if I choose to order you to remain here? It is a hard thing to sacrifice Colonel Mas alone. Must I lose you too? I need the advice of men I can trust.'

'At the moment your greater need is men who can set an example, sir,' Thomas replied. 'There are other good men in the Order whose advice you can rely on. In the past they may have been rivals, but there is no past now. Every man here has come to accept that we have one common purpose. Our places at your side will be filled by others.'

La Valette smiled sadly. 'It is true . . . I only wish that it had not taken this turn of events for our comrades to realise it. A pity that imminent extinction is the only thing that brings us wholly together in common cause.'

'Even then . . .' Colonel Mas cocked an eyebrow. 'I am sorry, I have been a soldier too long. It tends to harden a man's cynicism.'

La Valette stared at him and then smiled, and broke into a laugh. Thomas joined him, and even the scarred and battle-hardened Mas grinned. For a moment the grim burden of the last month lifted and there was a shared lightness of feeling that might have been close to friendship at a different time and place.

The boom of the Turkish cannon across the harbour broke the spell. La Valette rose from his chair and came round the table and embraced Colonel Mas.

'I thank you, Colonel. You are a good soldier. A good man. I am sorry that I recruited you to our cause. You deserve a better end than this.'

'There is no need to apologise. I am a mercenary, sir. I go where the fighting is, and in truth, my end is long overdue. Besides, not many of us find such an honourable exit. It's usually sickness or syphilis that does for us in the end. This is better.' He narrowed his eyes. 'Just be sure my contract is paid. I have a wife and children in Barcelona.'

'I will see to it. You have my word.'

'Thank you, sir.' Mas stood to attention, bowed his head in a final salute, and turned and strode from the room, leaving Thomas alone with the Grand Master. There was a moment of awkward silence as the older man regarded the English knight. A pained fondness filled his eyes.

'I count it a great pity to have lost your services for so many years, Thomas. I knew you had potential from the very first day you joined my galley. I had plans for you even then. I have given my life to the Order. I have denied myself a wife, a family.' His gaze dropped and his voice faltered. 'When you left, it felt as if I had lost a son . . . When you returned, it warmed my heart, for the first time in a long while. And now?' He looked at Thomas again. 'It is not too late to change your mind. I said that I need men like you at my side. I meant it.'

'Sir, my path is set before me. I will follow it to the end . . . But it does my heart good to know that I have meant something to you.' He took the hand that La Valette offered him and clasped it firmly for a moment and felt the tremor in the other man's touch. Then Thomas withdrew his hand. 'Goodbye, sir. Like the colonel, I too have affairs that I must settle before I leave.'

He stood outside the gate and stared at the brass knocker before him. He had been standing there for a little while in the thin light of dawn. A patrol of soldiers had passed him, with a curious glance, before continuing on their way, not willing to question a knight of the Order. Thomas breathed deeply, resolved in what he would do but unsure of the words he would use, and fearful of the manner in which he might be received. He had reached the house in the hour before dawn and remained out of sight inside a narrow alley between the houses standing opposite. Stokely had left the house at sunrise, wrapped in a cloak, and strode up the street in the direction of St Angelo. Once he was out of sight, Thomas emerged and slowly stepped across the street towards the courtyard wall and the stout wooden door framed by a limestone lintel.

He grasped the knocker and rapped it twice.

There was a short delay before he heard a door opening, muttering, and the patter of footsteps on cobbles and then the sound of the bolt being drawn back. The door opened just wide enough for a face to look out and Thomas recognised the maid who had accompanied Maria at St Elmo.

'The master isn't here,' she said.

'I know. I have come to see Lady Maria.'

The maid looked surprised. Then she shook her head. 'No one comes to see my lady.'

'I have. Please tell her that Sir Thomas Barrett is at her gate. Say that he begs a moment of her time and nothing more.'

The maid cocked an eyebrow and closed the door. The bolt slid back and her footsteps retreated towards the house. Despite his desire to control his feelings, Thomas felt his heartbeat quicken and a clamminess in the palms of his hands as he waited. When the bolt was drawn back again he was startled; he had not heard any footfall. The door opened and there was Maria. She wore an indigo gown and her long hair was tied back. Bare feet showed beneath the hem of the gown, an inch from the ground. She stared at him for a moment, without expression, and he feared that she might simply turn him away. But then the door opened wider and she stepped to one side.

'Please, enter.'

Thomas crossed the threshold and Maria closed the

door behind him. He looked round briefly and saw that the courtyard was no more than a small square in front of the house. But it was filled with potted plants and hanging baskets where flowers of every shape and colour waited to gleam in the full light of the coming day. To one side was a long, low seat, shaded by a trellis upon which bougainvillea had been trained. He looked at Maria again and saw a hint of a smile at the corners of her mouth before she turned to the maid. 'Lucia, leave us. Sir Oliver's boots need polishing. See to it.'

The maid bowed her head and primly hurried back up the small flight of steps into the house. Maria turned to Thomas and gestured towards the seat. They sat down at either end, leaving a gap of perhaps a yard of rich velvet cushion between them.

'Why did you not wait for me in the chapel at St Elmo?' Thomas asked gently.

She stared at him for a moment before replying hesitantly, 'I had time to think, and I became afraid.'

'Afraid? Of me?'

She shook her head. 'Of course not.'

'Then who? Sir Oliver?'

'No.' She tore her gaze away from him and looked at her hands, neatly folded in her lap. 'I was afraid of what I might do. That I might behave in a way I would regret.'

'What do you mean, Maria?'

She looked up again. 'You are not a fool, Thomas. You know precisely what I mean. And I know that you still feel for me as you did all those years ago. I could see it in your eyes, in your expression.'

Thomas nodded. 'And you? Do you feel the same?'

'Why should I after all that you caused to happen to me?' Her voice was suddenly cold and hard-edged. 'Before I met you I was destined to marry into one of the great houses of Sardinia. I would have had a palace and wanted for nothing. But then you stole my heart. I was publicly shamed and cast aside by my own family. I lost them, you and my child, and would have spent the rest of my days confined in a nunnery, or worse, had it not been for Oliver coming to my rescue. I owe that man a great debt. And so do you.'

'Why?'

'For the fact that I am here before you, and that you do not have more to trouble your conscience than you do.'

Her words struck deep into his heart and he glanced down at his hands lying limply in his lap. There was a silence between them that stretched out unbearably in the close warmth of the Maltese night before Thomas spoke again. 'I would give anything to have my time again and put right the grievous wrong I have done you.'

'But we cannot have our time again. What's done is done.'

He looked up quickly. 'Then what would you have me do to make amends?'

'It has gone beyond making amends, Thomas,' she said sadly. 'There is only living with the consequences left to us now.'

He swallowed. 'I understand. Then I should leave you be.'

As he made to rise, Maria quickly reached across to lay a restraining hand on his arm. 'You give in so soon? What has happened to the fearless knight I once knew?'

'Why should I stay?' Thomas asked bitterly. 'There is no love in your heart for me.'

'No?' She leaned across and kissed him gently on the lips, and then drew back as a smile flickered across her face. 'How can you doubt it?'

He felt a warm wave of relief and joy swell up inside his breast and his lips parted in a smile as he half rose to move closer to her. Maria's eyes widened in alarm and she raised a hand to stop him.

'No. Stay there.'

'But . . .'

'Stay there, I said. I mean it. Thomas, for the sake of the love you have for me, and for the love I still bear for you, keep your distance. I beg you.'

He sat back heavily, confused and anxious. 'Maria, you are my all. It has been a lifetime since I last held you. Please.'

She smiled sadly. 'As you say, it has been a lifetime. Another life has been given to each of us since then. You had your life back in England, and in many campaigns across Europe, so I hear. A rich life, no doubt.'

'An empty life, without you.'

'But a life none the less. And I have made another for myself. Once I had forced myself to accept that I would never see you again.' She paused and her smile faded. 'It was two years before I was ready to live again. In all that time Oliver took care of me. Despite being a knight, he has a gentle soul, Thomas, and he is a good man. I knew he loved me, and I was fond of him . . . more than fond. So we were married. In private, of course. The Order will turn a blind eye to many things but not to everything, as

394

you and I have discovered. I have been his wife ever since. I have even learned to be happy.' She stared hard at Thomas. 'And then you came back into my life, and it was like . . . a storm breaking in my heart. I will not lie. My first impulse was to take you in my arms and kiss you. I would have done if I had waited for you in the chapel. Instead I had time to think. Time to consider how much I would hurt Oliver. How you and I could never be happy as we once were.'

'Why not?' Thomas demanded in a strained tone. Every word she had uttered had been like a stone set about his neck.

'We are living under the shadow of a Turkish scimitar, my love. What life I have left I do not want sullied by being the cause of grief and suffering. I could not bear that. Nor could you, if you are honest with yourself.' She looked at him pleadingly. 'You must know that I am right.'

He shook his head. 'It need not be that way.'

It was a lie that seared his heart even as he spoke it. That very night he would be joining the doomed men of St Elmo and he would not be coming back. There were scant hours left in which to make his peace with Maria. He should not flame their feelings into a false promise for the future. She was staring at him, waiting. He nodded slowly.

'Thank you, Thomas.' She eased herself closer and then reached out and took his hand. The touch of her skin set off a tremor that rippled through his body. 'Now, let us talk. Without rancour. Without regret. There are things you should know.'

'I know. Oliver told me about the fate of our child.'

She looked surprised. 'Fate?'

'That he died in infancy.'

Maria frowned and a glimmer of anger shone in her eyes. 'He said that?'

'Yes.'

'He said that our son was dead?'

'Yes.'

'But he lives. He lives.' She looked confused. 'I could not raise him. I was not allowed. For the first years of his life we kept him a secret and Oliver told the Order that my child had died a few days after he was born. We passed him off as the child of one of the serving girls. Then we were betrayed. They were going to take him from me.'

'Who?'

'The knights. The Order was going to send the boy somewhere I would never find him. Where he would not bring shame on them. I begged Oliver not to let them. I begged him, and he promised he would find a solution.'

'What kind of solution?'

'He sent the boy to England to be raised by one of Oliver's cousins. That was the last time I saw him. But I have had news of him from time to time. I am told he has grown into a fine young man. Wait here . . .'

Maria rose quickly from the seat and walked back into the house. A moment later she returned and sat down and held out her hand. Opening it, she revealed a small locket on a delicate silver chain. She opened the locket with a warm smile and stared at a miniature portrait inside. Then, still smiling, she offered it to Thomas.

'This was sent to me when he turned sixteen. This is your son. This is our Ricardo.'

With a cold shiver of premonition Thomas took the locket and gazed down at the familiar features it contained. Younger, yes, and the wavy dark locks of hair that he had inherited from his mother were now tamed and neatly trimmed, but there was no mistaking the dark eyes and dark features of the man he had become.

CHAPTER THIRTY-THREE

'Dear God . . .' Thomas muttered through gritted teeth. His mind seethed with the currents of deceit and betrayal that had caught and used him. Then he looked up at Maria and her expression changed from the injured fondness of a moment before to anxiety.

'What is it? Thomas, tell me.'

'Have you ever shown this to anyone else? Has Oliver seen it?'

Maria looked confused. 'Why?'

'I have to know. Have you ever shown this locket to Oliver?'

'No.'

'Is there any chance that he knows of it?'

She shook her head. 'I do not think so. I keep it hidden from him. He is a good man, and has always been kind to me. Why should I wound his heart by reminding him of the past, of my affection for you?'

His heart was filled with fear as he closed the locket and placed it back in her hand. 'Keep this safe and let no one see it. I have to go. Now. I will try to return later today if I can, I swear it.'

She looked dismayed. 'What is it? What's the matter? Thomas, tell me!'

'I can't. Not yet. Trust me.' He stood up, made to leave, then turned and took her hand and pressed it to his lips, closing his eyes and breathing in the scent of her skin, holding it deep in his lungs before he was forced to exhale. Then he released her hand and turned away and walked swiftly towards the gate. He wrenched it open and stepped out into the street. As the gate closed behind him, Thomas had one last glimpse of Maria rising from the chair with a look of anguish etched on her face.

He strode quickly down the street and turned at the junction leading to the auberge. His mind was in turmoil over what he had just discovered and he was not paying particular attention to his surroundings. So it was that he missed the figure at the end of the street, partially hidden by shadow and standing still in the doorway of a baker, as if part of the small crowd of customers waiting their turn. For a moment the man stared after Thomas and then walked slowly towards the gate of the house.

'I know who you are,' Thomas said coldly as he closed the door to the cell behind him.

Richard looked up from the small desk where he had been writing. He was stripped to the waist and his skin gleamed where perspiration prickled out. He laid down his pen and casually drew an ink-stained rag across the sheet of paper to conceal several lines written in a small, neat hand.

'What are you talking about?' he asked calmly.

Thomas closed his eyes briefly and saw the image in the locket again, and Maria's face. He knew more than his heart could bear and was uncertain of his feelings now, and what precisely he should say to the young man before him. Walsingham's agent, his squire, his son. Even now, against all the certainties that filled his mind, it was still difficult to accept – to believe – it was real.

'Richard . . . Ricardo. I saw your picture in the locket that was sent to your mother.'

Richard frowned. 'What are you talking about? My mother? What madness is this?'

'I know the truth. There is no time for playing games. You may be in great danger.'

Richard cocked an eyebrow. 'Really? Why would I be in any danger in a town surrounded by Muslim fanatics?'

Thomas felt a burst of anger. 'Enough! I know that you are my son.'

Richard's eyes widened briefly and then his features fixed into a neutral expression. 'And what makes you think that?'

'I saw your portrait in the locket. Just now when I was speaking to your mother.'

Richard smiled coldly. 'That would be something of a one-sided conversation. My mother died years ago, when I was a child.' His expression hardened. 'But I know who you are well enough, Father. The man who used a serving girl for his pleasure and then cast her aside when she was with child. And never acknowledged that he had a son for fear of the shame of it.'

Now it was Thomas who was frowning. 'What?'

Richard narrowed his eyes. 'This locket, who showed it to you?'

'Maria, of course. Your mother.'

Richard breathed in sharply. 'No. That cannot be. My

mother was a servant. I remember her. I was told she died after I was sent to England, to be raised by Stokely's family, as an act of charity.' He clenched his teeth in bitter resentment at the memory. 'I suppose it was inevitable that you would discover my identity before the time was ripe for me to reveal the truth. Once the mission was over, and I had in my possession what I came here for, that was when I would tell you, so that you knew all, before I decided whether I would kill you.'

'Kill me?' Thomas felt an icy fist clench round his heart. 'Why?'

'Why?' Richard let out a cheerless laugh. 'Why not? You abandoned my mother, forced her to abandon me. Had me sent to be raised by strangers who treated me as if I should be ashamed to be alive. If it had not been for Sir Oliver's family and their patronage, I would never have gone to Cambridge and drawn the attention of Sir William Cecil.' Richard paused. 'He was more of a father to me than you ever were.'

'I swear to God, I never knew,' Thomas replied, 'else I would have moved heaven and earth to find you and raise you myself.'

'Of course. Like every other noble who takes on his responsibilities with respect to his bastard offspring.'

'No. It would have been different. You were – are – my son.'

'I am the sour fruit of your brief union with my mother, and neither of you ever wanted me.'

'That is not true.' Thomas took a step forward in anguish. 'I did not know of you, and your mother was forced to give you up. And she lives still.'

Richard snorted. 'Save your thin lies, Father. I know the truth. Walsingham told me, after he had investigated my past. He told me everything years ago, and when the chance for this mission came up, he chose me for the task and told me that I was free to do with you as I wished when it was all over.'

Thomas winced. 'You seek revenge?'

'Of course. It was the prospect of revenge that sustained me over the years. That was the reward that Walsingham offered me, as well as a most generous payment.'

Thomas was chilled by the cold-blooded calculation in Richard's voice, even as he swiftly reflected on the shadowy thinking that lay behind Walsingham's schemes. Then it struck him. 'My God, he has been planning this for years.'

Richard frowned. 'I don't understand.'

'Walsingham. He has been grooming you for this task. And watching me closely. He must have inherited the prospect from the men who served before him. Always waiting for the opportunity to put us both into play.' Thomas shook his head in wonder at the depth of the schemes hatched out by England's spymasters. It was a giddying realisation and with difficulty Thomas pushed it aside for the moment. He stared at Richard. 'He lied to you. Maria is your mother. He told you different to spur on your hatred towards me. It is your intention to kill me, then?'

His son stared back in silence for a moment before he replied, 'It was . . .'

'And now?'

Richard breathed deeply and dabbed the sweat from his

face with a strip of cloth. There was a slight droop to his shoulders as he spoke. 'Alas, I have spent too long in your company. Whatever your sins, and faults, as a father, I have come to know you as a man. I have seen your courage and recognised your sense of honour, and even your compassion for others. Walsingham warned me that to spend time with an enemy endangers the resolve to kill him. He expected this, and I was foolish enough to swear to him that I would not bend. That my thirst for revenge would not be quenched by such weakness. He was right, alas. I no longer wish to kill you. But I still wanted to hurt you, to punish you. That was my new intention. To tell you all, whether or not we survived the siege. I would have related how you had blighted my life, and cursed you.'

'And I am cursed,' Thomas replied, his throat strained with the tension of fighting back the grief that threatened to overwhelm him. 'I have twice lost a son. Once when told he had died as an infant, and now when I know of the years I have been denied as his father.'

'You are no father to me and never will be.' Richard shut his eyes for a moment. 'But, if you speak true, my mother still lives . . . My God, she is alive.'

'You must speak to her,' Thomas said gently.

'And what would I say? Where would I begin?'

Thomas shook his head. 'That I do not know, but perhaps the words will come when you are face to face.'

'I need time to think . . . Even if my mother lives, that changes nothing between us. I spurn you as a father. But, for all that, I admire you as a man. And that is all that can be between us now.'

Thomas stopped himself from pursuing the matter. There was still hope that his son might change his mind, there was still time for reconciliation. Then bitter self-reproach swept over him. Of course there was no time. Just as there was none for Maria. In a matter of hours he would leave for St Elmo, and there were preparations he must make before then.

He sat down wearily on the end of Richard's cot and gazed at his son, pained that he had not recognised those features he had inherited from Maria. He felt an urge to reach out and touch the young man's cheek, but stilled his hand for fear of the inevitable rebuff and that it would make him look like a foolish, desperate old man.

'Richard, I have volunteered to join the garrison at St Elmo, along with Colonel Mas. We leave tonight.'

His son stared at him and then his gaze wavered as he replied quietly, 'That is almost certain death.'

'It seems so. Unless Don Garcia and his army arrive in time.'

'That is unlikely.'

'Yes.'

There was a brief, agonising silence before Richard swallowed nervously. 'I will come with you.'

Thomas shook his head firmly. 'No. You will stay here, where you have a chance to survive. Besides, you have an obligation to return to Walsingham with your prize.'

Richard nodded. 'That is so. But I can make arrangements for it to find its way back to England if I die before Malta is saved from the Turks. And if it falls, then it is well enough hidden for the enemy not to find it. Does my . . . mother know that I am here?'

'No. But she may guess now that I have seen the locket and reacted as I did,' Thomas admitted.

'And if she knows then it is possible that others will learn the truth. If it is discovered that I am a spy, my life is forfeit.'

Thomas thought for a moment. 'Maria will not put your life at risk. She has kept the locket a secret. Even from Oliver.'

'Sir Oliver Stokely?'

Thomas smiled sadly. 'Her husband, as it turns out.'

'But he's a member of the Order. Marriage is forbidden.'

'So are many things but what is not flaunted is overlooked.'

Richard gave him a curious look. 'It must pain you to have discovered this.'

'As much as it did to discover I had a son. A son I would have been proud of.'

Richard looked away quickly. 'If Sir Oliver discovers the truth then I will be arrested, tortured and executed. Even if he does not have the stomach for it, La Valette will insist on it. I would rather die on St Elmo with a sword in my hand than on the rack or at the end of a rope. I shall come with you.'

'No.' This time Thomas did reach out with his hand and clasped that of his son. 'It is certain death. I will not send you to such a fate.'

'You do not send me. I choose to come.'

'And I tell you to stay.' The words came out quickly, like an order, and Thomas regretted his tone at once. He lowered his voice and continued more gently. 'Richard . . . my son, I beg you, do not come with me. This is a fate I have chosen for myself. I can bear it if I know that it gives you, and Maria, a chance to survive the siege. If you were there with me, I would only fear for you. If you were to be harmed before my eyes, I would die a thousand deaths in St Elmo, not just one. Please.' He squeezed Richard's hand. 'Stay here.'

Richard was silent for a moment, deep in thought, then he nodded reluctantly and Thomas eased himself back with a sigh of relief. 'Thank you.' He withdrew his hand and stroked his brow. 'There is one thing I would know before I leave. This document that you were sent to find. What is it?'

Richard looked at him with a slight air of suspicion. 'Why do you ask?'

'If I am to die then I would do so with a mind unclouded by doubts. Before I left London, Walsingham assured me that he needed the document in order to save many lives in England. He could have been lying to me. I would like to know if I was sent here on a dishonest pretext, or if I have done something for the good in this world. So, my son, tell me. What is so important that powerful men in England conspired for years so that we two might be brought to this place?'

Richard considered the request briefly, and nodded. 'I already know the contents of the document, assuming that Walsingham was telling me the truth.' He smiled. 'My trust in his word is no longer quite what it was. You had better read the document for yourself. Be good enough to stand up.'

Thomas did as he was told and Richard lifted the end of the cot and swung it away from the wall. The surface had been plastered long ago, but the boisterous activities of generations of squires had cracked the plaster in many places and bare bricks were exposed. Richard knelt beside a section of the wall that he had exposed and drew his dagger. He eased the point between two of the bricks and carefully worked one out far enough to get a grip on it and extract it. He placed the brick on the floor and reached his hand into the dark opening.

His expression froze, and he stretched his fingers as far into the hole as possible before he cursed under his breath.

'What's the matter?' asked Thomas.

'It's not there.' Richard looked round with a shocked expression. 'It's gone.'

CHAPTER THIRTY-FOUR

Ten days later, 22 June, Fort St Elmo

The enemy guns fell silent and for a moment there was silence across the scarred ground at the end of the Sciberras peninsula. The dust billowed slowly about the fort and settled on the bodies sprawled on the ground, making them look like stone sculptures. Some had lain in the open for many days and were bloated and corrupt with decay, the sickly sweet stench filling the air. It was mid-June and the heat of the day would soon begin to add to the discomfort, and bring the swarms of insects that settled to gorge themselves on the wounds and viscera of the dead and dying.

For the defenders, each day was torment as the sun beat down on them while they squatted behind the parapet, enclosed in padded jackets and armour that quickly became too hot to touch and as much a source of torture as protection from harm. Sweat streamed freely down their cheeks and dripped from their brows as they awaited the enemy. For some men, older or weaker than their comrades, the heat was too much and they collapsed, gasping for air as they tore at the buckles of their breastplates in an effort to remove their armour. Some died as their hearts gave out, gurgling incoherently while their swollen tongues writhed against cracked lips.

There was a sudden movement from the Turkish trenches and then a green banner rippled upright and drums and cymbals crashed out, accompanied by a throaty cheer. Heads appeared above the top of the trench and a moment later the first of the enemy swarmed into view.

'Here they come!' Captain Miranda yelled from the keep. He turned to the drummer standing ready beside him. 'Sound the alarm!'

The shrill rattle of the drum rang out across the crumbling walls of the fort. The men who had been sheltering inside the fort spilled out into the courtyard and raced up the steps to their stations on the walls to join their comrades on sentry duty. At once the two cannon and snipers waiting on top of the captured ravelin opened fire, striking down several men as they reached the top of the stairs.

Thomas was behind the barricade erected beyond the rubble slope that was all that remained of the north-west corner of the fort. And Richard was with him, for nothing would persuade him to stay in Birgu after he discovered that the document was missing. They had been called to the wall an hour before dawn when the first prayers of the imams had been heard by the sentries – a sure sign of a pending attack. Thomas looked round as the Spanish soldiers assigned to his position crouched down below the level of the parapet and bent double as they ran to their places. Along the barricade stood tubs of water big enough for a man to leap in and extinguish the fire of enemy incendiary weapons. There were also small piles of arquebuses, loaded and ready to fire, and the defenders' own stock of incendiary weapons – small clay pots filled with clinging naphtha, from which fuses protruded, ready to be lit before the pots were hurled amid the enemy. To each side of the barricade, where the parapet still stood and overlooked the ditches, other men readied the first of the fire hoops, and fanned the small braziers into flame in readiness to set light to them. Thomas and Richard squatted behind the centre of the barricade, beside the naphtha thrower and its two-man crew. One stood ready to operate the bellows while the other connected the leather hose to the keg containing the mixture that would burn with hellish ferocity once it was ignited by the flaming wick in front of the nozzle of the bellows.

'Careful with that,' said Richard. 'Unless you want us to go up like a torch.'

'I know what I'm doing, sir,' the Spaniard replied with a grim smile. 'Just keep out of my path, eh?'

The cheers of the enemy grew louder as they reached the edge of the ditch and started to scramble over the rubble that now filled it.

'Stay down!' Thomas shouted, waving back the handful of his men who had started to nervously glance over the edge of the barricade. The Turkish snipers kept up their fire until the last possible moment and, as if to justify Thomas's warning, a ball ricocheted off a block of stone and clanged off the fan crest of a morion helmet a short distance to Thomas's left. The man dropped back, dazed and blinking.

'Stay down until I give the order!' Thomas bellowed. He glanced quickly to each side; his men were watching him anxiously, clutching their arquebuses or pikes as they waited on his command. The clink of loose stones was clearly audible now amid the cheers and incoherent battle cries of the more fanatical of the enemy. Thomas controlled the impulse to rise up and peer over the barricade a moment longer, and then drew a deep breath, snapped the visor of his helmet shut and straightened up. For an instant he saw only the top of the rubble slope, then a pointed helmet and a turban to the side before suddenly a sea of faces as the Turks struggled to the top of the ruined wall, cutting off the line of sight of their snipers.

'Now!' Thomas thrust his pike into the air and with a roar his men stood up along the fifty-foot line of the barricade. There was a crash as the first of the arquebuses fired. The range was point blank and the swarm of targets impossible to miss. Thomas saw one figure in white robes and round shield lurch back amid his comrades, his scimitar spiralling backwards and out of sight as he fell. More shots blasted out on each side and several of the Turks fell as they clambered over the difficult ground towards the barricade.

'Ready incendiaries!' Thomas shouted and the men assigned to the task lit the fuses. 'Release!'

With a grunt the men hurled the pots out over the barricade and the fuses flared and trailed a thin line of smoke in the morning air as they arced up over the heads of the nearest of the enemy and disappeared amongst them before shattering on the rubble with a bright flash, engulfing the Turks closest to the impact in flame and smoke. Their loose robes caught fire and the men screamed in terror and then agony as they threw down their weapons and beat at the flames while their comrades leaped aside, fearful of also catching fire. To the right Thomas saw the first of the hoops set alight. The men on either side holding the blazing hoop in iron tongs heaved it up on to the parapet and over the side of the wall. The roar of the flames briefly filled the air before cries of panic rose from the ditch.

Then the first of the enemy incendiaries flew up and over the wall, falling a short distance behind the parapet. There was a loud crash and Thomas turned to see a pool of fire licking up from the stone slabs on the walkway. He thrust his hand out, pointing towards the nearby stock of incendiaries in a wicker basket. 'Move them! Quickly!'

The closest men were too preoccupied with firing their arquebuses to heed the warning. Seeing the danger, Richard dropped his pike and sprinted towards the basket, leaping over the flames. He grasped the handle just as some of the burning liquid reached it and small flames licked at the side. Thomas took a half step away from the barricade as his chest seized with fear. Richard gritted his teeth as he pulled the basket a safe distance away from the fire before stopping to beat out the flames on the wicker side. Thomas breathed out in relief and turned back to face the enemy.

The Turks, knowing that the only way to escape the fire and bullets of the defenders was to close on them as swiftly as possible, charged towards the barricade. But there was one final weapon standing between them and the Christians. Thomas waved the man with the naphtha bellows forward. He nodded and raised the long iron nozzle towards the enemy and pumped the bellows. A jet of naphtha liquid spurted out, and was instantly lit by the taper burning a short distance in front of the nozzle. A thin tongue of brilliant flame arced out across the attackers and rained down on them, searing heads, bodies and limbs. The defenders let out savage shouts of glee and triumph as their enemies roasted before their eyes. And still the Turks surged forward over the rubble, over their stricken comrades, and on towards the barricade.

Thomas held his pike ready. Richard hurried to his side, his weapon in an overhead grip. Then the Turks were all along the barricade, either side of the fiery avenue caused by the jets of the naphtha bellows. Through his visor Thomas concentrated his attention on an officer in brilliant scale armour shouting encouragement to his spearmen as they charged forward. Raising his pike, Thomas aimed at the man's chest and thrust hard. The point slammed home but the armour was well-made and the blow did not puncture the armour. Even so, the impact drove the breath from the officer's lungs and he staggered back, gasping. His men swept past and steel clattered and scraped on steel either side of Thomas as the two sides met.

Despite the overwhelming number of enemy the defenders had better armour and enjoyed a slight height advantage from their side of the barricade. Most of the Spaniards were armed with stout pikes which they thrust at the Turks to keep them at bay. Scimitars flashed as the Turks hacked at the shafts of the pikes, and any exposed hands or arms. A man wearing a lion skin over his head and shoulders burst through the crowd in front of Thomas and grasped the end of his pike just below the steel point. Instinctively he tightened his grip and wrenched it back. Another man grabbed the shaft. To his side Thomas saw a

Spahi warrior scramble up on to the barricade and raise his blade high, ready to strike at Richard who was battling a white-robed fanatic.

Seeing the danger to his son, Thomas released his hold on the pike and the two men on the other end tumbled back. Thomas snatched up a mace that was leaning against the inside of the barricade and swung it in a short, vicious arc at the shin of the Spahi before he could strike. The iron head smashed through flesh and bone and the man crumpled on to his side. Thomas swung the bloodied weapon again, this time smashing the Turk's skull open in an explosion of blood, bone and brains. Richard, still heedless of the danger that had threatened him, was thrusting his pike again, forcing his enemy to duck to one side to avoid being hit in the face.

A sharp blow to his left shoulder knocked Thomas round and he slashed out with the club, knocking his attacker's sword aside. Then, for an instant, there was no enemy within his reach and he glanced quickly to each side to see how the rest of his comrades were faring. Three men were down, sprawled on the flagstones behind the barricade. A man who had lost his hand clasped the bloodied stump to his chest as he staggered towards the top of the staircase. Then his head jerked to one side as a sniper on the ravelin picked him off. He fell headlong, only yards from the shelter of the staircase.

A flicker of motion to the right caught Thomas's eye and he just had time to step to one side as a curved blade slashed down. With a deafening clatter it deflected off his shoulder guard. He turned quickly and hammered on the blade with the mace, knocking it down on to a rock atop the barricade. The blade shattered and the Turk who had wielded the weapon screamed a curse and threw the guard and handle at Thomas, which struck his breastplate harmlessly. The man's curse was abruptly cut off as Richard piked him in the side of the chest. With a groan the man pulled himself free and staggered back into the throng of turbans, spiked helmets and robes.

An arrow whirled close by Thomas's head and he saw that some archers had taken position on the mounds of rubble and were shooting over the heads of their comrades. The defenders were higher up than the Turks and made clear targets.

'Watch out for the arrows!' Thomas bellowed the warning above the din of battle. It came too late for the soldier operating the naphtha bellows. An arrow struck him high in the shoulder and his hand spasmed and he released one of the handles on the bellows. The nozzle dropped down. At once the nearest of the Turks let out a savage cheer.

'Richard!' Thomas called out. 'Take the bellows!'

Richard nodded and dropped his pike as he ran across to the wounded soldier and took the weapon from him. On the other side of the barricade the Turks had begun to surge forward, sensing that the chance to overwhelm the defenders was within their grasp. Richard grasped the handles and hefted the bellows up on to the barricade, resting the nozzle on a flat stone that had been positioned there for the purpose. He pressed the handles together to prime the weapon and then again to pump the liquid out towards the enemy. It flared into a glittering arc as the taper ignited the mixture. Richard aimed directly at the mass of Turks surging towards the middle of the barricade and the fire burst upon them, lighting them up like walking torches that screamed and swirled as they burned to death. With a grim expression he worked the bellows, pivoting them from side to side, spraying fire into the terrified horde. Those at the back stopped advancing over the rubble, staring in fear at the horrific scene in front of them, and then they began to fall back, seeking shelter on the rubble sloping down into the ditch.

Their fear spread from man to man and soon even those who had reached the barricade fell back, until only an officer remained shouting his defiance at the defenders and contempt at his retreating men. He swung a heavy scimitar from side to side across the top of the barricade to drive his opponents back. Then he clambered up and stood, clearly visible to all, and waved his men forward. One of the Spaniards took up an arquebus, crouched down, took aim and coolly shot the Turkish officer under the chin. The ball burst through the top of his turban in a spray of blood and he stood for a moment, still as a statue, then fell back amid the scorched and bloodied bodies of his men on the outside of the barricade.

Thomas saw with relief that they had broken the attack.

'Get under cover!' he ordered, waving the men down on either side. 'Richard, you too.' He was still standing in clear view behind the bellows.

Richard lowered the weapon and crouched down behind the barricade to pinch out the small flame on the taper and make the bellows safe. If the enemy attacked again, the taper could be quickly relighted from one of the slow fuses used for the arquebuses.

Thomas cupped a hand to his mouth. 'Sergeants, keep watch on the enemy!'

He made his way to the left of the barricade and picked his way along, counting the casualties and offering words of praise and encouragement to the Spanish soldiers whose grime-streaked faces cracked into grins at having driven off yet another assault and survived. Some had not been so lucky. Of the forty men who had held the position that morning, four were dead and another five wounded, three of whom were still able to bear arms and refused to quit their posts. The others crawled towards the stairs and made their way to the shelter of the infirmary.

When he returned to his place at the centre of the line, Thomas slumped down beside Richard with a weary sigh.

'Water?' Richard held out his canteen and Thomas gave him a grateful nod as he took it, removed the stopper and tilted his head back, taking a mouthful and swilling it around his parched mouth before he lowered the canteen and handed it back. He looked up at the clear sky. In a few hours the walls would be baking, with no shade for the men. He would have to ensure that there was plenty of water available to see them through the day. Now that the initial assault had failed, the enemy would take to sniping at the defenders, while their officers attempted to harangue them into forming up for another charge.

It had been several days since he, Richard and Colonel Mas had joined the garrison. In that time he had noticed the growing reluctance of the enemy to renew their attacks after each one had been thrown back. They had taken to sniping, and small rushes at the defences to try and hurl incendiaries in amongst the defenders. The garrison had once numbered eight hundred men. When Thomas had arrived in the fort there was barely half that number and now only three hundred remained. A handful of reinforcements arrived each night from Birgu, and it was clear to the defenders that the Grand Master was husbanding his resources for the struggle to come once St Elmo finally fell to the enemy. It would not be long now, Thomas reflected.

He looked at his son. 'You should have remained in Birgu.'

Richard shook his head. 'I didn't have much choice once I found the document was missing. Someone has discovered more about me, about us, than is healthy. I have failed in my mission and I would not have been safe if I had stayed in Birgu. At least no one is going to come after me here.' He chuckled drily. 'The trouble is, if the Turks don't annihilate us, and by some miracle we are relieved by Don Garcia, then it's likely that I will fall into the hands of La Valette's interrogators.'

'I rather think that is the least of our problems,' Thomas replied quietly. 'The Turks have completed the battery covering the harbour. There won't be any more reinforcements coming from St Angelo.' He glanced at the soldiers slumped behind the barricade. Many were injured and wore soiled bandages, and their haggard faces spoke eloquently of their exhaustion and resignation to their all but inevitable fate. He turned back to his son and felt a great sadness come over him.

'I should have escaped with Maria all those years ago and taken her back to England with me, whatever the risk. Then none of us would be here.'

Richard shrugged. 'It's too late for all that. Nothing can

be changed. There's no point in blaming yourself, Father.'

The word slipped from his mouth before he realised it and both men turned to each other.

'I was hoping you would call me that, before the end.' Thomas patted him affectionately on the arm. 'Thank you.'

'I am your son,' Richard said simply.

Thomas smiled. 'My son . . . It has a good sound to it. I'm proud of you. I know your mother would be too.' Thomas looked down at the ground between his boots and thought for a moment. 'What a mess we make of life. We have but a short time in this world and this is the result. Such a waste . . . I should have made a better life for us all. I am sorry.'

'There is no need to apologise,' Richard said wearily. 'Besides, if we die as martyrs for the cause, then we are assured a place in paradise, eh?'

Thomas was silent for a moment. 'Do you really believe in heaven, Richard? In God, our faith, the Bible?'

His son shot him a concerned look. 'It is dangerous to voice such questions in others' hearing. I'd keep them to yourself.'

'We are beyond worrying about such dangers now.'

Richard puffed his cheeks out and thought briefly before he continued. 'Are you saying that you don't believe in the Church of Rome?'

'No. Not the Church of Rome, nor any church or faith. It is all dead to me and has been for years.'

Richard stared at him and shook his head. 'Then what is the point of this struggle? Why are you prepared to die in the service of the Order?'

'I am here because I have nothing to live for. Maria is lost to me, and I cannot protect you. All that is left is to fight to prevent the tyranny of another false faith holding sway over the world. Suleiman threatens the world I know, that is reason enough to oppose him. Tell me, Richard. Do you believe in God?'

Richard was silent.

'You are no fool,' Thomas went on. 'Surely you must have wondered why every prayer goes unanswered, why God stays his hand from preventing evil?' He paused. 'Have you ever read the Epicurean paradox?'

Richard shook his head.

'I think it goes something like this:

> *If God is willing but not able,*
> *Then he is not all-powerful.*
> *If he is able but not willing,*
> *Then he is malevolent.*
> *If he is both willing and able*
> *Then why is there evil in the world?*
> *If he is neither willing nor able*
> *Then why call him God?'*

He waved his hand at their surroundings. 'If ever there was a need for God to show himself, to give the slightest encouragement to those who serve him, then it is here and now. And yet there is nothing but us and the enemy.'

Richard frowned. 'I have thought about it but I do not like the implications.'

Thomas nodded and let the matter drop. But there was one question he did want an answer to. 'This document that has been the cause of our troubles, what exactly is it?'

'It is better that you do not know.'

'But you were going to show it to me back in Birgu.'

'I was wrong. If you are taken alive, there is a danger that you will reveal what you know of the document. I'm sorry, I cannot say any more. Please, let the matter rest.'

Thomas felt a bitter pang of disappointment that Richard would not trust him. He was silent for a moment before he eased himself up into a crouch and peered cautiously over the top of the barricade. The rubble- and corpse-strewn ground in front of him was still. Then he saw a slight movement and saw the flicker of a feather behind a large chunk of masonry and ducked down just as the sniper fired. The bullet struck a rock close to where Thomas's head had been and then ricocheted overhead towards the heart of the fort.

The hours stretched out as they huddled behind the barricade and both sides sniped at anyone rash enough to expose themselves.

CHAPTER THIRTY-FIVE

Colonel Mas appeared at noon, moving from position to position gathering reports on the morning action and casualty numbers to pass on to Miranda. Despite holding a senior rank, Mas had chosen to defer to the captain. The garrison looked to Miranda and he in turn inspired them with his courage and coolness under fire and the colonel had the good sense not to disturb the arrangement.

He listened to Thomas's account of the assault and noted the number of losses on a creased sheet of paper, then refolded it and slipped it inside his haversack.

'How goes it elsewhere?' asked Thomas.

'Not well,' Mas admitted. 'They sent a party round the north of the fort under the cover of the attack and broke into the cavalier. It's in their hands now. The rest of the fort is surrounded, except for a narrow track leading down to the jetty.'

'If they have the cavalier then the route won't be safe.'

'It is safe. We're using a drain. The grate has been removed and the opening has been camouflaged. It gives us some means of communication with Birgu, for what it's worth.'

Richard peered across the rubble-strewn walls of the

fort towards the free-standing cavalier tower rising up between the fort and the sea. There was a green standard flying above the parapet and now and then a head bobbed up to look down into the fort. 'They'll be able to see right into the courtyard.'

Mas nodded. 'Have your men be cautious when they come down from the wall for ammunition, water or food. From now on Miranda wants the men to stay at their posts. They'll be safer that way. He wants the officers to meet at dusk in the chapel. Be careful getting there.' He nodded a farewell and then bent low and scurried towards the next section of the wall.

Thomas and the others sat in the afternoon sun, occasionally taking out a dry biscuit or strip of cured meat to chew on, as much to help the long hours pass as to feed any appetite. Overhead the sun beat down on them and sweat dripped from their brows as they slowly stewed inside their cumbersome armour. Several times there was a brief flurry of shots and shouting from one of the other sections of the wall and the men would stand to their weapons in case it heralded another general assault. But each time the fighting quickly subsided and the skirmishing resumed.

At last the sun dipped far enough towards the horizon to cast long shadows across the walls of the fort and give some relief from the heat the defenders had endured for several hours. As the light began to fade, a trumpet sounded from the Turkish lines and men who had been crouching amid the rubble of the fort crept away, returning to their trenches. As soon as the last of them was in cover, the batteries on the crest of the ridge thundered out again and resumed bombarding St Elmo. Instinctively the men lining the barricade flinched and squirmed down a little further.

Thomas touched Richard's arm. 'I'm going to report to Miranda, You take command here until relieved. I'll be back as soon as I can.'

'Yes, sir,' Richard replied and smiled at his formality. 'Yes, Father.'

'Keep your head down, understand?'

Richard nodded, and Thomas took one last look at him in case there was never another chance, and felt the familiar stab of guilt and affection as he turned away.

He moved at a crouch until the angle of the wall no longer concealed him from the cavalier or the ravelin. He glanced at both towers and saw heads bob up as the Turks kept watch on the fort. Then several shots were fired from the cavalier as the enemy caught sight of movement along the nearest section of the wall.

Thomas took advantage of the diversion and rushed across the open space towards the stairs leading down into the courtyard. There was a faint shout from the direction of the ravelin and a rippling volley of shots. Stone chips flew past him but Thomas ran on and started down the stairs, taking four or five at a time in a wild rush that threatened to make him lose his balance. At the bottom of the stairs he threw himself against a nearby stretch of wall that was out of sight of the enemy and gasped for breath. Around him the courtyard was filled with rubble and dust that caught in the throat. There were few men about, now that the enemy could reach most of the inside of the fort with their weapons.

When he had recovered his breath Thomas edged his

way round the courtyard towards the chapel, which was fortunately out of the line of fire. A small group of men sat to one side of the door playing a desultory game of dice and barely looked up as he passed them and entered the chapel. The building was quite unlike a normal church; it was built into the fabric of the fort, with a handful of windows high up on the walls which made it a gloomy place for the garrison to come and worship. Although it could hold up to four hundred people at a time, there were only a few men that evening, gathered on facing pews in the space before the altar. Most of the officers and the friar, Robert of Eboli, had already arrived as Thomas walked along the aisle, undoing the straps fastening the gorget to his helmet and then removing the helmet.

Captain Miranda was sitting on a chair. His left arm was in a sling and his right leg was fixed in place by splints sawn from the shaft of a pike. A bloodied bandage was wound tightly about his knee. Like the others his face had been burned raw by the sun and his skin was red and peeling. Colonel Mas had also been wounded since midday and was barely recognisable under the bandage that covered one eye and half of his head. Most of the other officers had also been wounded and Thomas reflected that the scene was more like an infirmary than a gathering of officers. All of them looked exhausted and filthy and what had once been neatly trimmed beards were now straggling and matted with blood and the remains of hastily snatched meals.

'Glad to see you are still with us, Sir Thomas.' Miranda forced a smile. 'You are one of the few who can still stand.'

Thomas nodded and took a seat on one of the pews,

trying to ignore the ache in his limbs and the discomfort of clothes he had been unable to change for over a week. There was no small talk as they waited for the last officer to arrive, and once he was seated Miranda addressed his subordinates.

'There are fewer than a hundred of us left to man the walls, and most are already wounded. The Turks have the cavalier, and with that they can provide covering fire for any attempt to cross the ditch using the trestle bridges they have thrown up against what remains of the parapet. Gentlemen, the end is near. We have all but run out of gunpowder. I doubt that we will survive the morrow.' He paused. 'We have fought a good fight against great odds. It is a struggle to be proud of. We have endured far longer than was thought possible. Let us hope that we have won enough time for the Grand Master to prepare Birgu and Senglea for the onslaught to come when we are no more. I have given orders for the chapel's tapestries and sacred objects to be destroyed or hidden. Once Robert of Eboli and the other brothers have carried out that task they will make the rounds of our positions and take confession and administer the last rites to those who wish it. Colonel Mas will oversee one last filling of the water butts before the cisterns are fouled with enemy bodies. The rest of you should destroy anything that might be valuable if it falls into enemy hands.' He paused and looked round at his officers. 'There is a signal fire prepared on the keep where it can be seen from across the harbour. If the fort falls then the last of us should set light to it. After that, it's every man for himself. Does anyone have anything to say?'

One of the younger knights nodded. 'Sir, is it too late

to evacuate the fort? We could ask for volunteers for a rearguard while we signal Birgu to send boats.'

Miranda shook his head. 'It's too late for that. The moment the enemy realised what was happening they would overwhelm the few men left and then slaughter the rest as we attempted to escape. Besides, there are too many wounded to evacuate. We must resign ourselves to our fate and resolve to go down fighting in a manner that reflects the highest standards of the Order of St John.'

'What of the wounded?' asked Colonel Mas. 'We cannot let them fall into the enemy's hands. I've seen what the Turks do to their prisoners.'

Thomas watched Miranda's reaction closely.

'The wounded will be brought in here. Each man will be given a dagger, to use to fight from where he lies, or to use as he will,' Miranda replied carefully, for suicide was a sin. 'When the Turks get over the walls, every man that can must fall back here. The chapel is where we will make our final stand. If any man decides to appeal for mercy, that is his choice, but I would expect none from the enemy. They have paid a high price in blood and are thirsty for revenge.' He paused. 'There is one piece of good news I will share with you. We captured a prisoner today who says that Dragut was felled by a shot from one of our men as he inspected their siege guns.'

The officers murmured their pleasure at the news.

'It is a sign.' Friar Robert stood and raised a hand and stabbed his finger at the ceiling. 'The Lord is watching us, and has reached out his hand to smite our enemy.'

'It was a bullet that killed Dragut,' Thomas said mildly. 'He was not swatted aside.'

Some of the officers smiled, but Robert turned and glared. 'Do not be impious, Englishman. We have prayed for deliverance and the Lord has begun to answer our call.'

'I am glad,' Thomas replied, just before a Turkish cannonball struck the roof of the chapel and plaster and dust fell on to the pews beside the entrance. The officers winced, and after a brief silence Thomas said, 'It seems that we might not have prayed enough.'

Robert pointed at Thomas. 'How dare you mock? Do you cast doubt upon the Lord, our God?' His eyes narrowed. 'This smacks of heresy. Captain Miranda, this man should be arrested and his faith examined.'

'Don't be absurd,' Miranda growled. 'Right now I would give my weight in gold for a company of heretics to fight at our side.' He sighed and rubbed his brow. 'I imagine that exhaustion has clouded Sir Thomas's mind. He meant nothing by his comments. If you like, Robert, you should say a prayer for him while you are praying for further divine help.'

For a moment the priest held his ground, an angry frown on his face. Then his expression eased and he bowed his head and sat down. 'We are all tired, sir. And so I forgive Sir Thomas.'

Thomas gritted his teeth and responded in an ironic tone, 'And I accept your forgiveness.'

The door of the chapel opened and a sergeant ran inside and called out, 'There are boats, sir. Heading out from Birgu!'

Miranda frowned. 'Boats? That's madness. La Valette must not know that the enemy have covered the harbour with their guns. Sir Thomas, get up on the wall and try to warn them before it's too late. Go!'

Snatching up his helmet, Thomas ran down the aisle towards the sergeant. 'Show me.'

Thankfully it was dusk and the snipers could no longer easily pick out their targets inside the fort. Thomas and the sergeant hurried up the stairs on to the section of the wall overlooking the harbour. It had suffered little damage and they stood at the parapet and stared out across the darkened harbour towards the mass of St Angelo. Thomas searched the water and then saw them, six dark blots edging towards the peninsula. A moment later the Turkish gunners saw them too and there was a roar to Thomas's right as a gun unleashed a blast of grapeshot at the small flotilla. A faint loom of spray lifted from the gentle waves in front of the boats.

Thomas cupped his hands to his mouth and shouted as loudly as he could, feeling his lungs strain and burn with the effort. 'Turn back! Turn back!'

Still they came on, and another gun fired, and missed. The third shot tore into the lead boat and the shattering of timber and the cries of the stricken carried clearly to the men on the wall.

'Dear God,' the sergeant muttered. 'They'll be cut to pieces.'

'Turn back!' Thomas shouted again. 'For pity's sake, turn back! Save yourselves!'

The boats were halfway across the harbour now but close to the Turkish battery and more easily visible against the dark grey of the sea. More shots ripped up the surface of the water, then another boat was blasted, its bow shattered by the storm of iron fragments. It began to sink and some of the men still aboard jumped over the side and struck out for St Angelo. Others were wearing armour and carrying weapons and struggled to rid themselves of the burden before the water swallowed them. Then the boat, and the men, were gone. Thomas felt sickened by the sight.

The sergeant thrust his arm out. 'They're heading back!'

The last of the boats had turned aside and as they watched, it began to stroke back towards Birgu. A second boat followed it but the other two held their course.

'Row faster, damn you,' the sergeant muttered.

Thomas willed them on. Any moment they would pass out of sight of the Turkish guns and be sheltered by the cliff. Another gun blasted out, thrashing the surface of the harbour just behind the rearmost boat. Then they were safe from the cannon. But there were still the enemy snipers perched in the rocks surrounding the fort. Thomas turned to the sergeant.

'Find five men and join me by the drain at the back of the chapel. You know the place?'

'Yes, sir.'

'Then go.'

They separated, Thomas making for the chapel while the sergeant hurried along the wall towards the corner of the fort overlooking the harbour. As he ran into the chapel the other officers turned to him.

'Well?' asked Colonel Mas. 'Did they get through?'

'Just two boats, sir. Pulling towards the jetty now. I'll take a party out through the drain to guide them in.'

Mas nodded. 'I'll have a guard placed on the drain until you return.'

A moment later the sergeant returned with his men, Maltese militiamen, and Thomas led them to the rear of the chapel. There, in the corner behind the altar, was the drain cover. He bent down to lift the lid and pulled it aside. The stench of human waste wafted into the air but Thomas ignored it and let himself down into the low tunnel. There was a dim glimmer where the drain passed out of the fort and where a linen screen painted to look like rock hid the opening. Thomas splashed along the drain and the other men followed him. At the screen he paused and cautiously eased it aside. There was no sign of movement in the rocks below the wall. The drain followed a narrow channel down to the sea, not far from the path to the jetty.

'Follow me,' Thomas whispered and led the way out into the cool night air. The party stole quietly across the rocky ground until they reached the path. Ahead Thomas could hear the splash of oars and hurried on. They had almost reached the steps leading down to the jetty when a figure emerged from the rocks ahead and offered a friendly greeting in a tongue Thomas did not recognise. He raised a hand in response and continued forward as the man carried on speaking. Only at the last moment did the other man's tone change to one of alarm, and then he was cut off by a blow to the head from Thomas's mantlet before he could call out. One of the Maltese soldiers quickly cut the enemy's throat and the small party hurried on down the steps. At the bottom Thomas saw that the two boats had reached the jetty and the men were climbing out. One of them froze as he saw Thomas and his party approaching.

'Who's there?'

'I'm from St Elmo,' Thomas called back as loudly as he dared. 'Come to escort you into the fort. How many of you are there?'

'Sixteen. The last of the volunteers from Birgu.'

'Who is in command?'

'Me.' A tall man eased his way towards Thomas. There was no need for him to give his name. Thomas had recognised his voice and now nodded in greeting.

'Welcome to fort St Elmo, Sir Oliver.'

CHAPTER THIRTY-SIX

Once Stokely had reported to Captain Miranda, Thomas drew him to one side and said earnestly, 'We must talk.'

'Yes, we must,' Stokely replied. 'But it would be best if it was somewhere more private.'

'Follow me.' Thomas led him from the chapel and across the courtyard to the mess room.

'Not the most commodious of accommodation,' said Stokely as he glanced round the large chamber that had once served as the garrison's dining hall. Earlier in the siege Captain Miranda had set up some gaming tables and a makeshift bar where the men could buy the finest wines from the cellar. Now that the men had given up any hope of leaving the fort alive, they no longer tried to win money from their comrades and had abandoned the hall. Instead it served as a dressing station and bloodied rags and baskets filled with strips of cloth littered the floor. A handful of candles provided dim illumination and there were occasional moans and coughs from men lying on biers along one wall. Thomas found an unopened bottle of wine behind the counter and settled at a table in the corner of the hall where he poured them each a cup and pushed one across the table to Stokely.

Stokely hesitated a moment before he picked it up and forced a smile. 'What shall we toast?'

Thomas raised his cup. 'Maria.'

'Ah yes . . . Maria.'

They took a sip, each man watching the other warily. Then Thomas set his cup down gently. 'Why are you here, Oliver?'

'I volunteered to join the last effort to reinforce St Elmo.'

'And La Valette gave you permission to come?'

'He didn't know. I suspect he will soon enough. But it's too late to prevent me. For better or worse I am here.'

'For better?' Thomas laughed bitterly. 'How can it possibly be better here? You are on a fool's errand, Oliver. There is only death here.'

'I know that.' He sipped his wine. 'That is all I seek, now that I know, and accept, the truth.'

'And what truth would that be?'

Stokely held his cup in both hands as if his fingers were delicately poised about someone's neck. 'Before you left Birgu, you discovered where Maria was living and went to see her.'

Thomas hesitated. He did not want any harm to befall Maria as a result of his need to speak to her, yet what difference did it make now? Stokely was as doomed as any man in St Elmo. 'Yes, I did.'

Stokely nodded slightly. 'Thank you for your honesty. The fact is, I saw you leave the house.'

'I see.' Thomas felt the dread stirring in his heart. 'What did you do? Oliver, if you have done her any harm . . .'

'After I saw you leave our house, our home, my mind

was filled with the most painful imaginings. Though Maria and I have been married these many years I have never asked her about her feelings for you. Despite her grief at losing you, and her child, she was strong enough to go on. In time she grew to accept what had happened and resolved to make a new life for herself.' Oliver paused, and then sighed. 'When she agreed to be my wife, I knew that I was a poor shadow of what she truly wanted but that was enough for me. Besides, we lived happily together, and she seemed content with what fate had left to her.' He paused and the lightness of tone with which he had spoken his last words suddenly hardened. 'That all changed the moment she saw you here. Maria said nothing when she returned to the house, but I knew at once. I had tried to keep her away from you, at our estate near Mdina, but from the moment the enemy fleet was sighted, I knew that Maria must take shelter in Birgu and there would come a time when she discovered you had returned. When I questioned her she told me what had happened.' He glared at Thomas. 'I cannot tell you how the situation tore at my heart. I demanded that she never see or speak to you. I feared that she might yet want to be with you. I would have fallen at her feet and implored her to stay with me. I wanted to say I would die rather than lose her. Instead I did something more foolish, something so demeaning that I shudder to think of it even now.' Stokely took up his cup and drained it. 'I threatened you.'

'Me? How?'

'I said I had information that I could use to have you arrested and condemned as a spy. You, and Richard . . . her son.'

The earlier sense of dread returned, colder and more dangerous. Thomas leaned across the table. 'What information?' he hissed.

Stokely did not flinch. He regarded Thomas with disdain. 'Did you think I did not know about the locket? The instant I saw Richard I knew exactly who he was. What surprised me was that it quickly became evident that you did not. Of course, I suspected from the first that you answered the Grand Master's summons for reasons beyond a mere desire to serve the Order. But Richard? The last news I had of him from my cousin was that he had left Cambridge to serve a patron in London, no less a person than Walsingham. It is clear why he is here. Young Richard has sold his soul to the devil and become one of Walsingham's creatures. The theft of the document from Sir Peter de Launcey's chest was final proof that he is a spy.'

'You knew he was a spy?'

Stokely nodded. 'I suppose I could have had him arrested as soon as I recognised him, but he was Maria's son. If anything happened to him and she discovered my hand in it, she would never have forgiven me. Besides, I was determined to discover his purpose here. As soon as I heard that an attempt had been made to enter the archive I checked the chest and discovered that the locks had been broken and the will had gone.'

'The will?' Thomas tried to hide his surprise. At last the true nature of the document had been revealed. If he played his hand right, Stokely might reveal more. 'So you know about that?'

'I have known about it for years. Ever since Sir Peter

brought it to Malta. He knew exactly how dangerous the will would be if it fell into the wrong hands. He suspected that he might have been followed from England so he entrusted me with its secret, in case anything happened to him. Alas, it was a simple accident that did for him. Afterwards I arranged for the will to be placed in the chest and stored in the archive where it would be quite safe, and from where it could be retrieved if there was ever a need to use it. When it was taken, I knew at once where I might find it. I searched Richard's cell while the two of you were on duty. I have to say that I am not very impressed with his choice of hiding place, but then I knew exactly what I was looking for and the space required to hide it. The will is safe again. No one knows where it is but me. There it shall stay. One day it may be discovered but perhaps it is better that it is lost.' Stokely paused. 'I take it that Walsingham told you about the will before you left England.'

Thomas hesitated. 'He discussed it.'

Stokely stared at Thomas. 'You don't know the contents of the will, do you?'

'Walsingham said that it would cause great loss of life if it was misused.'

Stokely laughed bitterly. 'He only said that? My poor Thomas, you have been little more than their tool.' He glanced over Thomas's shoulder at a figure approaching them. He smiled faintly. 'Why don't you join us, Richard?'

Thomas turned swiftly and saw the young man watching them with a cold, detached expression. He stood still for a moment before he picked up a stool and positioned it at the end of the table, between the two knights.

Stokely smiled thinly. 'We were just discussing the will. It seems that you, and your superiors back in England, have not deigned to apprise Thomas of the full details. That hardly seems fair, given that he is soon to die because of it. So, why don't you tell him, or shall I?'

Richard did not reply.

Stokely nodded. 'Very well.'

He folded his hands together and collected his thoughts quickly before he began. 'We were both young men, and you, Richard, were not even born, when King Henry dissolved the monasteries in England and sold, or gave away, their vast landholdings as well as their gold and silver. Many noblemen garnered great fortunes as a result of the dissolution. Another effect was to deepen the division between Catholics and the growing numbers of Protestants, a division that has led to the deaths of hundreds in England and tens of thousands across Europe. It seems that at the end of his life Henry recognised the damage that he had done and sought to return both himself and his kingdom to the Church of Rome. After the great hurt he had done to papal authority the Vatican decided that it would exact a price for its absolution of the King. They would accept England back only if all the property that had once belonged to the monasteries was returned to the Church.

'All those nobles who had gained so much from Henry's largesse would be stripped of their fortunes. They would surely revolt against their King and plunge England into civil war. Henry was dying, and his only priority was that he be admitted to heaven. He no longer cared for worldly affairs. But his courtiers did and would have been horrified if they had discovered his intentions. So he wrote his last will and testament in secret. Only his closest advisers knew about it. The will was entrusted to Sir Peter de Launcey to carry to Rome.

'He duly set off, aware that as soon as he was missed the King's closest advisers, some of whom would suffer great loss if the dissolution was reversed, would send agents after him to retrieve the will. Knowing that the routes to Rome would be closely watched, he travelled via Spain to Malta where the Order would protect him. By then he had begun to have reservations about his mission. He understood the implications of the will and was torn between the needs of his country and those of his faith. That was when he confided in me and asked my advice. Before I could come to a decision he was drowned.' Stokely paused. 'I had Henry's will in my hand and could easily have turned it over to the Grand Master of the day. But I chose not to. I would not have the blood of tens of thousands of Englishmen on my conscience. So I put the will in Sir Peter's chest and had it placed in the archive.'

'Why didn't you just destroy it?' asked Thomas.

'It was too powerful a thing to destroy. As long as it was safe, no harm could befall the heirs of the King. And I was content to leave it be. But since then, I have watched the number of Protestants swell in England, and the persecution of the Catholics increase every year of Elizabeth's reign. I resolved that if necessary I would find a way to use the will to stay the hand of the Protestants.'

Thomas was astonished. 'You would blackmail the Queen?'

'I sincerely hoped that I would never have cause to.'

Richard finally spoke. 'And you think the will is safe in your hands?'

'Safer in mine than in Walsingham or Cecil's. They would use it to protect their position at Elizabeth's court. She would hardly defy the will of men who could threaten to make public the dying wishes of her father.'

'Better that my masters have the will than it should remain in the hands of a Catholic or fall to the Muslims, as now seems likely,' Richard responded bitterly.

'A Catholic I may be but I am an Englishman before that,' Stokely countered.

For the first time Thomas's heart warmed slightly towards Stokely. Then he recalled that this was the man who had made Maria his wife, and done all in his power to prevent them meeting again.

'One thing puzzles me,' he said. 'Why was it necessary for you to threaten Maria with my arrest? She told me that she could not leave you. She said it was too late to change the past. She was your wife now and that was how it would remain.'

Stokely stared at him with a stricken expression. 'She said that?'

'Yes.'

Stokely closed his eyes and his face twisted in pain. 'Dear God, I spoke too hastily. I was angry. After I saw you leave the house I confronted her and said I knew you had been there. I said I knew that she had been unfaithful to me.'

'No. She was not,' said Thomas. 'I would have given anything for that, but she refused me.'

'She refused you?' Stokely slowly shook his head. 'What

440

have I done? Dear God, what have I done? I raged at her. I accused her of faithlessness, of harlotry. She stood there and took it all in silence. Then she said she did not love me. That she had only ever loved you.' Stokely swallowed. 'I lost my temper. I struck her. So help me God, for the first time in my life I struck her.'

Thomas clenched his fist and fought to control the rage that welled up inside.

'She fell back on the chair.' Stokely trembled as he recalled the moment. 'There was blood on her lip, and then I saw fear in her eyes. And worse, disgust and pity. I wish she had struck me back, screamed at me. Instead she just looked at me. I walked out and went to the cathedral to pray for forgiveness. When I returned to the house she and her maid had gone. There was no note. She just disappeared. I searched Birgu for the next two days before I realised I would not find her again, and even if I did she would not have me back at her side.' Stokely smiled weakly. 'She was all that ever mattered to me. That was when I resolved to come here, and die along with you. Not for any affection I bear you, but for hate. You are the cause of my misery, Thomas. If providence is kind I shall see you die before I fall.'

'Then I had better guard my back,' Thomas responded. 'It seems I have enemies on both sides.'

'No. You need not fear me.'

'I don't fear you, Oliver. I pity you.'

'And I hate you, I have always hated you. But, as is so often the case with hatred, it was imperfect. I see that now. Before, I wanted to hurt you and then destroy you, as if that would somehow resolve the matter. But it never could. My hatred is unquenchable. Harming you would in no way diminish it.' He smiled. 'It is a strange thing, but I feel almost at peace now. I do not fear death. I only ever feared the prospect of a life without Maria. This is where it ends. Here in St Elmo. For me, for you, and for your son. Poor Maria. She still thinks that Richard is safe in England. For her sake, I hope she never discovers the truth.' He drained his cup and stood up. 'There, that is all that needs to be said. I shall find somewhere to rest, though I shall not sleep. There is only one release from my torment now.'

Without waiting for a response he got up and walked out into the courtyard.

Richard, his expression dark, made to rise from the table but Thomas grasped his wrist firmly.

'Leave him be.'

'You heard him,' Richard hissed. 'He harmed my mother.'

'Stokely has suffered enough. In any case, he is like the rest of us, walking in the shadow of death. It serves no purpose to hasten his end.'

Richard shook his head. 'Are you so lacking in heart that you are not moved to act?'

'My heart is replete, my son. Did you not hear him? She loves me, and always has. And you already know that she loves you. I would rather you were with her and spared this death but that is not to be.' He released Richard's wrist and took his hand. 'At least we will be together at the end.'

Richard stared at his father, struggling to control his emotions, and nodded. 'Together, at the end.'

CHAPTER THIRTY-SEVEN

23 June

In the hour before dawn, the enemy's preparations for the coming assault were clearly audible to the survivors thinly spread out along the ruined walls of the fort. Most were clustered about the breach that had opened up when a section of the wall had finally collapsed under the weight of the Turkish cannon. Murmured exchanges carried up to the defenders as the Turks gathered in their trenches that surrounded the fort. Across the water, oars splashed and there were occasional cries from the men at the bows as they sounded the depths of the harbour. The dark mass of the galleys was easily visible in the darkness as they took up position to add the weight of their cannon to the preliminary bombardment of St Elmo.

Thomas, like most of the others, had not slept at his station. During the long hours of the night he had lain down, his head resting on a rolled-up gambison, and gazed up at the stars. The night sky was clear and the stars shone brilliantly. As he stared at them Thomas found some comfort in their eternal serenity. They had been there before he ever breathed and would be there still the following night, hours after he and the others had fallen.

Their cold aloofness seemed to mock the petty tribulations of mankind. All the grand causes, all the heroic efforts, the religious fanaticism that motivated men to kill others and willingly face death, seemed trivial when considered in the round, Thomas reflected. He did not wish a martyr's death. He wanted more than anything to live, now that he felt sure of Maria's love. Thinking of the life he might have had caused him to smile sadly. When his mind drifted towards the coming day, he could not help fearing his death. He hoped it would be quick, and that he might die before Richard and be spared that hideous spectacle at least.

He turned to look at his son, sitting against the parapet a short distance away, his chin resting on his breast, breathing easily. Despite the circumstances, Richard's exhaustion had got the better of him and had embraced him with a few hours of merciful oblivion. The sight moved Thomas unbearably and his throat tightened with grief at the thought of losing what he had only just been given, the most valuable treasure a man could find in life, the gift of a child. He had only had a handful of days in which to know his son and it was bittersweet to discern those precious virtues and quirks of character in him that would never have the opportunity to mature further.

Some distance along the wall beyond the breach Thomas could just make out the still form of Stokely hugging his knees as he stared across the heart of the fort. Thomas could only wonder at the private despair of that tormented soul and hoped that Stokely would also find peace in a swift death.

As the sound of muttered prayers rose around the fort

like the sound of surf on a distant shore, Thomas leaned towards his son and gently shook his shoulder. There was no response and Thomas shook him again, more forcefully, until Richard snatched a deep breath and sat up quickly, startled and confused. He blinked for a moment and then stared at his father.

'You let me sleep.' His tone was accusing. 'My God, you let me sleep through my final hours.'

'It is better that you slept.'

Richard was still for a moment before he rolled his neck stiffly. 'I dreamed I was back in England, as a child, hunting rabbits on a clear autumn morning . . .'

'Ah, rabbit,' Thomas mused. 'Now there's something I could willingly eat.' He paused and raised an eyebrow. 'It's the eve of the Feast of St John. 'Tis a shame that we will not be free to take a seat at the banquet.' Thomas smiled at the image, then his expression hardened. 'Get down to the chapel. Tell Mas and Miranda that the enemy are coming.'

'Yes, sir.'

'Then come back here directly.' Thomas felt a pang of anxiety. 'Hurry. I want you here at my side, whatever happens.'

Richard nodded. 'Yes, Father.'

He eased himself into a crouch and edged away from the shelter of the parapet, keeping close to the piles of debris and the bodies that had been dragged together to remove the risk of the survivors tripping over them once the fighting began. At the edge of the wall Richard slipped over the rim and dropped out of sight on to the stairs below. Thomas turned his attention back to the enemy.

From the sounds on all sides their intention was clear enough. When the signal was given they would charge the fort, scaling what was left of the walls by ladder, and at the same time launching an assault through the breach. This time there would be little to hold them back. There was only enough powder left for a few more shots and only a handful of incendiary weapons remained. All of the naphtha had been used up. Once the defenders had expended the last of their firepower they would take up their hand weapons and fight to the end.

Along the wall the defenders stirred and here and there a bright glow showed where the arquebusiers were readying their fuses. Others pulled on their helmets and fastened the buckles securely beneath their chins; those with armour checked the straps and made minor adjustments. Some held pikes while others readied swords, daggers, hatchets and maces. Thomas glanced across the breach and saw Stokely take up the heavy two-handed sword he had chosen from the fort's armoury – a cumbersome weapon but deadly in the right hands.

There was a pause in the gloom before dawn, a silence, a stillness, as if the defenders were part of a tableau composed of shadows. The sky to the east was smeared with the faint pearly hue of dawn and as the veil of darkness began to fade, Thomas made out details on the scarred landscape in front of the wall. The flags planted by the enemy to mark the ground they had taken hung limp in the still air. Discarded weapons and buckled and shattered shields and armour were strewn across the rubble before the walls amid bodies that had not yet been recovered for burial. Some were hideously swollen by corruption, made worse by the heat of the sun, and limbs stuck out at an angle, grotesquely. And then there was the stench of the month-old battlefield, a cloying stink of blood and decaying flesh, overlaid with the acrid odour of burning and the gritty tang of masonry dust. For some reason it seemed to Thomas more pungent and revolting than ever this morning. Or was it that his senses were heightened now that he knew he was living through his final hours, he wondered.

He looked towards the stairs, willing Richard to return before the enemy launched their attack. Briefly he considered leaving his position to go and find him, and then chided himself. What example would that set to the men under his command? He hardened his resolve and stared in the direction of the enemy.

The first of the Turkish drums began to beat, quickly swelling out of the shadows as more joined. A crash of cymbals and the wailing of pipes added to the din and then, as the first rays of the sun pierced the eastern horizon, the imams led their worshippers in the *shahada* – the Muslim testament that there is no god but God, Mohammed is the messenger of God. A soft murmuring surrounded the fort as the men within braced themselves, knowing that the assault was imminent.

A faint scraping drew Thomas's attention away from the enemy and he was relieved to see Richard returning from the top of the stairs, dragging a chair in either hand. A moment later more men appeared: four soldiers, half carrying and half dragging Colonel Mas and Captain Miranda. Richard set their chairs up a short distance to one side of the breach, close to Thomas's position, and then helped to ease the two officers on to the chairs.

'My sword,' Mas ordered, holding out his hand.

A soldier unslung the scabbard from over his shoulder and passed it up. Another weapon was passed to Miranda.

'I am ready.' Mas gestured to the men who had carried them up on to the wall. 'Get to your positions, and may God be with you.'

The soldiers bowed their heads in a final salute and crept away along the wall. Richard crouched beside his father.

'What are they doing?' asked Thomas, gesturing towards the two officers. 'Why are they up here?'

'It was the colonel's idea. When I gave them your message he said he'd rather die where the men could see him than down in the chapel. Miranda agreed.'

Thomas shook his head as he regarded the two men sitting erect, their wounded legs sticking out in front of them, swathed in soiled and bloody bandages. 'Madness . . .'

The murmuring from the Turkish trenches died away and the din from their instruments rose up with renewed fervour. Thomas turned his attention to his son, taking a last opportunity to regard him closely, with affection.

'I wish . . .' He tried to continue but there were no words adequate to the moment.

Richard smiled and briefly squeezed his hand. 'I understand, Father. There is much I would have wished for if we had been granted the time.'

A single gun roared from the top of the ridge, the signal to begin the attack. The deep boom rolled round the harbour and then was drowned out by a frenzied roar as the Turks burst from concealment and rushed the short distance towards the battered mass of St Elmo. The defenders replied at once, without waiting for an order, and spurts of fire darted from the barrels of their arquebuses. The mass of enemy soldiers surged across the broken ground and up the mound of rubble lying in the breach. Thomas fixed his attention on them. The first died, shot through the head, and he crashed forward and was immediately trampled by those behind him. More men fell, shot in the head or chest, easy targets at such close range.

Thomas cupped a hand to his mouth and bellowed, 'Incendiaries!'

The fuses smeared low arcs in the air before the pots shattered amongst the enemy in savage sheets of flame that set men ablaze as they screamed in terror and agony.

'Give it to 'em, lads!' Colonel Mas shouted, punching his sword into the air. 'For the Holy Religion!'

Miranda echoed the cry and then his lips drew back in a fierce grin. 'Kill them!'

Thomas raised the tip of his sword and held it ready. Beside him Richard hunched over his pike. The Turks came on, heedless of their comrades struck down by bullets, incendiaries or the rocks hurled at them from either side of the breach. The steep gradient of the rubble began to slow them down and they took several more casualties as they struggled forward to close with the defenders.

Thomas stepped forward, sword held ready, keenly aware of Richard close at his side, lowering his pike, ready to thrust. A Spahi, a few paces in advance of his comrades, rushed up towards the parapet, mouth open wide as he screamed his battle cry. He carried a spear in an overhand grip and thrust it towards Richard. The young man deftly parried the spear aside with a sharp clack as wood struck wood. Then he thrust home with all his weight and the steel point tore through the Spahi's robes and punched deep into his chest.

More men surged up the rubble slope and Thomas hacked at a man's turbaned head, stunning him even though the tightly wound material resisted the keen edge of his sword. A thrust to the throat ripped through an artery and his adversary fell back. Thomas looked for the next opponent. He felt an impact on his shoulder and something flickered past his eyes – the shaft of an arrow. More arrows whipped up from the throng at the bottom of the mound of rubble, and then Thomas saw flashes and billows of smoke as the enemy arquebusiers picked their targets. The head of a Maltese militiaman close to Stokely burst like an overripe watermelon, spattering blood across the face of the English knight. Richard stabbed his pike into the shoulder of a wild-haired man in animal skins who howled in pain, then pulled himself free and slashed at Richard's helmet with a club. Using his pike like a cross-staff, Richard blocked the attack then lowered the base of his weapon, hooked it round his foe's leg and tipped him on to his back before ramming the point through the man's chest.

From behind him Thomas could clearly hear Colonel Mas's roar. 'For God! For St John! Fight! Fight!'

Stokely stepped boldly into the breach to give himself space to wield his sword and swung it above his head in both hands before he slashed at an officer rushing forward madly to seize the honour of being the first man through the breach. He saw the dull gleam of the blade in the pale dawn light and raised his round shield to block the sword. The weight of the blade, together with the savage strength with which it was wielded, were more than a match for the best of shields. With a shrill clang Stokely's sword shattered the shield and cut through the Turk's elbow and on into his flank, tearing through scale armour, leather, jerkin and flesh and driving the air from the officer's lungs. The blow sent him reeling to the side and he stood dazed, looking down at the blood pouring from the stump of his arm. Then, teeth gritted in a snarl, he swung his sword at the English knight. Stokely moved his blade to ward off the blow and then swung again, this time at the Turk's neck. There was a wet crunch and the officer's head leaped into the air and spun back above his men, spraying them with blood before it fell to the ground.

A groan rose from the lips of the enemy and for a moment they wavered. Already the Turks had lost a score or more of their number and more fell as they were caught between the defenders' fire from both sides of the breach. They began to fall back down the rubble slope, stopping only when they found shelter to crouch behind.

'Take cover!' Thomas shouted.

His men moved back from the breach towards the safety of what remained of the parapet on each side as Turkish bullets ricocheted off the masonry. One of the Maltese volunteers was not quick enough and let out a cry as a ball smashed into his hip. He fell on to the rubble, dropping his sword. He struggled to sit up and examine his wound, then a second shot struck him in the face and the impact threw him back. Stokely stood alone for a moment, sword raised, defying the Turks. A shot deflected off his breastplate and nudged him a step to the side. Another shot glanced off the thick armour on his shoulder before he turned and picked his way steadily out of the line of fire and crouched down behind the parapet close to where Thomas and Richard squatted, breathing heavily.

Those men armed with arquebuses kept their attention on the breach and carefully picked their shots with the last of their gunpowder whenever an enemy showed himself. The Turkish snipers returned the fire with interest, firing several shots at any man risking a quick glance over the parapet. Looking along the line of the wall, Thomas could see that the perimeter still held. Mas and Miranda kept up their shouts of defiance and encouragement from their chairs, punching their gleaming blades into the cool morning air.

'Ah, I thought so,' Stokely said softly and Thomas turned to see him looking down at blood smeared across the tips of his fingers and the gleaming steel of his mantlet.

'Are you wounded?'

Stokely nodded and gestured towards the midriff of his breastplate. There was a small hole there, below which a thin ribbon of blood had been smeared by Stokely's hand. He smiled weakly as he met Thomas's gaze. 'I felt the impact of a third shot but thought the armour had kept it out. Alas, not.'

'Richard!' Thomas turned to his son. 'Get Sir Oliver down to the chapel.'

As Richard made to lower his pike, Stokely raised his hand. 'No. Leave me.'

'But you're wounded, sir.'

'So I am, and soon I shall be dead. Better up here in battle than cut down like a dog with the other wounded. Leave me, I say. The wound does not pain me unduly just yet.'

Thomas saw the dark stain on the surcoat beneath the armour and guessed that the wound was mortal. Even if, by some miracle, St Elmo held out, Stokely would die from loss of blood or suppuration of his wound from any fragments of metal or cloth that had been driven into his body. Stokely's expression was calm as he wiped the blood from his fingers on the hem of the surcoat and gripped the handle of his sword tightly.

'I shall die a better man than I lived.'

Thomas said gently, 'There is no need for such remorse. You have done your duty and more . . . I wish it had been possible for us to call each other friend, Oliver.'

'Friends?' Stokely smiled and shook his head. 'Never.'

The sound of firing along the wall began to decrease and one by one Thomas saw his men putting aside their arquebuses and taking up hand weapons until, no more than an hour after the sun had risen clear of the horizon, there were no more shots fired from within St Elmo. It took a moment more for the enemy to realise that they were no longer under fire. A shout rose up from the trench in front of the breach and they emerged from cover and came on again.

'Hold the breach!' Miranda yelled. 'Hold your ground, brothers!'

The sound of feet scrambling over the rubble and loose masonry grew closer as Thomas helped Stokely back on to his feet. Together with Richard and the handful of other survivors, they took position along the edge of the breach and readied their weapons. Thomas could see the heads and shoulders of the leading ranks of the enemy. Above them gleamed the curved blades of their swords and spear points. Amongst them were several archers and arquebusiers, no longer fearful of being picked off by the defenders. Even as Thomas watched, one of the enemy lowered his stand and took aim before applying his fuse to the firing pan. The weapon leaped as it spat flame and smoke, and Captain Miranda lurched in his chair. His sword arm slumped down and the blade slipped from his grasp as he looked down at the pigeon-egg-sized hole over his heart. His jaw sagged, then worked a moment as he struggled to speak. Then he threw his head back and uttered a last shriek. 'Fight, brothers!'

More shots rang out and two of the defenders were struck down.

Richard brandished his pike. 'Come and fight me like men, you cowards!'

At that moment Thomas saw a blur of motion and instinctively turned towards it. An incendiary pot was flying through the air towards him. There was no time to jump aside and the pot shattered against his breastplate. At once there was a bright flash of light and burst of heat and fire engulfed him from head to foot in glittering flames of red and yellow.

CHAPTER THIRTY-EIGHT

For a brief moment there was only the glare and the heat, and Thomas staggered back, out of the pool of fire on the wall. He dropped his sword and started to beat at the flames and then saw that his hands were alight. The pain hit him like a blow – a tearing, nerve-searing agony across the right side of his face and on his left arm and leg.

'Father!' Richard's voice cried out.

Thomas did not reply but felt his throat tighten as a keening cry rose up in his chest and fought to escape his clenched jaw. He felt hands beating on the flames and he was grasped tightly by the arm and dragged away across the parapet. A short distance from the top of the stairs leading down into the courtyard was a tub of seawater prepared for just such a moment, and before Thomas was aware of what was happening, he fell heavily into the water. At once the pain on his face subsided, and there was the sharp tang of saltwater on his lips. Then his head broke the surface and the raging pain returned. His right eye refused to focus and he clenched it shut, wincing.

'Help me!' Richard called out. 'We have to get him down to the chapel!'

Some part of Thomas's mind reacted violently to the words. 'No! I will stay and fight!' He struggled out of the tub and on to his feet, dripping. Through the pain of his burns he forced his mind to focus. 'My sword, give it to me!'

Richard stared at him in horror, and it was Stokely who pressed the weapon into his hand. 'There.'

Without hesitation Thomas stepped forward, towards the line of men locked in a bitter fight for the breach. Some of the Turks had forced their way on to the wall and two Janissaries had set upon Colonel Mas. He wielded his sword desperately, parrying their attacks and stabbing one of his opponents in the throat. Then he was struck by a bullet and fell from his chair. At once the other Janissary leaped forward and hacked at the colonel's exposed face, cutting his proud features to bloody ribbons. Before Thomas could rush to his aid, he felt a blow to his left shoulder and spun round and fell on to his knees. Again, hands grasped him and pulled him back.

'We have to get him out of here!' yelled Richard.

'Take him,' Stokely growled. 'I'll protect you both.'

Dazed and blinded by terrible pain, Thomas felt his arm pulled over someone's shoulder and then he stumbled down the stairs, barely conscious as wave after wave of agony and despair swept over him.

A desperate cry went up. 'The breach has fallen! The Turks have broken through!'

Richard tightened his grasp about his father's body and glanced back as he struggled down the stairs. The Turks were spilling out of the breach and running along the walls on either side, cutting down the few men still in their way. All around the perimeter of St Elmo, more Turks were appearing and those defenders who could ran for the cover of the storerooms to make their final stand, or try and hide. Close behind Richard limped Stokely, holding his sword out, ready to strike down any of the enemy who came within reach.

As they reached the courtyard they joined a handful of men fleeing towards the entrance to the chapel. The bell had begun to toll, the rich tone struggling to be heard above the enemy's shouts of triumph and the cries for mercy and despair from the defenders. But there was no mercy. The Turks had lost far too many men over the previous month and wanted only to satisfy their desire for bloody revenge. With Stokely protecting his back, Richard staggered on towards the chapel. To one side he saw a Spanish soldier fall to his knees at the top of the stairs and clasp his hands together as he was surrounded by several Turks. They did not hesitate for a moment before hacking at the Spaniard in a frenzy of blades and sprays of blood.

'Come on, Father,' Richard muttered. 'A little further.'

A bullet struck the door of the chapel as they approached, splintering the dark wood. There were two soldiers with drawn swords at the entrance, desperately beckoning.

'Inside, quickly!' a sergeant in the surcoat of the Order shouted.

Richard increased his pace, half dragging his father across the threshold.

'Close the door!' Stokely ordered as he followed Richard inside. It was too late for their comrades still outside. A handful fought in a cluster at the top of the stairs while the rest were run down and slaughtered by the Turks. The door thudded shut and Stokely helped the sergeant drag the nearest pew against the inside of the door. Then he turned to Richard and pointed to the far end of the chapel. 'Take him over there, behind the altar. Quick!'

Richard nodded and continued to support the dead weight of his groaning father down the aisle of the chapel. On either side the pews had been pushed back against the walls to make way for the wounded. Many of the men were sitting up and staring anxiously towards the entrance as the jubilant shouts of the enemy echoed inside the fort's walls. Richard dragged Thomas up the steps at the end of the chapel and made his way round the altar before gently releasing his burden on to the flagstones beside the drain cover.

'Oh God . . .' Thomas groaned through clenched teeth. 'It hurts . . . it hurts.'

Richard grimaced as he saw the raw blistered flesh covering the right side of his father's face. Working quickly he unfastened the buckles and removed the helmet and armour, leaving his father in his quilted gambison and thick hose and boots. Thomas let out a cry as his gauntlets were removed, taking some flesh with them where the material had been burned through to the skin. Then Richard turned to the heavy iron grille of the drain cover, straining his muscles to lift it aside and expose the opening.

There was a thud from the chapel door and a cry of alarm from the sergeant. 'They're right outside!'

'Hold them a moment,' Stokely ordered as he staggered towards the altar, clutching at his bloodied side with one hand and dragging his sword along the floor with the other.

He panted a moment when he reached Thomas and

Richard. 'One last thing, Richard . . .' Stokely reached up to his neck and pulled out a key on a silver chain. He tugged it sharply, breaking the chain, and thrust the key into Richard's hand. 'Here. There's a false bottom to my writing desk . . . inside is a small chest . . . That's the key to it.'

'Henry's will?'

Stokely nodded. 'It would be best for all if you destroyed it . . .'

Richard stared at the key and then quickly thrust it inside his shirt.

Stokely gestured towards Thomas who was moaning pitifully on the floor. 'Save him . . . Get out of here.'

Richard nodded, and lifting Thomas under the arms he dragged him to the drain and eased him down before letting him drop the remaining distance. He sat on the rim and looked back at Stokely.

'You're not coming?'

'No.' Stokely indicated the blood oozing beneath the bottom of his breastplate. 'The wound is mortal. I'll stay here, with the others.'

Richard shook his head sadly. 'God save you, sir.'

'Go!' Stokely waved him away.

As soon as Richard had disappeared from sight, Stokely hobbled over to the grille and heaved it back into place before taking up position in front of the altar, leaning on his sword for support as he gasped for breath. The pounding on the door had increased and despite the weight of the bench and the desperate efforts of the two soldiers, the door began to edge inwards. The tolling of the bell died away and Stokely saw Robert of Eboli emerge from the door leading into the chapel's small bell tower. The friar carried a silver cross before him and raised it high as he strode into the middle of the chapel and turned to face the entrance before kneeling down. The Turks outside the door pressed forward, steadily forcing it open. As the gap widened, a shaft of light pierced the gloom and fell upon the symbol in the friar's hands and reflected a giant ghostly cross on the wall above the entrance.

'See?' Robert cried out. 'The Lord is with us! We are saved!'

The door lurched inwards and the two sergeants leaped back and readied their weapons as the Turks burst into the chapel. With a wild shout one of the sergeants swung his sword and struck down a robed warrior, splitting his skull open. Before he could recover his weapon, the enemy swarmed round him and the other sergeant, hacking and stabbing with their weapons until the two men were cut to pieces on the floor. More Turks spilled into the chapel. Stokely shook his head to try and dispel his giddiness.

'Stop, infidels!' Robert bellowed, in the same rich voice that had captivated his congregation. He thrust the cross towards the oncoming Turks. 'The Lord God commands you to stop. In his name I order you to leave his house and quit this island, never to return.'

A Janissary officer approached the friar and sneered in French, 'Where is your god, Christian?' He glanced round, as if looking, and some of his men laughed. Then he raised his sword high and swept it round in an arc with all his strength. Robert had time to utter a shriek of terror before his head toppled to the floor at his side. His body collapsed and the cross clattered beside his head. The officer turned to his men and shouted an order. With a cheer they spread out across the chapel and fell on the wounded men lying on the ground, butchering them even as they begged for mercy.

Several approached Stokely. He gathered what was left of his strength, raised his sword and swung it round above his head to build up its lethal momentum. 'For God and St John!' The bloodied tip hissed through the air as the first of the Turks approached, a heavily built man with a broad-bladed scimitar and large round shield. As the blade swept round behind Stokely, the Turk rushed forward. Stokely had anticipated the move and stepped back with him so that his sword cut below the rim of the Turk's shield and smashed through his knee, shattering the bone. As the Turk collapsed he swung his own blade and caught Stokely on the side of his helmet.

The force of the impact caused an explosion of light in his head and before his vision could clear the other Turks were upon him. They snatched the sword from his hands and knocked him down. Daggers pierced his flesh through the gaps in his armour before the officer bellowed at his men to stop.

'This is one of the accursed knights, you fools! Why kill him like this when you could slaughter him like a pig? Take off his armour and put him on the altar!'

Stokely, still dazed, felt his limbs pulled about as the Turks stripped him of the plates that had protected him, then his clothes, until he lay naked. Then he was hoisted up from the floor and placed on the cold stone of the altar, his ears ringing with the screams and cries of the last of the wounded to be killed. He tried to move but strong hands held him down. As his vision began to clear he saw the officer leering down at him, a dagger held up for the knight to see.

'This is what we do to the pigs who dare to defy Suleiman and Allah.'

He raised the dagger above Stokely's chest. Summoning the last of his strength, Stokely opened his mouth and screamed out, 'God save the Holy Religion!'

Then the blade slammed down, cutting into his breast. The impact drove the breath from his lungs and Stokely rolled his head to one side as he felt the blade rip down through his breastbone to expose his heart. Blackness rushed over him as he felt the Turk's fingers close round his living heart. Sir Oliver Stokely's lips moved one final time as they framed the words, 'Dear God, protect Maria . . .'

CHAPTER THIRTY-NINE

Down in the drain Richard heard Stokely's last cry of defiance and glanced back in the direction of the grille. At any moment some Turk was bound to become curious and search the drain. His only hope was that the overpowering stench of human waste would put the enemy off long enough for him to drag his father out of the tunnel and into the cover of the rocks beside the path leading down to the jetty. He reached under Thomas's shoulders, took firm hold of the gambison and pulled. The material caught on the burned flesh of his arms and Thomas let out a groan.

'Quiet!' Richard hissed. 'Do you want to get us killed?'

Thomas clamped his jaws tightly shut to bite off the urge to cry out. He began to tremble as the shock hit home and his strangled moans echoed faintly along the drain. Richard bent down close to his ear.

'Father, for pity's sake, please be quiet.'

He pulled on the dead weight of Thomas's body, dragging him through the trickle of fluids that ran amid the stinking slurry along the bottom of the drain. It was only a short distance to the screen that concealed the opening where the drain passed under the wall. Easing his father down, Richard gently moved the screen to one side and peered out into the daylight. The sounds of cheering came from above, carrying over the walls of the fort. Occasional shots added to the enemy's celebrations, but there was no one to be seen on this side of the fort which faced across the harbour towards Birgu and Senglea. Richard pushed the screen aside and crawled from the drain. He glanced quickly to both sides and saw only a handful of men some distance away, too far for them to make out any detail of Richard's attire. He stood up and waved his arm casually. A moment later one of the enemy waved back and then turned his attention back towards St Elmo.

Richard pulled Thomas out, eased him on to his feet and raised his unburned arm across his shoulder.

'Not far to go. Hold on to me.'

They picked their way across the rocks and stepped on to the path. At any moment Richard expected to be seen from the walls above and hear the alarm raised. But they continued their slow progress without being discovered and Richard guessed that the Turks were busy hunting down the last of the defenders inside the fort and looking for the loot that many of them had been promised in return for joining the campaign. There would be scant pickings, he reflected. Almost everything of value had been thrown into the fort's well the night before when the defenders had accepted that all was lost.

Richard was steering Thomas towards the steps that led down to the jetty when he heard the scrape of boots on rocks. A figure stepped out immediately in front of them and Richard's hand flew to his sword handle. Then he let out an explosive sigh of relief as he saw it was one of the

Maltese militiamen. The man stared wildly at the two Englishmen and then turned towards the sea.

'Wait!' Thomas called after him in Maltese. 'I need help.'

'Too late,' the man replied. 'It's every man for himself now.'

'Help me,' Richard pleaded. 'For pity's sake, help me.'

The man hesitated and then stepped to the other side of Thomas and lifted his arm before Richard could stop him. At once Thomas threw his head back and let out a cry. Before they reached the top of the steps a voice called down to them from the wall.

'Don't look back!' Richard hissed. 'Keep moving.'

The voice called out again, louder this time. Then there was a short pause before a challenge was shouted down to them. They kept going, Thomas's feet bumping down the steps between the rocks until they reached the jetty.

'Oh no . . .' Richard muttered in despair. There were no boats moored alongside the jetty. Only the bows of a sunken craft bobbed low in the water, all that remained of a boat pounded to pieces by the enemy guns that had been sited to sweep the sea between the Christian forts. There were more shouts from the direction of the wall and Richard glanced over his shoulder, but there was no sign of a pursuit yet. They continued to the end of the jetty and set Thomas down against a post before stripping off their clothes, down to their loincloths. Then Richard did the same for his father, wincing as he saw for the first time the full extent of the burns on the exposed flesh. Much of the right side of Thomas's face and neck was raw and red, like freshly butchered meat. So was most of the left side of his body. Patches of skin had peeled back and now lay on his flesh in puckered skeins of white and grey. The removal of most of his clothes caused fresh agonies and Thomas bit down as hard as he could to fight the urge to cry out.

'We're going to have to swim for it,' Richard said.

'Leave me,' Thomas said through his teeth.

'No. Not now.' Richard shook his head and forced a quick smile. 'I would not lose a father so soon after finding him.'

Then he took Thomas's right arm and leaped into the sea. The Maltese soldier dived in close by. The water closed briefly over Thomas's head and then his face burst clear of the surface. The water was cold and instantly dulled the sharpness of his agony. Even so he could not move his left arm or leg to swim without being tormented by pain.

'I can't make it, Richard. Please . . . please save yourself.'

'Float on your back,' Richard ordered. 'You there, take his other arm, and let's get moving.'

Thomas lay staring up as his companions struck out for the far shore, some four hundred yards across the harbour. For a while Thomas let himself be borne slowly along, then he strained his neck and looked towards St Elmo. He could see the full extent of the side of the wall facing Birgu and Senglea. The parapet was filled with figures shaking their swords and spears in the air, shadows against the morning sunlight. A few thin trails of smoke lifted a short distance into the sky before dispersing. Then, as he watched, the flag of the Order gracefully billowed away from its staff, and was pulled down rapidly. A short moment after, the green flag of Islam rose up above the fort to renewed cheers.

'What happened to Sir Oliver?' Thomas blurted. 'Where is he?'

Richard lifted his head clear of the water to reply. 'Dead. He made his stand in the chapel.'

The three men edged across the channel and were already a hundred yards from the jetty when Thomas saw a party of Turks armed with arquebuses running down the steps. They rushed to the end of the jetty where two of them set up the stands for their weapons and took aim. A small cloud of smoke engulfed the first man and the bullet slapped into the sea six feet to Thomas's side, throwing up a tall plume of water. The second shot was closer, in line, but overhead and it struck the surface some distance in front of the swimmers. More shots followed, some missing by a wide margin while a handful struck close by.

The Maltese soldier suddenly cried out, 'Look there! The Turks are coming!'

Richard craned his head and stared across the light swell. A boat had set out from one of the small batteries running along the shore of the Sciberras peninsula. There were men armed with arquebuses on board. More were filling a second boat.

'Damn,' Richard growled. 'They're certain to reach us before we gain the other side.' He turned to the Maltese man. 'Swim for your life!'

They struck out, dragging Thomas through the sea behind them, his mind slipping in and out of lucidity. They were halfway across when there was a rolling boom from the direction of St Angelo and Richard looked up to see a cloud of smoke swirling from one of the towers. He turned his head quickly and saw a pillar of water collapse close to the nearest of the Turkish boats, less than a hundred yards away. The near miss shook the men at the oars and the drag on the blades to one side caused the boat to swing round. The soldiers crowding the bows struggled to retain their balance and one dropped his arquebus which bounced off the side and splashed into the sea. An officer drew his sword and shouted orders at the crew. They swiftly took up their oars again and the boat turned back towards the swimmers and resumed the chase.

The cannon in the fort fired again and this time Richard saw the shot slap into the sea just behind the stern of the boat, throwing up a column of spray and sending a small wave over the transom. Still the officer urged the rowers on and the boat rapidly closed the distance. The next time Richard looked back he was horrified to see the enemy a scant thirty yards away. One of the men in the bows lowered his barrel and took aim, bracing his legs to take account of the movement of the boat beneath him. His right eye squinted as he raised the length of smouldering match up to the pan above the barrel.

At that moment the boat seemed to leap from the sea and lengths of wood and water exploded into the air. With cries of terror the Turks were pitched into the harbour. There was a flurry of splashing as the soldiers thrashed about and wreckage dropped into the water about them. Richard saw the officer struggling to stay afloat as his robes and armour dragged him down. His hands thrashed to the surface before he disappeared, along with the other soldiers who were encumbered by their equipment. But the second boat was still rowing hard, some distance behind.

Richard felt a painful cramp seize his right leg but forced himself to swim on. It seemed that every muscle in his body ached and felt heavy and for the first time he feared that he did not have the strength to reach the far side of the harbour, still some two hundred yards away. He could see men on the walls of St Angelo waving them on and the cannon fired again, aiming for the second boat.

'Richard . . .' Thomas spoke feebly, spluttering as seawater washed across his face. 'Son . . . Leave me.'

'No.'

'I am in such pain . . . I would rather die. Save yourself.'

'No, Father, I will not leave you.'

'I am dead already. I will not survive these wounds.'

Richard tightened his hold on his father and kicked out, using every last reserve of his failing strength to move forward.

'Leave me.'

'I will not. You will not die.' Richard spat out a mouthful of seawater. 'Think of Maria. She is there in Birgu. Waiting for you. Hold to that thought.'

'Maria . . .' Thomas muttered, barely conscious.

'Sir!' The Maltese soldier raised a hand above the water and pointed. 'Look!'

Richard craned his neck and followed the direction of the man's finger and saw a boat putting out from St Angelo. Sunlight glinted off armour and weapons as the craft surged across the slight swell in the morning sun. Richard took renewed hope from the sight and forced himself to continue on even as his lungs and muscles burned from the effort. As the cannon fired again, he glanced back and saw that the enemy had not given up the pursuit, clearly intent on running down their prey and ensuring that not one man of the garrison of St Elmo survived its destruction. The men on the boat from St Angelo were equally determined to save their comrades and rowed desperately. It was impossible for Richard to guess who would win the contest as he struggled on, with increasingly feeble strokes. The rocks at the foot of the fort and walls rising up still seemed impossibly far away.

Then he heard a voice cry out to them, urging them on, and soon there were splashes close at hand and a surge of water and then the long overlapping planks of the boat filled Richard's field of vision.

'Get 'em aboard! Quickly does it!'

Hands grasped his arms and hauled him bodily out of the water, over the side and down. He lay on his back staring into the blue heavens, gasping for breath, his heart pounding in his chest. There was a crash as an arquebus fired, and then another. The fire was returned from the enemy and bullets cracked into the prow of the boat. More shots were exchanged and then a chorus of jeers filled Richard's ears.

'They're bolting! Good shooting, lads. Now, back to St Angelo.'

As he felt the boat turn, a shadow loomed over Richard. He took a deep breath and propped himself up and saw that it was Romegas, the Order's senior captain.

Romegas nodded grimly. 'You're Sir Thomas's squire.'

'Yes, sir.'

'Your master is in a poor way.'

'I know.'

'Are you all that's left of the garrison? Did no one else get out?'

'I didn't see anyone else. There may be some who also managed to hide in rocks or the caves down by the water. I don't know, sir.'

'I see.' Romegas handed him a wineskin. 'Here. Take this.'

'Not yet.' With great effort Richard sat upright and saw his father lying on his back, trembling. Beyond him the Maltese soldier was sitting upright, arms wrapped round his knees. Richard crawled over to his father's side and took his hand. Thomas's eyes flickered open and he turned his head with a wince and squinted at his son.

'We're safe?'

Richard nodded, averting his gaze from the terrible burns on his father's body.

'Safe?' Romegas shook his head as he turned to gaze across the harbour at St Elmo, battered and ruined beneath the flags and standards of the enemy. 'The prelude is over. Now Birgu and Senglea will face the full weight of the enemy. Unless Don Garcia comes to our aid soon, I fear the worst is yet to come.'

CHAPTER FORTY

Many days passed before Thomas became coherently aware of his surroundings. He sensed the daylight through his eyelids and heard the irregular boom of artillery and the distant crash of heavy iron shot striking home. His body felt so weak that he could barely move his fingers, and any attempt to move his head caused a sharp stabbing pain down the side of his face and neck. So he lay still and silent, breathing deeply in a steady rhythm as his mind attempted to take stock of his situation. He knew where he was well enough, but the last thing that he could recall in detail was the final assault on St Elmo. The charge of the enemy up into the breach, the deaths of Miranda and Mas, and the burst of fire as the incendiary struck him and set him alight. After that, all sense of time was lost.

He recalled the burning agony that had consumed every fibre of his being, the fleeting impressions of the wounded lying in the chapel, Stokely, his expression waxen, leaning on his sword as he struggled for breath. Then the stench of a dark enclosed space, the relief of the sea as it cooled his burns and then a brief moment of confused serenity as he floated on his back staring into a peaceful azure sky and accepted that he was dying. Then agony as he was dragged from the sea.

After that he lost consciousness and his existence became a long, delirious nightmare of pain and fever. His head was swathed in bandages and there were long days when he lay sweltering in the heat, staring at a plaster ceiling curving overhead and a shaft of sunlight falling through a window behind him. He remembered voices, one that was stern and matter-of-fact as it discussed his treatment, then another, Richard, and last that of a woman, unmistakably Maria. Their words were confused and he could make no sense of what had been said. When he was alone his mind was filled with troubled images of fire, blood, sword and smoke, of terrible injuries. His head swelled with a cacophony of imagined noises of drums and cymbals, harsh cries of men locked in deadly combat and the screams of the dying . . .

Now all of that had begun to fade and Thomas was aware that his mind had emerged from a dark period of chaos. He took a long, deep breath and opened his eyes. At first his vision was blurred and the light coming through the window was too bright and painful and he blinked and closed his eyes. After a moment he opened them again, more cautiously this time. Slowly, the vision in his left eye cleared and he saw the stained white plaster of the ceiling. His right eye merely detected patches of light and shadow without any specific form. He moved his limbs carefully and winced at the tightness and pain that lanced down his left arm and side. Around him Thomas was aware of other men lying on beds, some in silence, while others moaned or mumbled incoherently to themselves. Now and then figures moved amongst them, men in the robes of friars and monks. Finally one came to Thomas and bent down to examine him.

'You're awake again.' The monk spoke French and smiled as he dabbed at the sweat pricking out at his hairline. 'And your fever finally seems to have broken.'

'Finally?' Thomas frowned and tried to speak again but his throat was too dry and he could only make a soft croaking sound. 'Where . . .'

'You're in the infirmary of St Angelo. Quite safe. Here, let me help you.'

There was a faint gurgle of liquid and then the monk gently slipped a hand under Thomas's head and raised it slightly. With the other hand he held a brass cup to his patient's lips and helped him to drink. Thomas gratefully swilled the water around his dry mouth and swallowed. He took a few more mouthfuls before he nodded and let his head slump back. The monk eased it down on to the bolster and withdrew his hand and placed it on Thomas's forehead.

'Yes, the heat has gone from your brow. That's good.' He smiled again. 'When you were first brought in here I was certain that you would not survive. Your burns are severe and there is a bullet wound to your leg. It seems you were struck as they pulled you from the water. Between the burns and the loss of blood I fully expected you not to survive through the night. You have a strong constitution, Sir Thomas. Even so, it was a close thing. You developed a fever and for many days I feared we might lose you. That you survived is due to the tireless efforts of the woman who nursed you.'

'Woman?'

'She's the widow of the late Sir Oliver Stokely, as I

understand it. She also claims to be your friend.' The monk tried to stifle a knowing smile and Thomas felt a passing irritation at the man.

'What is your name, brother?' Thomas asked huskily.

'Christopher.'

'Well then, Christopher, Lady Maria is indeed my friend, and a woman who is beyond reproach.'

'Of course. I meant no offence.'

'Where is she?'

'Resting. She has hardly left your side these last weeks. She saw to all your needs, though she did have the help of your squire from time to time, when he could be spared from his duties. She fed you, washed and bathed you and changed your dressings. The poor lady is exhausted. Once I saw that your fever had abated I sent her home to rest. That was this morning. She said she would return at dusk.'

Thomas nodded. Then he looked at the monk. 'You said weeks. How long have I been here? What date is it? What month?'

'Why, it is the twenty-second day of August, sir.'

'August?' Thomas started in alarm. 'Then . . . then I have been here almost eight weeks.'

The monk nodded. 'And for four of those weeks it was doubtful that you would live, despite your solid English constitution. For the last two weeks we have been fighting your fever. It was only a few days ago that I became confident that you would recover. Though when I say recover, you will have to live with the consequences of your injuries.'

'But what of the siege?'

The monk pursed his lips. 'The Turks are pounding us from all sides. At night they fire into the heart of Birgu and have killed scores of women and children. We still hold every one of the bastions and the wall, though barely. The Grand Master has less than a third of the men with which he started. Food and water are running short and morale is poor. There was a rumour that Don Garcia and his army would land at the end of July, but nothing came of it. And every day the guns continue to reduce the walls. Each time the Turks open a new breach they launch an assault, and we throw them back.' The monk paused and shook his head in wonder. 'God knows where they get the courage to hurl themselves on us time and again. They've tried everything. They even hauled their small galleys over the Sciberras ridge to attempt a landing on Senglea. They were cut to pieces along the shore, and their boats blasted by our cannon. Those we didn't cut down, or shoot, drowned in their hundreds . . . At least morale is as much a problem for the Turks as it is for us. According to the prisoners we've taken, Mustafa Pasha is finding it increasingly difficult to get his men to attack. There is sickness and hunger in his camp. Soon I fear that the dead will outnumber the living on this Godforsaken rock.' He closed his eyes briefly and rubbed his jaw wearily. Then he sighed and forced a smile. 'But enough of the siege. You need to rest.'

'No. I need to know about my wounds. When will I be fit to fight again?'

'Fight?' The monk seemed taken aback.

Thomas felt a chill course down his spine. He struggled for a moment to sit up in order to see his body but he was too weak and slumped back with a hiss of frustration. He reached out with his left hand and clasped the monk's arm. 'Tell me.'

The monk sucked in his breath. 'You had extensive burns to your left leg and hip and on your left arm and the right side of your neck and face. Your eye was scorched and damaged and I doubt that you can see much out of it. Am I right?'

Thomas nodded. 'Just shadows.'

'As I feared.' The monk gestured down Thomas's left side. 'Your skin and muscle tissue were badly damaged and will take many more months to heal. There will be a permanant tightness in your arm and leg and they will not flex as fully as they once did. And they will be painful. I would say your fighting days are behind you, Sir Thomas. Even though the Grand Master is short of men and is filling out the ranks with boys, dotards and any man still fit enough to hold a weapon, I have to say that this present conflict will be over before you recover enough to play any useful part.'

'Bring me a mirror,' Thomas said quietly.

'Later. You should rest. Then I shall bring you soup, and some bread.'

'I want a mirror. Now.'

The monk hesitated a moment, and then nodded. 'As you wish, Sir Thomas. A moment then.'

He stood up and walked out of the chamber. While he was gone, Thomas gritted his teeth and edged himself up the bed so that his shoulders were on the bolster and his head rested against the stone wall behind his bed. For a moment he had to fight off the pain from his side. The monk returned with a small square mirror of polished steel and handed it to Thomas.

'There. Though you may not like what you see.'

Thomas raised the mirror above his face and stared at his reflection. A short distance from the mid-line of his features the skin was tight and glossy like highly polished marble streaked with red and purple. The skin round his right eye was swollen and red, and the eyeball was blood-shot and the lens appeared milky. He adjusted the angle and saw that there were only tufts of hair on that side of his skull and his ear looked withered. Moving the mirror again he drew the sheet covering him aside and examined the left of his body, shocked by the tortured flesh he saw there. Swallowing, Thomas handed the mirror back and covered himself again.

'She saw me like this?' he asked softly.

'You looked far worse for the first two weeks.' The monk gestured towards his head. 'The scarring is permanent but the colour will fade. Most of the hair will grow back but some patches will remain bald. You may find that your vow of chastity will be a little easier to keep from now on.' He smiled to show that he was making a joke, albeit a harsh one.

Thomas turned his face to the wall at his side. 'I am tired. I need to sleep.'

'Yes. Of course, Sir Thomas. Do you wish me to send a message to Lady Maria to say that you are awake?'

'No,' he replied quickly. 'Let her rest too.'

'Very well. I'll bring you food later, once you have slept.'

Thomas heard the scuffing of the monk's sandals as he

moved off, and then he shut his eyes tightly as they filled with tears of grief. He no longer felt like a man. He felt repulsed by what he had seen in the mirror, and shamed by the idea that he would no longer be fit enough to fight or hunt or take part in the myriad pastimes of other men. Worse still, if the Turks carried the day and captured Birgu, then he and all the others too helpless to defend themselves would be butchered where they lay, like swine.

He eventually fell back into a troubled sleep and awoke close to midday, as far as he could calculate from the angle of the light streaming in through the window. As he stirred and his eyes flickered open, he saw Richard sitting on a stool beside his bed. The young man's head was slumped on his chest and a thick stubble of dark hair covered his jaw. His hair was matted with sweat and dust and the skin round his eyes was dark with fatigue. His doublet was filthy and torn in several places and there were scabs from cuts and scrapes on his hands and face.

Thomas reached out his left hand, wincing at the sting the movement caused, and gently touched his son's cheek. Richard twitched as if to discourage some bothersome insect and Thomas could not help smiling at the gesture as he let his hand drop back to his side.

'Richard . . .'

The young man's eyes flickered open at the mention of his name and he stirred wearily, then his lips parted in a warm smile. 'You're back with us at last.'

'Did you doubt I would be?'

'Not me.' Richard chuckled. 'Just that monk. He was certain we were wasting our efforts and that you should just be given the last rites. I told him I had served you long enough to know that you would not die half so easily.'

Thomas glanced round the room and saw that they would not be overheard. 'Does he know that I am your father?'

'No. Any more than he knows that you are a man without faith.'

Thomas nodded with relief. Either one of those truths could be dangerous and it was impossible to know what he might have revealed in his delirious condition. He gestured to the table beside Richard. 'Some water please.'

He managed to drink it unaided this time and once his throat and lips were moistened, he felt more able to converse. 'The monk gave me some idea of what has happened since I have been recovering, but tell me, how is the Grand Master coping?'

'Him?' Richard smiled thinly. 'La Valette is as hard as steel through and through. He is everywhere, encouraging the men and promising that we shall live through this trial. I tell you, he is a man possessed by the idea of confounding the will of Sultan Suleiman. He has also made it impossible for there to be any thought of surrender.'

'How so?'

Richard chewed his lip briefly. 'It was something that happened after St Elmo was taken. The next morning, at first light, a lookout on St Angelo saw some objects floating in the water close to the wall. They turned out to be the bodies of four knights and that of Robert of Eboli, nailed to crosses, all of them beheaded. When they were fished out of the sea we saw that plaques had been nailed to the crosses naming the men – Mas, Miranda, Stokely and Monserrat, as well as Robert of Eboli. Besides hacking their heads off, the enemy had torn their hearts out.'

'Sweet Jesus,' Thomas muttered. 'What happened then?'

Richard pursed his lips. 'La Valette repaid them in kind. He had all of the Turkish prisoners brought from the dungeons and taken up on to the walls of St Angelo where the enemy could see them. There they had their throats cut, one by one, and when it was over La Valette gave the order for their heads to be loaded into cannon and fired across the harbour into the enemy lines . . . A day later Mustafa Pasha sent a herald to announce that henceforth there would be no quarter given. If Birgu and Senglea fall, he promises to kill every living thing his men encounter.' Richard paused. 'So it is death or victory for us now.'

'It always has been. La Valette was at Rhodes when it surrendered to Suleiman. I think he resolved then never to taste such a defeat ever again.' Thomas was silent for a moment before he reached out and took his son's hand. 'You saved my life. I am in your debt. And it is one I fear I shall never be able to repay with this body.'

'Father, you gave me life. What man can ever repay that? Think no more on it. It was my duty, as your squire, and as your son.'

Thomas gently squeezed Richard's hand. 'If only I deserved to be your father . . .'

Richard looked away and withdrew his hand. 'I would not take too much pride in me. I have done questionable things in my time. Don't forget, I am Walsingham's man. I came here for Henry's last will and testament, and I have it. Stokely told me where to find it. If I live, then Walsingham will expect me to take it back to him.'

Thomas thought for a moment. The will would always be a potent weapon in the hands of whoever possessed it. The Catholics would use it to shatter the grip that Elizabeth held over many of the most powerful men in her realm. Walsingham would be only too willing to use it to blackmail the Queen into sanctioning his persecution of the Catholics in England, whom he saw as his enemy.

Thomas looked directly at his son. 'You could take it back. Or you could destroy it. You understand full well the implications of the will. The choice is yours. I trust that you will make the right decision.' There was a moment of silence before Thomas went on. 'No man is beyond redemption. Just as no man is immune from doing the wrong thing. Son, I know this better than most. Think on it. I would not have you go through life carrying a burden like I have. Learn from me.'

Richard gazed at him and then glanced towards the door. 'I had better go. I need to prepare my men for a patrol tonight. I'll come again, when I can. Goodbye, Father.'

He stood up and walked away. At the door he paused and then Maria stepped into view and held his arms and kissed him on the cheek. Richard received the kiss awkwardly before he raised a hand to touch her arm gently. Then he bowed his head and eased himself from her grasp and strode off down the corridor. Maria stared after him fondly, then turned back towards the room, towards Thomas, a smile lighting up her face as she saw that he was awake. The image he had seen earlier in the mirror was still fresh in Thomas's mind and he angled the scarred side of his face away from her as she approached and sat down.

Neither spoke at first and then Thomas swallowed nervously and cleared his throat. 'I am sorry for your loss. Oliver was a good man.'

'Yes . . . Yes, he was.' The sadness in her tone was genuine. 'He was kind to me, until the end. It was your presence that changed him. It could not be helped. I was never able to give him what he wanted from me. What you always had.' She reached out and tentatively cupped his cheek. Her skin was smooth and cool and Thomas closed his eyes as he breathed in the faint scent of her.

'I should have been a better wife to him.' Maria glanced in the direction Richard had gone. 'And Oliver should have let me be a better mother to my . . . our son. He knows the truth but he cannot forgive me for past wrongs.'

Thomas laughed drily and she turned to look down at him with a frown. 'What?'

'It's just that we have all made such a mess of things. Me, you, Oliver, Richard. There is no escaping the past. Not for us. Nor for La Valette or Suleiman. We are all the prisoners of our history, Maria.'

'Only if we choose to be.' She leaned closer to him and kissed his brow. 'There is time to change.'

A shot struck the fort and the impact was felt by all in the room and dislodged some plaster. Thomas could not help a wry smile. 'Not for those involved in this struggle.'

'For us, and for Richard, there is still a chance to mend the bonds that were broken. I would have that. I would hold you in my arms again, my love.'

'Even like this?' Thomas said harshly as he turned his head for her to see the livid scars on his face and scalp. He flicked the sheet back to reveal his left side. Maria's calm expression never wavered.

'Do you think I have not seen your injuries? It was I who changed your dressings and cleaned your wounds. I saw to your most base needs. I know your body more intimately than your own mother ever did. I grieved for your suffering even as I tended you and I prayed each night that you might live. And God, in his infinite mercy, has answered me.'

Maria's words struck a cold chord in Thomas's heart. 'If it is God's will that we should have endured all that we have, then what does God know about the quality of mercy? I am done with God, Maria. All that now matters to me is you, Richard and the men at whose side I fight.' He paused and smiled grimly. 'Though I should say, fought. For I am destined to be a poor soldier now.'

Maria stared at him. 'You have no faith?'

'Not in God. And, until recently, precious little in people. Yet I have seen the best and worst in men these last months. I count it a great pity that it takes a conflict over something as insubstantial as faith to test the valour and venality of men.'

'It is God's test then,' Maria countered fervently. 'His test of our resolve. He still has a purpose for you, Thomas.'

He took her hand and gazed into her eyes. 'Maria. I am what you see before you and that is all. I would not be a burden to you. I love you, and always have. But I am a changed man from the young knight you once knew. To me, you are still the same Maria and I wish nothing more than to be at your side until the end of my life. But I would not want to be there under any degree of sufferance.

Not for my body, or my character, or my beliefs. I would have you think on that before you choose to be my wife, if that is your desire.'

'But it is, my love.'

Thomas touched her lips with his fingers. 'Hush now. I would not have you give an answer before you have thought it through. And I am tired. Very tired. Go now and we can speak again when I have rested, and you have reflected.'

She made to speak, then stopped herself. Her lips pressed together in a thin line and she nodded. Maria leaned forward to kiss the puckered skin of his scarred cheek and stood up. 'Until tomorrow.'

'Tomorrow then.' He nodded.

She smiled and left the room hurriedly, cuffing her cheek as she passed through the door and out of sight. The soft slap of her sandals quickly faded and Thomas stared up at the ceiling, his heart heavy. Until Maria had considered the realities of what he had become, he would not have her. To accept her as his wife, only for her to come to wish she had chosen differently, would be the worst fate of all, Thomas reflected.

'I see your visitors have gone.'

Thomas opened his eyes and saw Christopher smiling down at him. He held a small wooden tray bearing a bowl, cup, spoon and a meagre hunk of dry bread.

'The meal I promised you. Can you sit up, or should I help?'

'I can do it myself.' Thomas gritted his teeth and eased himself up the bed until he was propped against the wall. The monk placed the tray on the stool beside him and

Thomas found that the pleasant odour of the soup made him feel hungry. As he carefully took a few sips with the spoon, the monk looked out of the window.

'There are clouds to the north. There's rain coming. A storm perhaps. Yes, a storm, I think. The end of the season is almost upon us. Pray God we hold out until the autumn arrives.'

CHAPTER FORTY-ONE

For the next two days Maria returned each morning and on the third day Thomas felt strong enough to venture on to the walls of St Angelo. The air was still and the flags and standards of both sides hung limply. Dark clouds loomed over the island, a sign of the abrupt change in the weather that portended the end of the summer. The enemy guns were concentrating their fire on what was left of the defences that protected Birgu and the walls of the fort were safe to walk, for the moment. Maria had not mentioned the exchange that had taken place between them that first day after Thomas had recovered from his fever, and such talk as there was between them was pleasant enough as they cautiously felt their way towards each other. It only became halting when they spoke of the future.

The last time he had beheld the vista of the harbour and the surrounding landscape from St Angelo, the peninsulas of Senglea and Birgu had been largely untouched by the siege. Now Thomas gazed out over an apocalyptic panorama of death and destruction. The outworks of St Michael and Birgu had been flattened and the main walls were little more than piles of rubble stretching between the battered bastions. Nearly all the buildings in the town of Birgu had been damaged by roundshot and many had collapsed. Masts and rigging emerged from the sea off the eastern shore of the peninsula where La Valette had given orders for ships to be sunk to prevent the Turks attempting to land there. Although it had been a month since the Turks' failed seaborne assault on Senglea, the channel between the two peninsulas held by the defenders was still littered with the shattered remains of galleys, and hundreds of bloated and discoloured corpses which created a nauseous stench in the streets of Birgu when the hot breeze blew in from the open sea.

Turkish batteries had been sited on every vantage point and kept up a steady fire on the defenders, levelling what remained of the out defences and occasionally lobbing a shot into the town to harass the civilian population and eat away at what was left of their morale. The landscape between the walls and the Turkish trenches was scarred by the passage of cannonballs and scorched by the incendiary weapons hurled by each side. The usual courtesies of war had been abandoned; any parties that dared to venture out to collect and bury the bodies were immediately fired on. As a result, thousands of corpses and shattered limbs lay beyond the walls of Birgu, carrion for the gulls to feed on.

Thomas beheld the scene in shocked silence. Even though he had witnessed the savage struggle for St Elmo, that had been on a small scale compared with what now lay before him. It seemed hard to believe that the enemy could not easily scale the rubble that was all that was left of the defences of Birgu. Only the hastily constructed inner works that blocked off the streets leading into the town would then stand in their way.

disappeared. He filled his lungs with the untainted air and felt as if a ray of hope had pierced the brooding gloom of the landscape.

A soldier emerged at the top of the staircase from the fort. He glanced round at the world briefly washed clean and smiled faintly to himself. Then he caught sight of them in the sentry's shelter and hurried across the slick flagstones towards them.

He stopped outside the entrance and bowed his head. 'Sir Thomas Barrett?'

'Yes?'

'The Grand Master sent me to find you. He desires that you attend him now that you have recovered sufficiently to resume your duties.'

'Recovered?' Thomas cocked an eyebrow.

'What madness is this?' Maria demanded. 'Can you not see that Sir Thomas is badly injured? He needs rest and time to recover.'

The soldier looked at her. 'Every man is required to defend Birgu, my lady. That includes the walking wounded. From now on, if they can walk then they're not wounded.'

Maria opened her mouth to protest but Thomas held up his fingers to touch her lips gently. 'I will go willingly to battle. I have everything to fight for now.' He turned to the soldier. 'Where is the Grand Master?'

'His forward command post, sir.'

Thomas gestured towards the dressings on his left arm. 'I have been out of the fight for a while. I am not familiar with the latest position.'

The soldier nodded. 'The Grand Master and his staff

are at the merchants' guildhouse on the main square, sir. I'm returning there now. I can show you the way.'

'Thank you.'

Thomas felt Maria grasp his hand tightly and when he looked round he saw that her face was filled with anguish. 'Stay here, Thomas. Stay with me. Please . . . I beg you.'

He gently squeezed her hand and then pulled himself free and smiled. 'I will come back and find you as soon as I can.'

The soldier turned away and made for the head of the staircase. Thomas followed, forcing himself not to turn his head and look back.

The two men left the scarred walls of St Angelo and made their way through Birgu. There seemed to be hardly a building left undamaged. Heaps of bricks, plaster and tiles lay everywhere, and the charred remains of buildings showed where the Turkish bombardment had caused fires. Occasionally there was a deep whine of a shot passing overhead and the crash and clatter of debris as it struck home. Some effort was being taken to keep the centre of the streets clear of rubble to permit passage, but lately the scale of destruction had overwhelmed the defenders. Several times Thomas and the soldier were obliged to clamber over heaps of bricks and shattered timbers.

Thomas was surprised to see that many people were prepared to brave the dangers of the streets and were busy searching through the remains of collapsed buildings, pausing only to look up at the sound of an incoming cannonball and hunch down behind the nearest cover until the danger had passed. Gaunt faces watched them warily as they went by.

'Scavengers,' said the soldier. 'They're looking for food, and valuables. The Grand Master has issued an edict forbidding looting, but there are too few soldiers left to enforce it. Besides, the people are on the edge of starvation and the edict means little to them.'

'Starvation?'

The soldier nodded. 'The rations were cut again three days ago. They're on a quarter of what they were given at the start of the siege. If it goes on much longer then the poor bastards will start dropping dead where they stand.'

'How is the spirit of the local people holding up?'

'They're a tough lot, the Maltese,' the soldier conceded. 'Not one word about surrendering or even seeking terms from any of 'em. They're ready to follow the old boy right to the end. He fights alongside them, shares the dangers, and only allows himself to eat what they do. So he's their hero. Here we are, sir.'

The soldier indicated the shell of a large building across an open expanse of rubble-strewn ground and with a start Thomas realised that he was looking across what had once been the neat lines of Birgu's main square. They picked their way over to the entrance of the merchants' guildhouse, stopping once to duck down as a cannonball moaned overhead. They listened for the crash of the impact but it never came.

'Overshot,' the soldier said with satisfaction.

They stood up and hurried across the square. A sentry at the guildhouse door recognised the soldier and he waved them through. Beyond the wide arch of the doorway was the hall where the island's merchants and cargo-ship owners had met to do business. Windows high up in the walls had once illuminated the whitewashed plaster walls upon which hung portraits of the most influential of the guild's members. Now the flagstone floor was covered with dust and grit, and where the roof had fallen in, shattered roof tiles lay in heaps. The soldier led Thomas across the hall to where stairs led down into the storerooms beneath the building. A corridor stretched out on both sides at the bottom of the stairs and was illuminated by candles guttering in iron holders mounted on the walls.

'You'll find the Grand Master down at the end.' The soldier pointed to the left.

Thomas nodded his thanks and the soldier turned to the right to join a small group of men sitting at a table, drinking and playing dice. Arched openings lined the corridor and as Thomas passed by, he could see that some were being used to treat the wounded. Others were filled with weapons, armour, powder kegs and small baskets of ammunition for arquebuses. A short distance down the corridor Thomas saw that a hole had been knocked through the wall and a stretch of tunnel led to the cellar of another building. There was an open space where a number of tables had been set up. Two men sat at one table upon which a map of the island was spread.

By the gloomy light of the candles Thomas could make out the features of Romegas in urgent conversation with a thin man with a matted white beard. It was a moment before he recognised the Grand Master. La Valette looked up at the sound of footsteps and he smiled wearily as he waved Thomas towards a stool beside the table.

Romegas nodded a greeting. 'I'm glad to see you again, Sir Thomas. I feared the worst when I heard of your injuries. You were lucky to escape from St Elmo at the end.'

Thomas sensed a hint of criticism in the man's tone and indicated the scarring on his face. 'You have a singular view of what constitutes luck.'

Romegas shrugged. 'You and a handful of men survived, when all others were killed. I would call that luck, for want of another word.'

Thomas felt his anger stirring. 'And which word would that be? What exactly would you accuse me of?'

The Grand Master cleared his throat. 'Gentlemen, please, that's enough. There are too few of us left to waste our efforts on petty fractiousness. That is why I summoned you from the infirmary, Thomas. I need every man who still has the strength, and the heart, to fight the Turks. We have lost so many good men, including my own nephew, and Fadrique, the son of Don Garcia. At least your squire still lives. He has proved to be a fine warrior, as brave as they come.' He smiled briefly before his expression became sombre once again. 'You two are the last of my advisers. Save all your anger for the enemy.'

Thomas was shocked. 'Just the three of us? I know about Stokely, but Marshal de Roblas?'

Romegas stroked his creased brow. 'He was shot through the head several days ago. But you would not have been aware of that, Sir Thomas. Much has happened while you were recovering from your wounds. Birgu and Senglea came under attack soon after St Elmo fell. You have seen the damage done to the town, but let me tell you that the wall is largely a ruin, destroyed by bombardment and the mines dug by the enemy's engineers. Only the bastions still withstand the enemy's guns. We have built an inner wall but it is a poor defence that is barely ten feet high, and there are no more than a thousand men left to hold the Turks at bay. Most of our soldiers are wounded and all of them are exhausted and hungry. Our powder is running short and there is still no sign of the relief force Don Garcia promised us.'

Thomas pursed his lips. 'If it is as bad as that then we shall surely be defeated.'

'No, Don Garcia will come,' La Valette said firmly. 'My good friend Romegas is inclined to dwell on our difficulties at the expense of our opportunities. Our situation is bleak but it is only half the picture. We know that the enemy camp is wracked with sickness and their spirits are at a low ebb because of the heavy losses they have endured since the siege began. And now the season is changing and the rain has come to add to the enemy's discomfort. If we can hold Mustafa Pasha back for a little longer, he will be forced to quit the island before autumn sets in.' He paused and narrowed his eyes shrewdly. 'If I were the enemy, I would throw everything into one final assault, whatever the cost.'

'Why?' asked Romegas.

'Because I would know that my master, the Sultan, would not be merciful if I were forced to return to Istanbul having failed to carry out his orders. I would do anything to keep my head on my shoulders. Therefore I believe Mustafa Pasha will attack us with all his might very soon.' La Valette looked at his surviving advisers. 'When the Turks come, they will be more desperate than ever to wipe us out. We shall need to be more than their equal in determination, or else they will slaughter every man, woman and child in Birgu.'

'There is something else we could do,' Romegas said quietly. 'We still have St Angelo. We can defend that, even if we can't hold Birgu. Sir, I suggest we withdraw what is left of our fighting men into the fort. We can hold out there for a month or so yet, until Don Garcia and his army, or autumn, arrives.'

Thomas shook his head. 'What about the civilians? We couldn't possibly fit them all into the fort. Are you suggesting that we abandon them to the Turks?' He thought of Maria and turned to his commander. 'Sir, we can't do that.'

'We might have to,' Romegas insisted. 'How else can we make our supplies last long enough? The people are already starving. Our men will not have the strength to fight on in a few weeks' time. The fort is more readily defended than the town and wall. It makes sense. It might be our only chance to save the Order, sir.'

'Only at the price of our reputation,' Thomas retorted. 'Our name will go down in the annals of infamy if we leave the people to the mercy of the Turks. There will be no mercy, just massacre.'

Romegas smiled coldly. 'This is war, Sir Thomas. A war that I, and the Grand Master, have been fighting through all the years we have served the Order. What matters, above all, is the survival of the Order.'

'I thought that what matters is stemming the tide of Islam,' Thomas countered.

'While we live on we will always be the sword thrust into the side of the enemy,' Romegas replied. 'To ensure that, we must be prepared to make sacrifices. For the greater good.'

Thomas saw the strained expression on the Grand Master's face as he reflected on Romegas's suggestion and gave his response. 'It's true. We could hold St Angelo far more easily than Birgu, and perhaps long enough to see out the siege . . . And yet, what Sir Thomas says is also true. We should never forget that the Order was set up to protect the righteous and the innocent.' He thought for a moment and then sighed. 'I think I already know what I must do. Yes, I am certain of it.'

Romegas glanced at Thomas and smiled, believing that he had won the argument. 'It is for the best, sir.'

'You mistake me,' said La Valette. 'There will be no retreat to the fort . . . once I have seen to it that the drawbridge is blown to pieces.'

CHAPTER FORTY-TWO

The gloom of dusk was broken by the brief brilliance of a savage explosion and Thomas's good eye squinted at the sudden glare. The sheet of flame and smoke was accompanied by an ear-shattering roar that echoed across Birgu. Pieces of the drawbridge spun lazily into the air, hung there for an instant, and then collapsed in a shower of debris that clattered across the roofs of the nearest buildings and splashed down into the channel that had been cut between the fort and the town of Birgu.

The Grand Master, his advisers and senior officers watched in silence for a moment.

'There will be no retreat for us now, gentlemen,' La Valette said. 'That is the message we send to the Turks just as much as to our own people. With God's help we will hold Birgu. If we fail in that duty then we shall perish in its ruins. The final test is coming.' He turned to survey the enemy-held heights above the town. 'An enemy officer was captured this morning. He revealed that the Turks are steeling themselves for one last attack. That is why there have been no assaults for the last eight days and why Mustafa Pasha has concentrated his cannon fire on what is left of the walls. The enemy will strike at first light tomorrow.' He paused while his officers took in the news.

'If the attack fails then I believe Mustafa Pasha will not find it possible to stir his men to further action and we may yet survive this siege. Rest well tonight and be at your posts an hour before dawn.' He looked round at his followers with a grim expression. 'I am too weary to make fine speeches. I have only a few words to offer you now. We have battled the Turk in the best traditions of the Order. I count myself honoured to have commanded and fought alongside you and all those who have fallen defending the Holy Religion. Heroes all. No men could have done more to win a greater share of honour and glory. If it is our fate to die on the morrow then so be it. Our martyrdom will inspire the rest of Christendom to fight the infidels. They will avenge us. If we should live then we shall have a tale to tell that will stir the hearts of men for generations to come. All who hear of our great deeds will stop and wonder, and say with full heart that in the long history of our struggle *this* was our finest time.' He stepped among his officers and clasped each man's hand in turn. 'God go with you. I shall be at prayer in the cathedral if I am needed.' Then he turned and walked stiffly back into the heart of Birgu.

Thomas stared after him, aware of the change in the Grand Master. Over the last months, as the strain told on other men, La Valette alone amongst the defenders had seemed to grow stronger and more fiercely determined. But now his long years had finally settled their burden upon his shoulders and for the first time he seemed thin, frail and weak, which was only to be expected in a man of seventy.

'I'm surprised he has endured the strain for so long,'

Richard said softly, echoing Thomas's thoughts. 'Now I believe he has given up hope.'

'No. Not him. Never him,' Thomas replied. 'He may be exhausted but his heart is as strong as ever.'

'I hope you're right. Without La Valette the Turks would have defeated us long ago.'

'I trust you are content with the Grand Master's decision?'

Thomas turned and saw Romegas standing at his side. Romegas nodded towards the shattered remnants of the drawbridge. 'You should have supported my advice, Thomas. La Valette has only left enough men in the fort to man the guns. If Birgu falls tomorrow St Angelo will stand little chance of holding out for more than a few days. A stronger garrison might have endured for weeks, even months. But it's too late now,' he concluded bitterly.

Thomas shook his head. 'You are wrong. If we had abandoned Birgu we would have lost the heart to fight and the enemy's will to continue their attack would be renewed. This way, there is no retreat for our men. When they face the enemy tomorrow they will have iron in their hearts and will die before they give one inch of ground to the Turks.'

'We shall see.' Romegas turned and walked across the open ground to the fort, where he stood and stared at the splintered lengths of timber along the edge of the cutting forced up by the explosion.

The small gathering of officers began to disperse and Thomas beckoned to Richard.

'Come, let us go back to Stokely's house.' They set off down the street, moving at a slow pace due to the continuing pain in Thomas's leg. 'I am unsure if I should say anything to your mother about the coming attack,' Thomas muttered.

'Why not?' Richard was surprised. 'She has a right to know. A right to make her peace in case tomorrow is the end. Surely?'

Thomas nodded. 'I was thinking more about her fear for me. I have not fought since that last day at St Elmo.'

'Are you fit to bear arms?'

'La Valette thinks so.'

'What do you think?'

'My right arm is weak from lack of exercise. I can only see out of one eye and the flesh on my left arm and leg feels tight and it is painful when I flex the muscles.' He glanced at Richard and forced a smile. 'So I am no worse off than many men who will take their place on the wall. You must lead a charmed life. There's hardly a scratch on you.'

Richard shrugged. 'My luck will not last. I will be struck down one day soon.'

Thomas stopped and took his arm. 'Are you afraid?'

For a moment Richard considered denying it. Then he nodded. 'Of course, Father. I am not a brave man by disposition.'

'That is not what I have heard. La Valette tells me that you fought like a veteran while I was in the infirmary. You have nothing to prove concerning your courage.'

'On the contrary. I fight hard mostly because I am scared. So scared that I want it to end more than anything else. A bullet then would be a mercy. I face every attack with fear in my heart and cold sweat on my palms and running down my spine.' He stared at Thomas. 'I would not be surprised if you are ashamed of me.'

'Ashamed?' His heart was torn by a helpless desire to protect his son, to shield him from his torment. He rested his hands on the young man's shoulders. 'I could not be more proud of you, Richard. You are the bravest man I have ever known.'

Richard shook his head. 'I am a coward.'

'A coward is one who imagines the risks and turns to run. Courage comes from having the will to stay and face peril. I know it better than most, Richard. It is the standard against which I have tested myself throughout my life.'

Richard looked at him sceptically and Thomas chuckled.

'Did you think I was any different to you? Fear is the spur which drives men like us on. How else could we tame it and not let it become the master of our fate? It seems that we are alike in this, father and son.'

Richard nodded, his lips quivered for an instant and then he looked away awkwardly and hurriedly brushed at the corner of his eye. Thomas felt a stab of pain at his distress, which he took for shame.

'There is no need to reproach yourself.'

Richard laughed nervously. 'It is not reproach. I am happy. Happy to have a father . . . Happy to have *you* as my father.'

The distress inside Thomas instantly gave way to a serene joy and he drew his son close to embrace him and kiss his brow. Then, as if they had just shared a joke, he released him and punched him lightly on the chest. 'We shall drink together tonight. God's wounds! If ever there was a true test of courage, it must surely be the preserve of those who consume a bottle of the local wine.'

Richard grinned and they continued along their way, with Thomas contentedly resting his injured arm across his son's shoulder.

When they reached the gate of Stokely's house, Thomas stepped forward to reach for the latch. He raised it and pushed the gate inwards. Glancing back he saw that Richard was standing in the street.

'What's wrong?'

'Nothing.' Richard smiled. 'Nothing at all. I'm not coming in tonight. I'll sleep at the auberge.'

Thomas frowned. 'Why?'

'I have had my moment of closeness to you, Father. It is well that you should be alone with my mother tonight. I will see you tomorrow, on the wall. Good night.' Richard nodded with a fond expression and then turned away into the gathering shadows of the street. Thomas stood on the threshold of the small courtyard, tempted to call after him.

'Thomas?' Maria's voice came from the house. 'Is that you?'

He turned away from the street and closed the gate behind him. He saw her standing in the doorway of the house, outlined by the pale glow of the candlelight in the small entrance hall. Above her the walls of the house rose up to the skeletal remains of the timbers that had supported the roof, before it had been dashed to pieces by a Turkish roundshot. Most of the tiles had crashed through to the floor below and now only one room above the ground floor was habitable. Thomas slipped the bolt across to lock the gate, crossed the courtyard and climbed the steps to take her in his arms and kiss her on the lips.

When they parted she asked, 'Where's Richard?'

'He's staying at the auberge tonight.'

'Why?'

'He wanted to give us the chance to be together.'

'Why?' A faint frown creased Maria's brow. Thomas took her hands and stroked his thumbs across her soft palms. Maria looked hurt for a moment and then nodded. 'As he wishes. It is a pity as I have prepared a meal to share with my family. I found some salted pork in the cellar, together with some cheese to go with the bread ration.'

'A veritable banquet,' Thomas said lightly.

Maria gave a laugh as she drew him inside and closed the door behind them.

Later that night they lay naked on a couch behind the open wooden lattice of the balcony outside the surviving bedroom and looked up at the sky. The starry heavens were streaked with thin silver shreds of clouds. To the north a dense mass of shadow covered the horizon and steadily edged closer to the island. Despite the change in season the night was not so cold that it discomforted them. Their bodies still radiated warmth from their earlier love-making. Maria lay against his right side, head resting on his chest as she ran her fingers lightly through the hair that covered his stomach.

'I want, more than anything, to talk about the future,' she said softly. 'But I know it is a luxury we cannot afford. Not for a while perhaps. Only when the siege is over.'

Thomas smiled sadly. 'We should not look to the future, my love. We should not.'

She was silent for a moment and then propped herself up on an elbow. 'The future is my only comfort, my dear Thomas. There is little but peril in the present and only darkness and despair in the past. There is too much pain there. All we have is this moment.'

Thomas touched her cheek, uncertain whether he should unburden his mind. He had no right to hide the truth from her. 'Sweet Maria, this night may be our last together. The Turks are coming tomorrow. La Valette thinks that this will be their final attempt to crush us. Every gun and man will be used in the attack. We must meet them on the same terms.'

'You will be fighting as well?'

'I must. To defend the Order, Birgu, and most of all you.'

'Then I shall fight with you.'

Thomas shook his head. 'You can't. There is no place for women on the battle line.'

'Really? Do you think we shall stand idle while the Turks overwhelm you, and then turn their thirst for blood and lust upon us? I can assure you, Thomas, that every woman and child knows what is at stake. We shall do all we can to defeat the enemy.'

'No. You will stay here, where you are safe.'

'Safe?' She laughed bitterly. 'If the defences are breached then all will die, or be enslaved. I would rather die at your side than wait here to be raped and butchered. I will not have my life end like that. I will choose my own end.' She pressed her fingertips gently on his lips. 'That is my final word. You cannot dissuade me.'

'I would not dare,' he replied in a mocking tone. 'No more of that now. Just hold me . . .'

She lay her head on his chest again and pressed her body against his and Thomas closed his eyes and let his mind dwell on the sensation of warm closeness. Outside, a bank of cloud closed over the island, steadily blotting out the stars. Shortly after the cathedral bell struck midnight, the first drops of rain began to patter on to the ruined town, swelling into a rattling hiss as the downpour passed overhead accompanied by a chilly breeze that blew drips in through the trellis. They rose from the couch and went back to the bed and held each other beneath the warmth of its coverings.

In the hour before dawn the rain had not abated and seemed to be falling harder than ever, accompanied by lightning and thunder. As the bell struck the appointed hour, Thomas lit a candle and rose and dressed, aware that Maria was awake and watching him. When he had buttoned his jerkin he turned his head.

'Will you help me with my armour?'

She nodded, and reached for her gown as she sat up. She followed him downstairs to the hall where the armour and weapons lay on a chest by the door. Thomas pulled on his breastplate and held it to his chest while she fitted the backplate and fastened the buckles. She helped him with his gauntlets and fastened the mantlets to protect his arms and hands. When she reached for his thigh guards, Thomas shook his head. 'I cannot wear those over my injuries. It is too painful. Just my helmet now, please.'

She carefully placed the padded cap on his skull and

then lifted the morion helmet and eased it down and fastened the chinstrap. 'There.'

Thomas tested the movement, concentrating hard on not betraying the agony flaring down his left side. He nodded with satisfaction and reached for his sword, slipping the strap across his shoulder. Maria hurried back upstairs and returned shortly afterwards in a boy's gambison and breeches, her hair tied back. She slipped on a pair of soft boots and laced them up. Lastly, she took a belt and dagger from the weapons still lying on the chest and fastened it about her midriff, then faced Thomas. 'I am ready.'

The wan glow of the candle flame made her skin look rosy and smooth and he smiled. 'There is one last thing I would ask of you before we go. There is a letter I have written for Richard. I have left it on the chest by the bed. If anything happens to me, please see that it is given to him.'

Maria nodded.

'Good.' Thomas smiled. 'Then let us go.'

A wagon, its sides reinforced with stout planks of studded wood, acted as the gateway of the hastily constructed inner wall. The wall was built from materials taken from demolished houses and rubble from sections of the wall that had collapsed. It stood no higher than ten feet along its length, curving in at each end to join two battered bastions that still held out against the Turks. A fighting step had been constructed behind the wall and women and children, together with old men, filed out along its length, heads hunched against the rain, and took up their positions under the orders of a handful of soldiers assigned to command this final line of defence. They carried a mixture of light pikes, swords, hatchets and studded clubs, together with baskets filled with rocks to hurl down upon the heads of the Turks should they force their way over what was left of the main wall.

Maria parted from Thomas at the wagon and took up a club before climbing the small ladder on to the fighting step. He passed through the gap. Ladders were ready on the far side, in case the men on the main wall were forced to retreat. Richard was waiting for him on the open ground beyond. Together they climbed on to the stretch of wall where the Grand Master had already taken his position, under the sodden banner of the Order. La Valette stood at the parapet, gloved hands resting on the glistening stonework, staring out towards the Turkish trenches.

Richard glanced up at the sky and blinked away the raindrops. 'There'll be no gunfire today. No one can keep their powder dry in this downfall. It will be a fight, man to man. There'll be no threat to the Turks as they charge the walls.'

'Not so, young man.' La Valette turned away from the enemy. 'It may be too wet for our cannon and arquebuses but not for our crossbows.'

Thomas looked down the length of the wall and noticed in the first hint of daylight that the men who would usually be armed with arquebuses were holding crossbows and carrying quivers at their sides packed with quarrels.

La Valette chuckled. 'You reminded me of them the other day, Sir Thomas. Stored in the dungeon amid the relics of earlier wars. I had them ferried over from St Angelo during the night. Let's hope our men can put them to good use.'

The Grand Master turned back to the parapet and the defenders waited in the rain as dawn struggled to break through the dark clouds obscuring the sky. As the thin light slowly strengthened, Thomas could see that the ground in front of the remains of the wall was slick and muddy. A hundred paces away the Turkish trenches were marked by their drenched standards. Faint movements could be seen as the enemy prepared for their assault. Every so often a faint chorus of prayer could be heard through the din of the rain as lightning lit the battlefield in a harsh silvery glare.

If there was a moment when the sun had risen, no one could know it because of the heavy clouds. At length a figure climbed out of the trench opposite the Grand Master's standard and took several paces forward before he stopped and drew his jewelled scimitar. Despite his wet clothes, it was clear that he was a man of significance. He wore a large turban and a finely decorated breastplate.

'It is Mustafa Pasha himself,' said Romegas, squinting into the rain.

The Turkish commander's chest puffed out as he drew a breath and bellowed an order that cut through the hiss of the rain. At his command, figures swarmed from the trenches, letting out a roar as they charged forward all along the length of Birgu's battered defences. Lightning burst overhead, freezing the tableau of thousands, grim-faced, mouths open in savage cries as they half ran, half slithered over the dead ground, determined to wipe the defenders off the face of the earth.

CHAPTER FORTY-THREE

'Ready crossbows,' La Valette commanded.

Romegas cupped a hand to his mouth and bellowed the order, struggling to be heard above the slashing rain. The order was repeated along the line of the wall and the crossbowmen raised their weapons and took aim.

Thomas looked to the side. There seemed to be more breaches than stretches of intact wall and the rubble from the damaged sections had tumbled into the ditch in front of the walls to provide practicable causeways leading up to the defenders. Some attempt had been made to create crude breastworks across the breaches but they would provide only limited shelter before they were torn down by the enemy. He glanced back towards the inner wall, looking for Maria, but it was impossible to tell her apart from the other sodden figures along the fighting step.

'The Turks will get a nasty surprise once they come within range of the crossbows,' Richard commented with cold satisfaction.

Thomas nodded. Before the rains, the attackers would have had to endure a hail of cannon and small-arms fire from the walls. This morning they would charge into battle unscathed. Or so they thought. The swiftest of the enemy were already drawing ahead of their comrades and the broad mass of Turks came on behind, providing a target that was impossible to miss. La Valette raised his right hand and waited until they were no more than a hundred paces away, then swept his arm down. 'Now.'

Even as Romegas relayed the order, those who had been watching for the signal bellowed the command and there was a chorus of dull cracks along the wall as the arms of the weapons sprang forward, unleashing the short heavy bolts in a shallow arc through the driving rain towards the enemy. A moment later Thomas saw scores of the Turks stop in their tracks. Some pitched forward and writhed on the ground, while others staggered and struggled to remove the barbed heads. A handful of men were killed outright.

At once the defenders lowered their crossbows, placed a foot in the iron stirrup at the end of their weapons and strained to wind the drawstring back ready to load the next quarrel. The strongest of them were the first to shoot again and more of the Turks were struck down as they increased their pace to close up on the wall before more of them fell victim to the antiquated weapon.

Thomas looked for the enemy commander and saw Mustafa Pasha's large turban bobbing amid the drenched ranks of his men. The veteran general of the Sultan trudged forward, sword waving from side to side above his head. A small party of Janissary bodyguards kept up with him, one of them holding aloft the personal standard of Suleiman and waving it from side to side so that the sodden horsetail crest would be more easily visible to the rest of the men.

The first Turk reached the ditch to one side of the bastion and Thomas watched as he scrambled over the wet masonry, his robes hanging on his body like loose folds of skin. One of the crossbowmen on the wall beside the breach aimed down at him and shot a bolt into his back, just below his neck. The Turk fell face first and his legs began to twitch violently. More of his comrades followed, clothes, armour, skin and weapons sleek and glistening in the rain. Scores were struck down by the quarrels as they struggled over the rubble to close with the defenders. At the last moment the crossbowmen threw down their weapons and snatched up clubs, swords and pikes. The air around the bastion was filled with the thud of weapons striking shields, the scrape and clatter of blade on blade and the mingled war cries, curses and howls of agony from the wounded, all underscored by the hiss of rain and light pinging as the heavy drops burst on helmets and plate armour.

'Stand ready!' Romegas ordered those on the bastion and a moment later an assault ladder slapped against the parapet. Thomas raised his sword and stepped over to the ladder as a pair of dark-skinned hands grasped the top rung and a spiked helmet appeared. Thomas swung his sword down hard and the edge bit through the cloth of the man's shoulder but was held by the chain-mail vest beneath. The impact drove the Turk's body down and numbed his arm enough to loosen his grip on the ladder. With a grunt he swung off the ladder and hung there for an instant before the strength in his other hand gave out and he dropped out of sight. At once, another Turk took his place and clambered up, warily looking over the parapet.

'Richard,' Thomas called out. 'The ladder! Use your pike. Quick, my boy!'

The Turk raised a shield to protect his head as he struggled up the ladder. Thomas's blade glanced off it and he drew the sword back to attempt a direct thrust instead. But the Turk was good and easily parried it aside. He reached a hand up on to the parapet in readiness to haul himself on to the bastion. There was a blur of movement as Richard lowered his pike and caught the crosspiece against the top rung, and thrust the ladder back with all his strength. The Turk's eyes widened in alarm as he swayed back from the parapet and then, with a vigorous push from Richard, the ladder fell back into the breach, together with the three men who had been coming up behind.

Hundreds of men were locked in a deadly fight along the line of the wall and Thomas could see that the weight of numbers must inevitably force the defenders back. More ladders were placed against the sides of the bastion and the Grand Master and the officers and men with him were drawn into the desperate battle to hold their ground. As Richard drove his pike into a man's face, Thomas looked round and saw La Valette brace his feet as he lowered the shaft of his pike and advanced on a Janissary who had gained the top of his ladder and had already swung his foot down over the side of the parapet. The Grand Master drove his point forward and the Janissary just managed to swing his scimitar across in time to parry the pike. La Valette drew his weapon back and, as if he was practising on a drill ground, calmly thrust again. This time, he dropped the point at the last moment, so that the other man's blade failed to make contact and the point of the weapon stabbed into his stomach. The Turk's face contorted in agony and he dropped his sword and grasped the shaft of the pike as La Valette pressed home. The Janissary toppled back over the parapet and the point ripped free from his wound. Romegas pushed his commander aside, grasped the top of the ladder and wrenched it to one side, unbalancing those below who shouted in alarm as the ladder fell into the breach.

Looking down from the bastion Thomas saw that the defenders were already being forced back from the breastworks in several places. At once the Turks pushed the stones forward, collapsing the crude obstacles before clambering over the ruins to press the defenders back. Then his attention was drawn to another ladder appearing close by. He slashed at his enemy's hand the moment it appeared above the edge of the parapet, cutting through the knuckles before splintering the wooden rung beneath. There was a howl of agony and the ruined hand was snatched back. Again Richard used his pike to thrust the ladder away from the wall.

'Over here!' Romegas bellowed and Thomas turned to see the senior knight and two sergeants battling several men who had managed to gain a foothold on the far side of the bastion. Thomas turned to Richard.

'Go! Help Romegas. I can hold this position.'

A flicker of concern crossed the young man's rain-streaked face before he nodded and turned to run across the bastion to assist Romegas. There was a clatter of wood against stone as another ladder appeared in front of Thomas. The Turk who scaled it wore a spiked helmet with a turban tightly wound about the rim and his eyes glared above a thick beard dripping water on to his breastplate. He was waist high to the parapet and raising his shield when Thomas struck. The blade forced the shield down before it deflected to the side and with a sharp clatter the end broke off.

'Ha!' the Turk exclaimed and immediately swung his leg over the parapet and drew his scimitar. Thomas saw that only a scant eighteen inches of blade, ending in a jagged point, was left to him. Too little for a conventional fight. He launched himself at the Turk. His left foot slipped on the wet flagstones and there was no impetus to his blow when he collided with the other man. They were pressed together, against the parapet, face to face. The Turk's thin lips parted in a snarl as he struggled to wrench himself free and win enough space to wield his scimitar. Thomas tried to use his left hand to grasp his opponent and hold on. A fiery agony shot through the limb and he had to release his grip and let the arm hang uselessly. He stretched his right arm out, angled the broken blade in and thrust it under the rim of the Turk's shield. The tip jarred against the bottom of the breastplate and Thomas drew it back, aimed lower and thrust again, feeling it drive home into the Turk's groin.

His opponent let out an explosive groan and spittle struck Thomas in the face. Then the Turk hammered the side of Thomas's helmet with the hilt of his scimitar, smashing his head again and again as Thomas desperately worked his blade deep into his opponent's vital organs. Then his left foot slipped again and he fell back and the Turk came with him, landing heavily on Thomas and driving the air from his lungs. As the Turk tried to rise, Thomas wrenched the sword to one side and the man's face contorted with agony. But with a huge effort he pulled himself up and rolled to the side. The blade came free of the terrible wound with a sucking noise. Blood smeared the hilt of Thomas's weapon and covered his mantlet as far as the wrist. The Turk's wound was mortal and he knew it as he loomed over Thomas, balanced on his knees. He batted the broken sword aside with his shield then his eyes glinted with rage as he raised his scimitar and aimed the point at Thomas's face.

For an instant the terrible din around him seemed to fade to silence and the dull gleam of the sword point above seemed to be all that existed for Thomas; every ounce of his flesh froze in absolute terror.

Then the Turk lurched back as the point of a pike stabbed into his throat. He collapsed against the parapet, gurgling as blood spurted from the wound and sprayed from his lips. Thomas struggled to his feet as a hand supported his arm and helped him up. La Valette looked into his face with a concerned expression.

'Are you wounded, Sir Thomas?'

He was badly shaken but felt no pain other than the burning sensation in his left arm. 'No, sir.'

'Then find yourself another weapon.' La Valette clasped his pike, ready to fight, as he glanced round the bastion and then over the parapet. Thomas could see that the Turks were gaining footholds on the remaining sections of the wall and steadily forcing their way through the breaches. The weight of their numbers was proving impossible for the defenders to contain.

'We cannot hold the line,' said La Valette. 'We must fall back to the inner wall.' He turned to look for Romegas. The senior knight and Richard were just finishing off a

Turk who had climbed on to the tower. They tipped the body down on to those still attempting to scale the bastion and a quick thrust of Richard's pike sent the ladder reeling back. For the moment the bastion was cleared, although two of the bodies lying amid the puddles on the ground wore the surcoats of the Order. Another lay propped up against the parapet, his face a bloody mask of crushed flesh and bone, his body and limbs trembling uncontrollably.

'Romegas!' La Valette called. 'On me!'

As soon as the knight reached him La Valette pointed towards the men desperately struggling to hold the line along the wall. 'Give the signal to fall back to the inner wall once I have taken my position there by the gate, together with the standard. You stay here with the others and hold the bastion.'

Romegas gestured towards one of the bodies on the ground and Thomas saw the standard lying beside the corpse. 'He's done for, sir.'

La Valette nodded and turned to Thomas. 'Then the honour falls to you. Take up the standard, then you and your squire come with me.'

Thomas called Richard over and picked up the standard in his good hand and rested it against his shoulder. The three of them descended the stairs to the base of the bastion. Two men were guarding the entrance and they heaved the iron bolts back at La Valette's order, and pushed the sturdy door open. Thomas and Richard followed the Grand Master as he crossed the open ground behind the line of men still fighting to hold the Turks back. There was a narrow gap left open by the wagon, just wide enough for two men to go through at a time, and they passed inside the last defence of Birgu. Grunting with the effort, La Valette clambered on to the fighting step and Richard helped Thomas up beside him before joining them himself.

La Valette turned towards the bastion and raised his hand and waved. Romegas waved back and a moment later the sharp blast of a trumpet cut through the sounds of battle and the rain. Those men who were behind the fighting line immediately turned and joined the wounded making for the safety of the inner wall. Those still fighting began to disengage, backing warily away from the enemy before turning to hurry down the steps from the wall or scramble away over the loose rubble towards the clear ground.

As soon as the Turks realised what was happening a cheer rippled along the battle line and they surged forward, desperate to pursue and overwhelm the defenders and put an end to the dreadful siege that had cost the lives of so many of their comrades. They poured into the breaches, cutting down those too slow to answer the signal to fall back or too maddened by battle rage to retreat, spitting their defiance into the faces of the Turks until they perished under the savage blows of enemy blades.

'Here, take my dagger.'

Thomas turned to Richard and saw the handle extended to him. He nodded his thanks for the weapon and shifted the standard to his left, hooked his leg round the base of the staff and then tucked the shaft against his left shoulder.

Richard lowered the point of his pike over the rough stonework of the parapet and stared grimly towards the enemy struggling down the piles of rubble towards the open ground. To his left, twenty yards beyond the Grand

Master, Thomas saw Maria helping a soldier climb over the wall. More were hurrying up the ladders and on to the inner wall, while others hurried through the gap beside the wagon. La Valette watched intently as the last of the defenders and wounded made for the ladders. The first of the Turks had reached the open ground and began to race after them. Thomas heard the dull whack of a crossbow and saw one of the Turks throw up his arms and tumble forward as a quarrel shattered his knee. More bolts darted across the open ground, most finding their mark at such close range. Those Turks alert to the danger hunched down and raised their shields, and came on more warily. It bought the defenders a sliver of time in which to reach the ladders.

Just then Mustafa Pasha appeared in one of the breaches, together with his standard bearer. He thrust his scimitar towards the inner wall and shrieked a command to his men. The cry was taken up and the Turks charged forward. A handful of men still stood at the bottom of each ladder, waiting their turn to climb to safety. Some turned towards the enemy and lowered their pikes, or swung their swords and clubs in preparation to strike.

'Raise the ladders!' La Valette called out. 'Quickly!'

There were cries of despair from the men still on the far side, and the last few that could raced up the rungs and threw themselves over the parapet. Then the ladders were pulled up by their comrades. Some of the men still on the other side clung on and had to be shaken loose. Thomas saw one of the ladders fall to the side, a gift to the enemy.

'Close the gate!' La Valette shouted to the men waiting

by the wagon and they put their shoulders to the timbered frame and heaved it across the small gap, sealing the opening, before securing it in place with chains. Then they climbed up on to the bed of the wagon and took up their crossbows to shoot into the bedraggled horde charging towards them. All along the final line of defence the crossbowmen took a last chance to pick off the Turks and scores more fell into the mud and puddles, pierced by the deadly bolts. Thomas caught sight of one last defender in a futile struggle to reach safety before he was engulfed by the enemy. The man had been wounded in the leg and limped as fast as he could, one arm reaching out to his comrades on the wall, imploring them to save him. Then he tripped and fell. At once a bare-headed man in animal skins rushed over to him and raised a spear in both hands. The soldier pushed himself up, his face plastered with mud, mouth hanging open in a last cry. Then the Turk rammed the head of his spear down between his victim's shoulder blades. The point burst out of his chest and the man's face contorted in agony before he collapsed, instantly lost from view as the enemy surged over him.

There were enough men on the inner wall to displace most of the women and children and they dropped back behind the fighting step and snatched up rocks and stones to hurl over the wall. With shrill cries of hatred they threw their missiles and Thomas saw them clatter off the helmets and shields of the enemy. But some struck home, striking men in the face, injuring many of the unarmoured fanatics who had joined Suleiman's army to kill the enemies of Islam and find martyrdom for themselves. Then the Turks reached the wall and cut down the last of the defenders trapped there before they jabbed their spears at the faces looming above them.

Thomas saw La Valette lean forward and thrust his pike into the shoulder of a man below, then wrench the point back and thrust again. Richard cried out as a spear point caught in his sleeve and then cut into the flesh of his arm. His jerkin ripped as he tore his arm free and stabbed his pike into the man who had wounded him. For a short period the Turks were caught tightly against the base of the wall, easy prey for those above them who thrust and stabbed into the tightly packed mass of robes and armour. The first of the men carrying assault ladders forced their way through the throng and ran the ladders up against the wall. At once their comrades began to climb, desperate to get at the defenders of Birgu.

Thomas raised his dagger as a ladder clattered against the wall to his right, just between himself and Richard. It swayed a moment as the first of the Turks swarmed up. Thomas leaned forward and stabbed at his hand. The Turk seemed to ignore the pain; he hauled himself up and his wild eyes beneath the rim of his helmet stared at Thomas with hatred. He pulled his hand free with a rush of blood and drew his scimitar. His blade arced towards Thomas's neck and he just had time to throw his weight to one side and duck the blow that would surely have struck his head off if he had not moved. The Turk shouted a curse and made to swing again. Before he could, a rock caught him on the bridge of his nose and blood spurted from his nostrils. He blinked and shook his head. Richard swung the butt of his pike and knocked him back amid the swords, spears and spiked helmets of his comrades.

Mustafa Pasha urged his men on, his sword punching out, his mouth stretched wide as he bellowed encouragement. Then he moved forward towards the inner wall, his bodyguard parting the press before him. For a moment Thomas could only follow his progress by the horsehair standard weaving above the sea of helmets, turbans, bare heads, points of spears and sword blades.

'Sir,' he shouted to La Valette and pointed out Suleiman's standard. 'Look there!'

The Grand Master followed the direction Thomas indicated and saw that the enemy commander was making directly towards him. 'He means to kill me.'

Thomas nodded. 'You must get off the wall, sir.'

'No. Our fate hangs by a thread. I must stay here, where my people can see me.'

La Valette turned away as a spear thrust glanced off his shoulder plate. One of the Turks had climbed up on to the shoulders of his comrades to strike at the Grand Master, and now La Valette coolly turned his pike on the man and ran him through.

Thomas watched the steady progress of the enemy's standard as it picked its way closer. Then the sea of faces before him parted and a squad of Janissaries pushed through, making space for their commander and his personal bodyguard, tall, well-built warriors, in fine armour and carrying heavy scimitars – hand-picked men from the elite corps of Suleiman's army. Two of them grabbed a ladder from their comrades and placed it against the wall, directly in front of Thomas and the standard of the Order of St John. Now he could see Mustafa Pasha, his weathered face wet with rain as he shouted orders to his men and pointed at Thomas. The first of his men rushed up the ladder. Thomas stabbed at him with the dagger but the Janissary was quick and dodged the blow. He caught Thomas's wrist in his hand and clamped tightly as he continued up the last rung and swung his muddy boot over the parapet. He reached for his scimitar. Thomas tried to pull himself free but the other man was too strong for him and his lips parted in a cruel smile.

'Protect the standard!' La Valette shouted in alarm.

Richard was two paces to Thomas's right, thrusting a ladder back. The moment it fell away he turned and lunged at the Janissary. The man saw the danger and released his grip on Thomas's wrist. He threw up his arm to ward off the blow and knocked the steel point aside. Thomas moved at once and stabbed his dagger into the man's arm, and again. With a bellow of pain and rage, the Janissary thrust his sword hand out, smashing Thomas in the chest and unbalancing him so that he tottered on the edge of the fighting step for a moment and then fell back, the standard falling with him.

At once a groan rose from the lips of the nearest defenders, matched by a shout of jubilation from the other side of the wall. The Janissary swung his other leg over the wall and rushed at Richard, slashing wildly with his scimitar. Richard desperately blocked the blows with the shaft of his pike. Another Janissary came over the wall and turned towards La Valette, warily eyeing the lowered point of his pike as he closed. Two more men came over the wall and then a fifth, carrying Suleiman's standard which he planted on the parapet and waved from side to side. Thomas scrambled to his feet and snatched up the standard of the Order in his good hand, leaving the dagger on the ground.

'Stand firm!' he bellowed to left and right. 'Stand firm!'

'Drive them back!' La Valette yelled. 'For God and St John! Kill them!'

Figures surged past Thomas and he saw a young boy, no more than twelve, pull himself on to the wall and throw himself at the Janissary attacking Richard. His puny fists clawed at the Turk's face and he bit into the bare skin of his arm, above the gauntlet. The Turk glared at the boy, then grabbed his hair and wrenched him away before dashing his brains out on the parapet and flinging the wretchedly skinny bag of bones down beside Thomas. A shrill cry of grief and rage cut through the air and a thin woman stepped over the body and hurled a rock at the Janissary. The sharp-edged stone split his eyebrow open and blood coursed over his eyes, forcing him to pause and wipe them clear. The moment's distraction cost him his life as Richard rammed his pike into the Janissary's stomach, twisted the point to both sides and ripped it free. The Turk tumbled inside the wall and at once the woman leaped upon him, another rock in her hand, which she punched into his face repeatedly, pulverising flesh and bone as tears streamed down her cheeks and an animal keening strained at her throat.

More women and children charged forward, snatching and tearing at the Janissaries, pulling them from the wall and beating them to death. The enemy standard bearer on the wall looked down aghast as the Maltese slaughtered his comrades like wild animals. Then Richard cast his pike aside and rushed at the man, striking him in the face with his mantlet, the metal finger guards tearing into the Janissary's cheek. He struck the man again and again and then seized the shaft of the standard in his left hand in a desperate struggle for its possession. There was a sudden lull in the fighting around the two men as the combatants on both sides watched the struggle.

The Turkish standard bearer clung on to the shaft as he endured Richard's blows. He tried at first to ward them off with his left hand, and then suddenly thrust it forward, clamping his fingers round Richard's throat. Thomas saw his son's face contort in agony. Richard renewed his efforts, punching with all his failing strength. Then the man's head snapped back with a deep groan and he staggered, dazed, his fingers releasing their grip on Richard. He stumbled and fell across the parapet and Richard tore the enemy standard from his hand before thrusting him over the side. At once Richard held the standard aloft and a wild cheer erupted from the defenders on and behind the wall. Richard waved it back and forth for a moment, taunting the Turks, and then contemptuously hurled the standard back towards Birgu where it landed in the mud.

The Turks fell silent. Then the first of them began to back away, and the motion rippled through the ranks as the rest followed. Thomas climbed up beside Richard and held the Order's standard high in the air and added his cheers to those of the other defenders. Below him he saw Mustafa Pasha threaten his men with his sword as he screamed at them to continue the attack. Some stopped and turned back, and then a rock struck the enemy commander on the chin and he stumbled and fell to his knees, blood pouring from a deep gash. A wail of despair rose up from those immediately around him and the urge to retreat became unstoppable. Mustafa Pasha's bodyguards hurriedly picked up their commander and bore him away, towards the breach. Around them the Turks fell back across the open ground to the main wall.

'After them!' La Valette commanded. 'Drive them out! They must not be allowed to hold the wall!'

His order was repeated and the defenders slid over the parapet and began to chase after the Turks. Knights, soldiers, women and children all joined the pursuit, sprinting after the enemy and falling like wolves upon those that lagged behind their comrades. Watching from the wall Thomas felt sickened by the sight. This was not a war any more, but a savage, bloody massacre. Women and children attacked their prey with knives, axes and clubs, splattering blood and gobbets of flesh across the ground where the rain struggled to wash them away. An old woman hacked away at a fallen Janissary and then leaned down to clench his beard in her fist and raise the bloodied head aloft with a shrill cry of triumph.

'Richard!' La Valette called out. 'Take up the enemy's standard. The trophy is yours. Then follow me.'

The three men waited briefly while the wagon was unchained and rolled aside. Then they emerged from the wall and picked their way through the bodies scattered across the open ground and returned to the bastion. Romegas greeted the Grand Master with a wide smile, then waved his arm in the direction of the enemy trenches. The ground in front of Birgu's outer defences was covered with a sea of fleeing figures. Ranged along the wall and standing on the piles of rubble in the breaches the soldiers and people of Birgu stood in the rain, cheering, waving, and shouting their contempt at the backs of the enemy.

'Thanks be to God,' Thomas heard the Grand Master mutter. 'We survive.'

CHAPTER FORTY-FOUR

11 September

The rain stopped and for several days the sky cleared and the sun shone down on the devastation of the battlefield. The Turkish bombardment resumed, interspersed with a handful of attacks that were not pressed home and quickly disintegrated under the withering fire from the defenders crouching in the rubble along the line of the walls of Birgu and Senglea. The Grand Master no longer held meetings for his advisers. There was nothing to discuss. Rations were running short, their numbers were so diminished that one more determined assault was bound to result in defeat and annihilation. It was simply a matter of holding on for as long as possible.

Each morning Thomas rose before dawn to take his position in the bastion, alongside Richard and the other defenders, and then watch and wait, senses straining to pick up any warning of another assault. But eventually the attacks stopped coming and only a few of the enemy batteries still maintained their bombardment of the defences. To Thomas it seemed as if the enemy no longer had the heart to continue the siege and for the first time he allowed himself to hope that he, Maria and Richard might yet survive. They would return to England, he resolved, and begin to live the life that had been denied them for so long. There was a rightness about the quiet fantasy he allowed himself to indulge in. It was meant to be, Thomas told himself with a smile of contentment, surely, after all that they had endured?

He would not pray for such an outcome, though he knew that Maria prayed for little else, and she prayed fervently. He had watched her, kneeling before the small shrine that she had erected in the cellar of the house, rosary beads clenched in her hand, eyes gazing at the small statuette of the Virgin Mary, lips working faintly as she muttered her imprecations. She paused whenever a Turkish cannonball droned overhead, or smashed into a building nearby. Thomas looked on with a fatigued sense of disappointment in Maria, and in all those who held to their conviction that this world was the creation of a loving compassionate God. But her religious convictions did not extend to denying herself the full pleasure of their relationship, one of many compromises among the faithful that Thomas took as a sign of the emptiness of religion.

He was aware that he no longer felt the burden of guilt that had formerly accompanied his abandonment of belief, when he had felt that he had failed himself and all those around him. Now it was as if a cloying mantle had been lifted from him and he felt free, and just a little afraid of the idea of the finality of death. At the same time, it served as a stark reminder of the need to live fully in the moment. There was no eternity of reward in the afterlife, just a shallow promise of paradise to sugar the bitterness of the brief span of life that for many was little more than a struggle against starvation and violent death. What better way to hold people in thrall, Thomas thought to himself, his expression bitter.

'What is it?'

Thomas blinked as his thoughts refocused. Richard was watching him curiously where they both sat behind the parapet of the bastion.

'What were you thinking?' Richard asked.

'It was nothing. A passing fancy.' Thomas stiffly eased himself up behind the parapet and cautiously peered towards the enemy trenches a hundred paces away. The Turkish marker flags were still in position, hanging limply from their standards in the calm morning air. There was no sign of movement there, nor further back beyond the trenches where there were usually small parties of men carrying supplies from the ships to the enemy camps. Richard rose up too and peered over the edge of the parapet, eyes scouring the ground for any sign of enemy snipers.

'They're quiet today.'

'Quiet be damned,' Thomas muttered. 'They've gone.'

'Gone?' Richard scrutinised the enemy's entrenchments. 'It could be a trick.'

Thomas pursed his lips. 'Let's see.'

He sat down again and unbuckled the chinstrap of his helmet. Then, taking up one of the loaded arquebuses that were leaning against the parapet ready for use, he balanced his helmet on the butt and slowly raised it behind the crenellation so that its plume would be visible above the top of the stone. Then he eased the helmet sideways round the masonry until it was in clear view of the enemy's trenches.

'If there's any of them out there, they'll not pass up the chance of trying a shot at one of the knights,' said Thomas.

There was no response to his bait. He waited a moment longer before he lowered the arquebus and retrieved his helmet.

'Have one of the men report to La Valette. Tell him that there is no sign of the enemy to our front. I'll confirm that when I return.'

Richard sucked in a quick breath. 'You're going out there?'

'Of course. We need to be sure.'

'What if it's a trick? An attempt to lure us from cover?'

Thomas tapped the brim of his helmet. 'You saw. Not a single shot. They've abandoned their trenches, I'm sure of it.'

'But why?'

Thomas smiled. 'I would hate to tempt fate, and I will not say what my heart hopes, not until I have seen it with my own eyes.' He patted his son on the shoulder. 'No more tarrying, Richard. Send word to La Valette and then keep watch for me. I might just return somewhat more swiftly than I set out.'

He did not wait for a reply but scurried a short distance along the parapet towards the nearest breach where a low breastwork had been hurriedly thrown up. Easing his head up, Thomas swept his gaze over the ground in front of him. Satisfied that there was no movement, he snatched a quick breath, slid over the breastwork and scrambled down the rubble slope and dropped into the ditch where he pressed himself against the ground, breathing hard. He waited, his ears straining for any sound of voices or movement. A short distance to his right he saw a corpse, half buried in dust and rubble. There was a dried brown stain on the turban and torn cloth where a bullet had passed through his skull. His head lay back and his eyes stared into the clear heavens as flies buzzed lazily about the blotched skin of his face and walked undisturbed across his rotting flesh. From the sight and smell of the corpse, Thomas estimated the body must have lain there for at least ten days, one of many that the Turks had not dared to retrieve for a proper burial according to their custom.

Satisfied that he was safe for the moment, Thomas crept up to the rim of the ditch and peered over. Before him the rocky ground was scarred by the rough furrows of enemy shot that had grounded in front of the wall and ricocheted on into the defences. Broken ladders and abandoned weapons and armour lay scattered on the ground, together with the dead, their stomachs grossly distorted by mortal corruption under the glare of the sun. The shattered remains of a siege tower were no more than twenty yards away and Thomas slowly eased himself up before rushing across the open ground towards it, head and shoulders hunched down. Still there was no shout of alarm, nor the crack of sniper's weapon. He squatted down behind the shelter of the solid timbers and caught his breath before he glanced back towards the bastion. There was a brief glitter of sunlight on steel and he saw Richard watching him.

'Keep your head down, you fool!' Thomas hissed and gestured furiously with his gloved hand, but Richard continued to expose his head above the parapet. Fearing for his son, Thomas moved out from his shelter and ran for the nearest Turkish flag indicating the front line of their trenches, trusting that if there was a sniper lying in concealment then he would find him an easier target than Richard. He did not run in a straight line, but zigzagged across the open ground. All the while his heart pounded with a mixture of exertion and fear. Then he suddenly found himself on the parapet of a trench and he dropped into it on his hands and knees, splashing into the muddy water pooled along the bottom. At once he pressed against the side, hands splayed against the stony surface, gasping for breath. He looked quickly from side to side.

Nothing moved. He was alone.

Once his frantic breathing had calmed, Thomas drew his sword and cautiously headed for an opening that he guessed would lead into one of the approach trenches. The Turks had left little behind them, merely broken tools and rags. Edging round the corner, Thomas followed the trench towards one of the batteries that had fallen silent three days earlier. As he made his way through the silence and stillness, he saw soil- and rock-filled wicker baskets that made up the embrasures of the battery, but no sign of the muzzles of the cannon that had been pounding Birgu for the last two months.

At length the trench sloped up and entered the battery. The air inside the fortified position was thick with the acrid odour of burning and Thomas saw the blackened remains of gun carriages, barrel staves and lengths of timber used to construct the platforms for the Turkish guns. A short distance behind the battery was a large mound. Near the top, a handful of wild dogs had scratched away at the thin scraping of soil that had been quickly thrown over the mass grave, and the half-starved animals were feasting on the dead limbs they had exposed.

From the raised platform in the centre of the battery Thomas could see puffs of smoke from the batteries on the other side of the harbour, but there was no sign of activity from the batteries facing the defences at the end of each of the promontories of Senglea and Birgu. He felt a surge of hope, and then exultation at the realisation that the enemy were abandoning their siege. He took a last look round at the heights on either side and then sheathed his sword and hurried back down the trench towards the bastion, a quarter of a mile away. He had thought about striding directly across the open ground but there was still a possibility that the enemy had left a handful of snipers behind to harass the defenders the moment they ventured too far outside their defences.

By the time he returned to the bastion, the Grand Master was waiting for him, an excited gleam in his weary face. 'Well?'

'They have gone, sir.' Thomas crossed to the parapet and stood in full view of the enemy trenches as he indicated his route. 'I went as far as that battery, there. I saw no one, and the Turks have carried away whatever equipment and supplies they could and burned the rest. They have abandoned their positions on this side of the harbour, I'm sure of it.'

La Valette nodded. 'The lookouts on St Angelo have also seen some of their guns being withdrawn from the batteries on the Sciberras ridge.'

The dull roar of intermittent cannon fire from across the harbour proved that some guns were still in position.

Thomas turned towards St Elmo and the peninsula stretching out beyond. He watched the flashes and puffs of the next few shots and said, 'There's not more than one gun left in each of those batteries, sir. No more than six in total. They've been left to keep our attention and cover the withdrawal of their army to their ships.'

'Then we've beaten them!' Richard exclaimed and smacked his gloved fist into the palm of his other hand. 'By all that's holy, we've done it.'

'No.' La Valette stroked his chin thoughtfully. 'Mustafa Pasha must know that we are on the edge of defeat. He only has to wait until hunger, or the failure of our will, brings about our surrender. If I were him, I would stay here to the bitter end and have a prize to hold out to the Sultan. There can only be one reason for this. The Turks know that our relief force is coming. Don Garcia has stirred at last.'

There was a brief silence as they contemplated the Grand Master's conclusion.

'Then what should we do, sir?' asked Richard. 'Sally out from our defences and harry the Turks?'

La Valette frowned slightly. 'Young man, it would be a pitiful force that marched out from Birgu to do battle. A company of scarecrows swathed in dressings. No. If Don Garcia is coming, then we shall await him. Except for one thing.' He turned his gaze in the direction of St Elmo. 'We shall take back our fort. I would see the standard of the Order flying there again. As soon as can be.' He looked at Thomas. 'We have ten horses left in the stables. All that is left. Take them. You, your squire and eight picked men. Ride to St Elmo. If you find no Turks before you, then occupy the fort and raise the standard from the cavalier. Have two of your men climb to the crest of the ridge to observe the enemy, and look for the first sign of Don Garcia's army. There are still fresh troops at Mdina. I'll send a man there with orders for the garrison to make ready to march to Don Garcia's support.'

'Very well, sir.' Thomas bowed his head. 'We'll ride out as soon as we are ready.'

The huge camp that had sprawled across the land around the Marsa was abandoned and littered with equipment and smouldering heaps where the Turks had taken the time to burn what they could. Thomas and his small party of horsemen entered the camp shortly before noon. The sun beat down from a clear sky and locked the scene in a stifling embrace. The stench of burning was matched by the foul odour of the enemy's latrines and Richard pressed the back of his gauntlet to his nose as their bony mounts clopped through the camp.

As they approached the far side, where the track led along the Sciberras peninsula to St Elmo, they came across several tents, the only ones remaining. The air was thick with the sickly sour smell of rotting flesh and Thomas swallowed as he edged his horse over to the open flaps of the nearest tent. The buzzing of flies through the still air was the only sound apart from the scraping of the horses' hooves and their soft champing. Through the flaps he could see rows of men lying on soiled bedrolls. Every one of them was dead, many with cut throats; the Turks had clearly resolved not to let any of their men be captured or left to the mercy of the vengeful Maltese.

'Good God . . .' Richard muttered as he leaned from his saddle and glimpsed the horror inside the tent.

Thomas turned to him with a weary expression. 'I wonder that you can still utter those words.' Then he turned his horse and spurred it into a trot to quit the deathly scene as swiftly as possible and fill his lungs with untainted air.

They continued along the track, the ridge rising up to their left, the waters of the harbour sparkling to their right. There was no sound of life from the ridge. They rode past four of the batteries from where the enemy's guns had pounded Senglea and Birgu, and St Elmo before that. Two of the guns had suffered damage to their carriages and had been left behind, their barrels split by a blocked charge to render them useless.

At last the track rounded an outcrop of rock and there before the riders lay the ruined walls of the fort. Thomas reined in and grimly surveyed the scene. The ground before the fort was scarred by the lines of enemy trenches. A ramp of compacted rock and soil had been laid up into one of the breaches so that the Turks could mount their guns on the surviving walls to fire across the harbour. As before, there was no sign of life. Thomas waved his hand forward and the small column trotted towards the fort. As they drew closer Thomas saw a line of stakes at the top of the ramp, each one topped with a dark, withered orb. His stomach clenched with disgust and rage as he realised what they were.

'Aren't those . . . heads?' asked Richard.

Thomas nodded once then urged his horse to a trot so that Richard and the others would not see his grief. After two months in the sun there was little to recognise in the dried features of the faces on the stakes. Thin lips curled back from teeth and the skin had shrunk against the bone. Wispy tendrils of hair clung to the scalps and the eyes had long since been devoured by gulls. Thomas felt sickened by the sight. These pitiful remains were all that was left of the comrades who had given their lives to hold St Elmo far longer than anyone had thought possible. They had paid with their suffering and death to save their comrades in Birgu and Senglea. As he looked upon them, Thomas felt a pang of guilt that he still lived. He tried to push the feeling aside, reasoning that he had fought on for as long as he could and that to stay and die would have been pointless – worse than pointless now that he had Maria and his son to live for. But the mute testimony to sacrifice of the heads mocked his reason and shamed him.

He passed the last of the grisly trophies and rode into the fort, followed by his men. The clop of the horses' hooves echoed off the pitted walls surrounding the courtyard.

Thomas cleared his throat. 'Who has the standard?'

'I do, sir,' one of the sergeants replied.

'Then dismount and follow me.' Thomas released his reins and slid from the back of his mount. He looked up at Richard. 'Send two men with good eyesight to the top of the ridge. I want to know what Mustafa Pasha is up to. He can't have finished embarking his men already. Also, they're to look out for any sign of the relief force. Is that clear?'

Richard nodded.

'Then search the fort. They may have left someone

behind, their wounded, a prisoner perhaps. If so, we might gain a better grasp of what the Turks are up to.'

Thomas gestured to the sergeant to follow him and then made his way across the courtyard to the entrance of the main tower. Behind him he heard Richard giving his orders in a muted tone. It was understandable. Both of them had seen the full horrors of the bitter fighting for possession of St Elmo and it was as if the ghosts of all those who had died here were looking on in silence. When Thomas reached the top of the staircase and emerged on to the tower he saw at once that the flagstaff raised by the enemy had been stripped of the Turkish banner that had been flown to taunt the defenders across the harbour.

'Raise our colours, Sergeant. If there are still Turks on the island then let them know that St Elmo is ours again.'

'Yes, sir.' The sergeant took the tightly folded flag from his haversack and approached the base of the mast. He worked quickly to attach the Order's standard to the halyard and when all was ready he raised it up the pole. The light breeze that blew across the harbour caused the red cloth to billow slightly. A moment later Thomas could hear the faint sound of cheering from across the water and saw the garrison of St Angelo waving their arms in jubilation. Already, boats were setting off across the harbour, loaded with men, their equipment and a few days' rations to sustain them through the endgame of the siege. He turned to look down at the corner of the fort where he and his men had endured the bombardment and faced the fire and steel of the enemy day after day. He felt a stab of pain as he fixed his attention on the spot where Colonel Mas and Captain Miranda had faced the last assault, propped up on chairs, holding true to their promise to defend St Elmo to the last.

'Sir, look there.' The sergeant was shielding his eyes and squinting to the north. Thomas joined him. In the shimmering haze of the distance a cloud of dust hung over the dry countryside in the direction of Mdina, stirred up by the passage of a large body of men.

'Who are they?' asked the sergeant. 'Ours, or theirs?'

Thomas clenched his jaw. 'It's the Turks. They're moving against Mdina.' He tried to gauge their numbers from the cloud of dust that surrounded the main column. 'They must have every available man under arms. It looks like the Grand Master might have been mistaken about the relief force.'

The sergeant spat over the side of the tower. 'If Don Garcia hasn't landed, the enemy will take Mdina, sir. There're no two ways about it. The food supplies there might be enough for them to return to Birgu and starve us out.'

'Then we'd better hope that Mdina holds out,' Thomas said. The hope that had been building inside him began to fade. He turned his gaze away from the dust cloud and stared out to sea. A faint haze covered the water a mile offshore but he could just make out the masts and sails of the Turkish fleet steering towards the northern tip of the island. 'They're making for St Paul's Bay. We shall know the reason for it soon enough. Stay here and keep watch. If the enemy column changes direction then come and find me in the courtyard. If the Turks decide to re-occupy St Elmo then we'll need to quit the fort in good time.'

The sergeant nodded and Thomas left him on the tower and descended to the square. As he stepped out of the tower and into the glare of the sun, he shielded his eye and glanced round. Two of his men were holding the reins of the horses and had retreated to the narrow strip of shadow along one of the walls. Richard emerged from the chapel and Thomas beckoned to him.

'Remove those.' He pointed up the ramp at the impaled heads. 'Take them down and place them in the chapel for now. They can be given a proper burial later.'

Richard did not move but stared at the heads for a moment before he turned back to face his father. 'We should let them stay there. So that our people understand the true nature of the Turks.'

'No,' Thomas said firmly. 'We must remove them. They are an affront to humanity.'

Richard laughed bitterly. 'This entire struggle is an affront to humanity. Let the heads act as a reminder of that for now. They are the real fruits of war. Let that be the lesson for all those who see them so that they know what war has made of us.'

Thomas paused before he replied gently, 'You think to teach our men the terrible cost that has been paid here? They already know, my son. Their hearts are filled with the tragedy of it. What is the purpose of letting them see this fresh atrocity? It will only inflame them further. They will thirst for revenge and their violence can only beget more violence.'

'Then let it be so. Until the world is purged of Islam.'

A leaden despair weighed Thomas down as he beheld the disfiguring, dark rage in his son's expression. 'Richard, at some point we must put an end to such conflict, else it will put an end to us. Can you not see that?'

Richard looked down and responded in a strained tone. 'I can see it right well but I cannot help my feelings. Not now. Not after this.'

'Don't waste the rest of your life hating. There are better things to embrace. It has taken me too long to learn that. I would not have you repeat my failings, Richard.' He rested a hand on his son's shoulder. 'Help me to remove them, please.'

Richard's lips pressed into a tight line but when he looked up, he nodded. Thomas ordered the other men to continue searching the fort and then the two of them made their way up into the breach to the first of the heads. Thomas paused in front of it briefly and waved his hand to ward off the flies, and the air filled with a disturbed droning. Now, at close quarters, he could recognise enough of the features to know who it was.

'Captain Miranda . . .'

For a moment his mind filled with an image of the lively Spaniard who had inspired his men to fight on against impossible odds: Miranda, sword in hand, sun glinting off his blade and armour as he shouted his defiance at the enemy. Then the image faded and there was nothing left but the shrunken discoloured remnant in front of Thomas. He took a deep breath and reached out with both hands.

A clatter of hoofbeats caused him to turn and he saw one of the men he had sent up to the ridge riding hard across the open ground towards the fort. Temporarily abandoning the unpleasant task he was about to perform, Thomas strode down the ramp with Richard at his side. The rider reined in at the last moment, spraying grit and dust into the air. He thrust his arm to the north as his report spilled from his lips.

'The relief force has come, sir! There, towards Naxxar. They are deploying to give battle.'

Thomas felt his pulse quicken at the news. 'How many men?'

The soldier estimated quickly. 'Seven, perhaps eight thousand.'

'Eight thousand?' Thomas's brow creased with concern. 'And the enemy?'

'Twice their number, sir.'

Still the odds favoured the Turks, Thomas reflected anxiously. But set against that, the men in the relief force would be fresh, unlike their weary, famished enemy.

'There are boats putting out from St Angelo,' he said to the rider. 'Ride down to the shore and take one back across the harbour and tell the Grand Master all that you have seen.'

As the horse pounded towards the far side of the fort, Thomas turned back into the fort.

'What now?' asked Richard.

'Now?' Thomas smiled thinly. 'There is only one place to be on this day, Richard. The fate of Malta, and Christendom, rests on the result of the coming battle. If Don Garcia wins then the Turks are crushed. If he fails, they will return to the siege in the knowledge that they can starve us into surrender without any threat of further intervention. Don Garcia will need every man he can find to fight for him today. Naxxar is where our fate will be decided. Come!'

CHAPTER FORTY-FIVE

The horses were spent by the time Thomas and the six men he had brought with him reached the command post of the relief force. They had ridden round the northern harbour, circling behind the Turkish army before making their final gallop across country to join the men forming up on the slope in front of the small village of Naxxar. Their approach had been noted and a company of pikemen had turned to face them, but they moved back into line when they saw the distinctive red surcoats worn by the riders.

Some of the Spanish troops raised a weary cheer as Thomas and the others rode down the rear of the line, but most were too hot and thirsty as they leaned on their weapons, slowly cooking inside their breastplates and helmets. Less than a mile away the Turks were forming up to give battle. Thomas briefly noted that the enemy only had two small squadrons of cavalry, one on either flank. The rest of the army was composed of infantry, mostly Spahis, corsairs and the surviving fanatics, and Janissaries. There was little sound of the drums and shrill pipes that had accompanied their early attacks on the forts around the harbour, and none of the cheering that they had once used to bolster their spirits. The Turkish line extended across the uneven ground, overlapping that of their opponents.

A short distance behind the centre of the position, Thomas saw the Spanish commander of the relief force and his officers, their armour sparkling in the sun's harsh glare, bright red plumes flicking from side to side like spatters of blood. He steered his blown mount over towards the officers and as they became aware of his approach they turned to stare. Thomas reined in and bowed his head.

'I have come from Birgu. From the Grand Master.'

'He still lives?' asked one of the officers.

Thomas nodded, then looked round briefly. 'Where is Don Garcia? I should report to him.'

'Don Garcia is in Sicily,' a tall officer with a neatly trimmed beard answered. 'I am in command here. Don Alvare Sande at your service.' He nodded in greeting before continuing testily, 'And might I know your name?'

'Sir Thomas Barrett. I had thought to meet Don Garcia.'

'The King has ordered Don Garcia not to place the fleet or himself at risk. The Turkish fleet would overwhelm our galleys with ease. Don Garcia was therefore obliged to sail back to Palermo as soon as the army had landed.' Don Alvare made no attempt to hide his frustration. 'I have orders to raise the siege and drive the Turks from the island.'

'I see. Is this all the men you have, sir?'

'All that could be spared, yes. With these I am expected to sweep aside the Turkish host. As you can see, Sir Thomas, my King continues in his unfounded optimism over what can be achieved with the minimum of resources. But tell me, how goes it with La Valette and his followers?'

'We still hold Birgu, Senglea and Mdina, sir. St Elmo was lost, but is now ours again.'

'Indeed.' Don Alvare's expression lightened. 'Then you must have many thousands that you could add to my strength. Is the Grand Master marching to join forces with me?'

'Alas, no, sir. Half the knights are dead, and many of the others are wounded. Of the rest, only some six hundred of the militia and mercenaries are left. There is also a small garrison at Mdina, but they number a few hundred.' Thomas turned towards the distant town and pointed out the small force atop a hillock a short distance from the walls of Mdina. 'There, sir.'

Don Alvare's gaze fixed on the garrison of Mdina. 'Ah, I had thought them to be more of the enemy. So we are grievously outnumbered.'

Thomas hesitated a moment and then asked, 'What are your plans, sir?'

Don Alvare gestured to the small hill upon which his army was formed up. 'We have the advantage of the high ground. This is where we should make our stand and let the enemy come to us. That is what I would do in the normal course of events. But the Turks seem weak. They have suffered the same privations as you in these last months.'

'Your men are fresh, sir. Attack now, while they are still forming up,' Thomas urged.

Don Alvare blinked sweat from his eyes as he considered his options. 'My men have been at sea for nine days while we waited for a chance to land unmolested. They are still suffering from seasickness. But we may never get a better chance to crush the Turks . . .'

'There is no time to prevaricate, sir,' Richard said irritably. He thrust his arm out and pointed in the direction of St Elmo. 'Our comrades died there while we waited for the promised relief force. Your delay has been paid for with our blood, sir. Now you are here, it is time to do your duty. Attack the Turks and drive them into the sea!'

Don Alvare's eyes blazed. 'How dare you address me so, you impudent pup!'

'Forgive my squire, sir,' Thomas intervened. 'It has been a hard siege and all our reserves of patience have worn thin. But he is right. The time to strike is now. The longer you wait, the weaker your men will become and the greater the chance of defeat. Strike now, while they still have the heart and strength for it.'

Don Alvare was silent for a moment before he nodded sombrely. 'Very well. I think we must attack.'

Thomas felt the tension in his heart ease and a great sense of relief wash over him. But he knew he must act before Don Alvare changed his mind or lost his nerve. Thomas spurred his horse away through a gap between two companies of pikemen and emerged in front of the relief force. He felt the blood racing through his veins, hot with desire to strike at the enemy. Drawing his sword, he waved it above his head to draw the attention of all.

'Hear me! Hear me!'

Despite the soul-sapping sweat that coursed from their brows the men of the relief force turned their attention to him. The line extended along the slope so it was possible for almost all of them to see Thomas clearly. He paused briefly to marshal his thoughts and readied himself to speak.

'For long months you have waited for this moment,' he began. 'And for years before that. I warrant there is hardly a man amongst you whose family or friends have not suffered from the raids of the corsairs who serve Suleiman. They have butchered your brethren and carried many off into slavery. You all know the dreaded names that have frozen the blood of our people – Barbarossa, Dragut . . .'

There were angry shouts and curses at the mention of the corsairs' names and Thomas indulged them a moment while he drew breath to continue. His chest felt tight and strained under the weight of his breastplate.

'Now those two demons are dead and gone, and Suleiman's power is on the wane. The vast host that he sent against Malta was full of Turkish arrogance, ambition and avarice. They thought to make an easy conquest of my brother knights and the people of this island. They thought to wipe us out within a matter of weeks . . . We held them off for four months, at great cost to the base servants of the Sultan! But also at great cost to us . . . Many of my brother knights are gone, and other soldiers known to you all. Captain Miranda for one.'

There were cries of surprise and grief from the mercenaries who had served under Miranda in previous campaigns. Thomas waited until the noise abated before continuing.

'The noble captain died a hero's death. As did Colonel Mas.'

More cries of anger rippled along the line.

'Heroes both.' Thomas thrust his sword in the direction of the harbour. 'They died together defending the breach in the walls of the fort of St Elmo. They died, and then their bodies were cruelly mutilated by the Turks. Less than an hour ago, I beheld their heads mounted on stakes as trophies, cut off and left to rot under a merciless sun!' He stabbed his blade towards the enemy battle line. Again the anger welled up in the throats of the soldiers and the relief force began to edge forward, down the slope.

'Remember St Elmo!' Thomas shouted. 'That is our battle cry. Remember St Elmo!'

Richard and the others urged their mounts through the line to join him and take up the cry, which quickly spread through the ranks. Don Alvaro hurriedly issued orders to his officers while he still had some control over them. Thomas grasped his reins and turned to face the Turks. 'The time has come for revenge!'

'No prisoners!' Richard yelled harshly. 'Take no prisoners!'

The handful of mounted men walked their horses down the slope towards the enemy, and as if with one will, the rest of the relief force surged after them, pikes lowered and swords drawn, the colours of their standards swirling through the shimmering air. Glancing back, Thomas saw the fixed expression on Don Alvaro's face before he gritted his teeth, drew his sword and joined the advance with the rest of his officers.

The Spanish soldiers kept the line as they marched down towards the waiting Turks, shouting out Thomas's battle cry and calling on the names of the saints to protect them. Beyond the Turkish line Thomas could see that the

Mdina garrison was also on the move, striking towards the enemy's rear without regard to the odds against them. Beyond his feeling of exhilaration, tainted as ever with fear, he felt a deep inner calm, as if this was the moment he had waited for all his life. His doubts about faith and the righteousness of religious causes fell away and all he saw was the need to defeat the enemy. At his side rode Richard. His sword was sheathed as he guided his horse, fastening the buckle of his gorget so that only his eyes, gleaming with ferocious intensity, were visible. Thomas drew his sword once more and urged the others on.

Ahead, the Turks closed ranks and readied their weapons. A thin screen of men armed with arquebuses moved forward fifty paces and set their weapons up on iron stands. They took aim at their opponents and waited until they came within range. Then they touched their smouldering fuses to the firing pans and with a puff of smoke and a dart of flame the weapons fired. The initial range was long and Thomas saw only a handful of men struck down. The Turks reloaded quickly and efficiently and continued their fire, with ever greater success as the relief force drew closer. Over a score of men, dead or wounded, lay on the dry stubble of the slope behind their comrades. Some propped themselves up and shouted encouragement.

A loud clang drew Thomas's attention and he turned in his saddle to see one of his men slump over his saddle. He struggled feebly for a moment as blood seeped from beneath his holed breastplate, then his lifeless fingers dropped the reins and he fell from the saddle, lost from sight amid the pikemen advancing either side of his horse.

The relief force reached the bottom of the slope, no more than a hundred paces from the enemy. The Turkish arquebusiers pulled up their supports, shouldered their weapons and hurried back to their battle line. The heat of the day and the blinding sweat that dripped from the brows of the Spanish meant that there was no wild charge into action. Instead they paced steadily forward. The pikemen lowered their weapons and drove into the Turkish line with a rolling chorus of thuds and clatter of blades. There were hoarse cries from both sides, rising to a feverish crescendo as the hand-to-hand struggle began.

Thomas held his sword slightly to the side, ready to strike, as he urged his mount into the throng of turbans, pointed helmets and the flickering blades of scimitars brandished by the Spahis massed before him. Fixing his eye on the nearest of them, Thomas thrust his sword out and pierced the man's shoulder, ripping the blade free before it might be twisted from his fingers. At once he chose another target, a tall, dark-skinned man whose crooked teeth were clamped together in a snarl as he turned towards Thomas. He raised his spear and plunged it towards Thomas's chest, ripping through the material of the surcoat before it was deflected by the breastplate beneath. Thomas struck at the spear shaft, knocking it down, and then stabbed the point of his sword into the Turk's throat before spurring his horse forward and ripping the blade free.

A space opened up in front of him and Thomas took the chance to glance to each side. The attackers had driven deep into the Turkish line, led by the pikemen who methodically thrust their weapons into the lightly protected bodies of their enemy before pulling the deadly points free and looking for the next foe. A pall of choking dust was swirling about the combatants but Thomas could already see that some of the Turks were backing away from the fight. He opened his mouth to urge the pikemen on when his horse let out a shrill whinny of pain and terror and reared up, hooves lashing at the Turk who had slashed into the beast's neck with a scimitar. Thomas threw his weight forward, clutching the reins tightly as the wounded animal kicked and reared and men of both sides retreated from the horse's wild death throes. Its legs buckled and it slumped to the ground, snorting frantically. Thomas quickly kicked his boots free of the stirrups and scrambled aside before the horse could roll on him. An instant later, as it sensed the pressure from the saddle ease, the horse jerked over and kicked out.

Thomas stepped away and turned to face the Turks. He picked out two Janissaries amid the figures flitting through the dust. They saw him at the same instant and charged, their ostrich plumes dancing above their white headdresses. Thomas thrust his sword up over his head to ward off the first blow and saw the sparks fly from the blades and a deafening clash filled his ears. The impact jarred his wrist and the scimitar scraped down his blade and glanced off his shoulder guard. Thomas saw the other man leaping round his comrade, sword rising, and he knew that there was no time to attempt a riposte on the first man. Instinctively he punched the guard of his sword into the Janissary's face with all his strength and felt the blow strike home, crushing the man's nose and gouging open the flesh of his cheek. The Janissary staggered back then lurched upright and the bloodied point of a pike exploded through the material covering his stomach. The man collapsed on to his knees and Thomas saw a Spaniard behind him, teeth clenched in a triumphant grimace before he braced his boot against the man's back and wrenched his pike free of the body.

Thomas had no time to nod his thanks. The first Janissary was balanced on the balls of his feet, ready to strike. For an instant the surrounding battle seemed distant, as if the two of them were engaged in some private duel. Then the spell was broken and the man leaped forward, his scimitar slicing through the air. Thomas stepped quickly to the side and struck at where he anticipated the Janissary's arm would be as the scimitar came down. The steel glittered as Thomas's blade struck the Janissary's wrist and cut clean through it. The hand and sword spun several feet away on to the dusty ground. With an animal howl the Janissary threw himself at Thomas, clawing at his gorget with his remaining hand. Thomas felt fingernails digging into his skin and clenched his eyes shut as he struggled to tear the man's hand away. As soon as he had prised the fingers loose Thomas thrust the Janissary back and then ran him through with his sword. His opponent fell on to the ground and lay gasping as the blood pulsed from the wound over his heart and the stump of his wrist.

'Father!' Richard approached him through the dust haze with an anxious expression. 'You're bleeding.'

Thomas could feel it, the warm flow on his cheek, running down to the corner of his mouth where he tasted the salty gore.

'I'm fine,' he panted. 'Fine.'

Sword raised, he looked round, but no more of the enemy loomed nearby out of the dust and the sound of fighting seemed to be fading. He turned back to Richard. 'Where is your horse?'

'Shot through the head. I lost my sword when I fell, hence . . .' Richard held a pike up. 'Which way?'

Thomas had lost his bearings in the fight and now the dust obscured the surrounding landscape, but the afternoon sun was angled towards the west. 'This way. Stay with me.'

They followed the sound of the fighting, stepping over bodies and pausing only to finish off the enemy wounded who might yet pose a threat. The dust began to thin out and then there was open country before them in the direction of St Paul's Bay. It was clear at once that the Turks had broken. They were streaming away from the men of the relief force, many throwing down their arms and equipment in order to hasten their escape. Behind them came their Christian opponents, mercilessly butchering any Turk too slow, or too weak, to flee. The first of the horsemen from the garrison at Mdina joined the pursuit, charging in from the flank, shouting with cruel glee as they rode down and killed the enemy who had caused so much fear and suffering over the long months of the siege. As he watched the unfolding massacre, it seemed to Thomas as if a swarm of wild and ravenous beasts had been let loose upon the helpless Turks. There was no longer any semblance of order in either army, just figures scattered across the barren landscape.

With Richard at his side he followed the direction of the rout, across baking fields, past the blackened remains of farmhouses torched by the Turks. His armour weighed him down and every step forward seemed to take a great effort, and all the while sweat coursed from his brow and caused his linen undershirt to stick to his flesh and chafe the skin. At length, after three miles, they came to the top of a small rise overlooking the bay where St Paul had once landed to convert the island's inhabitants to the new creed of peace and universal brotherhood. But on this day, the scene was from the darkest and most bloody of nightmares.

The Turkish soldiers were trapped along the edge of the bay. Small clusters had turned on their pursuers and bitterly contested the shore-line. Elsewhere hundreds had waded out into the sea towards the fleet of galleys anchored in the bay. Small craft were desperately rowing between the galleys and the shallows to try and rescue as many of their comrades as possible. In amongst those waiting to be taken off waded the men of the relief force, pitilessly cutting down those they could reach and then looting their bodies before moving on. A score of Turks had crowded around the bows of one of the rowing boats and were fighting to get aboard. The small craft rocked crazily and the crew was trying to beat the soldiers back. Then the boat tilted violently and capsized, spilling men into the sea. The shallows of the bay were stained red and a pink froth washed up on the pebbles as the gentle waves lapped the shore.

'Look there,' said Richard, pointing out one of the bands of Janissaries still fighting at the edge of the water, a quarter of a mile away. There were perhaps a hundred of them, most holding off their pursuers with spears while a handful steadily fired and reloaded their arquebuses, picking off easy targets. In the middle of the loose crescent of soldiers stood an officer in silk robes and a bejewelled turban.

'That's Mustafa Pasha.' Thomas breathed heavily through cracked lips, his voice hoarse. 'If he is taken, then the Sultan's humiliation is complete.'

'Come then.' Richard started down the slope, holding his pike in a firm grip. 'Let us take him.'

'Wait!' Thomas rasped as he followed his son. 'Wait for me.'

The late afternoon sun was low in the sky, and cast long shadows across the carnage and burnished the grime and blood-spattered armour of the Christian soldiers as they went about their murderous business. Thomas saw a handful of Turkish boats setting out from the enemy flagship, steering towards their commander and his bodyguards. As the boats approached the shallows, scores of men converged on them, surging through the bloodied tide. Those on the boats were clearly under orders to permit only the Janissaries to board; they ruthlessly slashed out with their scimitars at any man who came within reach as they approached the shore. Mustafa's standard had drawn the attention of his pursuers and a vicious struggle was taking place between the Spanish pikemen and the Janissaries.

'We must hurry,' Richard panted. 'Before he escapes.'

Despite their leaden limbs, the two of them broke into a trot, their scabbards slapping at their sides. Only a handful of the Turks were still resisting along the edge of the bay. Some threw down their arms and dropped to their knees to surrender but were cut down without mercy. Other boats were picking up the last of those still in the water and Thomas could see activity on the bows of the galleys as their gun crews loaded the cannon ready to fire on the Christians in one last act of defiance before the Sultan's humiliated host was driven from the island.

Mustafa Pasha, accompanied by his standard bearer and two other men, waded out towards the flagship's boats. Behind him his bodyguards fought on, to buy him time.

'This way!' Thomas panted, striking out at an angle towards the enemy commander. They splashed into the shallows and then waded towards the personal standard of the Sultan, the horsehair tail flicking from side to side as the man carrying it struggled towards the boat. Mustafa turned towards the splashing in the water nearby and saw the two knights making directly for him. He snapped an order to the two bodyguards protecting him and they instantly turned towards Thomas and Richard, raising their scimitars. Richard held his pike clear of the water and feinted towards the nearest of the Janissaries. The Turk made to dodge to one side but failed to make allowance for the drag of the water and the pike tore into his side. Richard thrust home, and then worked the tip free. Thomas caught up with him and waded past to engage the other bodyguard. There was no finesse to his actions as he struck out at the Janissary, just brute force and determination. He hacked again, and again, driving the man back. Then the Turk missed his step on the seabed and fell back with a splash. At once Thomas pushed forward and pressed the man down with his left hand, holding him under the surface of the bay as he stabbed with his sword, and blood billowed up through the water.

Thomas turned to see that Mustafa had reached the prow of the nearest boat, not twenty feet away, and two of the sailors were struggling to drag him aboard. Richard, too, saw that the enemy commander was on the verge of getting away; he cast his pike aside and the water boiled around him as he reached out for the shoulders of the standard bearer waiting in the water behind his master. Richard grasped the man roughly and turned him round before striking his fist into the Turk's face. The man clung on to the shaft of the standard with one hand and lashed out at Richard with the other. Richard blinked, momentarily disorientated, and then he growled angrily and struck the man again in the face with all his strength and the Turk's head snapped back. His grasp on the standard slipped and with a triumphant shout Richard ripped it from his hands and raised the standard up so that all could see it had been captured.

Thomas saw that Mustafa Pasha had been hauled into the boat and sat in an undignified heap near the bows as the crew lowered the oars and began to pull away from the shore. Just beyond Mustafa a soldier stood up, bracing his legs as he raised a light arquebus and took aim at Richard.

'No!' Thomas shouted, his voice cracking. Without thinking he pushed Richard aside and surged between his son and the boat as the flame flashed out. There was a small ring of smoke, a loud crash in the hot air, and Thomas felt a blow, like a vicious punch, in his stomach. The impact drove the breath out of him. He saw Mustafa Pasha's lips part in a cold grin as the boat drew away.

Richard burst out of the sea with an enraged expression.

He still had the standard clasped in both hands and he glared at Thomas. 'What are you doing? Why did you . . .' His words dried up as he stared at the hole in Thomas's breast-plate.

With a sick feeling of certainty, Thomas was aware that he had been shot. He looked down and saw the indent in his armour, just above where it curved towards the flange above his groin. Blood oozed from the hole and dribbled down the polished steel.

'Oh God, no,' he muttered. 'Not this. Not now.'

'Father!' Richard hurled the standard towards the shallows and waded towards him. 'Father, you're hit.'

Thomas shook his head, not wanting to believe it but knowing that the wound was mortal. The numbing impact of the shot began to fade and a terrible pain spread through his stomach. He staggered towards his son, stumbling into his arms before the strength in his legs gave out. A dark veil blurred his vision and he wanted to vomit as he felt his consciousness slipping away.

Richard held him under the arms, struggling towards the shore. Thomas was dimly aware of his son's voice as he called out desperately, 'Over here! Help me! For pity's sake, help me!'

CHAPTER FORTY-SIX

'There's nothing that can be done to save him,' La Valette said gently as they approached the door to the infirmary. Maria did not reply but stared fixedly ahead. The glow of the rising sun lit up the battlements on the wall above them, and in Birgu the bells of every church continued to ring, as they had done ever since news of the defeat of the Turks had reached the town. The courtyard of St Angelo was filled with the wounded who had begun to arrive from Naxxar the night before.

'It is a miracle that he has lived through the night,' La Valette continued. 'When his squire brought him in, he had lost much blood. But all he said was that he wanted to see you. I sent for you at once. I can only imagine the strength of will that is still keeping him in this world. He has made a final request of me.' La Valette stopped on the threshold of the infirmary and turned to face Maria. 'A strange thing, and you should know of it before you see him.'

'What is it?' Maria frowned.

'He asks for two things. That you are married here and now, and that I prepare and sanction the adoption of his squire as his legal son and heir. That young man has not left his side since he brought Sir Thomas back from the battlefield, but there is more to this than merely rewarding loyal service, I think.' La Valette shook his head. 'A peculiar situation. But the Order owes a great debt to Sir Thomas and I am happy to fulfil his wishes. The question is, are you?'

Maria said nothing, her lips pressed together in a thin line as she nodded.

'Well then. All is in readiness. I have a priest at hand and I shall witness the ceremony, together with his squire. But it grieves me that you should become a widow so soon after becoming a wife.'

Maria swallowed and held her head high as she responded, 'I can think of no greater happiness than being the wife of Sir Thomas. Now take me to him.'

An hour later the ceremony was over. Thomas slipped back on his bolster with a smile of contentment as his wife and son sat either side of him, each holding one of his hands. His hair was plastered to his scalp and sweat gleamed on his pallid skin and the scar tissue on his face. He felt cold and what was left of his strength was steadily failing. Only the agony in his stomach kept his thoughts coherent. He knew that there was little time left to him and felt a burst of rage until he recalled that because he was dying his son was still living. He nodded to himself and whispered, 'It is a fair fate.'

He turned his head towards Richard and moistened his lips so that he might speak clearly. He found the effort a strain and his voice was thin and frail. 'Swear to me that you will look after your mother. She has been wronged all through her life. Swear to me that you will care for her.'

'I swear it.'

Thomas smiled. 'I am proud of you. Any man would be honoured to call you his son.'

Richard swallowed hard and gently laid a hand on his father's chest. 'I know. And to you I owe it all.'

'No. I should have been a better father. A better man.' Thomas turned to Maria, his eyes filled with pain and longing. 'A better husband.'

She tried to fight back tears, then leaned forward to kiss his cheek and whisper in his ear, 'There is no better man. You are my all . . . my love.'

Thomas's vision began to blur and he had barely enough strength to breathe. His expression twisted in agony. 'And you . . . are mine. Always . . . Always. Forgive me.'

Then his eyes closed as his breathing became more laboured, and with a last sigh, he lay silent and still. There was no mistaking the moment of his death; that final stillness of body and spirit from which there was no return. His son and wife stared in silence and each shed tears. Their grief was raw and they sat a while together as the hours passed.

As dusk closed over the island, La Valette returned to the infirmary to pay his respects. Maria eased her hand away from the growing chill of Thomas's fingers and rose stiffly. She stared down at his scarred face and leaned to kiss him on the brow before she turned and walked slowly away, her hand resting on Richard's arm. La Valette accompanied them outside.

'Rest assured, Sir Thomas will never be forgotten. Nor will any who endured the siege.' La Valette breathed in deeply as if savouring the air. 'When the rest of

Christendom hears that the Turks have been thrown back from Malta they will gain heart and common purpose. Suleiman and his empire have been humbled, but soon he will be back. Yet Europe will no longer fear the prospect of living under the shadow of the crescent. Because of what happened here, on Malta. Because of those who died, like Thomas, and those who fought and lived, like you, Richard.'

He embraced the young man, then stood back and smiled curiously. 'You are a worthy heir to Sir Thomas's name. It is almost as if you were born to take on the mantle.'

La Valette turned to Maria and bowed deeply. 'My lady, I wish that this had ended more favourably for you. But God's will be done.'

Maria's lips parted as she made to reply, but she could only nod.

'There is one more thing.' La Valette reached inside his doublet and pulled out a folded sheet of paper, sealed with the Barrett crest. He offered it to Richard. 'Sir Thomas gave me this several days ago. He requested that I give it to you, should anything happen to him.' He smiled sadly. 'I doubt that he really expected the worst, but . . . here.'

Richard took the letter hesitantly and nodded his thanks. La Valette bowed his head and then strode back towards his quarters where the end of the siege had produced an endless list of new problems that needed urgent resolution. Richard waited until he was out of sight before he turned to Maria.

'Do you mind?'

'No. I'll wait for you on the wall. There's a pleasant breeze tonight.' She bowed her head and slowly walked over to the bottom of the stairs leading up on to the wall of the fort. Richard moved into the pool of light cast by a torch flickering in an iron bracket and opened the letter and began to read.

My dearest Richard,

I am not a man of great learning. Nor am I any more a man of noted deeds and actions. Nor, I fear, do I have much time left to me to be a man at all. If I should die then let this brief note be my testament to you. If I should live, then perhaps these poor thoughts might still carry some of the weight and value that I purpose for them.

I would have you know, and tell your mother, that she was right about the incorruptible truth that lives in our hearts. Tell her she was always what I loved most in the world, though you, my son, are what I valued most. The two sentiments are not the same, but nor are they mutually exclusive. Indeed, they both form part of the bond between lovers and the product of their love. This alone is what matters. Everything else is a poor shadow by comparison.

My son, you have become as dear to me in a few short months as any son could have become in a lifetime. I have come to look on you with well-earned pride. You have great courage, and compassion and wisdom. I would not have you squander such gifts in the ignoble service of a reptile like Walsingham. There is a better path for you, should you choose to take it. If there has been any worth to have come out of the trials that we have endured here on this barren rock it is that the real document that fate intended for you to bring away was not that for which you were sent, but this that you now hold in your hands.

I have lived a full life. I have done much that I regret and I have learned something of the limits of the ambitions and beliefs that men, and women, live by. Know that I have tried to be a good man, and that the measure of that goodness is wholly human. I have forsaken the idea that there is any God in this universe, let alone a Christian one, or one conceived by the Muslims. There is nothing godly in the bloodshed and cruelty that we have both witnessed.

Of all the causes that preoccupy the minds of humanity, of all the works of science and faith that have been set down in words, in my life there is only one truth of any value that I have learned and now entrust to you.

It is this: that I have loved, and been loved. And I have sired a child. That is all the divinity that any man requires in this world.

Your adoring father.

Richard read the letter again, more slowly, and then folded it carefully and placed it inside his doublet, next to his heart. He climbed the stairs to join his mother and gazed out across the harbour towards the ruined mass of St Elmo.

He felt the touch of her hand on his shoulder. 'Richard, are you all right?'

Richard swallowed his bitter grief at the unrequited gratitude he owed the man who had been his father, and friend. Then he turned to her with a forced smile and nodded. 'I am.'

He leaned forward and kissed her cheek and then held her hands. 'Mother, let us go home.'

'Home?'

'England.' Richard felt a pang of longing as he uttered the word. But there was one final task he must perform before he could put his affairs to rest. 'There is a gentleman I have to see in London first. After that there is a fine house awaiting us. And a family name and a title.' He opened his hand to look at the ring, a painful lump in his throat. 'I shall do all that I can to be a worthy son of Sir Thomas Barrett, Knight of the Order of St John.'

She forced a smile but could no longer meet his eyes and looked away. 'I am sure he would have been proud of you.'

'I wish for nothing more.' Richard was silent for a moment before he cleared his throat. 'You will have to make preparations for the journey. I will leave you to it.'

Maria turned back to him anxiously. 'Where are you going?'

'There is something I must attend to. Something important. I'll come to your house as soon as it is done.'

'Promise me.'

'I swear it, Mother.'

She was silent for a moment before she nodded. 'Very well. But don't be long. You are all that I have now . . . my dear son.'

Richard felt a pang of affection swell up in his breast

569

and he took her hand and squeezed it very gently. 'I'll be as quick as I can.'

He shut the heavy door of the auberge behind him, muffling the sounds of the bells that pealed across the rooftops of Birgu and echoed in the streets filled with excited people, still stunned by the realisation that they had come through the greatest trial of their lives and survived. The hall was still and gloomy, the only light coming from the window high up in the wall. Richard stared round briefly, and then made his way down the corridor leading to the kitchen. There he took a candle and lit it, using Jenkins's tinderbox. With the small flame held out before him, he descended into the cellar that ran beneath the auberge, a greater place of safety for King Henry's will. In a small, neglected alcove he removed a loose brick and set it aside before he groped into the cavity beyond and extracted the aged piece of parchment that he had been sent to find and take back to England. It seemed strange that this had once seemed a great and dangerous treasure to him. Richard held it in his hand and gazed at the smooth vellum by the wan glow of the candle for a while. Then, without any further hesitation, he held the corner of the will to the flame and watched as the flickering yellow tongue licked along the edge of the document in a bright line that spread rapidly and left grey and black ash in its wake. He held it for as long as possible before the heat caused him to release his grip and the letter dropped to the floor, flaring briefly before it struck the ground with a small flurry of sparks and then quickly faded into darkness as the last of it was consumed by flame. With a sigh, Richard turned away and headed back up into the kitchen.

As he passed down the corridor he was aware of the sound of movement from the hall. He continued as quietly as he could until he emerged from the corridor and saw Jenkins struggling to set a ladder up against the wall.

'Jenkins.'

The old man started and turned round. He puffed his cheeks in relief as he saw Richard and then smiled. At once the smile faded and he shook his head sadly. 'It's good to see you again, Master Richard . . . though I wish that Sir Thomas was with you.'

'You know then?'

Jenkins nodded. 'I heard it from one of the servants at St Angelo, while we were offering our thanks to God at the cathedral. I came back here as soon as the service was over. There was something I had to do.'

'As did I.' Richard smiled. 'What are you about?'

Jenkins stepped over to the table and picked up a small bundle of red wool. He unwrapped the folds and took out a small wooden shield bearing a coat of arms and held it up for Richard to see. 'I put it safely aside after the auberge received the instruction to take it down. I hoped that one day it would be returned to its rightful place, sir. It has been a long wait. I think there is no better time than now. Would you give me a hand, sir? My limbs are not as steady as they once were.'

'Of course.' Richard held out his hand. 'Let me do it.'

Jenkins stood still for a moment before he gave the small shield to Richard. 'Thank you, sir. You can see there's a small hook on the back.'

Richard turned it over to look.

'You can hang it on that nail up there.' Jenkins pointed to the gap on the beam, a short distance from the ladder. 'Where it used to be.'

'Very well.'

Richard climbed, one-handed, holding his father's coat of arms in the other. When his head drew level with the beam he reached out and carefully slipped the hook over the nail and then adjusted the shield so that it hung straight. Satisfied, he climbed back down and then stood beside Jenkins. They looked up at the coat of arms. The paint had not faded during the long years of storage and the design seemed as fresh as the day it first hung in the hall.

'It is good to have things in their rightful place,' said Jenkins.

Richard nodded.

They were silent a moment longer before Richard turned and offered his hand to the servant. 'I have come to say farewell, Jenkins. I'm returning to England.'

'Really, sir?' The old man looked disappointed. 'I had hoped that you might stay. Now that the last of the knights has gone, the auberge needs new blood.'

Richard's expression hardened at the unfortunate choice of word. He forced himself to smile faintly. 'Perhaps one day. Not for some years. I have earned a respite from war. But if ever the Order calls on me, I shall come. Look for me then.'

Both men smiled, knowing full well that Jenkins would be long in his grave before that day.

'Goodbye then, sir.' Jenkins bowed his head, and

shuffled over to open the door. Richard stepped out into the bright sunlight bathing the town. As the latch clacked behind him, he felt a lightness in his being, as if all manner of burdens had been lifted from his shoulders. He breathed in deeply, then glanced over his shoulder for one last look at the auberge before he turned away and went to join his mother.

For Tom

After life's fitful fever he sleeps well.
Treason has done his worst. Nor steel nor
poison,
Malice domestic, foreign levy, nothing
Can touch him further.

William Shakespeare

AUTHOR'S NOTE

Few sieges in history are as significant as that of 1565. It took place at a time when the Ottoman Empire was at its height and there was little doubt that Sultan Suleiman ruled the superpower of the age. The kingdoms of Europe did not dare stand in his way and lived in fear of his all-conquering armies. For those nations with a shore on the Mediterranean Sea – or the White Sea as the Ottoman Turks referred to it – there was the added terror of the Sultan's sea power, often exercised by his proxy fleets of corsairs led by legendary characters such as Barbarossa and Turgut, whose very names caused Christians to quail in terror. Descending by night, the corsairs raided coastal villages and towns, killed countless thousands and carried many more off into slavery.

There is little doubt about the Grand Strategy of Suleiman. He aimed to crush his Christian enemies between the pincers of his army and his fleet. He believed he had been divinely chosen to complete the long-standing ambition of the Muslim world – to subject all other nations to the will of Allah, under the rule of the Ottoman Empire. The Kingdom of Spain was a mirror image of the same ambition, and just as ruthless, and equally ready to use religion to justify its actions. It was fitting that the most celebrated act of the great struggle between the two powers should be played out on Malta, the island in the very heart of the sea so bitterly contested for hundreds of years.

At that time the Order of St John was little more than the garrison of an outpost in the Christian world. The Order was in decline, its numbers falling as the wars in Europe claimed knights it might once have attracted. It was comprised of many nationalities and there were always tensions within its ranks, which was not helped by a long history of defeats and retreats in the face of the forces of Islam. Given that the knights of the sixteenth-century Order were single-minded fanatical warriors, it is hard to believe that their origins date back to the twelfth century when a simple priest wished to offer food and shelter to pilgrims travelling to the Holy Land. As part of that service the Order soon extended its scope to offering armed escort to pilgrims, before evolving into an extensive paramilitary force that went over to the offensive with considerable relish.

Ultimately, the military Orders proved insufficient to the challenge they faced and were driven from the Holy Land in 1291 (when they were all but annihilated). Regrouping on Cyprus they invaded Rhodes in 1310 and used the island as a base for naval operations against the enemies of Christendom. Eventually, in 1523, the newly crowned Sultan, Suleiman, sent a powerful fleet and army to overwhelm the Order. It was not an easy task since the knights had built a vast array of fortifications around their headquarters, which visitors to Rhodes can still see today. Suleiman was young at the time, and inclined to rather more chivalry than was wise. Instead of crushing the Order that had been a constant threat to the Turks, he took pity and permitted them to quit the island alive, taking with them their portable belongings. It was a mistake that would cost him dearly, for the knights went back on to the offensive the moment they secured a new base on Malta.

By the time Mustafa Pasha and Piyale Pasha launched their assault on the island detailed in this book, the Sultan had become older, wiser and more ruthless. This time there would be no mercy shown to the Order. Whereas Rhodes had been less than a day's sail from the shores of Turkey, Malta would present a far more demanding set of logistical challenges. Besides requiring far longer lines of communication, there was also the nature of the island itself to contend with. Malta was a dry rock whose people had to scratch a living on its thin soil. Consequently the Turks had to bring timber with them to construct their siege works. That, and adequate supplies of food and munitions to see them through. In the event, they underestimated the task and were decimated by hunger and sickness in the latter stages of the campaign. Equally debilitating was the Sultan's decision to split the command. By contrast, the unquestioned authority of La Valette, bolstered by his courage, meant that the defenders had a strong sense of mission. Neither side was lacking in courage, and when one considers the exhausting heat and privations suffered by the combatants it is hard not to be awed by their bravery and endurance.

The achievement of the Order in humbling the Sultan made them the toast of Europe. The victory was even celebrated in Protestant England. As a result, money and men flowed in, to such a degree that the Order was able to level the Sciberras ridge and build a brand-new fortified city, which was named in honour of La Valette. The example of the Order inspired the European powers to unite against the Sultan and his navy was crushed at the Battle of Lepanto six years after the humiliation on Malta. The shift in power led to the long decline of the Order. They remained in control of the island until the arrival of Napoleon and his army, en route to Egypt, in 1798. In rather stark contrast to their heroic forbears the knights of the Order who faced Napoleon surrendered after resisting for some ninety minutes. Thereafter the Order was forced to leave Malta and shifted its headquarters to Rome, where it has remained ever since.

Although the scene is very different today, one can still get a sense of the challenge that faced the Turks by exploring the harbour. When I first sailed into Valetta I was struck by the predominance of Fort St Elmo, and it is easy to understand why the Turks would have chosen it as the target of the first assault. Although the city is heavily built up, the main features of the harbour are intact and it is easy to picture the scene as it would have been in 1565. There is an excellent museum in the Grand Master's palace with a fine collection of armour and weapons dating back to the siege. For those who wish to read more about the siege and the wider historical context, a good starting place is Tim Pickles's *Malta 1565: Last Battle of the Crusades* from the ever excellent Osprey series. There is also an utterly gripping first-hand account by Francisco Balbi Di Correggio. Part diary and part commentary, it is a detailed summary from the point of view of a common soldier caught up in events. Ernle Bradford's *The Great Siege: Malta 1565* provides a very readable overview of the siege, and more recently Roger Crowley's *Empires of the Sea* admirably sets the siege in a wider context.

On the question of the document at the heart of the tale, it is clear that King Henry VIII became increasingly concerned about his prospects for the afterlife as he grew older. His break with the Church of Rome had left England isolated from the heart of Europe and late in his reign he was keen to rebuild relations with the Catholic powers. The sticking point was the Pope's demand that the possessions the Catholic Church had lost during the Reformation should be returned. Any attempt to strip the assets from those who had profited from the confiscation of Church property would have split the English ruling class right down the middle and the threat of civil war would have been unavoidable. Hence the desperate attempt by Sir William Cecil and Sir Francis Walsingham to secure the will that I have depicted in this novel.

Q&A WITH
SIMON SCARROW

Writers of historical fiction are often asked how true to the thinking of the time the views of the contemporary characters can really be. How have you bridged the divide between sixteenth-century thinking and your own in the characters in the novel?

This is the central problem that all writers in the historical fiction genre have to grapple with. Authors want to reproduce the era they are depicting with the greatest possible fidelity. That is part of the unwritten contract with the reader and it is why we spend so much time on research to get the details (large and small) correct. Readers, myself included, like to be immersed in the everyday apparatus of the past.

But the more subtle layer of historical reproduction in fiction, which presents the greatest challenge to writers, is trying to get inside the minds of those who lived hundreds – or even thousands – of years ago. While there is no doubt that we share many of the emotions and thought processes of our forebears, modern readers would find a great number of the nuances of earlier mindsets incomprehensible at best, and would be frankly appalled by some of the views and opinions that made up the 'common sense' of those living in previous centuries.

We don't even have to go very far back before we come up against ideas that run counter to our own. I have often been struck by the differences between my view of the world and that of my parents, and even more strikingly, my grandparents. It is a little sobering to think that the present speed of change means that my children are already starting to look at me in that mildly surprised way that intimates that my views are out of date, and already vaguely 'historic'. If we can't get inside the minds of people who lived only a generation or two back then what realistic hope have we of understanding those who lived centuries ago? Of course we have plenty of contemporary documents which can be used to attempt a reconstruction of the way people thought and treated each other, but the results would be pretty abhorrent in the main. By modern standards our ancestors would be considered a thoroughly cruel, sexist, racist and religiously fanatic bunch and we would find it pretty tough to empathise with them, let alone actually like them.

Which is where the difficulty for historical novelists comes in. We write stories that we are fascinated by and we hope to share this interest with others. We create characters we are fond of (even the villains!) and we want to cheer them on through the challenges they face and overcome. It would be very difficult to identify with such characters if they were absolutely true to the mind-set of their age. So historical novelists have to tread a wary line between realism and romanticism in depicting these characters against a given backdrop. The setting can be rendered as realistically as possible in every sordid detail and that will delight the reader. But when we are to inhabit the minds of those who walked in the past then there must be some minimal common ground of language, thought and morality for the novel to be comprehensible, let alone enjoyable, for a contemporary reader.

In the present novel, this was not as difficult a task as it might seem thanks to the virulent religious conflicts that are still being waged around the world today. The kind of extreme beliefs that motivate fanatics today were prevalent in the sixteenth century. Thanks to Walter Scott and Hollywood, the knights who took part in the original crusades have been romanticised to such a degree that the modern usage of 'crusade' or 'crusader' tends to carry positive connotations of fixity of purpose and purity of motivation. The horrific barbarity of many aspects of the original campaigns has been frequently glossed over in the western world. The men who fought in the military orders of the Hospitallers and Templars were ruthless professional warriors who dedicated their lives to defending their faith and obliterating any threat posed to it. To modern readers, there would be little to distinguish the Knights of St John from any other holy warriors. Nor were their opponents any less ruthless or dedicated to their cause. That is why the conflict between Islam and Christianity took on an increasingly bitter edge over the long centuries of warfare. With that in mind, and, regrettably, with extensive evidence of ongoing religious strife, there was plenty of material to draw on in depicting the characters in my novel.

How would the weaponry and tactics employed in this book compare to those in play in your Roman novels?

One of the reasons why I originally became interested in the Roman period was the struggle I had in imagining how ancient warfare would have played out. In the modern era the distance between combatants has tended to increase and the process of war has become depersonalised in the main. Before the advent of firearms most combat was hand-to-hand and brutal in the extreme. In the age of Rome, those who fought in battle would see every detail of their opponents' expressions. They would see the fear, horror, rage and pain. They would smell their sweat, blood and filth. And they would feel the impact of their blows on the flesh of their enemy, and stand amid the carnage of battle as they fought, and later as the fighting ceased. Such realities are a challenge to the imagination.

With the advent of gunpowder, that began to change. Killing at a distance became possible. By the time of the Siege of Malta in 1565 the Turks and the Christians both had access to accurate firearms as well as artillery. Fortifications were no longer determined by the height of the walls so much as their depth. When I visited Fort St Angelo I was astonished by the thickness of the defences protecting the outer bastions, fully thirty feet in places.

Added to the perils of traditional hand-weapons and firearms was a panoply of other devices such as the fire-hoops and the trumps: a primitive version of the terrifying flame-thrower. Combining all these weapons with the implacable religious fanaticism of both sides, it is hard to think of a bloodier and more bitterly contested battlefield in history.

The Maltese people were at the mercy of opposed forces in the Siege of Malta. What was their view on events, and how has history affected them at other critical times over the years?

By the time the Order of St John took charge of Malta in 1530 the Maltese people were accustomed to being used as part of the loose change of the great powers. At that time the island was a possession of the Spanish Crown and King Charles V was content for the knights to use it as a forward outpost in the war against the Turks. The Maltese had suffered greatly from the raids of the corsairs operating from their lairs on the north coast of Africa and so were relieved to accept the protection offered by the knights. When the island was besieged in 1565 they willingly offered to fight and despite the Grand Master's misgivings about their quality the Maltese proved to be courageous and tenacious defenders of their homeland. Not just the men, but the women and even children too. The same qualities were to see the islanders through the much longer siege they endured during the Second World War when the island was subjected to the heaviest bombardment of the conflict.

What became of the Order of the Knights of St John following the Siege of Malta?

Following the Siege the Order was showered with gifts and rewards by the powers of Europe who had belatedly realised its significance. It was at Malta that the tide of Ottoman expansion was turned back, and the victory emboldened the Christian nations and gave them unity and a sense of purpose. At the Battle of Lepanto in 1571 they were able to assemble a coalition of fleets powerful enough to overcome the Ottoman navy. As the danger from the East diminished and the European nations gained in power, the Order became something of an anachronism from the start of the seventeenth century. The age of the crusades was over, and the Order's activities came to look more and more like simple acts of piracy. With the receding of the Turkish threat the knights began to live lives of luxury on the back of their loot and sold their services as mercenaries to the great powers.

Outdated and decadent, they were no match for the French army that landed on the island in 1798 under the command of young general Napoleon. The knights put up a feeble resistance that lasted a matter of hours before capitulating. Napoleon removed them from the island and the survivors of the Order were homeless for many years before being offered shelter by the Czar in St Petersburg. Eventually, they were given a base in Rome where the headquarters of the Order remains to this day. The era of the warrior knights is long gone and now they devote their energies to the peaceful service of the Catholic Church and the wider community through organisations such as St John's Ambulance and the St John's Eye Hospital in Jerusalem.

Yet the link with Malta is not completely broken. Even now there is a knight of the Order living in what used to be the quarters of the Grand Master Jean de la Valette in Fort St Angelo. Surrounded by the slowly crumbling remains of the vast fortifications, he still enjoys the views across the harbour and the island that his forebears gave their lives to defend, changing the course of history.